NEVER ENOUGH TIME

A Novel

Kimberly McMillan

ISBN: 978-1-957723-85-3 (hard cover)
       978-1-957723-86-0 (soft cover)

Edited by: Erika Nein

Published by Warren Publishing
Charlotte, NC
www.warrenpublishing.net
Printed in the United States

For Codi and Cara, you are my inspiration.
For Aaron, you are the love of my life.

PROLOGUE
Marni

The sun blasts its warming rays into the crisp October air. Not a wisp of a cloud threatens the serenity of this bluebird day. The wind whispers through the trees and tousles my hair, tickling the back of my neck like gentle kisses. The colors' vibrancy glitters all around me, confusing my senses as they try to decipher how to balance today's perfection against this great loss. Squinting, I numbly comb through my purse for my sunglasses, hoping the armor of my oversized shades will block my pain.

Loose dirt slowly starts to rise around the pointy heels of my shoes as they sink farther into the ground, but I just can't make myself move. I watch as men and women slowly navigate the rows of concrete love notes, permanent markers that will remind us of the love shared, the laughs had, and the memories we made along the way. The people arrive at the white tent protecting a polished mahogany casket adorned in white and yellow roses. Bodies scrunch together like sardines while a hushed chatter slowly ripples through the sea of black. My heels, now stuck in soft dirt clods, keep me planted toward the back of the tent as I wait for this nightmare to end.

All the family are seated, but one empty chair remains. I anxiously look around, unsettled, until she spots me in the crowd. Our eyes lock, and a conversation is conducted without either of us saying a word. Her emotions bubble at the surface, as tears cascade over the bottoms of her eyelids. Her chest rises as she takes a deep inhale. I can see her strength is being tested. I know this test—I remember it well—and I hate it!

She shuffles through the watchful congregation, making her way to me. The crowd parts like the Red Sea, not wishing to be an obstacle in her hour of need.

"Marni, please, there's a chair up front for you," she says, beckoning me with a slight lilt in her hoarse voice.

My shoulders slump forward as tears escape the outside corners of my eyes, falling freely down my cheeks. "This is too much," I confess, feeling the uncomfortable weight of empathetic eyes.

"I know." She pats my arm gently. "But I need you with me," she whispers in a tired voice.

I look down at my disappearing heels and nod. She offers me her arm so I can stabilize myself as I attempt to discreetly wiggle my heels free. Then, with a satisfied smile, she encircles my arm with hers and escorts me to our seats.

Violins begin playing a familiar song, instantly transforming me back into that scared fourteen-year-old girl, wondering what's next. Sixteen years later and the same fears rush over me like a crashing wave. Has it really been that long? Some days, it seems like a lifetime ago. But other days, like today, life exposes my old wounds, tricking my tender heart into feeling every ounce of sorrow as if it all happened yesterday.

Today, it starts all over again, a vicious cycle that preys on the innocent notions of would-be happily-ever-afters. Sixteen years later and I still fantasize about what we could have done with more time. But time has proven, once again, it recklessly tumbles forward, completely disregarding my feelings or plans.

I close my eyes as the preacher opens the service in prayer and find myself asking the same question I did all those years ago: *What do I do now?* Silently, I pray, *Lord, how can I go through this again?*

CHAPTER 1
Marni

I know black is all I'll see—black suits, black dresses, black hats. The appropriate color symbolizes the end—the color of doom, of loss, of emptiness—the absolute absence of light, my light.

It's impossible to dress for such an occasion. Who would put effort into looking their best to say a final goodbye—a goodbye to everything that defines life as I know it?

"I'm not ready," I say to my reflection as I replace the weight of my grief with fear of the unknown. This can't be my new reality. If I refuse to leave this room, maybe this will all go away, and I'll awake from this relentless nightmare. But I hear my patient aunt's heels steadily clicking down the wooden hallway, stopping just outside my locked bedroom door.

Aunt Jo tickles the wooden door with her ragged but clean fingernails. "It's just about time, Marni." She pauses, and I hear her staccato breathing catch at regular intervals as she tries to maintain her composure. Then she adds, "My friend, Trey, is here to drive us." She doesn't move, surely listening through the door for a response I cannot produce. Time mocks my pain as it propels me forward, never stopping to allow me what I desperately need—solitude.

Aunt Jo twists the door handle but stops when the lock responds with a hitch. Why can't she let me barricade myself in my room to wallow in self-pity?

She whispers, "This is gonna be hard, the hardest thing ever. But I can't do it alone." I hear her take a couple of deep breaths before adding, "Marni, I need you with me." Her voice cracks with emotion.

Reluctantly, I nod my head, catching my reflection in the mirror. I tuck my hair behind my ears like Mom used to and walk to my closet. I put on my best dress, the black-and-cream watercolor floral print with a wide scoop neckline Mom snagged at a garage sale in one of the fancy neighborhoods. Before slipping my feet into my black peep-toe pumps, I double-check their lackluster surface, satisfied every scruff mark and scratch has been buffed out. I smile, recalling how Mom excitedly proclaimed me old enough to wear a small heel last year on my thirteenth birthday, surprising me with a shopping trip to the "good" Goodwill. I cherish the memory of us trying on secondhand heels, remembering our joy when I discovered these pumps hiding behind a pair of boots. I pull my curly hair up, showcasing the dainty silver cross necklace Mom gave me last Christmas, an heirloom piece she'd inherited from her mom. With one last look in the mirror, I am confident Mom would be proud of her "sweet girl."

Aunt Jo escorts me down my stoop, toward a shiny, black limousine sitting by the curb. Before I climb in, I notice a couple of older great-aunts I barely recognize, staring at me with handkerchiefs in hand. Sadness fills the empty space between us as the broken women across from me continuously dab the water from their eyes. I close my eyes briefly to ward off their piercing stares, then force myself into the limo.

I shift in my seat just enough to easily look out the tinted window running the length of the vehicle. The pictures in my mind of limo travelers look nothing like my present company. Aren't limo riders celebrities, or super-rich people who bounce from one spectacular party to another, or newly married couples who cuddle with each other as they head toward their lavish honeymoons? Maybe, but not this time.

I sit, unmoving in this dark cave, feeling the road quietly thud under me. I watch the world outside steadily move forward at its regular pace like nothing of significance has happened—what an insult to my heart. So, I gently lay my head inside the crook of my propped elbow and shut my eyes, willing visions of Mom to fill the space around me until the limo comes to a stop, and I'm shuffled out of the car and into a cushioned seat under a large white tent.

On this hot June day in Chicago, my sorrow and the sweltering heat persuade every pore in my body to release water. Fresh tears stream down my scorching cheeks, sprinkling the newly disturbed ground. I can't focus on the preacher—the finality of it all overwhelms me. His comforting words promise us we'll be reunited again someday in heaven, stressing that this isn't the end. Hopeful friends and family punctuate his hopeful words with animated responses of "Amen," "Yes," and "Praise Jesus." But I just stare into space, remembering Mom.

When she wasn't working, Mom loved to sing, cook, and be with those she loved most—me and Aunt Jo. She also loved being outside and enjoyed God's beautiful creation. But what I remember the most is how she loved me. Mom always called me her "best-kept secret the world hasn't met yet." But Mom was my world, and now my world lies motionless, crammed into a carved wooden box meant to be buried and never opened again. I know Mom is with Jesus, and I do believe I'll see her again. But right now, at fourteen and with so much of my life ahead of me, that's a hard pill to swallow. Now, all I have to keep her alive is our memories and the stories Aunt Jo shares of her sister, her best friend—my mom.

***

I've always heard death comes like a thief in the night. In my case, the perpetrator was not death so much as it was the sickness that stole Mom from me. I remember the day like it was yesterday—everything was fine, nothing momentous or out of the ordinary. Sometimes it actually feels like the entire journey covered a single day. One long, bad day.

It was payday, the only day she permitted us to splurge, even if that just meant a small, single-topping pizza. After spending her days and nights in a hot kitchen, Mom justified eating out as a well-deserved brain-break. She wanted someone else to handle our dinner, clean up the messy kitchen, and end their day on tired feet. So, we ate pizza in a greasy hole-in-the-wall joint around the block from our apartment, entertaining each other by reenacting our week in short-story format, laced with juicy dramatizations. I always had the same goal—make Mom's belly ache with laughter. I remember so clearly the sound of her joyful laugh after my spot-on portrayals of a specific teacher and her quirks. I'll never forget how Mom's hands pressed against the table's edge, stabilizing her overly giggly body as her weight teetered, threatening her ability to stay balanced in her seat. We were both rolling with laughter, but not for long.

Without warning, her laughter ceased. Her sparkling, brown eyes suddenly changed to register shock and confusion. Her body fell heavily out of the wooden chair and flopped violently on the greasy floor.

Frantically screaming for help, I flung myself next to her, trying my best to calm her hysterical movements. Sal, owner of the pizza place, rushed over and rotated Mom on her side before pulling me away. Another customer must have dialed 911. After what seemed like forever, Mom stopped shaking. Exhausted and confused, she glanced at me with glazed eyes before she closed them again. Within minutes, the ambulance came.

As the paramedics strapped her in, anxiety flashed across Mom's face, and she protested. Trying to convince them this wasn't worth their trouble, or the cost, I heard her whisper to the woman in uniform that we couldn't afford this. Tears slipped out of the corners of my eyes as she begged me to send them away. "Marni, I'm fine. It's only my head. Nothing a little at-home rest can't fix." Scared to death and tongue-tied, I shook my head. This was bigger than frugality, so off we went to the emergency room.

A couple of days later, Mom seemed to be herself again. The doctor had warned us seizures could come on unexpectedly, so they prescribed her an antiepileptic drug, claiming, "Early treatment is our best form of defense." Mom hated depending on any medication, but she registered the fear in my eyes and decided to trust the doctor's advice. "We've had great success with these treatments." He paused as he glanced back down at the chart in his hands. Sounding confident, he added, "Success in preventing and controlling future seizure incidents, that is. However, you both still need to be prepared … always."

I sat on the cold vinyl chair, twisting my folded hands into a nervous knot as Mom casually listened and took notes she would later share with Aunt Jo. The doctor instructed us on what to do and what not to do in the event of another episode, but I processed nothing except fear.

Before the doctor left, he slouched down to my level to look me square in the eyes and asked, "Do you have any questions?"

His directness snapped my focus back to my mom who stared at me with concern. I quickly shook my head as I answered, "No, sir."

As he stood to leave, Mom stopped him. Embarrassed by her situation, she admitted, "I appreciate all you're doing, but I don't know how I'm going to pay for all this."

His expression softened as he reassured her. "Don't worry about that right now. There are always ways to work those details out."

It seemed the pizza incident might be Mom's only seizure—a single episode—or maybe the medication was working. Either way, Aunt Jo and I breathed a little easier when Mom hit the one-week mark without any recurrence. We watched her like a hawk, but Aunt Jo carried the bulk of the weight on her shoulders, trying to protect us both from the what-ifs. As Mom's younger sister, Aunt Jo was used to Mom's care and guidance, but she immediately stepped up and wiggled her way into our apartment at every opportunity, trying to keep tabs on Mom's health.

After a solid week of interference, Mom convinced Aunt Jo to leave us be. "I'm fine. Go home." She softened as she pleaded with Aunt Jo. "You're going to scare Marni with all this hovering. We're fine."

With Mom's insistence, we both let our guards down and silently chalked her seizure up to a scary fluke. But our naivete barely lasted a day beyond Aunt Jo's departure. Thereafter, Mom's singular episode became a frequent event. Aunt Jo kept a calendar indicating when Mom's episodes occurred—which was every two or three days—and the details of each event. She noted how the seizures consumed her, leaving her body exhausted, temporarily paralyzed, while also noting my reaction to each event.

As Mom's condition rapidly worsened, so did our reality. Since Mom was unable to work her jobs at both the school and nursing home cafeterias, her anxiety over a possible eviction consumed her. During the week, I went to school and came right home, and then I stayed by her side all weekend, every weekend. Both of us were afraid to go out in public, terrified an unexpected episode would ruin our day, so we stayed home. Our routine felt safe yet stale as we confined ourselves within our tiny apartment—an in-home prison sentence. The fear we carried prohibited us from living our lives. We stopped laughing, stopped venturing out, stopped being us, which scared me just as much as the seizures.

After a couple of exhausting weeks, it was abundantly clear Mom needed further medical help, but she reminded Aunt Jo, "I've already seen a doctor, remember?" Mom argued this point as she methodically paced a circle around the kitchen table while I strained to listen, crouched behind my bedroom door.

"You saw an ER doctor, but you need to see a specialist," Aunt Jo persisted.

"You and I both know that I don't have that kind of luxury. I have no money coming in right now, and I'm already drowning under all of these bills. We just can't handle any more," she said, her voice trailing off, barely audible.

Silence filled my ears as I imagined them staring at each other, communicating wordlessly as only sisters can.

Aunt Jo's pleas became more desperate. "Don't do it for me. Do it for Marni. Please, Gabby. I'll set everything up."

I heard footsteps in the hall, approaching my bedroom. Satisfied I was sleeping, Mom returned to the kitchen. "Don't use my daughter against me," she snapped. "Besides, I already have the meds, which clearly aren't working. What can they really do except cost me more money? Money I don't have." I heard the creak of our unstable kitchen chair as she sat down. Her voice cracked as she said, "I just can't afford to keep piling up more debt."

"Can we just concentrate on getting you better? A second opinion?"

Walking the thin line between natural fear and her stubborn personality, Mom reluctantly gave in. "You're right, we do need some answers ... and I want my life back."

A few days later, while I was in school, Mom met Aunt Jo at the hospital for her appointment—a full day of tests, bloodwork, and scans. Three days later, after the doctor had studied and mulled over all the collected data, his office called.

Three days. That was all it took to turn my world completely upside down.

After school, Mom and I sat patiently in the waiting room's plush navy-and-tan plaid armchairs. Neither of us spoke as we mindlessly thumbed through various magazines, waiting ... and waiting. When we were finally escorted into the doctor's office, he politely dismissed me, saying he wanted to speak privately with Mom. My stomach flipped, and my mouth went dry. She and I stared blankly at each other for a moment before she waved me out the door.

I slouched just outside his office, trying my best to listen through the thick wooden door. Mimicking how spies uncovered marvelous secrets in the movies, I pressed my ear against the door, held my breath, and sat quietly, hoping to decipher their secret conversation. Muffled sounds escaped the sealed room like chatter from Charlie Brown's teacher, unrecognizable gibberish.

My need to know what was happening in that room was fierce, and I hated being in that hallway. I felt disconnected, adrift, alone. I understood why Aunt Jo couldn't be there. She had pulled a lot of strings to get Mom in to see the specialist so quickly, so she couldn't ask for time off from the hospital unless it was absolutely necessary. Mom had understood too.

I sat there, staring blankly down the hall as couples walked by, entering and leaving rooms, hand-in-hand. I was on the outskirts, watching a perfectly balanced world pass by where the patient and their significant other equaled a solid team. Two separate people with one purpose: to help the other, support the other, and to just be there for each other.

For as long as I can remember, Mom and I have always had each other's backs. But, once again, I couldn't help but wonder what it would be like to have my father on our team. Someone Mom could turn to for help, and someone who could console me through all this uncertainty. If he were here, surely he would have held Mom's hand as they listened to the doctor. He would have insisted I go hang out at a friend's house where we'd eat ice cream and talk about nothing, blissfully unaware of Mom's doctor appointment. No matter how I would have liked for my family life to have played out, the truth was, he wasn't here. He couldn't squat down beside me, hold my hand while gently reassuring me everything would be all right. He couldn't. I silently blinked a stream of tears out of my eyes as another husband-and-wife team walked past my curled-up body.

My brain, switching back and forth from daydreaming about what-ifs to my present situation, slowly focused on all the unknowns awaiting me in the doctor's office. I cringed, knowing whatever Mom was hearing, she had to process it alone. She didn't have the comfort of a husband holding her hand, but we had each other. With Aunt Jo, there was nothing the three of us couldn't tackle together. Still, me not being in there with Mom felt wrong.

How could the rest of this office—the world, for that matter—keep going like nothing was happening behind that door? Nurses kept busy by steering patients into designated rooms and completing paperwork. The staff exchanged jokes while discussing their plans for the upcoming weekend. Life seemed quite normal and jolly to everyone except me.

The distraction of being isolated in that bubble of normalcy ended when the door finally opened. Mom was sitting by a pile of crumpled tissues. Her red splotchy face and puffy eyes triggered a fresh stream of salty tears of my own. The doctor ushered me back into his office, lightly patting me on the back as if to pre-comfort me for the train about to slam into my world. His words, far from soothing or reassuring, were surgically cold and blunt.

He reported with scientific authority that Mom had a massive tumor pushing on her brain. His words never veered from her problem to a hopeful medical solution because there was no treatment plan—nothing could be done. I heard him say, "It's inoperable and growing at a brisk rate," and then my mind went blank.

I drifted in and out of the conversation through a dense fog.

"More seizures ... more and different medications ... hopefully slow or diminish the severity ... keep her comfortable."

I'm not sure he took a breath as he foretold our future. In hindsight, his medical monologue felt like ripping off an adhesive bandage, as if he wanted to just get through the horrible diagnosis.

A few long moments after the bomb dropped, I sat like a statue in the overly plush office chair. The doctor broke the silence, recognizing how the weight of this news smothered me. "Nothing about your situation is ideal. In fact, it's going to be very difficult. Caring for someone is not something that should be handled by just one person, especially a child. But your choices are limited. Ideally, there would be more family around to lighten this burden, but as it stands, it's just you and your aunt." He paused. "I understand resources are limited, so hiring help is not an option, so lean on your aunt for support. Don't exhaust yourself trying to be a team of one," he said insistently. Then his voice softened, like he was talking to his own kid. "I know this must be scary for you, but do you understand what I've just told you?"

I looked up, confused and shocked. I understood his words, I just didn't understand why those words were being spoken to me.

He continued a little softer. "Do you have any questions for me?"

I looked over at Mom's pile of wet tissues and understood she had already been through this question-and-answer session. Mom squeezed my hand in hers as she focused her watering eyes on me, waiting for my reaction.

Of course I had questions. "Could this all be a big mistake?" I blurted out in a delusion of hope.

"No," he explained. "All the tests verified the same findings."

The other questions I had—*When did I have to say goodbye? When was she not going to be with me anymore? When was my life going to shatter to pieces?*—how could I ask those questions in front of my mom? My voice cracked as I barely verbalized a single word: "When?"

His eyes left mine and went to Mom's. His body visibly deflated in the chair. I kept my eyes on his, never giving him a chance to gloss over the question. I needed his honest, professional opinion. He took a deep breath, leaned forward as if he was about to share a secret and said, "Time is a gift, Marni. Take advantage of every moment you have together." I stared blankly at him, waiting for him to offer me something concrete I could brace myself against—a real answer—but he said nothing else. Mom nodded and stood, signaling the end of our discussion.

Time is a gift, but it turned out to be a brief gift. Aunt Jo moved in with us almost immediately. I was so thankful for her help, especially when Mom became bedridden a few short weeks later. I spent every moment possible lying next to Mom in her room. We watched movies, listened to music, laughed as we recalled classic moments together, and talked about the future's infinite possibilities. I was always hesitant to talk about any future, unsure and scared of what lies just beyond my sightlines. But it was important to Mom to constantly remind me of all the plans and dreams she had for me. She would always smile and say, "Marni, never lose sight of the path where God has placed your feet." Gently pulling small sections of my curls through her delicate fingers, she'd continue, "Don't worry about the future, sweet girl. You are dearly loved and will always be taken care of. I promise."

When our words ran out, we continued lying side by side, peacefully tucked into each other, cuddling. I wanted to remember how she felt, her warmth, the fragrant smell of her clean skin, how her loving embrace could erase all my fears and sadness. I wanted to capture these moments on a canvas or create something concrete that would instantly transport me back to us cuddling and laughing, but I couldn't waste time. Instead, I prayed my mind would etch Mom's essence so clearly on my heart and brain so I'd never lose sight of her.

The day she left me, I whispered in her ear that I'd always love her and miss her, but it was okay to go. I snuggled up next to her and positioned her arms around my shoulders for one last hug. I gently placed a kiss on her still-warm cheek and listened to her heart slowly fade away, one beat at a time.

Devastated and scared, lost and alone, I couldn't imagine life without her.

***

I try to shake off the memory of her last moments and focus on the end of the service. Numbly, I stand and bend over Mom's casket to whisper, "I love you, Mom, always and forever." I rest a single pink rose on top of the wooden casket—warm from the summer heat—and stand there, frozen in fear, the weight of the past months anchoring me. Staring into my new unknown, I cannot force myself to walk away because moving means leaving Mom behind in an attempt to move forward. But what will life look like for me? All I see is a girl whose security, love, and family lays shattered into a million unmatchable pieces around her feet. The silent tears shed during the service by friends and family now freely flow as they witness my inability to say goodbye. The weight of my grief tethers my helpless body to the casket. I hear sniffles as the tightly packed crowd shuffles in their seats, waiting for a signal from someone, probably Aunt Jo, to indicate the service is over.

A few quivering breaths later, Aunt Jo brushes her body next to mine and gently grabs my hand as she nods, fully feeling the depth of our loss.

"She loved you more than you could ever know," she states with 100 percent authority.

"I know. I just miss her so much, Aunt Jo." I turn and bury my head into her pillowy, soft shoulder.

"Of course you do, sweet girl. Of course ..." Her voice trails off as she rubs my back softly in a circular motion. "But it's gonna be okay, Marni, I promise." She whispers her assurances in my ear. I feel her gaze shift to the preacher who then releases the seated crowd from their quietude without a word. Soon, gentle murmurs break the unbearable silence. Aunt Jo lifts my face to meet hers, saying, "I need to go talk to the preacher. You want to walk over there with me?"

I just shake my head. "No, I think I want to be alone for a moment."

She slowly unfolds me out of her embrace, lifts my chin with her thumb to look me in the eyes, and then says, "I'll just be a minute." She approaches the preacher who's standing under a large shade tree at the back of the crowd. My wish for solitude barely lasts longer than the four hurried strides Aunt Jo takes toward the preacher. People I barely know—practical strangers, distant relatives, and close friends—interpret Aunt Jo's departure as an invitation to bury me in their deepest sympathies and unsolicited comforting remarks. "I'm so sorry, dear," and, "she was so young," or, "if you need anything—" and of course, "she's in a better place."

No one should ever tell a kid at her mother's funeral that her Mom is in a better place because the truth is, she would rather be here with me. The well-wishers and hug-givers descend on me like bees on honey. Overwhelmed, I stand silently as Aunt Jo gently elbows her way through the huddle to secure me in her protective arms. Shielding me, she guides me back to the sleek black car. I tumble into the limo and begin, for the umpteenth time, to process the sequence of events that led to this horrible day. Too surreal. As Trey carefully pulls away, Mom's fresh grave slowly fades from my blurry vision, a new memory I will never forget. My chest tightly twists into a knot, my throat swells with a massive lump, and the weight of the stale air crushes me further into my personal pit of despair. Everything has changed now. I am all alone, and Mom is in the ground.

Aunt Jo and I sit quietly in our cushy limo seats, both distracted by our thoughts. She lightly blows her nose, and for the first time today, I step outside my sadness and recognize her pain. Her bloodshot eyes produce a steady flow of tears that leave trails streaking down her face, carrying away squiggly lines of makeup. Her nose is raw and swollen from constantly wiping at the drippy faucet. She looks lost and almost as alone as I feel. Until this moment, I never appreciated the depth of their bond. Mom always said, "We're more than sisters, we're best friends." I would roll my eyes at the two of them as they laughed. But now I see their relationship more clearly. Mom was Aunt Jo's only sister and best friend, and now she's gone, leaving a huge void. I can see how much Aunt Jo and I need each other now more than ever.

I stare out the window as the world keeps moving forward in a blur while I sit suspended in time. It dawns on me that, in the midst of my heartbreak, my devastation, the loss of my mother means nothing to all the people I see enjoying this hot summer day with their families. Are they so caught up in how life exists right now that the possibility of it ever disappearing seems as unreal to them as flying pigs? I can honestly say I used to be that naive. I close my eyes, wishing I could rewind time back to that innocence, to my normal life when all was right in my world. Instead, I grant myself permission to envy them and the silent luxury of an ordinary day.

My fragile heart sinks deeper in my chest as I fully acknowledge that I have no parents. Thankfully, I have Aunt Jo. I know things will be different with her, even though we'll probably still do the same things we always did with Mom. Our routines will become ritualistic as we silently and intentionally honor Mom and look for traces of her in those everyday moments. But no matter how hard we'll try, she'll always be gone. I'm sure I'll move into Aunt Jo's apartment since it's closer to her work, but it's even smaller than mine and Mom's. I guess we'll figure it out, and I'm sure Aunt Jo will be the loving mother figure Mom imagined. It offers some peace, knowing Mom was content leaving me with Aunt Jo since she's always been more like a second mother to me than an aunt. But it still doesn't change the fact that my mother and father are both dead.

As we turn the corner onto Aunt Jo's street, I can't believe how many cars edge both sides of the road. I don't remember seeing all these cars at the funeral. The limo cautiously glides through the street. Trey narrowly misses someone's car bumper that juts out past the curb before he stops the limo and opens our door. As Trey frees us from our quiet cave, Aunt Jo thanks him profusely for his generosity, and then we make our way to her front door where, thankfully, no one stops to talk to us or offer more condolences. But I know people are lurking inside, waiting for us.

Just inside, sweaty bodies dressed in black greet me with half smiles and a cumulative stout stench. The crowded mass tried soaking up as much air conditioning as the small window unit could provide, but the magnitude of heat being emitted from their bodies in such close quarters made their efforts counterproductive.

Aunt Jo and I wiggle our way through the crowd to discover a veritable banquet provided by the church ladies. Aunt Jo's kitchen table is dotted with plates of cookies, cakes, brownies, and sandwiches. I don't think I've ever seen so much food in my life. The inviting smell of freshly baked food and the escalating noise from the crowd confuse my senses as the scene conjures up images of a party, not a funeral. My nose and lungs open wide, allowing the sweet sensations to fill and entice my body, which my stomach responds to with a loud growl. After grabbing a plate of food, I look for a quiet place to retreat. I've already heard enough pleasantries for a lifetime—right now, I just need some space.

I park myself in a small midcentury wooden armchair tucked into a corner next to my grandmother's secretary desk—a cherished piece of furniture Aunt Jo was proud to have inherited. I set my plate on the desk and admire my choice of foods. "I will indulge in all the sweets I can handle," I half-whisper to myself, justifying my food choices. There will be nothing of nutritional value on my plate today. No sense in letting the heart hurt alone. I may as well upset the stomach to round out the amount of pain I can tolerate in a day. I savor my desserts while my ears pick up stories of Mom and how much everyone loved her. It's satisfying to hear others remember her in a way so personal to them without having to be cornered and listen to story after story. I'm fascinated at the depth of their love for her and her love for them.

After completely stuffing myself, I dig through the few drawers in the secretary to find the notepad and pencils Aunt Jo keeps for my entertainment. I grab the cream-colored paper and two pencils and sneak behind the worn-out curtain barely separating the apartment's living area from my aunt's tiny bedroom. I peel off my peep-toe pumps, massage my toes, and wriggle between two layers of mismatched blankets. The weight of today presses against my body. I stretch out my hands to make sure the walls aren't shrinking around me and am surprised to find I can almost touch the wall's crumbling texture.

It has been a long day. Actually, it has been a long journey. A yawn tempts my body to give in to the exhaustion, promising an escape through dreamland. But I fight the urge to slip away and begin doodling images of the flower I laid on Mom's casket. My fingers draw without thought as they create, erase, recreate, and eventually add value to a small sketch showing the outline of black pumps beside a long wooden box. Delicate fingers pinch the thorny stem of the rose as it is being placed on the shiny box. But the focus of the sketch, matching the tone of the day, is the lonely rose petal falling unnoticed, unprotected to the ground.

Confident no one will miss me, I drop the pad and pencils on the floor and effortlessly fall asleep.

CHAPTER 2
Marni

M om always said it was rude to whisper secrets. Which was why Mom and I didn't whisper. We didn't need to since there were no secrets between us. In reality, overhearing a whisper makes you feel isolated and unimportant, building the psychological illusion that you've been intentionally uninvited to the party. But, there's something about overhearing a whispered conversation. You want to be in on the secret, carefully doing whatever it takes to learn what forbidden words aren't being uttered out loud. This is how I slowly come back into consciousness—waking up to whispered secrets.

Their secret conversation plays around me like irritating elevator music. The words are mostly unrecognizable, but what I can hear, I hate. What I can't make out makes me increasingly anxious. What is going on? I bolt upright out of bed, throw the curtain aside, and scare the fool out of Aunt Jo and her best friend Tiffany. They were the only ones left in the now oppressively quiet apartment.

"What were you just saying?" I ask with quiet caution.

"Nothing that's any of your concern right now, Marni," Aunt Jo calmly states.

I'm not buying her attempt to sidestep my question. Obviously, they are discussing something that concerns me. My ears clue in to Aunt Jo's word selection.

"What do you mean, not my concern *right now*?" I ask, my voice tense.

"If I wanted you to know something, I'd tell you."

"So, you are hiding something," I say through a snarky laugh. "Don't you think you owe it to me and to Mom to be open and honest with me? I mean, seriously, what are you? Nine years old, whispering to your BFF?"

"Our conversation is none of your business," Aunt Jo says through clenched teeth. "Besides, if I say not now, I mean *not right now*."

I stare suspiciously at them. They look at each other, trying to conduct a private conversation. Silence fills the air.

Nodding at the papers she's failing to hide under her clasped hands, I turn to Tiffany. "What's that you're reading—"

"Marni!" Aunt Jo interrupts, perturbed at the direction our conversation is heading. "Show some manners."

"Huh!" My audible blurt suggests *what goes around comes around*.

Our eyes meet; her expression more than suggests I drop it, but I can't.

Just minutes ago, they were whispering to each other, probably about whatever Tiffany is clutching. They obviously had no idea I was in the same room behind a flimsy curtain.

I watch panic wash across Tiffany's features, a sure sign she's been caught. Noting she might be the weak link, I change tactics.

"That's right, Tiffany. Show some manners," I parrot. "I heard you talking about me. Is there something in those papers you want to share with the class?" I let the last word hiss out of my mouth. Tiffany looks to Aunt Jo, who just shakes her head, slowly, intentionally, and in control.

I break the distance between Aunt Jo and me, stand right under her nose, and snarl. "Mom always said it's not polite to keep secrets."

Aunt Jo bristles at my sassiness. "Enough, Marni!" She profusely apologizes to her friend on my behalf.

Tiffany's stricken face projects a deep sadness I can't understand, like she holds the key to some unforeseen heartbreak. She puts the pages in a folder I hadn't noticed, and her eyes lock on mine. A fresh wave of pain hits me in the face as she says, "Marni, again, I am so sorry for your loss."

Handing the folder to my aunt, Tiffany puts her hand on my shoulder. "Jo loves you, Marni. Never doubt that." She hugs my aunt goodbye and walks down the hall.

Aunt Jo shoots me a look of disapproval before shuffling after her friend. There is something more in her look, though, a message I can't quite decode.

A small pain starts to throb at my temples as my brain tries to solve the riddle I'm left to ponder. *What is in that folder?*

I know Mom handled all this before she passed. I remember her saying, "Everything's been taken care of, Marni." Then she inhaled another large breath, stared into my eyes, and continued. "You'll be loved and taken care of." I can still feel the sensation of her warm breath brushing across my cheek as she pushed out her words. In the quiet moments, these phrases broke our silence as they rolled off her tongue in a repetitive loop. It was as if her peace was unattainable until she was confident I had heard her words and understood their meaning. She would always finish these mini monologues by promising me, "Everything will be okay, sweet girl." And I would answer, "I know, Mom," as I pet her arm in soft strokes.

My head starts to spin, causing the room to tilt at odd angles. I'm dizzy. My growing anxiety increases my heart rate. I put my head between my knees and take a few deep breaths, trying to slow everything down as my heart rate gradually finds its normal rhythmic pattern just in time for Aunt Jo to reappear in the doorway, hands fixed on her hips.

I glare at her. "You can't wait to get rid of me, is that it?"

CHAPTER 3
Marni

After basically accusing my aunt of putting me up for adoption, I watch the color drain from her face. Her reaction makes my heart sink, but the following "conversation" rips my heart right out.

"Marni, we do need to talk, but it can wait until morning when we're both not quite so fragile. We just buried your mother …." Aunt Jo's voice is firm, but her eyes are soft pools of sadness.

"No," I say. "Now," I add aggressively, elongating the word into multiple syllables.

My aunt's shoulders sink. "I'm so tired," she says and picks up a white napkin to dab the wetness off her cheeks.

"Me too." Sarcasm drips off my tongue. "I'm tired of the crappy hand life has dealt me." I turn and stare at the framed picture of Jo standing between Mom and me. I grab it and set the frozen memory in front of her. "You're all I have left, Aunt Jo. Mom would want you to talk to me, to tell me the truth about whatever is going on. I can handle it."

Jo takes a finger and lightly brushes off the tears that have silently landed on the frame. She looks heavenward as she raises a shaking fist into the air and screams, "This is all your fault!"

Unnerved, I slam my hands on the table and yell, "Just tell me already!"

Aunt Jo pushes herself away from the table, flings her flimsy bedroom curtain out of the way, and begins rummaging through one of her dresser drawers. I hear her slightly cursing under her breath but not at me. She's mad, madder than I've ever seen her, but, strangely, I understand she's not mad at me. I collapse and sit rooted in my chair as fear tries to suffocate me.

My aunt peels around the corner and, with gritted teeth, slams an envelope on the table. "You wanna know so bad? Here, have at it." She nods to the letter. "But this isn't on me, so don't accuse me of nothin'."

I unfold the familiar stationery, and my heart pounds as I recognize Mom's handwriting. My fingers trace over each cursive letter of my name. As tears well up in my eyes, my heart skips a beat, and my brain tries to prepare itself for her final words. I nervously look to Aunt Jo, but her demeanor sends a chill up my spine.

"Go on and read it," she says.

My dearest Marni,

If you're reading this letter, then I am gone. I am gone in the physical sense of this world, but I'm with you always in your heart, memories, and spirit. You have been my greatest gift from God, full of never-ending joy and surprises. To be your mom was a blessing that I will forever be thankful for. I have only one regret: I should have told you about your father.

But I was hurt a long time ago and so angry at someone who should have been in your life—your father. The details are hazy now and have become distorted with time. Please understand, despite the fact of my broken heart, the love that created you was real.

I met your father the year before you were born. We were two very different people, from different worlds, but it didn't take long before we talked of having a family and dreamed of a future ... together. Forever.

Work eventually drew him away, but we knew it would, and we had a plan. He headed home to Texas, and I was going to join him shortly afterward. Two weeks before I was to leave, I found out

I was pregnant with you, sweet girl. I couldn't wait to tell him ... but I wanted to give him the news in person! Three days before I was supposed to leave, he shattered my heart.

I was devastated.

I made the decision to keep you all to myself. I always told you that you were my best-kept secret, but now it's time to share my secret.

Your father is alive, and he wants you to live with him.

I'm sorry for this secret. I should have told you about each other sooner, but I didn't have the strength or courage to share you. I took away his privilege and right to be your father, and I'm sorry. You deserved better.

You have every right to be hurt and angry. But you need your father now. It is my last wish that you go and get to know him, let him love you as much as I do. After six months, if it is not working out, Aunt Jo will become your legal guardian.

I'm sorry for the pain I'm causing you.

I'm sorry I didn't tell you face-to-face.

I'm so, so sorry, but I love you, and I will forever be watching over you.

Mom

I drop the letter and watch as it flutters innocently to the ground, carrying my shattered heart with it. Stunned, I look up at Aunt Jo, my mouth hanging open in disbelief. She stares at me—waiting, watching, bracing for my reaction. But my only response, the only thing I can utter is, "What?"

I need more space, so I pull myself up and point my body toward Aunt Jo's lumpy, shabby couch. Although Mom never uttered my father's name, she always insisted I was the product, the evidence, of their great love. For fourteen years, I longed to know anything about my father. I asked, begged, and even pleaded with Mom for details about him.

Sometimes all I wanted for my birthday was to know more about him, not just the generic details Mom volunteered. My questions were always the same:

"Who's my father?"

Mom would answer with a smile on her lips. "He was my prince charming."

"Well, where is he?"

"Wishing he could be here with you, sweet girl," she'd say.

My voice would soften in concern. "What happened to him?"

Mom's response was always soft, yet definitive, and there was a hint of sadness in her eyes. "He was taken away before we could have our happily ever after."

"Did he ever get a chance to know me?"

"Only in my dreams, Marni."

As it turns out, Mom *did* have all the answers. I don't remember how or why it happened, but somewhere along the way, I invented my own answers concerning my father's disappearance. I naturally assumed he was dead, which explained why he never came to see me or sent me birthday cards or even a gift at Christmas. I concluded that the subject of my father was too painful for Mom to talk about since he was dead and never coming back to us. All this made perfect sense to me, which satisfied most of my curiosities. My imagination created a truth I could handle, one that solidly filled in the gaps haunting my heart and mind. I understood that any other explanation besides death translated into a truth I would never be ready to process—I was unwanted, rejected by my father. But my truth, the truth I authored, is a lie. He's not dead.

I stare at Aunt Jo, the keeper of Mom's secrets. "Why did she hide the truth from me until now? When she's gone?"

"It's complicated, and it was a long time ago," she tries to appease me in her soft-spoken voice, which irritates me to no end. Because the truth is, Mom being gone makes this even more complicated. She will never be able to answer any of the questions swarming inside my head, rattling me like a hive of angry bees.

As my mind tries to digest my newly defined reality, I feel my aunt's eyes on me, waiting. I stare down, studying the deep scuffmarks that pattern her dingy wooden floors. I sit uncomfortably, anchored to the threadbare couch, trying to take it all in. My chest pounds an angry beat as Aunt Jo slides next to me, tears streaming down her makeup-ruined face.

Attempting to offer strength and comfort, Aunt Jo rests her hand on my back. She leans in, causing my body to sink down, tipping my shoulders toward her chest while her fingertips create irregular circles along my back. I feel the heat from her breath as she says, "I'm here with you, sweet girl. It's okay. It's going to be okay." She tries reassuring both of us, but who is she kidding?

I look up at her, push off her cushiony belly, and say in a gravelly voice, "Traitor."

"Marni, watch your tongue. You have no idea what you're saying," she says, her voice trembling with mixed emotions.

"Did you know I have a dad?" I ask. "A dad!" I screech.

She nods silently. "Yes. And he's just as shocked as you are."

"So what? I'm expected to live with this complete stranger, call him "Dad," and pretend that all this isn't totally insane?"

Aunt Jo grabs me by the arms. "Take a deep breath and listen. I've already talked with your dad, explained everything—"

"What did he say?"

"He is truly excited to get to know you." She pauses. "Of course, he couldn't believe that your mom kept you from him all these years." Quickly she adds, "But he knew he had hurt her and now just wants to honor her wishes. Oh, and he has two young daughters, so you have sisters!" She adds emphasis to the last detail, playing on the knowledge that I always wanted to be a sister and not an only child.

The 411 on my newly discovered father is quick, but the bottom line is, he wants to meet me and is expecting me in just two short weeks.

The words pile up, one on top of another, creating a mountain of information my brain isn't ready to accept. My hands slink behind my neck, fingering through the tangles at the base of my curly hairline, pulling sections of hair into smooth lines. My nervous habit always irritated Mom. She used to warn me not to pull my hair out. Her words float in my head, but I push them aside, hurt now by what she never said.

"So that's it? I have no say in all this?"

"Not really. All the arrangements have been made," Aunt Jo admits. She tries to sweep some loose hair out of my face, but I dodge her hand. Her hands freeze inches from my face before she gently folds them in her lap.

"Marni, honey. Do you have any questions?" she asks matter-of-factly. I lift my gaze as my hands retreat into my lap.

I stand, lean over her, and scream hysterically, "My father is dead!" I straighten up, take a breath, and add, "Maybe he's not actually dead, but to me ... he is." I pick up Mom's letter. "This letter is wrong! This could not have been her plan." My voice cracks as my anger melts into fear. "Please, Aunt Jo. Tell me that the plan was always that I'd be with you." Tears flood my face as I grab up her hand in mine, illustrating we are a team.

But Aunt Jo can't talk ... or won't. For what seems like minutes, her tears come faster as she breathes in an agitated staccato rhythm. Finally, she encircles me in a hug.

"This *is* what your mom wanted."

My jaw drops, and I jerk away from her. "Liar!" I yell. "Liars ... both of you—" The pain choked my final word like a defeated cry. "Aunt Jo, why don't you want me?"

"Sweet girl, if it were just up to me, you'd be with me forever. But this was your mom's decision," Aunt Jo answers, eyes puffy and red. "You'll always have me, Marni, no matter what happens. Do you understand that?"

"I understand that you're sending me to live with complete strangers ... that my life and my future mean nothing to you ... that my whole world has been one big fat lie." Growing angrier by the second, my chest tightens. Through messy sobs, I say the one thing I never thought I'd say: "I can't believe you'd give me up, Aunt Jo." My voice cracks with emotion. Shock ripples through my body, the current carrying me into a state of disbelief and sheer terror.

"That's not fair, Marni. This was your mom's plan, not mine." Her tone is sharp and defensive. The edges of her body language soften as she offers her two cents. "Nothing about this will be easy for any of us, but this is something that should have been done a long time ago."

"Tell that to my mom," I say quietly.

Tired from all the crying, screaming, and heartbreak, we sit in awkward silence until she says, "I know your father is going to love you to pieces ... just like I do."

I look into her eyes. She seems to recognize the pain, the fury, and the fear coursing through me. She lays a hand on top of my hands and calmly says, "Honey, I don't know what's going to happen or how it will all turn out, but this was your mom's dying wish."

My heart, my identity, my future. Everything I once knew and believed to be true ... *poof*, gone. The damage is irreparable, the pain ... unimaginable. Why would Mom do this to me? How can I *ever* forgive her?

CHAPTER 4
Kyle

"I don't understand," Lauren says, numbly setting down her lemon and mint iced tea. "What do you mean you *have another daughter*?"

The words, I know, taste just as sour in her mouth as they did in mine when I uttered something similar. I imagine her head is starting to spin, grasping at what I've just said. I know the feeling. I close my eyes for a moment, trying to steady myself.

"Lauren, I don't know what to say. I'm still trying to process all this too."

"Process? What exactly is there to process?"

How do I explain everything I'm feeling without making this harder than it already is? How do I get her to see this is more than just an inconvenience for her? It's, first of all, a damn injustice to me. I mean, who does this sort of thing? Who deletes a perfectly healthy, sane, and capable person from their child's life out of spite?

I search Lauren's pale, shocked face, hoping to find a speck of empathy, but the fiery glint in her blue eyes tells me all I need to know.

"Lauren, I'm so sorry. So, so, sorry!"

"Sorry for what, exactly?" she demands in a sharp tone. "Sorry you never told me about *her* or sorry you have another daughter or sorry it all caught up to you?" She waits a few beats, tears betraying the depth of emotions swirling inside her. She closes her eyes, her fingertips making small circles at her hairline. "History is repeating itself all over again."

"I know how this must feel to you, but it's not the same," I insist. "I promise, I would never betray or hurt you like that. Never!"

Her eyes narrow onto my clasped hands before looking me straight in the eye. "Twelve years ... twelve years. Why didn't you ever tell me there was another woman, an obviously important woman, before me?" Her voice pitches up as she lands on her final word.

"I can't go back and do what I should have done. I should have told you everything, but what did I really have to tell? That I met a girl in Chicago? We dated and briefly dreamed of a future together? Would that have helped?" The blunt question rolls hot off my tongue.

Her eyes widen as she slowly nods her head. "Maybe."

I pull myself off the beige chenille couch piled high with down-stuffed throw pillows and walk to the bar caddy tucked in the corner of the room. I pour a thick stream of honey-colored bourbon into a weighty crystal glass and return to sit on the couch next to Lauren. As if in a trance, I stare into the glass like it's a crystal ball, searching for something, some truth, some reason, some answer. I try to find the right words, but my tongue stiffens. I thought she'd immediately recognize the betrayal engulfing me. But I should have known better than to play to her own experiences. I take another sip and feel the heat slide down the back of my throat.

"I'm not perfect, Lauren, but I'm not deceitful." I push out an audible exhale, cradling my heavy head between my thumb and middle finger. I need her to see that the only person who should be mad is me. "Look, that woman didn't get her way. She didn't get me and all this," I say, my hand and my bitterness punctuating the air. "I guess this is her form of punishment." I hope my words appease Lauren's anxiety by reiterating that I chose her and our life together. But she sits like a statue, unresponsive to me.

"Lauren, say something. Talk to me," I plead softly.

She turns her head and looks me square in the eye. "No more pussyfooting around," she spits out, her consonants pop from her lips. "Tell me about *her.*"

"There's nothing much to tell. Really," I state, trying to calmly reassure her as my mind travels back in time. I haven't thought about her in years; I tried not to. "We were both so young. I was fresh out of law school that summer, trying to prove to myself and the firm that I was a serious lawyer and not just my father's son. Dad sent me to Chicago to sink my teeth into a three-month project—said it was my opportunity to cut my teeth in the real world. I first met her at a taxi stand, funny enough."

"If she was no big deal, then why did you keep her a secret for twelve years? Better yet, why did you keep your Chicago adventures bottled up so tightly?"

She's picking a fight. I understand her need to open every emotional cavity and just release it all, but I try to rein her in. "I never … I mean, I didn't think …" I shake my head as memories flash across my vision, and I try to compose my thoughts. "She had just graduated high school and was waitressing in a café a block from my firm's office. She loved to cook though. She wanted to be a chef. In fact, her boss allowed her to create a lunchtime special each week."

A smile starts to lift at the corners of my lips, remembering the first time she served me. She slid a hot ciabatta Italian sub in front of me and said, "It's a Gabby special. Spicy, colorful, and one of a kind." She had the brightest smile I'd ever seen. She was so vibrant and spunky … I was captivated.

"Hello? Kyle?" my wife says snarkily, trying to drag me out of my head.

I sigh. If I let them, the memories will all come burning back. But something—perhaps it's not wanting to hurt my wife more than I already have or some deep-seated anger toward Gabby—hinders me from reaching in and pulling them to the forefront.

Lauren's anger keeps me in the present. "You knew about my past relationships," she says. "Didn't I deserve the same courtesy?" she blurts out and doesn't bother waiting for a response. "You lied to me. Lied by omission … which still hurts. I feel so deceived."

"There's just nothing I can say that will change any of this." My words slice through me because I know there was a lot I could have done differently ... with Gabby.

"It might change the way I see things," she says through gritted teeth, eyeing me.

"I didn't betray you, Lauren. I didn't even know you back then." I tip my glass back, flushing down a healthy sip of bourbon. "Do the math—she's older than our marriage." I try not to sound defensive, but I'm exhausted. I expected this conversation to be a nightmare. I can't believe that for a part of the afternoon, I was genuinely excited about this news. I mean, of course I was stunned, hurt, angry, and even suspicious. But after the fog cleared, I was excited. I had rose-colored visions of Lauren hugging me, asking motherly questions about the girl, and putting her best maternal foot forward. I even contemplated calling Lauren and giving her a heads-up that I had some wonderful and astonishing news to share with her. Looking back, I'm glad I didn't go that route. Stretching one arm across the top of the couch cushions to pull her closer to me while caressing the top of her leg with my fingertips, I half-whisper, "Please, Lauren."

She holds up a hand to silence me and pulls back. She asks point-blank, "Did you love her?"

I stiffen as her question marinates inside me, and I break eye contact as I'm forced to dig through the memories I shoved into a dark corner of my brain. I squeeze my eyes shut, demanding to see everything clearly, but it remains fuzzy, just out of reach. Every emotion, every kiss shared, every stolen look ... yesterday, they were all lost to time, but today, they're fighting for my heart's recognition. Still, I can't come up with an honest answer because I'm not sure anymore what I truly felt for Gabby back then, or maybe I am just shielding myself from some truth I'm still not ready to acknowledge.

At least some part of me thought we both knew the deal, that I was paying my dues until I could get back to Texas, and Gabby was waiting to hear back from some culinary school to become a hotshot sous chef in some fancy Italian restaurant. Neither of us really believed we'd stay together ... I don't think. It was all just kid talk, right? But, no, that doesn't feel right. My brain rejects that scenario as a small voice threatens to expose what I buried and why. All I can acknowledge with 100 percent certainty is that I ended things terribly—and that truth might be what impugns all others.

I pull my arm back from Lauren and answer as honestly as I can. "There was love, I think, or maybe it was just young romance disguised as love." I search her eyes for a flicker of understanding. "This has all been so sudden and shocking. I wish I could tell you without a doubt what she meant to me, but I was just as confused back then as I am today." She tries to stand, to leave, but I grab her hands, keeping her beside me. "What can I say to help alleviate your fears?"

With tears sliding in rivers down her face, she says, "I can't help being mad, jealous, and a little bitter about the fact that you have a child with a woman you loved and never mentioned to me."

My heart breaks in half as she bends her head to look away from me. I gently cup her face with my hands, tuck a stray piece of hair behind her ear, and say, "It was never anything like what we have. I promise you that."

"But you have a child with *her*. Your first." She looks up at me with flushed cheeks.

"I know. But it doesn't change anything."

"That's where you're wrong, Kyle. This child changes everything. She's your love child."

Her words rip at my heart. "That's not right, and you know it." My voice rattles under the building heat in my belly.

"It is right. We worked hard to create our perfect little world, and now she's coming to blow the whole thing up. What do you think people are going to say?" She pauses for effect. "Because I can already hear it. Our family will be the laughingstock of society. They will pity me and the girls, never accept this other child, and will drop-kick you clean off your high horse."

"People are more understanding than you give them credit, Lauren. It doesn't have to be like that."

She leaps up. "Kyle, don't be so naive!" She sounds scared. And broken. "How are we going to tell our girls, your parents, and our friends without feeding our family to the gossips?"

Southern women know they hold the power to control the room, control the dialog, and control the situation. So, I remind her. "We both understand the power of details and how to successfully control the release of sensational news to 'the wild,' or the Southern busybodies. You understand the personal impact rumors and misinformation can have on a family's reputation. So, we need to handle this with care."

"Are you asking me to create a cover-up story for you?"

"Of course not. We just need to concoct a short and accurate version of the truth to temper destructive tongues. I would hope that you would discourage any nasty untruths from being circulated for pure storytelling enjoyment." I cock my head slightly, hoping to jar a memory she wouldn't want our girls to experience. "We are going to just tell 'em like it is and introduce Marni as one of the family," I say with shaky optimism.

She arches her right eyebrow, tips her chin up, and challenges me. "Are you going to just blurt out to your parents, 'Hey, guess what? You have another granddaughter, and it's not with Lauren'?" She smirks, knowing this idealistic approach will not work with my parents. I flinch at the mention of my parents, but she's too worked up to notice. She holds a finger up in the air and says, "Or first, let's see how it goes with the girls. It's every girl's fear to be forgotten and unloved by their father, so you tell them they have a sister in Chicago that you never knew about." She nods in satisfaction and adds, "That'll get them asking some bigger questions."

In a deep, calm voice, I say, "Or we can have my parents over for dinner in a couple of days after we—you, me, and the girls—have digested everything. Telling them in person, with the girls, will be the best way."

"Oh, I see," she huffs. "You expect the girls to buffer your parents' reaction, knowing that this will hit them like a ton of bricks."

"Maybe ... I don't know. But we have to tell them." I pause, fidgeting and spinning my gold wedding ring nervously around my finger. I finally ask the questions I hoped I wouldn't have to ask: "What do you want, Lauren? Want me to be a deadbeat dad to this girl? Want me to ignore her and the fact that she just lost her mother?"

Her shoulders slump as the realization of our options hit her. "Of course not. I'm sorry for Marni and sad for anyone who loses a parent or loved one. I am. But are you ready for the fallout when our girls become less important than your new daughter?"

"Stop it, Lauren. That will never happen. I won't let that happen." My tone is sharp and terse, punctuating my intense exhaustion.

"You don't know that. I know you—you will want to make up for lost time. I'm not blaming you. Ask yourself, though, at what price will you try to make amends with Marni? Will it cost you a healthy relationship with our girls or with me? You have a responsibility to *our* family, to *our* girls, and to me."

My belly boils with anger and frustration. I want to scream at her. *Can't you see that I'm trying to do what's right here? I'm trying to make things right. I'm trying ... if you'll just meet me halfway, maybe this will work out. I don't need another vengeful woman in my life, I need the opposite. I need my other half—my better half, the woman I chose to marry—right beside me.*

"You know I'm not *that* man. I don't run from my mistakes. I don't shirk off family. I know this must feel like a cruel repeat of your past, but it's not. This is different. You and I are different." I reach out to take her hands in mine, marveling at how perfectly our hands fit into each other. "It'll all be fine, you'll see." My voice cracks slightly.

She yanks her hands free, walks to the bookshelf across the room, and stands with her back to me. I assume she is looking at one of our many framed family photos because she softly says, "I just can't see how we will all meld into this newly defined family without some serious damage being inflicted."

I stare back at her in disbelief, hoping she will turn around as I try to understand what she means. She reaches for a small silver frame showcasing our family at the beach last summer. She turns, hugging it to her chest and tries to speak, but nothing comes out.

I understand. *I* can't fully grasp the changes coming our way, and I've had a whole day to think on this; she's only had hours. I walk to her, take the photo from her hands, and set it back on the shelf. I lift her chin up with my thumb, forcing her eyes to meet mine. "I'm so sorry, Lauren. Sorry I never told you, sorry this bomb has been dropped on us so suddenly, and sorry Marni lost her mother and never had a father figure. And honestly, I'm sorry for me too. I missed out on knowing my child, Lauren—nearly her whole childhood! Can you imagine losing out on all that time with Annabelle or Lila? I'm just … just heartbroken about all this. You have to believe me. I didn't know anything about her. Once I left Chicago, I left all of Chicago behind me. You are the love of my life. You and the girls are my top priority, but … Marni's one of my girls, too, now, and she's all alone."

Lauren turns for one last look at the photo, like she's saying goodbye to something already dead and gone. She doesn't speak, or can't, just cries.

"We will make this work," I promise.

She nods reluctantly then lays her head on my shoulder. I feel her body's tension begin to unfold as I wrap my arms around her, holding on to her for dear life.

"I need you, Lauren, now and forever." Tears slip gently out of the corners of my eyes as I admit, "I can't do this without you."

CHAPTER 5
Lauren

In a full stupor, I draw a steaming hot bath, dumping half a bottle of lavender bubble bath and a handful of fragrant dried rose petals into the basin, hoping my spa-like concoction will trick my tired and tense body into relaxing. All day had felt like an amazing kickoff to summer, only to end in a nightmare.

The girls and I had started our day at the club's pool with friends. We ate burgers under a teal cabana and enjoyed being outside for hours. The first week of summer means swimming is still a welcome treat, one that feels like a mini vacation. The chlorine and sun teamed up, zapping everyone's energy, but it was worth it to enjoy the beautiful day. I had planned a full day for the girls with an ulterior motive. I wanted us to have fun, but I also hoped to guarantee myself a short evening after our dinner routine.

While we were at the club, Kyle had called to prepare me for some important news we needed to discuss. He sounded more nervous than optimistic, so I thought I'd boost his mood by serving one of his favorite meals—barbecue chicken and stuffed baked potatoes, followed by my homemade pound cake topped with strawberries and fresh whipped cream. As I watched the girls jump off the diving board, I smiled to myself, anticipating a relaxing evening of cuddling next to Kyle on the couch.

I laugh bitterly as I slip out of my knee-length summer dress and slide into the almost-scalding bathwater. The iridescent bubbles softly settle on my body until they completely cover me in a magical foam. I rest my heavy head on the wide porcelain lip of the tub, close my eyes, and try to force myself to go somewhere peaceful in my mind. Instead, I hear one sentence replaying over and over on a loop: *I have another daughter.*

As I rub the delicate bubbles into my arms and neck, I search my memory of this evening for any warning lights, signs, or hints of the impending doom. I can't find a single moment from our practically perfect day that seemed amiss. Kyle was happy, which ignited our tired bodies with brighter spirits. It wasn't until after we tucked our little princesses into their beds that the truth came out, little by little.

After our talk, by the look of him, you'd have thought he was sick. His sandy-colored hair, normally groomed to perfection, had been disheveled, highlighting the gray strands that stand higher and curlier than their darker counterparts. His bloodshot eyes were magnified against the pale tones of his ashen skin. His shoulders stooped over like a beaten dog, a posture he quickly assumed after my knee-jerk reaction to his news. A perfectly normal and reasonable reaction to the unexpected news that my husband is bringing his unknown love child into my home.

Fresh tears start to fall as I remember how he tried to tell me his news in one fell swoop, but my brain kept glitching. His story proved to be too complex for me to process all at once. But I got the gist of it. To be blunt, this news is not good. In fact, I was horrified ... still am. A drum begins to pound in my head as I filter through the memories of our courtship. From the beginning, he had been an open book. He brought me into his world, shared his life memories and family dreams with me. There were no secrets between us, or so I thought. I can't help but wonder why he purposefully erased this chunk of time off his timeline.

Surely he can see how terrible this will be for us and our family on multiple levels. I'm having a hard time swallowing it all as a lump swells at the back of my throat. I assume this child's mother accurately identified Kyle as the father years ago and, for whatever reason, failed to inform him he had a daughter. I don't want or need someone else's daughter living in my house, even if she is Kyle's. Besides, I'm already the mother of his two girls—our girls. How could that woman do this to us—go off and die and *then* tell Kyle he has a child to raise?

I sink farther into the bathwater as unspoken questions drown my rational thoughts. *Isn't there anywhere else she could land? Maybe with someone who, at the very least, knows her middle name and birthday? Anywhere but here, with us.* I wanted to say all this earlier, but I sensed Kyle's inner struggle, so I kept my mouth shut. At least, I am sealing it for now.

I wish I could be more supportive. However, the wind has just been violently sucked out of my sails. I know in my heart all this had happened before I entered Kyle's life. But I can already hear that major detail conveniently being omitted in the colorful renditions whispered not-so-softly behind my back. This will ruin us, brand us as "that family," the not-so-put-together family ripped apart at the seams. I know this trivial fear should be at the bottom of my worry bucket, but it's not. And I will not apologize for caring how we're perceived around town because I have lived on the wrong side of that line. I know how gut-wrenching it is to be the object of nasty rumors women blather as they chew the fat.

And what if she's a terrible teen? Surely there will be anger and resentment. What will the ramifications be for my girls and my marriage? What if she can't, or won't, adjust to us? What if *I* can't adjust to her?

The what-ifs begin spinning out of control, making me lightheaded. I draw circles in the iridescent film that clings to the water, trying to make sense of it all. I had demanded and deserved answers. Kyle owed me at least that much. But I knew he wasn't telling me everything. I saw it in his face when he closed his eyes. He was a million miles away, opening a locked door to his heart, a door I never knew existed. I noticed how his body relaxed slightly as a faint smile tried to form at the corners of his mouth. He remembered her ... fondly. Fresh pain and anger suffocate me as I wonder what he's not telling me and why.

An inner demon from an old battle rears its nasty head and hisses in my ear, *You'll never be enough.*

I reach for a towel and slip out of the tub and into my silky nightgown. Staring into my bathroom mirror, I give myself permission to play out the endless possibilities. It is dangerous to let my imagination run wild, but better to gear myself up for the worst versus being surprised and caught off guard by it.

My mind wanders through the dusty maze of old memories, and I am back in high school. Why can't these memories just disappear? I thought I had wiped them out of existence, pushing them so far away, they virtually vanished into thin air. I refuse to give this part of my past any attention! I need peace and answers, not the resurfacing of old pains that compound the effects of my perceived personal deficiencies. So why now? Is there some parallel worth noting that tethers today's discovery to the personal devastation, the personal F5 tornado that tore me apart back then? Feelings and memories I thought I had replaced long ago now bubble to the surface.

***

She was the new girl in town the summer before my senior year, and we lived in a town that rarely saw an influx of newbies. I didn't know anything about this girl, had no personal experience with her, but my loose-tongued friends kept me up to speed while I spent most of the summer at church camp. She was beautiful in an exotic and mysterious way—a practically unknown junior who I assumed wouldn't be in my way. I didn't put much effort into thinking about her because why would I? It was my senior year, my year to shine and make memories. Looking back, I see how that blinding promise of a flawless year was too idealistic. I should have anticipated that nothing goes as planned. It doesn't matter how intentional and well-constructed your plans are, something always threatens to throw everything off-balance. Now I know that all too well.

Living in a very small town in East Texas, there wasn't much to do except talk or find a way to get into trouble. Boys seemed to live on the edge of trouble while girls sharpened their razor-like tongues.

Gossip is a Southern pastime, a learned behavior I'd seen perfected in the generations of women who shaped me. The price for all gossipers is simple: keep your personal matters private. Gossip feeds off the dramatic. So, if you wanted to stay off the gossip radar, you didn't chance anything that could give you negative press because if you were discovered, loose lips would ruin you. I admit, I never gave my gossipy nature a second thought. After all, it was the solid platform that securely defined my popularity. Most of the time, the gossip was a means to an end—try to fit in or be one of the outcast girls. Acknowledging how my words ripped others apart didn't faze me as long as I got the reaction or attention I craved.

Texas in August is always sweltering. The heat smothers your entire body by wrapping itself around you like cling wrap. Just one look outside triggers your conditioned pores to start sweating, or *glistening* as some girls insist on calling it. But my body's reaction was not a consequence of the blistering Texas heat. At first glance, my face flushed, and water gushed out of my pores, my jealousy boiling hotter than the air around us. Rosemary, the new girl, was undeniably beautiful, which I immediately deduced would definitely ruin my senior year. I just knew it! Rosemary was the newest, shiniest thing to happen in our small town in years. Yes, families came and went, but this felt different. In a conservative town that thrived on the power of a nuclear family, Rosemary and her mom were an anomaly. Since it was just the two of them, they didn't fit the town mold.

As far as anyone knew, there was no man in their household … at least to date. A vibrant woman in her midforties, Rosemary's mom stood out from the other women, flaunting her stylish relevance with her trendy hair and fashion-forward wardrobe. The everyday housewives felt threatened by her modern edge and the obvious availability she posed to any breathing male in town. So, with their hackles raised in unison, they formed a Southern alliance against her. It started with a gossip train designed to be simple: keep an eye on your husbands. Then the warnings and the cattiness grew and took on a life of their own. In truth, we all wondered why they moved to Pine Hills, Texas.

It was a lingering question that encouraged their meddling curiosity and prompted a new tactic: an infiltration. The alliance started inviting this woman to teas, book clubs, and other social gatherings under the false promise of friendship. However, they used the lighthearted socials to keep tabs on her while they hoped to uncover her questionable history. Even though everyone wanted to know this woman's story, they kept her an arm's-length away from them. Friendship is a sincere two-way street. Since their efforts were calculated and fake, she remained a mystery to them, living safely outside the circle of social acceptance.

As anticipated, Rosemary was front and center for the remaining weeks of summer. She was everywhere—the pool, the lake, the movies, the pizza hangout—everywhere! I couldn't escape this new beauty who mysteriously *poofed* her way into town and stole my spotlight. My senior year was planned to perfection: nominated president of Student Council, guaranteed lead roles in all musical and theater performances, and dating the quarterback of our winning football team. I had it all in the palm of my hand. I had worked too hard to have my senior year ransacked by this no-name junior. This was my show, and I didn't need or want anyone else stealing my spot! She could have her turn at my life next year, once I'd graduated.

So, like any good Southern girl, it was time to play nice. I bit my lip and decided I would "make friends" with Rosemary in an attempt to keep my enemy close. That's the Southern way of manipulation. Luckily for me, Rosemary, being from the Midwest, was completely unaware of this cultural norm and took the bait. I allowed her to be seen with me in public, making it my mission to be in the hub of all her activities as well as my own. I spent the last few weeks of summer teaching her the ins and outs of our town, the people, and school. She was going to owe me big for all my time. But I didn't expect her to latch on to me so obsessively in the process. It blew my mind how much she thrived on our time together, but I didn't let that distract me from securing my perfect senior year.

It didn't take long for people to notice us spending time together. Questions concerning my motives were raised by my longtime friends while praise dripped like honey from mothers' lips for graciously taking her under my wing. It seemed my hospitality was a win-win situation … that is, until the first day of school.

***

Staring at my now-middle-age reflection, I see an insecure girl looking back at me. My mind unscrambles the distant image as I remind myself that was a long time ago. Despite all my preemptive efforts, my past still haunts me. I sigh, gently lifting the outside skin around my puffy eyes, tight and firm. Today has taken its toll on me. I walk into our bedroom, pull back the covers, and grab my journal. I write one sentence, the only one I keep uttering. *How will I live with my husband's love child?* I close the journal and sink into the covers, listening to my husband's solid footfalls moving toward me.

CHAPTER 6
Marni

"Yes, yes, *yes*! I'm getting it all! Geez!" I exhale dramatically, releasing pent-up frustration and pain. I once read that breathing in deep patterns can improve your health or current state of mind, but I don't think anything will help me now. Even though I know what I want, no one cares. My vote won't count until I'm eighteen years old. So here we are, less than two weeks after Mom's funeral, and today marks another end to a lifelong chapter: the last day in my apartment—in Mom's apartment. It wasn't much, but it was where our memories were created, and our life together was lived. I can hardly bear to say goodbye ... again.

I feel the world is taking a magic eraser to my life, forcibly trying to wipe away all evidence of Mom and me. A darkness swallows me like a black hole as I imagine a different life, a faceless future that waits for me.

My hands robotically grab some shirts and jeans, and I throw them in my four-year-old backpack. My closet was never filled to begin with, and now it resembles an empty cavity. I yank one more shirt off a hanger, then notice a banged-up box tucked into the corner. Water stains dot the bottom, and chunks are missing from two corners of the lid, but I sit down and put it gingerly in my lap, at once excited and fearful of what I'll find.

I open the box to find Mom's personal treasures. Tears sting my eyes as I pull out all the things I have made for her over the years—drawings, paintings, handprint art, and personal letters. I flip through each piece and discover her careful documentation with dates, context, and its impact on her heart. I flip over a pencil sketch of an old farmhouse and read her words:

> *Marni gave this to me after seeing a picture at Jo's of our grandma's house where we spent our childhood summers. Warms my heart thinking back to those innocent and carefree days. Thank you, God, for the beautiful memories stirred up from this beautiful picture Marni created.*

My jaw drops. I had no idea. I read her notes on the back of the top few pieces of art, remembering my inspiration behind each creation. Once she got sick, I barely picked up a pencil.

I'll ask Aunt Jo to store this for me. I swipe my eyes and stand to finish packing my room. It doesn't take long, and when my fingers slowly pull at the flimsy zipper around my backpack, my heart sinks. I never thought things could look bleaker than losing Mom, but I was wrong. This new loss of home adds more baggage to my heavy heart, an emptiness I can't explain. This is it, after all these years. All I'll have in Texas to remind me of my real life are a few outfits from the secondhand store.

It's ironic how little importance you place on the things that fill your personal world until the possibility of never seeing them again becomes a reality. We created a family here, just the two of us, with memories and love. I will miss curling up in the comfy barrel chair to drink my hot chocolate while Mom talked to me from the kitchen. I will miss smelling traces of her cooking wafting through the floor vents, the smell of home. Looking around, I try to lock every last detail, moment, and image into my memory vault.

Finally, I walk down the old hallway, thankful for the creaking floorboards as they gift me one last memory, a musical goodbye. Bouncing the wooden planks to make them sing one last time, I remember Mom. I smile as I remember how she tried so hard to walk soundlessly down the hall to my room every morning and each night to check on me. But the old floors always betrayed her presence. As I walk away now, it helps to imagine it isn't my creaky footsteps I hear but Mom's right beside me, like she's helping me say goodbye. I swallow the lump in the back of my throat as I acknowledge her comforting presence.

I stop in the kitchen and capture one last look at the growth tick marks laddering up the wall beside the green fridge. The landlord will probably repaint the walls, but I need to leave one more mark. I open the kitchen junk drawer and find a pen. I stand with my heels butting up to the wall next to the fridge, level the pen on top of my head, and draw a line from left to right. I step back and write, *Marni. Age 14. Last day in her home.*

I turn and look around the only home I've ever known. It's eerily quiet outside and uncannily empty inside.

I take a deep breath and hear Mom whisper to my heart, "I am with you, always and forever … you are my home." I feel her grab my hand as she leads me out the door for the last time. I walk down the few steps to the street and join Aunt Jo whose eyes are red and swollen. I pause, unable to speak as tears gush down my face, and drop the box at her feet.

Aunt Jo glances at it then swoops me into her huge embrace. "Shhh, shhh. It'll be okay, Marni. It's gonna be okay, you'll see."

I pull away and look at her with red, watery eyes. Then I turn back for one last look at my home, my memories, my life. "Goodbye," I whisper, my voice catching in audible breaths.

The next day is busy handling last-minute details. Aunt Jo dominates the phone without the simple courtesy of my feelings. I need closure, not airtight travel plans. I couldn't care less about what plane I'll be flying, where I'm going, and how I will be getting there. Doesn't she get it? All I really want is for my friends to call me, stop by for one last tearful hug, swear we'll never lose touch even though we know it's inevitable at fourteen. It matters to me that I will be missed. I just lost everything, and I want reassurance that losing me pains them as much as it does me. There is no doubt I will miss everything—Mom, home, Aunt Jo, my friends, school, Chicago. I know it sounds selfish and shallow, but I need someone to miss me in return. Twenty-four hours from now, I'll be leaving. The finality of it all is suffocating, yet it feels unimportant to everyone else around me. It's maddening.

"Aunt Jo, *stop*! Stop the crazy train! Why are you panicking about tomorrow when I'm still here with you today? Don't you want to spend our last day together, doing something memorable?" I plead, thinking it's the least she could do. A fresh wave of irritability washes over me as I try to bite my tongue. I don't want to spend my last day mad, but she's not helping things. She's too determined to get me on that plane and out of her hair.

Aunt Jo drops her head. Fascinated at how her wild, frizzy hair always remains glued into position, compliments of a can of ultra-frizz-control hair spray, I give her the best pouty look I can muster.

"Marni, honey, of course I want to spend time lovin' on you. But you're my responsibility, and I have to verify that everything is in order before I send you down to your dad. I won't be able to relax until I know all is right. This is just my way of showing you the depths of my heart—making sure all the questions and concerns have been answered and addressed." I'm unimpressed by this explanation, and reading my reaction, she adds with a smile, "Let's splurge and go out for a special dinner." She winks.

Slightly appeased for the moment, I politely excuse myself from her preoccupied presence and sneak outside for some fresh Chicago smog. Sitting on the stoop of her building, I close my eyes, trying to trigger my senses into memorizing the details and senses that characterize my Chicago. The thick, black exhaust from the delivery trucks down the road invade my lungs like a welcome visitor. Distant fire and police sirens create a reassuring ballad amid the constant chaos. My grumbling stomach and watering saliva glands instinctively react to the fresh pizza dough perfuming the air. Doors open and shut all around me in this city filled with constant motion. My Chicago, the heartbeat of my home, won't skip a beat when I'm gone. Somehow reassured by the city's durability, I tilt my chin up to the blistering sun and promise myself I will always remember Chicago as my home.

Aunt Jo and I walk a couple of blocks to her favorite neighborhood restaurant. She opens the door to guide me inside, but I hesitate. Mom always loved this place, but we could never afford more than a shared dessert for special occasions.

Aunt Jo leans down and says, "Did you know your mom loved eating here with your father?" I shake my head, eyes wide with surprise. "Let's go see what all the fuss is about," she says, ushering me inside.

We park ourselves by the window and both order the "famous" pesto pasta, but my mood—ever so volatile these days—has darkened. My aunt tries to camouflage the uncomfortable tension between us by filling the silence with her boring work stories. I tune her out, lost in thoughts of my mother and father. Our food finally arrives, and I put my head down and devour every last noodle. I start to soak up the green sauce with a puffy dinner roll when I look up at my aunt and ask her the question that haunts me: "Why didn't she tell me?"

Aunt Jo gently puts down her fork. She is slow to respond, probably trying to buy time to come up with another new explanation, maybe one that will satisfy me. "Tell you what, exactly?"

I take an obnoxiously loud slurp of soda and glare at her. She knows precisely what I mean because I keep asking her the same question every chance I get, despite her inability to give me a straight answer. "About my dad," I say, my voice growing in intensity. "About this crazy plan of hers. All of it."

"It was a long time ago, Marni." Aunt Jo looks out the window like she's looking back in time. "She was so young, had so many dreams …" She looks back at me. "I can't answer that for her. I don't know."

"But you knew."

She releases an exhaustive breath and moans like she's in pain. "We can't get into this again. Not now, not tonight. I wish she'd have told you everything before it was too late, before leaving all your unanswered questions up to *me* to field. I just don't know how to answer you." Her head hangs, defeated. "Can't we just enjoy this time together, please."

I shrug listlessly, letting her off the hook for now because deep down, I know she's right. My mother should have been the one to provide me with answers. She's the one who betrayed me for fourteen years.

"All right," Aunt Jo says with a swift slap on the table. "Want to go see a few friends?"

I nod slowly and start to feel my skin prickle with excitement. We pay the bill and head out the door in the direction of my best friend's house. When we get there, though, she's not home. We try another friend with the same outcome.

Jo looks at me and says, "I told them we'd be by after dinner. I'm so sorry, sweet girl."

The tip of my nose begins to sting as tears fall down my face.

Aunt Jo wraps her soft arms around me and says, "Let's go home."

As we turn the corner, I hear a loud commotion coming from the basketball court. A party of some sort. There are tons of people … wait, not people, my friends! Stunned, I stop and look questioningly at Aunt Jo. Her mascara slides messily down her full cheeks, which she pulls into a sad smile. Unable to talk, however, she flicks her wrist, quickly shooing me away from her and toward the expectant crowd. I run into my friends' arms, jumping up and down, hugging and giggling like this is just an ordinary day, which it's not. Happiness lifts my spirit as Mom's friends and, more importantly mine love me enough to give me a send-off celebration. I silence my brain and ignore my heartache to savor one more memory before everything changes.

The send-off party is the best hour and a half I've experienced since Mom passed. Aunt Jo pulls her phone out of her purse and snaps picture after picture of me and my friends. For a moment, I'm just a fourteen-year-old girl at the center of a surprise party. We celebrate with cookies and soda. My friends decorated the metal cage door with a few balloons and some handmade banners. I even receive a few going-away cards.

Being with my friends, laughing, replaying memories, sharing stories, all of it reminds me of who I am. For a moment, I'm the girl I used to be before my entire world shattered. What a gift—my last moments in Chicago are filled with friends. I almost forgot what it was like to feel so carefree and happy. But it all comes to an end too quickly.

***

"Plane ticket? Emergency phone numbers?" Aunt Jo nervously asks. She is a wreck. But who are we kidding? So am I.

"Check," I answer numbly. I can't believe this is it. In mere minutes, I will be flying away from home and into the unknown. Tears fill my eyes as Aunt Jo wraps her pillowy arm around my shoulders, gently guiding me to the correct gate.

Airport personnel mumble boarding instructions over the intercom. I throw my arms around Aunt Jo's warm body and cling to her, terrified to say goodbye. We hold each other, clasped in a tight embrace. How can we let each other go? I need her.

Through a muffled sob deep in her dress, I whisper, "Thank you, Aunt Jo. Thank you for loving me! I love you."

Wiping away her tears, she pulls back to look past my eyes and into my soul as she speaks, "I love you too, sweet girl. I'll always be here for you. I'm going to miss you so much." She seals her love with one last kiss on my forehead. As I tearfully board the plane for Texas, jitters from my belly awaken my nerves, and I pass happy families seated together on the plane. Why am I leaving the only family I have in this world to live with complete strangers? As I rest my head against the plane's uncomfortable headrest, I concentrate on Aunt Jo's last words—I'm loved, I'm not alone, and I'll be missed. Clutching my bag into my chest, I pull out Mom's letter and once again focus on her promise, my favorite line: *I will forever be watching over you.*

CHAPTER 7
Lauren

I always loved the first day of school, when even the smell of freshly painted hallways heralded the possibility of new beginnings. Everyone always put their best foot forward, excited to see everybody but also anxious to be seen sporting a new outfit, perfect makeup, and a fresh hairstyle.

As I look back on my senior year, though, the details that immediately spring to mind replace what that day inevitably represented to me—an end, not a beginning. I'm in awe of how my self-preservation has restructured the memories I've carefully cataloged. My senses travel through the dusty caves and cobwebs of my mind, recalling those events with haunting clarity. A memory I can easily retrieve is fixated on how I looked on the outside. There is no depth associated with this visual because a true Southern woman understands the importance of physical appearance. But that's an inaccurate account of that day. Why hide the truth from myself? I know it's acceptable to fall apart on the inside as long as no one is there to witness it.

I smile, remembering how that day started. I oozed confidence. I wore a flirty jean skirt that hugged my hips, flaring just enough to provide a decent swing without showing too much of my toned thighs. My cornflower-blue blouse matched my eyes. I finished my outfit with a skinny, iridescent belt, which added interest while accentuating my cinched waistline. My long, golden hair cascaded down my shoulders in loose curls I had neatly secured to one side with bobby pins. My makeup was flawless and fresh. This was the first day of my best year yet.

By third period, I had seen just about everyone. I relished the attention I evoked, noting how peers stopped to stare at me, envying my confident poise. The spotlight granted me the lead role, illuminating me as I pranced up and down the halls. All eyes were on me—mission accomplished. I was a success. However, after a few periods, the attention felt different from what I had expected.

The gossip swarmed me like mad bees as the intense buzz floated from one social circle to another in between class periods, but that was normal, right? The constant buzz spilled monumental news into everyone's ears except mine. But why was I left out? I watched as lips moved and eyes narrowed their focus on me—they were anything but discreet. Were they talking about me? I tried to understand, but the information flow conveniently ran dry before it ever reached my ears. I heard hushed snippets, but nothing made sense to me.

I hated the feeling of being out of control of the flow of information because I had always been the one in the know.

Being an egotistical teenage girl, I tried to assume the best. *Of course they're talking about me. And why not? I look fabulous.* I grabbed my lunch and walked over to the table my friends and I had claimed for the past three years. As I sat down, I heard our names—Rosemary and Lauren. The lunchroom whispers grew into a controlled roar, causing my head to spin. My friends sat quietly, awkwardly stealing glances at each other as if to ask, *What now?* They knew something they weren't telling me.

I calmly leaned in and asked my friends, "What's going on? Seems like there's some juicy gossip spreading. Anyone know what it is?" I took a sip of my water and watched them squirm in their seats. "Come on, girls. I'm pretty sure I heard my name mentioned ..."

"They're talking about you and Rosemary," my friend Angie said.

I laughed, wondering whose feathers I'd ruffled by taking her under my wing. My voice instantly lighter, I asked, "What about us?"

"It's the nature of your *relationship*," Angie said, raising her eyebrows.

I mocked her by stating the obvious. "We're *friends*," I said, stretching out the word. "She's new, so I helped her get acquainted and meet some people. What's the big deal?" I broke off a segment of my orange and popped it into my mouth. "I was just being a good senior to the school newbie."

"Is that all?" Angie's eyebrows peaked. "You sure there's nothing else you'd like to add?" She paused, her fingers spinning her loose hair mindlessly into a tight cord as she looked at the other girls at the table. With suspicious interest, she continued, "Okay, fine. Since you've spent so much time with her, what's her story?"

"Angie, I don't know her story, and I don't really care. Like I said, I was just trying to show her the ropes to make sure she knows who's in charge ..." I shifted in my seat, straightened my posture, and reminded them by pointing my thumb at my chest.

"Well, maybe you"—she paused, her eyes picking up everyone else's expression at the table—"should talk to your dad because rumors are spreading fast that she's your sister."

I dropped the carrot I was munching on and glared at Angie. Through clenched teeth, I growled, "What are you talking about?" I half laughed. The outrageous slander must have started by someone jealous of my standing at the top. What a joke! But I quickly read the faces of my friends and saw they were not joking. I pushed the palms of my hands onto the lunchroom table before I demanded, "Stop spreading these scandalous lies about my family!"

"I'm not spreading anything about your family! It's everyone else," Angie said, attempting to defend herself.

"Then be my friend and shut it down, stick up for me, do something!" I practically screamed in the now-silent lunchroom. Everyone's eyes were fixed on our table. They weren't envious of my outfit or social status in school. They were soaking in the deliciousness of my unprecedented meltdown. Their predatorial looks sent a shiver down my spine.

The cafeteria was notorious for breeding drama. It was the hour we all looked forward to, where everyone received a pass to be themselves with their friends. People talked, drama unfolded, and gossip spun out of control. The difference, though, was my gossip sessions were based on 100 percent truths, unlike these nasty rumors about my family. Ugh, this could be incredibly detrimental to my overall image and my family's reputation. Foul gossip in a small town had the ripple effect of a tsunami. I needed to get through the day without allowing outrageous slander to ruin it. Lies and jealousy—that's what I kept telling myself. Someone had concocted and spread these lies out of jealousy.

As soon as school let out, I found my little brother outside, talking with fellow ninth graders, and headed straight home. I should have known something was amiss when Dad and Mom were waiting motionless for us in the living room. Not that it was unusual to see them together, but it was out of the norm at four in the afternoon. Mom's face expressed heartache and anger. Her puffy, red eyes glowed with rage while streaks of exposed skin peeked through her previously perfect makeup in a zigzag pattern down her face. She was clearly upset yet unnaturally quiet for her perky personality. Dad slumped at one end of the couch, allowing a full seat cushion as a buffer zone to the other end where Mom sat perfectly still and upright. His hands constantly moved as if he were tying imaginary cords in knots. His face was drained of color except for the deep-blue eyes that still held traces of spent tears. My brother and I stood confused, taking in the scene. Mom motioned for us to join. "Your dad has something to share with you." We sat in the two chairs facing the couch as horrible scenarios raced through our minds.

Did someone die?

Did Dad lose his job?

Is someone terminally ill?

Are we moving?

Tension filled the room like thick fog as questions stormed my brain.

CHAPTER 8
Marni

Since this is my first time on an airplane, Aunt Jo made sure I'd have a window seat. Although, there really isn't much to see as we touch down in Dallas, except for a cluster of tall downtown buildings including one with a ball on top. The flight attendant tells me the giant ball is actually a spinning restaurant. She says she's eaten there before and hopes I can find the time to try it out. I think she must have sensed my sadness and was trying to perk me up. After the plane rolls to a gentle stop, I double-check my shoulder bag and my folder of instructions while listening as the flight attendant calls out connecting flight information. I quickly exit the plane where an older woman, probably someone's grandma, greets me. She makes a statement in her black uniformed dress with frosted hair styled and sprayed so high it could catch a baseball. Honestly, the amount of hair spray evidenced by the crystalized dots glistening in her hairdo astonishes me.

"Marni?" the older woman asks in an accent straight out of an old western movie.

"Yes, ma'am. I'm Marni," I cautiously answer.

"I'm Sue. I'll be helping you get on your next flight," she chirps as she glances at an electronic board overhead. "Here, honey"—she extends her hand—"I brought you an ice-cold drink," she announces, handing me a bright-red soda can.

As we maneuver through the terminals, Sue tries her best to initiate small talk. After several failed attempts, she enters into a monologue about all the wonderful things Dallas has to offer. Once she finishes talking food, entertainment, and recent celebrity sightings in the airport, she casually asks why I am visiting Texas.

"I'm not visiting," I answer bluntly. "My mom just passed away, and now I'm being forced to live with a man I've been told is my father." I hope my snippy answer will seal her lips shut.

"Oh, well ... I'm so sorry about your mother. But I'm sure you'll just love Texas. Everyone is so nice here," she continues with too much positivity, but since I appreciate her effort, I offer her a sincere smile.

Arriving at the gate, Sue wishes me good luck in her thick Texas twang and checks me in at the flight counter. Just one more flight, and I'll be that much closer to finding out what awaits me at the end of this stressful journey. The emotional anticipation causes my chest to tighten and my head to spin as a nauseating feeling builds from the pit of my stomach.

I curl into myself and whisper a silent reminder into my heart. *This is just a short visit.* I refuse to acknowledge this as anything other than a temporary stop with a definite expiration date typed in bold font. Since Mom and Aunt Jo promised me I could come back home after six months, I am guaranteed to be home by Christmas. I smile as my mind travels into the future to where I see Aunt Jo welcoming me back home. A single tear will slip from the corner of my eye when she promises me she'll never let me leave again.

Six months, that's all. It's one season of a TV show, one semester of school, practically a drop in the bucket of time—at least, that's what I keep telling myself. I've warped my mind into believing I'm on a much-needed vacation from life. In just six months, I will return to Chicago, back to Aunt Jo where I belong. Even though there is a light at the end of this tunnel, my heart twists in knots as a shadowy truth tortures my soul. My home, Mom, our family ... it's all permanently gone.

I continue to go through the motions like Aunt Jo instructed. Board my next plane to Waco—check. Watch the clouds drift by—check.

Now, as I stand beside my backpack, waiting for a cab, the reality and awkwardness of the situation hits me right between the eyes.

Why isn't my father picking me up? I think, once again.

Aunt Jo set up all my travel arrangements—though my "father" had paid for it all—and when I asked her that question, she took a few beats before responding.

"I think it'll be an easier transition for everyone if you meet them all at once, at your new house. Besides, sometimes planes get delayed, so this will be a more fluid plan." She sounded pleased with her thought-out explanation.

Within a few minutes of breathing in the Texas heat, my cabdriver pulls next to the curb, holds up a picture, looks at my face, and then asks, "You Marni?" He lifts a sign revealing my picture with my name in bold print across the top. I nod as he takes my old backpack and drops it into the trunk. I take a deep breath and slide into the back seat. Simple instructions I have followed to a T. Once all the boxes of my to-do list are checked off, my body relaxes into the crackled leather seat. I am in Texas, driving to meet my new family, or strangers—I'm not sure exactly what they are to me yet.

We pull out of the tiny Waco airport and onto a large road and head straight into the sun's line of fire. The rays briefly blind my vision as I lift my hand to cut the glare. There is nothing of stature big enough to block the sun's annoying presence, so I position myself behind the headrest in front of me, hoping it is up to the challenge. The streets are peppered with small buildings, gas stations, and shopping centers. Occasional fields dotted with livestock break up the monotony of the flat scenery. There is no skyline to speak of, nothing of real architectural or visual interest. This place seems so unreal and unlike home. How can this be my new city?

Squinting through the glare of the window, the cabdriver announces, "I'll have you home in about fifteen minutes." I refocus my eyes on his through the rearview mirror and nod.

The quiet drive is a stark contrast to the voices and noise in my head. I close my eyes, trying to channel my energy into preparing to meet my dad. My mind rewinds time to my younger days, remembering how I used to imagine all sorts of scenarios of things we'd do together. I used to lie awake at night and envision him sitting next to Mom at the edge of my bed as they told me bedtime stories. I would wake up Christmas mornings, hoping with all my might that my dad would be waiting for me by our tree, drinking his coffee next to Mom. I was convinced he'd have loved taking me to the zoo to quiz me on specific animal trivia or walk me to the library to check out my first book. Whatever dream day I had invented with my dad always ended the same: the three of us—Mom, Dad, and I—enjoying one of Mom's home-cooked meals around our small wooden table as a family, laughing and talking. But in all my dreaming, I never imagined this turn of events. A life without Mom, and now I find out my dad is actually alive? I had always imagined my happily-ever-after ending with me in the center of my completed family, surrounded by their love. My stomach lurches and contracts as I feel my childhood fantasy being uprooted and trampled on.

My mind replays Aunt Jo's words over and over. "He never knew you existed, Marni. He can't wait to meet you," she insisted, meeting my eyes as she squeezed my shoulder in affirmation. Fear punctuates my uncertainty. What if I'm an unwelcome interruption to the family and the happily ever after he's already created? As the what-ifs start to choke out any spark of excitement, I remember all the birthday wishes I made over the years—*I wish I could meet my dad*. My nerves jitter at the realization that those wishes, against all odds, are coming true. I picture his expression and reaction as we meet and immediately appreciate the gift of finally being able to replace the made-up face I've given him for his real face. I cross my fingers as I secretly make one more wish: *Please, Lord, help him love and accept me as his daughter.*

With barely two weeks to get used to the idea, I'm still struggling to process my mom's wishes and reasoning behind her decision. I understand she thought I'd be alone, all by myself, but why did she overlook Aunt Jo? Maybe she was too focused on providing me with my best shot at being a part of a normal family. I twist the skin around my fingers to channel my tension and nerves. I can't believe this is actually about to happen after fourteen years of wondering. Bowing my head slightly, I silently pray: *Lord, I hope I'm not a disappointment. Help me to be enough.*

The cab finally turns down a winding road leading to the entrance of the most beautiful neighborhood I have ever seen. Massive homes peek through pecan and oak tree-lined streets. Shiny cars sit neatly on brick-paved driveways like ornaments intended to be seen, not driven. Lush emerald lawns feature colorful flower beds expertly manicured underneath the protection of giant shade trees. I can't get over how different this is from what I expected. I'd gone from one extreme to another. Chicago was loud, cramped, and industrial, whereas every inch of this neighborhood appears perfectly put together, sophisticated, and clean. But all this perfection puts me on edge. What little confidence I had seems to be dwindling. How will I fit into this perfect world?

My stomach drops as we make our way down a long, curvy driveway and stop in front of an enormous red-brick house. I fumble getting out of the car on shaky legs as I adjust my shirt and inhale the thick Texas heat. My lungs gratefully accept the pure air as it pushes the last lingering taste of downtown Chicago's smog out of my body. Strangely, the street sleeps like a giant as I get myself situated. Nothing moves ... no wind, no squirrels scavenging, no annoying dogs barking, or rowdy kids zooming down the sidewalks on their bikes. The eerie quiet is disconcerting, which makes me jump when the driver slams his door shut. He opens his squeaky trunk and quickly retrieves my bag. Appearing uneasy, he shuffles up the flower-lined pathway and plops my backpack onto the wide wooden porch. He stares at me for a hard moment, raises an eyebrow, and carefully asks, "You sure this the right address, honey? Seems we might be in the wrong place."

I pull out my folder with the typed address and read it off to him, confirming this is the right house.

He asks hesitantly, "You think anyone's home?" His eyes scan the perimeter of the house. He continues with an empty offering, "Want me to knock?" He rocks apprehensively on his heels.

"Uh ...." I stammer, unsure. As I am wondering what to do, I notice the front window's curtains flutter and sway. I guess I hoped for more fanfare, not this ghostly welcoming reception. What am I supposed to do now?

I take in my alien surroundings and repeat to myself, *They are expecting me. They want me. They will love me.* At least, that's what Aunt Jo says, right?

I raise my voice for the cabdriver to hear. "Yes, sir. This is right. Thank you."

He hustles into his cab and drives out of sight before I can change my mind. This has to be right, but … what if …? Just then, the white plantation shutters from a second-story window quickly snap shut. It is obvious I'm being watched. What a strange sensation it is to know people are home and expecting you, but they've decided to spy before welcoming you inside. Beads of sweat start glistening on my forehead; my heart pounds to a quickening drumbeat in my ears. I can hardly breathe. Mysteries and answers stand on the other side of their elegant, mahogany and glass door. Light bounces off the cut angles of the diamond-patterned glass, throwing miniature prisms against the nearest wall. My fourteen-year wait will be over in just a few knocks. Straightening my shoulders, I whisper another prayer of strength as I timidly tap out three quick knocks with the back of my hand.

Just when the weight of my anxiety almost buckles my knees, shuffling footsteps approach from inside. The handle jiggles as the heavy door slowly swings open, and an older woman fills the doorway. With wide eyes, we stare at each other blankly. Her wrinkly skin sags under narrowing eyes that uncomfortably study every inch of me. I fidget, smoothing down the sides of my worn-thin shirt and attempt to cover the holes around the pockets of my shorts. My heart speeds up. Slowly, I meet her dark eyes and ask, "Um, Mrs. Mercer?"

Her eyebrows shoot up. "And you are?" Her curt response, cold and uninviting, catches me off guard. Struggling for air and the right words, I feel insecurity wrapping menacing fingers around my throat.

"Mrs. Mercer, I—I'm Marni." My voice cracks with uncertainty.

She drops her chin, peering at me over the top of her glasses, and shakes her head. I catch a barely audible but obviously disapproving sound as she turns away from me, pulling the heavy door almost closed. I stand there, stunned at my stepmother's reaction. I've read stories and watched movies about mean stepmothers, but I hadn't put much thought into my stepmom actually being a nightmare. I didn't think much past meeting my dad, a lifetime dream that is actually happening. At least, I thought so until now. What if she sends me away? She obviously wants nothing to do with me.

It took seconds for that haughty woman to decide I don't belong with them. A nagging voice inside my head chips away at my withering confidence and says, *Look at yourself. Can you blame her?* My clothes are far from fashionable, unless faded and visibly tattered is the new look. My hair is disheveled from a long day of travel. I am by no means put together, even though I tried hard this morning to wear something presentable. I wanted to make a positive first impression … I tried.

Embarrassed by the rejection, I turn to sit on the top step of their porch and bury my head into my knees. Silent tears fall as it hits me that I've absolutely nowhere to go. I don't know how long I sit there, cradling my bruised heart before I hear a commotion. I pull my head up and turn toward the door as four people appear in the doorway next to the rude woman. Flashing their perfect smiles, they look like they just jumped off a magazine page. I can't help noticing how beautifully put together they are with their color-coordinated outfits and perfectly styled hair. As I stand, the rude woman introduces me.

"This," she says, dragging out the *s* in what feels like an attack, "is Miss Marni."

My cheeks flush at her announcement.

The other grown woman gracefully waves her hand in the air. "We've got it from here. Thank you, Penny."

My eyes meet Penny's before she pivots to walk away. I want to ask who Penny is, but my tongue is tied by the presence of a man who might be my dad.

Tears fill my brown eyes as I politely make the first move. "Excuse me, sir, do you know Mr. Mercer?" My voice shakes under the awkward pressure. "He's expecting me."

The man steps toward me, and I stumble backward, a little skeptical of his motive. Noticing my tense response, he slowly tucks his hands into his designer jean pockets and shifts his gaze, staring a little too long at my ratty backpack. When his eyes meet mine, he clears his throat and softly replies, "Marni, I am Kyle Mercer." He gestures to the blond, blue-eyed woman and the matching set of girls. "This is my wife, Lauren, and our daughters, Lila and Annabelle. And you're absolutely right, we've been expecting you. Won't you please come in?" Mr. Mercer bends down to grab my bag and whispers, "You look just like your mother."

I just stare up at him for a few moments. Hesitantly, I relax the tension in my shoulders and then follow him inside their massive house. My mouth drops at the sheer enormity, at the abundance and the opulence I see all around me. I turn this way and that, rudely staring for long moments. This cannot be right. My father isn't this unbelievably rich man who lives in a mansion with servants. No.

My mind quickly jumps back to Chicago and the struggles Mom endured just to provide for me. *Did she know about his money? Surely, she must have. What would our lives have been like if she'd just told him about me from the beginning?* I shake my head, feeling ashamed and angry by my hapless upbringing and embarrassed and jealous of their privileged lifestyle.

Looking around at all of them, the differences between us feel palpable. It's hard to describe, but there's an aura around them. Everything about them screams affluence, and I'm not just talking about the mansion and their expensive clothes. They have an irreproachable poise. It's in the graceful way they hold themselves and in their confident gazes, as if they were inherently accustomed to this world of privilege from the moment they took their first breaths.

A shiver travels up my spine. *How is this going to work?* I wonder miserably.

I scan each face, trying to read their thoughts. Both young girls stand silent but obviously intrigued, understandably curious about me. I feel sympathy radiating from the man, my father, like he's sorry. I want to scream in his face, *You should be sorry! This life should have been*

Mom's and mine. Instead, I turn my attention to her, his wife, and notice the smile she greeted me with has turned uncomfortably strained, like she's forcing it. Tension is boldly painted across her face. But, it's more than that; it's like she's nervous about me or judging me. It makes my skin squirm. I stare down at my scuffed and weathered shoes and glance at her perfectly painted pink toes peeping out of crisp, white sandals. Yep, she feels it too—this doesn't feel right. I look back at her husband and wonder how he can be so calm. He squints his blue eyes and watches me assess the situation before he calmly addresses the elephant in the room.

"Marni, I can see all this is a shock to you. I'm sure it feels overwhelming, but we're just a normal family living a normal life, just like you and your mom."

I cut my eyes at him and say, "This is *nothing* like what Mom and I had. We had *nothing.*" My snide remark hangs in the air like a pungent smell.

"I'm sorry, Marni. I wish I had known …."

My shoulders drop as I hear exactly what he's not saying: Mom kept him out of my life. Mom kept us in the poorhouse. Even though I'm torn apart with grief, I've never been angrier at her. I want to scream at her, at him—at everyone! And it is in this moment that I feel it in my bones: I will never fit in here. Outside of this man's DNA contribution, this is not my family. This postcard-perfect household is not going to accept me and my life experiences any more than I can wrap my head around them and theirs.

CHAPTER 9
Lauren

I exchange a look with Kyle, then lightly tap Lila and Annabelle on the shoulder to usher them into the sitting room. "Marni, why don't you go in there and have a seat with the girls?" I point into the sitting room. I am cognizant of how pitchy my voice has become in the past few seconds since seeing her. My blood boils from within as I try desperately to keep up my polite Southern appearance. As I gently tug Kyle into the kitchen, I swivel my head over my shoulder to announce, "We'll be right back with some cold drinks and snacks."

My head spins as I try to regain my focus, but my whole body is reeling with just how difficult this transition is going to be. "Are you kidding me, Kyle? That's *our* Marni?"

"What do you mean by *that*?"

"You saw what she looked like. My stars, Kyle! What were they, dirt poor?" I shake my head in disbelief. "She's dressed in rags, literally dingy, holey rags. And how, *how* can fourteen years of her life fit neatly inside one small backpack?"

"So, we'll get her new clothes. It's not that big of a deal, Lauren."

"Not a big deal?" I hiss. How can he be so dense? "Do you have any idea what kind of life she has been living? Do you know anything about her mother or her parenting style?" My imagination runs wild as terrible thoughts and scenarios race through my mind. I gasp. "Was her mother on drugs? Oh, Kyle. What has Marni's life been like?"

I take a deep breath and brace myself against the kitchen counter. He puts his arm around me, trying to draw me in, but I just keep going, leaping to more ugly conclusions. "Has she been in school? Can she read, for crying out loud? Is *Marni* on drugs? Lord, should I be concerned about her stealing from us? My goodness, Kyle. What have you brought into our home?"

"Lauren, calm down."

I glare at him, hating to be told to calm down. I grind my clenched teeth and say, "Don't you dare say that to me. You have no idea what you're asking all of us to do, including Marni!"

His shoulders slump. "I know. But life has obviously not been easy on her. She has nothing, Lauren. Don't you see that I owe it to her and myself to make things right?"

I want to scream, *You owe it to your girls not to screw things up*! Instead, I control my temper. "This is absolutely not the way to set up our family for success," I say, my heart breaking with every syllable. "Just how will this emotionally distressed teenage girl, who we know nothing about, affect our family's stability? Affect our girls?"

He lets out a tired breath. "I don't know, but we can do this." He runs a hand through his golden, wavy hair. "Gabby never gave me the chance to be a father to Marni. I am not throwing this opportunity away, Lauren."

At the mention of *her*, Gabby, I let myself wonder what Kyle's first love looked like. I had seen pictures of the girls Kyle dated from his high school and college days. No surprise, they were all blue-eyed blondes with fit figures. I thought he had a type—I am that type—but it seems Gabby broke the mold. Judging by Marni's physique, her mom was far from Kyle's type. I try to bat away the green monster infiltrating my thoughts. I know she's dead, but I can't help wondering what set her apart from the rest us. How could she have possibly been *that* enticing to make him deviate from his "type"?

Maybe I shouldn't have been so naive when I imagined what Marni would look like. She's not a little girl—far from it. Her tall, lanky body flaunts distinctive curves that take me by surprise. Instead of resembling my girls with their pale golden hair and similar traits,

Marni is a stark contrast with dark, wavy hair, chocolate eyes, a sharp Roman nose, and high cheekbones. When I look at my girls, their father's features stare back at me—his blue eyes, the shape of his lips, the dimples that pop out when he laughs, and his slightly upturned button nose. No one would ever question he is their father; it's written all over their faces. I can't say the same about Marni. Without a visible trace of Kyle in any of her features, she could be any stranger off the street. I shake my head, trying to make sense of it all. The image of her standing a couple of inches taller than me, fully developed, and completely different from anything I expected overwhelms me. I am a mom of little girls. That's what I know. I don't know how to mother a nearly grown stepdaughter.

I groan aloud, remembering how Marni's pretty face had rapidly transformed from hopeful anticipation into utter fear. I guess we both had pictured each other as an extension of what we know, what is familiar to us. "Kyle, that introduction could not have gone worse. Witnessing her embarrassment at mistaking our maid for me, the shame flitting over her face as she visually compared herself to us, and the intimidation wafting off of her as she walked into our home … all of it made my heart ache."

Kyle slowly approaches me from behind and rubs his hands down the length of my arms.

My emotions are torn. As Kyle's wife, I am furious with his nonchalant approach that all of this will work out because I don't see that in the cards. As a mother, I can imagine all the questions the girls will have about Marni, and seeing poor Marni completely overwhelmed and lost … I grab my spatula and start transferring hot chocolate chip cookies onto a cooling rack while I think through the last few minutes.

I have to admit to myself that, yes, I had hoped Marni resembled us so she would easily blend in and make the transition a bit easier, a touch less noticeable. Now, though, it's not just about superficial, physical differences. It is the fact that we are raising our girls in a manner that is completely foreign to anything Marni has ever known. My agitation builds as I acknowledge I may not have the capacity or capability to help her—and all of us—bridge that gap to recreate a new, *happy* family. I don't want to admit defeat prematurely, but putting on a brave face and pushing forward may not be the right thing for everyone either.

I put the spatula down, close my eyes, and breathe. *In and out. In and out.* A stillness washes over me, and whispers of encouragement reassure my heart. *You are a mother. You are prepared for this.*

"What kept you from telling me about Gabby all these years? You know that I knew you had past girlfriends. So why did you hide *this* relationship from me until all this"—I fling my hand toward Marni—"forced your hand?" I huff in frustration. "I heard you tell Marni she looks just like her mother, a woman you keep mysteriously tucked deep inside your heart." I want to cry as I picture him pining for this woman, regretting his decision to leave her. Does he think of her when he should only be thinking and loving me? Without hesitating, I add, "Do you think you're protecting me? Because from my vantage point, it appears your sole focus is on preserving the memory of the two of you together." I pop a few cookie crumbs into my mouth, trying to stave off my jealousy without any success.

"It's not like that, Lauren."

Annoyed at myself as much as him, I slap my hand on the counter. "Honestly, Kyle? How do you expect me to believe that? This girl comes into our home and instantly stirs up images of *her* and the secret feelings you never dealt with. I don't know what to think anymore except that I'm scared to find out what else I don't know."

I turn away and start pulling glasses out of the cabinet. Knowing my husband, I'm sure Kyle's stare is boring a hole in the wood plank floors. He gently pulls me around to face him. His eyes look so tired. "Babe, I'm not trying to hide anything. I'm a man. Some stuff honestly never crosses my mind until it stares me right in the face."

I roll my eyes at this.

He glances down at my hands and starts gently stroking the inside of my palms with his thumbs. "I told you that Gabby was fresh out of high school when we met. She worked at the café near my office. Over a number of meals, I learned that she was from one of the nearby

Italian neighborhoods, her parents had died in a car accident a few years before, and she worked as many shifts as possible, saving money for her culinary dreams. I remember she worked hard for every penny she got and set aside what she could. That job—her determination— were her ticket out." He sighs. "Looking back on it, Marni is proof that we had passion, but I don't know if I'd call it *love*. Gabby was fiery and fun-loving and down-to-earth—so different from the girls my parents encouraged me to date. It was refreshing to meet someone who had no clue what my last name implied. She genuinely liked me. *Me.* Without all the clout."

I take a sharp intake of breath at his insinuation, but he shakes his head at me. "And I was young, too, and feeling a bit rebellious. I may have loved her, or at least, I remember thinking I could be moving down that path. But after confiding in my dad, he convinced me that she was just a temporary escape from my reality. I trusted him, and bought it, and ..." he blows out a hefty breath before admitting, "All I know for sure is that I ended things badly, like a coward."

"How so?"

"When I left, I knew we weren't going to work out, but I waited to break it off until I'd been home for a bit. I didn't want to hurt her. I think—I hoped—she knew it was coming." He looks down and squeezes his eyes shut. "Her sister, Jo, told me that she had been waiting to tell me she was pregnant in person." He runs his fingers through his disheveled hair. "Perhaps Gabby thought we would start our new life together, accomplish our dreams side by side, but the harsh reality is, I was the one who trapped her in the world she was trying to leave."

I feel my anger bubbling under the surface, but I tamp it down. "That isn't on you, Kyle. Gabby made her choice. It was a selfish choice, and it was hers alone. But now it's up to us—me and you—to figure out a way forward."

He nods but takes a minute to articulate his thoughts. "This is hard for me to admit, Lauren, but I honestly don't know where to begin to make things right with Marni. Who knows what's been said about me or what ideas she's conjured up in her head. Can you imagine how she must be processing all of this?"

Kyle's head falls to our entwined hands. "It's really just been her and her mom, but now she has a brand-new father, a stepmother, and two sisters. Not to mention, it's abundantly clear now that Gabby was barely able to keep them afloat. Marni's never had a fraction of what we can give her, and I want to give her everything. I really do ..."

I blow out a wave of pent-up air, releasing nervous energy. I tilt my head and look at my husband as I admit my own hard truth. "It's painful for me to think about you loving another woman. It's even harder for me to see this beautiful child without picturing you with her mother. How do you think Marni will tolerate seeing us together without constantly being reminded that *her* family is gone?"

"I don't know, Lauren." He takes a deep breath before speaking softly into my hands like a prayer. "But we have to make it work. We can do this—you and me. Together." He lifts his eyes to meet mine. "If you and I are feeling this overwhelmed, just imagine how my daughter is feeling?"

My eyes tear up, and my head begins to throb. I feel lightheaded and walk over to the table to sit. Kyle grabs my glass of iced tea, sets it in front of me, and joins me at the table.

I look up at him with imploring eyes. "This is a lot to ask of us, Kyle."

His eyes momentarily go wide.

"It's not just us—I'm concerned for her. All this"—I wave my hand to encompass us, the house, Texas—"it's a lot for her. Don't you think she'd be happier back home with her aunt?"

I'm not trying to upset him; I just want all the cards to be laid on the table. But determination flashes over Kyle's face like he's in the fight of his life. He lightly drums his fingers on the table, creating a steady beat before he answers. "I'm not certain where her aunt fits in, and I know this is going to be a huge adjustment for everyone, especially for Marni. Please try for her sake and mine." He reaches his hand across the table to hold mine and whispers with sincerity, "I'm not *your* father. I chose you and always will."

Deep down, I know he's right. I have no real claim to be mad or hurt. He met Marni's mom before we ever met. Marni's presence represents nothing unfaithful or dishonest toward me or my family. But he nailed it—the root of my pain. A deep wound had resurfaced when I first learned about Marni's existence. But after seeing that beautiful, lost teenager on my front porch, a new realm of uncertainty has forced me into another relapse.

Like my dad, Kyle had a secret romance he never once tried to share with me. He chose to keep his relationship with Gabby hidden until he had no other option but to tell me. The visible scars marking the landscape of my heart crack, exposing a wound I spent years tricking myself into forgetting. I look into Kyle's eyes, full of emotion, and am suddenly exhausted. I silently ask myself for the umpteenth time, *Will I ever be enough? Am I his heart's first choice or the sensible consolation prize?* I'm tired of contemplating and justifying my importance, my worth to the men in my life. For once, I need them to be enough for me, to stop disappointing me.

I carry plenty of psychological baggage from my dad's fling—a huge lack of trust and confidence in myself and others, especially men. Not to mention the toll it took on our once-perfect family. But because we're Southern, we kept our problems sealed behind locked doors, always portraying the outward appearance that everything was peachy. Sealed lips created sealed hearts, which was probably why I always wondered when Kyle was going to let me down and choose something better.

My dad's sneaky, selfish behavior banished my trust in men. Until Kyle. He changed everything. He renewed my faith in relationships through his kind, funny, and attentive love. I was comfortable by his side and felt truly seen when we were together. He helped me to realize that faithful love was attainable despite all the fears I kept bottled inside. Somehow, Kyle sensed my reluctance to release my heart fully to him. So, after months of talking about the future, our families, our goals, our beliefs, I opened up completely about my family's past and my deepest fears. He heard me and promised me truth would always be the foundation of our relationship, so I lowered my guard.

Before we married, I asked my dad what drove him to the arms of another woman. He blamed being burdened by tediously long days, new responsibilities that came with being a new father, and the lack of spontaneity. Love or the lack thereof was not the driving force; it was something intangible and unattainable that had seduced him. I can still see the sadness that crept into the cavities of his aging face as he was once again reminded of the domino effect that followed his selfish actions. I will forever remember him saying, "The truth is, I missed out on a sacred bond of love, trust, and confidence. Not only with your mother, but with you."

Suddenly, it dawns on me that Marni is sitting in the other room with my girls, waiting nervously for our return. I'm hit with the realization that we hold the power to navigate the course of her life. It's all in our hands, and I can make that choice.

Still processing, I mechanically pull out a shiny pewter tray trimmed in a beaded pattern. I plate a large stack of warm double chocolate chip cookies, fresh napkins, three glasses of iced sweet tea, and two juice boxes. Glancing over my shoulder, I catch Kyle watching me. He seems so afraid of so many things right now, but my reaction to Marni tops his list. I sense the overwhelming question that taxes both our minds: What's next?

Needing him to look into my eyes and really hear my heart, I turn to face him. "I'm sure Marni's exhausted from all of her travels and meeting all of us. This isn't going to be easy, but I'll do my best to help her see that she belongs here with us ... her family."

His eyes glisten with appreciation. Then he takes me in his arms and holds me close as he whispers in my ear, "You're amazing, Lauren. I love you more than anything. Never, ever doubt my love."

CHAPTER 10
Marni

"Did you know your hair almost matches your eyes? Except your hair is darker," the older girl states, moving too close to my face as she tries to confirm her observation. There is no judgment or ugliness, she's just baffled by our differences, like me. I feel positive that both our expectations have fallen very short. Disappointed, she probably envisioned an older, blue-eyed, blond version of herself. But that obviously isn't me. I plunge my fingers into the hair at the base of my neck, nervously pulling a small section of my coarse hair straight.

The younger sister, lost in her own world, suddenly adds, "She's like Snow White, except she's not wearing a poofy dress." I can't help it. I laugh at her comparison. I really am like her. The girls look at each other before the younger says, "What's so funny?"

"Well, doesn't Snow White leave her home to live with strangers in the woods?" They nod. "Sounds pretty close to what I've done."

The older one cocks her head. "We're not strangers. I'm Lila. I'm seven years old, and that's Annabelle, she's just five." I smile back at them. Without missing a beat, she adds, "And we live in this house, not the woods." Lila's tone suggests I might be crazy.

"I can see that. But, to me, it kind of feels the same. The home I just left had huge buildings towering over streets. But the tallest things around here are the trees ... like in the woods." The girls both laugh. Either they thought I was joking, or they had no idea what I meant.

Before I can change the subject, Lila digs through a large wicker basket nestled against the wall until she pulls out a rubbery, miniature figure of Disney's Snow White. Her delightful laugh breaks the awkwardness as she places the mini doll into my hands and turns to her sister. "Let's play."

Questions start to trickle out of them, one after another, without so much as a pause. How old am I? Why am I here? How long will I stay? Where have I been until now? It doesn't take long to interpret their banter as a method of making age-appropriate sense of our strange situation. I can't answer all their questions because these same questions and more swarm inside my head. So instead of making up creative answers, I tip my head closer to them like I'm about to share a secret and softly ask, "What have your parents said about me?"

Annabelle's eyes light up. She opens her mouth wide, formulating her answer. "Well, first they took us out for pizza, and then we came home and made gigantic ice cream sundaes. Mine had mini marshmallows, crushed chocolate chip cookies, chocolate syrup—"

"Annabelle, we don't care about your sundae," Lila interrupts, apparently easily exhausted by her sister's ramblings.

A little hurt, Annabelle crosses her arms and huffs at her older sister. I recognize the silent standoff, but I wanted to hear the rest of the story. I ask with sincere curiosity, "So what happened after you had the best sundae ever?"

Annabelle scrunches her eyebrows as she tries to remember the next detail. But Lila beats her to it. "We all cuddled up on the couch and watched the movie *Homeward Bound*. Have you seen it?" Lila's voice jumps an octave. A smile touches my lips as I remember Mom and I watching that movie together after she required me to read the book first. I nod yes. "Well, after it was finished, you know, when all the pets—the cat, the young dog and old one—finally make it back home, Mommy and Daddy said they had some incredible news for us too." Lila takes a breath to continue, but Annabelle interrupts her succinct flow.

"They told us we have an older sister! You!" Annabelle bursts.

"Were you happy to hear this news? I mean, what did you think?" I ask.

"Didn't really think much about it," Lila answers directly. "They said you're our sister, and that you're coming home." Lila pauses, her eyebrows furrow before she looks me in the eye and asks, "But why have you been gone so long?"

I stare into her inquisitive eyes, unable to speak as my tongue twists itself into a knot. This innocent question triggers spin-off questions I fear can never be answered. Why was I kept away? Was Mom ashamed of me? Tears start to sting the back of my eyes as fresh anxiety pushes into my heart. I take a deep breath as I attempt to refocus and am so thankful when Annabelle breaks the silence.

"I couldn't wait to meet you," Annabelle says. "Isn't it so exciting?" She squeals, and her fists come together under her chin.

I smile and nod at them, deciding to absorb their carefree, take-it-as-it-comes attitude. Ultimately, I think being able to openly voice their questions without any negative parental restrictions meant a lot. Nothing was cringe-worthy or outlandish; they just wanted their questions heard, which I completely understand. It's always nice to know someone hears you.

I glance at the large grandfather clock that stands at attention in the back corner. I can't believe I've only been in their house for twenty minutes, and I'm already pooped! Who knew these two girls could be so talkative? After the barrage of questions, they continue to overwhelm me with a highly animated all-about-us monologue. The highlights of what I've learned are as follows: Annabelle is five years old and loves everything Disney princess and fantasy. I remember my fairy-tale phase when everything always had a happy ending. The seven-year-old, Lila, boasts about her above-average reading skills and enjoys acting out her favorite books. Their vivid imaginations match their bubbly personalities. Since I always thought of myself as an only child, this constant bombardment of questions mixed with their need to sell themselves as my new and wonderful sisters has my head feeling like the inside of a tired pinball machine. As I start to detach my involvement due to sensory overload, I feel a slight shift in the room.

"So, do you?" Annabelle pauses, scooting within inches of my face, her blue eyes swelling with anticipation. Too impatient for my answer, she asks again with more force. "Do you want to, Marni?" Annabelle's polite insistence catches me off guard. She literally can't sit still as she bounces with excitement. But I zoned out for a few important seconds, and now I don't have a clue what she is asking me to do.

I crouch down, looking into her eyes, and confess, "I'm sorry, Annabelle. But what is it you want me to do?"

She frowns, releases a quick exhale, and sticks her pointer finger in the air as if to push pause on the conversation and darts out of the room. This very dramatic exit makes me wonder how she'll return. I shrug my shoulders and lift my hands questioning Lila, who deviously raises an eyebrow as she shoots me a you'll-find-out-soon-enough kind of smile. Of course, she knows what's going on—she knows her sister. My nerves heighten as I suddenly feel like I've become a game to them.

Just then, a swooping storm of sparkling pink twirls around the couch where I sit. Giggles break out between the girls as I receive a magical blow to my head thanks to Annabelle's silvery magic wand. Annabelle dances between the side table and chairs and stops in front of me. In her high-pitched, five-year-old voice, she chants a rehearsed spell three times, "Bibbidi-boo, you play princess too! Bibbidi-boo, you play princess too! Bibbidi-boo, you play princess too!" Each phrase is louder than the last. For fear of a princess meltdown, I accept her challenge. After all, I am a guest in her palace.

Lila bolts out of the chair and returns with a purple plastic bin dripping with princess paraphernalia. They drape me in pink-and-purple boas and top my head with a blue Cinderella tiara complete with large colored rhinestones dazzling across the top. Once I am deemed properly dressed, the girls host an imaginary tea party on the floor. Annabelle serves her favorite pink heart-shaped cupcakes with rainbow sprinkles while Lila makes the perfect English tea. Of course, it's all pretend, but it refreshes my soul to have some fun and laughs. I quickly submerge myself into their fantasy, remembering how Mom and I used to pretend. I look up and smile, hoping she can see my happy face enjoying this moment.

As Lila pours our third cup of Her Majesty's tea, Mr. and Mrs. Mercer walk back into the room. I'm not sure what startles them more—the chaotic transformation of their neat sitting room into a messy princess dressing room, or that I am on the floor, playing with their girls. A sudden fear grips me. Maybe they don't *want* me to interact with the girls? I nervously wait to see if I have done something wrong. But Mrs. Mercer eloquently interrupts our tea by asking the girls, "Would your majesties mind too terribly if we present the party with some refreshments?" The girls giggle and quickly grab their cookies and juice from the fancy silver tray.

I carefully put my wardrobe back into the basket when Lila unexpectantly asks, "Marni, promise you'll play with us again?"

I grin and nod. "I promise if you promise," I say, tossing her a playful wink.

"Girls, give us a few minutes to talk with Marni," Mrs. Mercer says. "Why don't you eat your cookies in the kitchen, please? Once we're finished, you can help us show Marni her new room."

The girls quickly obey, leaving me once again scared and uneasy. I quickly find my seat on the chair adjacent to the Mercers.

"Marni, would you care for a glass of sweet tea and some of Lauren's famous double chocolate chip cookies? They're still warm and gooey," Mr. Mercer asks while doting on his beautiful wife.

"Yes, please, Marni, help yourself." Mrs. Mercer graciously offers me the tray.

My stomach growls when the sugar-sweet scents hit my nose. "I am hungry, thank you," I admit as my cheeks flush in embarrassment. But I'm also a nervous wreck, which is making me feel queasy. I place two large cookies on a fresh napkin in my lap and set my iced tea on a light-blue geode coaster on the side table next to my chair. I am hopeful a little sugar and caffeine will hit the spot.

The Mercers sit directly across from me on a long camel-colored chenille couch. There are only a few moments of silence, but it is long enough for me to ponder this new life in Texas with the Mercers. *Do they really want me here?*

Just when my mind has almost convinced me to run out of the room, Mr. Mercer wraps his arm around Mrs. Mercer and says, "We are so happy to have you here with us, Marni! I know you must have a lot of questions, so please know nothing is off-limits. You can ask us anything, and we promise to always shoot you straight." He pauses briefly, lovingly tilting his head into Mrs. Mercer's. She smiles up at him before her blue eyes settle on me. I squirm in my seat as a hint of sympathy travels the short distance between us. Blinking her warm expression away, I shift my gaze back on Mr. Mercer. "We want you to make this place and all of us your home."

The oversize chair swallows my timid frame. Two fears flood my thoughts: a fear of the unknown—them—and my fear of the known, life without Mom. They both overwhelm me. I sink as the Y in my crossroads comes into full view, knowing one path has abruptly ended while the other one feels so wrong. However, these unknowns seem to at least be okay people. They appear to be kind and generous, but this could never be my family, which means this will never be my home. My family lives in Chicago. My home is two long airplane flights away. This entire scenario can't be further from the picture of home I hold in my heart. Thoughts of Mom fill my head, and my eyes begin to well with tears. Staring into my glass of iced tea, I dab the tears at the corners of my eyes and ponder, yet again, why she sent me here, away from everyone and everything I've ever known. Under my breath I mumble, "Why, Mom? Why?"

That's when it all hits me. For months, fear and tension have squeezed and wrung out every happy and innocent fiber in my body, leaving behind the brittle shell of a girl I don't recognize. Unable to hold it together for a second longer, I give into the tight knot in my belly and willingly let my emotions drown everything out. I lay the cookies on the table and bury my face in my hands, sobbing. My body shakes as my lungs gasp for fresh air, forcing my breathing to imitate an unstable staccato rhythm. I cry, devastated and unashamed, realizing just how alone I am in this world, in Texas, and in their house. As my depression sinks further into my skin, I feel someone's arms slowly wrap around my shoulders. My breath catches as my heart skips a beat, and I half-expect to see Mom's spirit cuddling up close beside me. I slowly lift my gaze up to find Mrs. Mercer trying to soothe my panicking soul with the trained empathy only found in a mother. Her comforting blue eyes, wet from her own tears, make me wonder if she truly understands the overwhelming pain life has thrown in my path. Or could her tearful reaction be as simple as Southern empathy? I watch Mr. Mercer wipe a trail of tears off his cheekbones with his thumb. Whatever they are thinking or feeling, one thing is certain: we are all in uncharted waters. We sit in silence together, staring into the unknown. Finally, I inhale a deep breath before I reach for my abandoned cookies.

I nibble on the delicious cookies as I try to refocus my thoughts. "I don't know what you want from me." The words, full of fear and uncertainty, fumble out of my mouth.

"Marni, I just want a chance ... that's all," Mr. Mercer responds immediately.

Turning to face Mrs. Mercer, I ask, "And you? What do you think?" If I were in her shoes, I wouldn't want an estranged daughter disrupting my perfect life. In fact, I'd hate the idea.

She raises a single eyebrow as her bright blue eyes go wide. Maybe she didn't think I'd ask her such a blunt question, but what have I got to lose?

"The truth?"

I nod, encouraging her.

Her eyes drop to her folded hands as she begins fidgeting with her giant diamond ring. "This has all been very unexpected ... and hard to swallow."

I shake my head and let out a *humph*. "Yeah, for me too."

"What I mean is," she starts, then looks to Mr. Mercer who nods for her to continue. "I mean, this situation, having you here ... makes me nervous." She bites her lip and looks away.

"Why?" I ask, surprised by her honesty.

"I don't know you, and you don't know me. We're strangers being asked to trust each other like family overnight. That's a little scary, wouldn't you agree?"

I nod. "If it makes you feel better, I didn't want to be here either."

She flinches at my words. She didn't say those exact words, but who are we kidding? Taking me in must be a nuisance for all of them.

Mr. Mercer speaks up. "Well, I'm thrilled you're here." I turn to look at the father I've always wanted to know. The muscle in my cheek twitches as a smile tries to break through. He's here, in front of me, wanting to know me.

"Marni, you being here will take some adjustments, but I'm on board," Mrs. Mercer states. Her Southern accent drawls out the words. Then, she leans in a bit, like she's letting me in on a secret and softly adds, "You're a Mercer."

Her honesty pierces my heart. I study them, unapologetically, allowing my eyes the freedom to boldly examine them. They sit, looking from each other to me, with a calm and peaceful expression resting on their faces. No one breaks the awkward silence. No one moves. The fear of not knowing what to do overwhelms me, producing a rogue tear that slides down my face. Her hand startles me as she makes small circles on my back, just like Mom used to do. I admire the fancy things around the room and the polished way the Mercers are dressed versus the worn-out clothes Mom could afford. I tuck my chin into my chest and whisper, "I'm not one of you. How can you think we're family?"

Mr. Mercer makes a guttural sound and starts to say something, but Mrs. Mercer holds up her other hand to stop him. Somehow, she understood my question wasn't aimed at him, it was meant for her. "I remember the first time I ever met Lila and then later Annabelle," she says. Her hand stops circling my back and drops back into her lap. "We loved them from the moment we knew they were coming. Right, Kyle?"

"Absolutely!" he agrees.

"Even though we had nine months to prepare for them and couldn't wait to meet them, our love for both of them started the moment we found out we were expecting them. They were ours, and we were theirs. A family."

I squint up at her, unclear how that compares to all this.

She nods as she continues. "Same with you. The moment your dad learned about you, he was over-the-moon excited and couldn't wait to meet his daughter."

"And you?" I ask.

She slowly exhales, possibly debating how to answer.

"Because I'm not yours, I'm his," I add.

"You're right." She reaches her hand out to touch Mr. Mercer's knee. "But we're a team. And that means if you're his, then you're ours."

My head starts to spin again as I contemplate what she's saying. We all know this is not going to be as easy as they're making it sound. Besides, there's a clock on all this, and I'm going to keep track until the day I can go home to Aunt Jo.

Thinking of home, a lump quickly forms at the back of my throat. I need some space to be alone, to think and process today.

Mr. Mercer must notice because he says, "You must be exhausted. Would you like some time to settle in your room?"

I nod appreciatively.

Mrs. Mercer smiles and calls the girls back into the living room. I watch Lila stroll in prim and proper while Annabelle skips through the doorway with chocolatey fingers and a chocolate-smudged face. A quick glance passes between the Mercers and I smile, thankful to see the parental attention now falling on the girls.

"Annabelle Mercer, how many cookies did you eat?" Mrs. Mercer reprimands.

"All of the ones you said to eat," Annabelle answers with perfected innocence.

"So, just two?"

"No, all the ones in the kitchen!" Annabelle beams proudly. A slight snicker escapes me as I envision her shoveling cookie after cookie into her mouth without thinking twice about the consequences. The whole scenario feels like something I would have attempted when I was younger.

Mr. Mercer senses Mrs. Mercer's patience teetering, so he quickly steps in to help deescalate the comical situation. "Okay, you little chocolate monster. You've had enough. Go wash your hands and face quickly so you can help Marni find her room." His calm approach prompts Annabelle to bolt out of the room, which makes me smile.

Lila giggles as she comes over to sit right next to me while we wait for Annabelle's return. Lila's serious eyes drift from me to Mr. Mercer and then back again. *What is she looking for? What is she seeing?* I wonder as I remain perfectly still.

When Annabelle returns, she grabs my hand, then Lila claims the other one. Together they pull me to my feet, and we shuffle out of the living room, through the kitchen, and up the back staircase. Everything is a clean, white blur as we trot through the house. I try taking it all in but realize that capturing those details will have to wait. At the top of the staircase, a narrow hall runs the width of the house with rooms branching off the right side. The left side of the hallway remains open, allowing us to see down to the living room where we just ate cookies. The first two rooms are large, princess-themed rooms.

Annabelle pulls me into her room. "My room is the color of Princess Aurora's dress in *Sleeping Beauty*! But Daddy thinks it looks as yummy as cotton candy." She giggles as her sugar high starts to take effect.

They tug me through a huge bathroom outfitted with two personal closets, two separate sinks, and a large tub-and-shower combo. They have a connected bathroom, and it's amazing! We walk through the expansive room and land in Lila's bedroom.

"My room is the color of Princess Jasmine's outfit in *Aladdin*. Daddy says my room is like a whole new world." Lila sings out the last few words, instigating ferocious belly laughter from both girls. I notice how quickly the devious sugar takes over their bodies.

We leave Lila's room and walk past a large, open space complete with two teeming bookshelves and toy baskets, a television, large beanbag chairs, and a game table. The girls identify this room as their playroom. Lila adds, "But you can play in here anytime you want!"

Annabelle agrees by vigorously shaking her head up and down, slightly losing her balance as she wobbles on her noodle-like legs.

The last room, my room, sits at the end of the hall on the right. I cautiously open the door to a room that is easily three times the size of my old room back in Chicago. I know my mouth must have hit the ground from shock. How can all this be for me? The girls struggle to read my reaction, not fully understanding why my face registers shock and disbelief instead of joy. Concerned but impatient, they insist on hearing my response.

"Well, Marni? Whachya think?" the girls ask almost in unison.

"It's like nothing I could have ever imagined! I don't know what to say. It's absolutely beautiful!" I admit in shock.

The room looks like it was ripped straight out of some fancy catalog. Creamy gray walls are accentuated with a white trim casing that surrounds the windows and doors. A queen-size bed is framed in a white, antique iron frame and dressed to the nines with a white, fluffy duvet and matching white, scallop-edged pillows. Several colorful throw pillows with fun sayings add a pop of color to the neutral pallet. Next to my bed sits a table with drawers for my books, an antique-inspired lamp, a new diary, and a full set of colorful gel pens. The luxury continues as I discover I have my own private bathroom, large walk-in closet, and several beautiful picture windows. This is too much. I don't know what to say.

"Well, Marni? What do you think?" Mrs. Mercer asks nervously. "We had to guess what you might like. So, if you hate it, we can return it all and find something else you prefer."

I turn around, taking it all in, baffled she is truly interested in what I like. My tongue is completely tied. I've never had such a beautiful room where everything is new and thoughtfully picked out just for me. She obviously poured a lot of time into preparing this special space for me. I am simply stunned.

"Mrs. Mercer, I ... I've never seen anything so beautiful or spacious. Are you sure this is all for me?"

She responds with a smile and an excited nod.

"Thank you, but this is too much," I say through the lump in my throat.

Pleased, Mrs. Mercer's beautiful smile illuminates her face as my thoughts drift back to the doll-sized room Mom and I decorated together with our flea-market finds and garage-sale treasures. Nothing matched, nothing was ever new, and nothing could ever be returned. I look around the room, still shocked there is a giant bathroom in my room just for me. Everything looks too pretty. I stand there frozen and stunned, afraid to mess anything up.

"We have something else for you, Marni," Mr. Mercer admits, his hands hiding behind his back. "We know you're gonna miss your Aunt Jo and friends from Chicago, so we wanted to make sure you have a phone to use anytime you want," he says as he hands me an expensive-looking cell phone. "It has an unlimited plan."

Holding my new phone in my amazing room, I choke up as another lump develops in my throat, and tears sting my eyes. I nod, knowing I can never articulate the words necessary to thank them for their kindness and generosity.

Seeing my emotional state, Mrs. Mercer starts to shuffle everyone out. "Girls, let's give Marni some alone time. She's had a very long day." She turns and adds, "We'll eat dinner in about an hour, and we'd love for you to join us, Marni."

Mr. Mercer stops in the doorway and turns back toward me. "Marni, I just want you to know that I'm so glad you're here. I'm sorry for the circumstances that brought us together today, but I'm so thankful to have you in my life. I can't wait to get to know you."

I can see the hope glimmering in his eyes. A sudden thought hits me, and before he leaves, I ask, "What should I call you?"

Maybe he hasn't thought that far ahead either because he just looks at me for a moment. "Well," he says cautiously, leaning his shoulder into the doorframe. "I hope that someday, you'll come to think of me as Dad, but there is no rushing any of this, Marni. Let's take things nice and slow, okay? You can call me and Lauren whatever feels comfortable for you."

"So, you won't be upset if I keep calling you Mr. and Mrs. Mercer?"

"Of course not. Call us whatever you like—just know that we're here for you and whatever it is that you may need or want. We want you to make yourself at home here." He slowly backs out of the doorway and quietly closes my door.

Alone at last, my brain flips through today's events and discoveries. How am I supposed to process living with a new and fully intact family, in their mansion, in a completely different part of the country? My head swirls with questions. It's just too different. What do I know of their world—a privileged, super wealthy, Southern dream? As my mind starts to race out of control around my tried-and-true pity party racetrack, I hear the small sound of skittering feet approaching my room. My doorknob turns slightly, creating a small sliver of space as big eyes dart around my room. I watch Lila's small frame quietly push open my door and sneak inside before softly shutting the door.

"Lila?" I ask.

"Shhh. Don't tell Mom because we're not supposed to bother you. But I wanted to see you," she pleads.

"It's fine, I won't tell," I answer. "Come on in."

Lila tiptoes across my room and hops onto the bed next to me.

"It's just that I've always been the big sister. Annabelle's always been the baby, and now I'm not the oldest, you are," she confesses, genuinely worried about her new predicament.

My eyes widen as I see exactly how my presence has thrown her world off-kilter. I understand the importance of family position. Mom was always the big sister to Aunt Jo, and that was important to her. I grab Lila's hands as I make a pact with her. "Lila, you'll always be Annabelle's big sister. No one can ever take your place. But, you know what? I've never had any sisters before, so I'll need you to show me what it means to be a great sister." I pause to give her time to take in this new information. "Will you help me?"

She takes a minute, trying to understand these new family dynamics, and answers decisively. "I really am excited to have a big sister." With her nerves somewhat subdued, and her concerns voiced, she lunges at me—half-tackling, half-hugging me—before leaping off my bed and leaving the room.

Slightly dazed, I sit back and reflect on our conversation. Of course me being here is hard for her. Me being here is disruptive in ways I haven't been able to process yet. Lila's concerns, though real and big in her world, are galaxies away from my concerns. But it's refreshing to hear I'm not the only one haunted by anxious thoughts. I admire her gumption in deciding we can solve this problem together and openly. Thankfully, it appears Lila will be someone who keeps it real with me. It's a comforting gift I didn't expect.

CHAPTER 11
Marni

With a full belly, I lean back in my chair, my empty plate showing little sign of the Southern-inspired feast they served. They dished out more food than I thought a family could eat, a three-course meal on an elaborately set table. First, Mrs. Mercer brought out chips and an avocado-and-corn dip for our appetizer. Then, we enjoyed a dinner of grilled chicken, roasted vegetables, and warm rolls. I only embarrassed myself a little; a red-hot flush bloomed across my cheeks when the girls had laughed at me, saying, "You can't use the dessert fork, silly." Like I knew what fork to grab? I've never had more than one fork next to my plate. It was an unmistakable reminder of just how unsophisticated I am compared to them. However, after Mrs. Mercer pulled a peach cobbler from the oven, everybody was too busy eating it to comment on if we were using the proper fork.

Turns out I was really hungry. I guess grief and nerves heightened my appetite because I've never eaten that much food at one sitting. The meals Mom used to make were delicious but very simple. She was a fantastic cook, especially considering we didn't have the money to create such elaborate dinners. She would always improvise, substituting cheaper ingredients for the "right" ones. To her, recipes were just a loose suggestion for her culinary artistry. But I don't recall ever having more than the main course and a simple side on our plate for dinner. Mom was creative but frugal.

Eating with the Mercers is as entertaining as play time. The girls' mouths motored nonstop with questions about Chicago and my life there. I tried to answer them all, but Mom always taught me never to talk with a full mouth. So instead of waiting for me to chew and swallow, the girls delighted in allowing their imaginations to creatively respond to their inquiries. I quickly understood how unimportant my responses were since, clearly, their questions were meant to be heard rather than answered. Mr. Mercer eventually instructed them to let me eat in peace.

It's been weeks, maybe even months, since I've enjoyed a tasty, home-cooked meal. Aunt Jo tried, but she's a terrible cook. She's notorious for burning our mac-n-cheese, which Mom used to say is the easiest thing to cook. But Mom was talented in the kitchen. She would scrounge together random things from our cabinet and fridge to create a feast. A salty tear slides down my face and lands on the corner of my mouth as fresh memories of Mom flood my senses. I can almost smell the delicious aromas wafting through our apartment and hear her contagious laughter as I shared the hilarious details of my day. I smile, knowing Mom must be happy seeing a warm, home-cooked meal in front of me.

Remembering my manners, I politely carry my plate to the kitchen sink. As Mrs. Mercer instructs me to set them in the sudsy sink, the girls ask, "Where's Ms. Penny?"

Mrs. Mercer says, "She's already gone."

"What did you decide to do for the summer?" Mr. Mercer asks.

Curious, my ears tune in to their conversation. "With everything going on right now, I gave Penny the summer off. I paid her a summer bonus so she could visit her family."

He nods his head, obviously agreeing with her.

I can't help myself. "Who's Penny? Is she an aunt or something?"

"Penny is our maid," Mrs. Mercer answers. "She normally comes every day except the weekends, but she'll be gone until school starts back up."

"You have a *maid*?" The question slips out before I can stop myself. Immediately, I see her stiffen, and I wonder if my comment rubs her the wrong way, like she thinks I'm judging her. It's just that I don't know anyone with a maid. And even if I did, who has enough money to pay for their maid to go on vacation?

Mr. Mercer clears his throat and smiles. "We do."

The girls, bored with the adult talk, run upstairs to start their nighttime ritual: bath, teeth, and reading. Before leaving the kitchen, Lila and Annabelle notify me that I am invited to join their reading time, but only if I "read in character." Mrs. Mercer lets out a soft chuckle before shooing them off.

"I'll be up in a few minutes, girls. No dilly-dallying," Mrs. Mercer firmly warns under a hidden smile. "Marni, I'm sure you're exhausted. You go relax. Walk around and explore; make yourself at home. And if you'd like, we'd love for you to join us upstairs to read, but only if *you* want to." She pauses, then adds, "No pressure. But just a heads-up, they will pick out a princess book." She smiles and winks.

I walk through the long kitchen and into the adjoining room where I find Mr. Mercer relaxing in his recliner, feet propped up, and watching some sports show. He looks up at me and smiles. "Come on in and have a seat," he says, motioning with a hand as his eyes turn back to the TV. The family room feels cozy and inviting, not pretentious or stiff. The comfortably furnished den welcomes me with a brown leather couch, two recliners upholstered in a navy-blue, patterned fabric, a woodburning fireplace, huge floor-to-ceiling windows, and a glass door leading to the backyard. The princess toys and dress-up clothes from earlier are neatly stored in gingham fabric-lined baskets tucked along the back wall.

I walk to the glass door, admiring the dimly lit, luscious green space spreading outside. Even in the near dark, I can see the beautifully landscaped yard boasts several monstrous, live oak trees with colorful flower beds woven around each tree base. A large swing set with an attached fort sits in the back corner of their lot. But the highlight is the gorgeous free-form swimming pool surrounded by wide patios and colorful planters. Mr. Mercer watches me looking outside and says, "It's different from Chicago ... all the space?"

I glance over my shoulder. "That's an understatement."

"I'm so sorry about your mother. I can't imagine how hard the past several months must have been for you. And now all this." He pauses, swallowing back visible emotion. "But I wasn't lying when I said I'm so happy you're here with me."

I move to the couch, feeling the weight of my body sink into the soft leather. What does he want me to say? That I'm excited to be one big, happy family? Instead, I ask, "Do you remember her well?"

"Of course I do. She was so talented, strong-headed, and vibrant. And you look so much like her."

I smile at his words, but it is short-lived.

He tilts his head. "What's wrong?"

"I'm sorry, really I am. I've always wanted to know who my father is, but ..." I pause, looking for permission to speak freely.

He nods, encouraging me to continue.

"It's just that her being gone is the only reason we know about each other."

"And you wish she were here with you, instead of me." He's not asking me a question, just bluntly stating a fact.

I nod.

"I understand."

We sit in silence, the only noise being the sports announcer on the television. I want to explain how for years, knowing him was all I ever wanted. But I can't speak.

He leans forward, hands clasped with elbows resting on his knees. "I wish our circumstances, the reason we finally got to meet, were different, Marni. I really do. But I'm thankful that your mom gave me this chance to be with you. Give *us* a chance, okay?"

Sincerity fills his eyes and hits me like a dagger in my heart. I feel the weight of today pressing down on me. I need to be alone. "I think I'll go upstairs and rest a while, if that's okay?" My voice quivers, highlighting my nerves.

"Of course, Marni," Mr. Mercer responds softly.

I hear the girls and Mrs. Mercer going through their routines. I sneak down the hall unnoticed and slip into my room. I still can't believe all this is mine! But I'd trade all this grandeur and beauty in an instant if I could just go back to the way things were.

I plop down on the fluffy bed and throw myself the best pity party I can imagine until my emotions overwhelm my body, resulting in sheer exhaustion. I imagine what Aunt Jo may be doing at this exact moment in Chicago. A twinge of pain hits me as I envision her all alone on her worn-out, lumpy couch, biting into a greasy slice of pizza. I cringe, feeling guilty, knowing how much food we just ate when I know how hard she struggles.

Just then, I remember the phone the Mercers gifted me. Hadn't they said I could call anyone I wanted, whenever I wanted? Yes, they did. I grab it, still astonished that it's *my* phone. I always wanted one, but Mom said it wasn't practical, which meant we couldn't afford it. Cradling the phone in my hands, I quickly dial her number. I need to hear Aunt Jo's voice.

"Hello," her voice rattles as she clears her throat.

I perk up at the familiar sound. "Aunt Jo, it's me, Marni."

"Marni? Oh, sweet girl! You don't know how bad I've been wanting to hear your voice!"

"I miss you so much," I blurt out as tears sting the edges of my eyes.

A silent pause hangs in the space between us. In an effort to sound cheery, I notice she lifts her voice half an octave to ask, "So, tell me. How's Texas?"

"It's okay, I guess. I mean … things are … definitely different down here. It's nothing like what I imagined." I half-whisper into the phone like I'm revealing a secret. On the other end of the line, I hear her make a *hmmm* sound like she's trying to act surprised. A new awareness suddenly hits me in the gut. "You knew, didn't you?"

"Knew what?"

"That the Mercers are filthy rich," I blurt out. "They live in a mansion." I take a breath to let that sink in. "With a maid, who comes every … single … day!" The pitch of my voice jumps up an octave.

I hear her let out a long sigh before she answers. "I assumed he lives comfortably given that he's a lawyer." She waits in silence on the other end while I process what she's just said, what she's known all these years. My head spins as anger grows white-hot deep inside me.

"For as long as I can remember, Mom barely kept us going. She worked her butt off! She didn't know I knew, but I knew we were barely getting by. She pinched every penny as she walked through brutal Chicago winters to one of her many revolving jobs, making sure I could eat and keep the heat turned on." I am so mad at Mom; I want to rip something to shreds.

"Marni—"

"No," I interrupt. "I hate her! She should have told him about me. Things could have been so much better. Instead, we lived in that crummy little apartment where everything we had was either found in the street, or she haggled for it at the secondhand store. Do you know that sometimes she tried fooling me that she wasn't hungry, just so I'd have enough to eat? She couldn't scrape two pennies together, never mind feeding us *both* dinner." I let out a nasty little chuckle, before continuing, "You should have *seen* all the food we had tonight!" I squeeze my eyes shut, trying not to scream. "Her stubborn pride makes me sick." I can't help being furious at her, knowing all her struggling probably killed her. I bark, "And here they are, with all this ... flaunting their money."

"Are you finished?" Aunt Jo's tone sounds tight and irritable.

I growl.

"Your mother did the best she could, and this is how you repay her? By hating her?"

"She was wrong. And so were you. You should have said something." I blink back the tears threatening to fall. "Haven't I been through enough without more curveballs being thrown at me?" My voice rises in anger.

"What should I have done?"

"You could have made her see reason. You could have convinced her that it'd be worth it to tell him about me. But you did nothing. You didn't even try to prepare me for all this, for feeling so out of place."

"It's been years, Marni, since your mom made her decision. Years. I fully supported her then, and I stand by my decision now. I did what she asked. But if what you need to hear is, 'I'm sorry,' then fine." She takes a dramatic inhale and with a tinge of sarcasm says, "I'm sorry."

"Whatever. You don't get it."

I hear a sloshing sound in the receiver as she takes a sip of something. "Who cares that they have money? He's your father. That's all that matters."

"It matters, and not just to me. I stick out like a sore thumb in this family of perfect blondes. You should have seen the way they eyed my appearance, like I knocked on their door straight from a dumpster dive! I'm so far below their standards." My voice dips into pools of anger, sadness, and frustration. "They're not going to want me around any more than I belong here."

She breathes out a deep sigh. "You're right. I should have warned you that he had money—his family always had lots of money and connections." Her words slow as her mind drifts, revisiting the past. "At least, that's what your mom said."

"So, why did you keep all of this a secret from me?" I wave my hand around the room as if we were talking face-to-face.

"I was asked to, sweet girl. Plain and simple."

"I don't understand. Why wouldn't she want to give us a better shot at life by asking for his support? I wish she'd never made you tell him about me because then I wouldn't be so mad at her betrayal. What kind of mom knows that her kid's father is alive, is able to help, and is a good person, but still makes her child think he's dead? That's psycho!"

"Marni, until you've walked a mile in her shoes, don't go thinking you would have done anything different."

"She robbed me of years with my father for reasons she took to her grave." The sarcasm drips from my tongue as I add, "How very selfish and narrow-minded of her. Or maybe ..." I start, thinking the awful thought I've been trying to push out of my mind, but it suddenly flies out of my mouth. "Maybe she knew what I already can see."

"And what's that?"

"That I'd be an embarrassment to him, a trashy addition to their perfect family."

A heavy sigh blows through Aunt Jo's lips. Then, silence.

"I knew it. I'm right, aren't I?"

"Why would you think a thing like that?" Aunt Jo snarls.

"Because it's true. We're in different leagues. I can't do their high-society, fancy-pants living, and they are certainly not coming down to my secondhand lifestyle level."

Aunt Jo laughs. "I bet you change your tune fast. You'll be surprised how easy a bit of money makes things. You might not even notice the transition."

I grit my teeth, irritated and ready to fight, when she asks, "By the way, I meant to ask. What number are you calling me from? It's not the number I have listed for their house line."

"It's my new cell phone," I admit.

"Hmm. You have your own cell phone?"

"They bought me one." I start to squirm as I hear her silently making her point. "They gave it to me so I can call *you* whenever I want." Feeling my cheeks start to flush, my eyes dart around my room, landing on the open closet door where a full-size mirror hangs. I stare at an out-of-place girl in her brand new room, scared to death of her new reality. "I could have had my own phone years ago if Mom had just been honest …."

I can feel my aunt's energy ebbing and flowing. If my words upset, anger, or offend her, she doesn't show it. Instead, she tries to untangle the invisible web I have spun myself into.

"Marni, she's gone. Try not to be too mad at her because there's no changing what she did."

"She always warned me that a secret would burn the tongue and scar the heart." I pause, feeling the hypocrisy of her words drown me like a turbulent river. "For someone who hated secrets, she had a whopper of one, didn't she?" I snark.

My aunt's sharp intake of breath precedes her attempt to justify Mom's actions. "Your mom spoke from experience. She knew firsthand how destructive secrets can be, eating away at your soul a nibble at a time. She never wanted that for you, and neither do I."

"That doesn't justify her lying to me."

My aunt groans, probably fighting off her own urge to be upset with Mom for leaving behind this mess to sort out. But finally, she answers, "Yes, she hid your father's identity from you and your existence from him, but," she carefully stresses, "not because he's rich. The plain and simple truth is that she was protecting herself. I watched her struggle to put him out of her mind for months, so when she ordered me never to mention him again, I respected her wishes." Aunt Jo's heavy sigh blows into the receiver before she continues. "She never wanted to lie to you. Her lies, my silence, they were both efforts in protecting her heart and yours."

"So why tell me now?"

"I think it wasn't the secret itself that finally got to her, it was what the secret became—you. When she found out how sick she really was, clarity and closure weighed heavy on her mind. She cried on my shoulder, hoping you and your father would forgive her one day."

Tears spill down my cheeks as I imagine her crying. It hurt so much to miss her with my whole heart while being so unbelievably mad at her. I'm not sure what to think as Aunt Jo's words pierce my soul. How could anyone hurt Mom so badly, she had to lie to protect me? I sniff back the lingering tears and ask, "Why not just keep me with you and protect me from all of this?" I back her into a corner, hoping she will tell me why she didn't fight for me.

"Because I made your mom a promise," she answers matter-of-factly.

I roll my eyes up to the ceiling and lie back onto the fluffy mound of pillows. It wouldn't have hurt anyone if she had broken that promise because who would even know enough to care? Surely, she can agree Mr. Mercer and his family would be better off not knowing I ever existed.

I was just about to voice my argument when she adds, "It turns out that keeping you from your father was a secret she couldn't bear to have buried with her. Time wasn't on her side, Marni"—her voice shakes—"but peace washed over her face the night I promised her I'd follow her requests to the letter."

I fiddle with the pristine white covers on my bed as I sit in complete silence. My heart thumps in my ear, and my brain swirls, trying to understand Mom's past. Pushing those questions aside, my thoughts return to my not-so-picture-perfect introduction to my father's family. Acknowledging the elephant in the room, I say, "That doesn't explain why you didn't warn me. That could have at least helped."

I wonder how Aunt Jo pictured our reunion. Did she recognize the fear that engulfed me from the moment I packed for Texas? Could she sense my building anxiety as I watched my nervous taxidriver speed off, or feel the sweat dotting my forehead and trickling down the sides of my body? The terror coursing through my veins immediately magnified as the front door revealed a cold, judgy woman, who I assumed was my stepmother, staring back at me like unwanted trash? A sinking first impression.

"Can you imagine what it feels like to meet your father for the first time on his doorstep? All the dreams and scenarios I imagined my whole life, and none of it came close to reality. Everything felt so unnatural, so formal, especially with him standing next to his *real* family. He already has the perfect, loving family. He definitely doesn't need another daughter." Heat fills every inch of my body as my mind retraces those uncertain moments.

"I'm sorry you felt that way, but I think you're wrong. If he is the family man you think he is, how could he *not* want you in his life? You are his child, his firstborn. I'm sure he needs you in his life just as much as his other children. And, Marni, don't forget how important this was to your mom." Aunt Jo sniffled and cleared her throat. "I *know* my sister deeply regretted her mistakes regarding your father, and she wasn't certain you meeting him face-to-face without talking beforehand was a great idea, but she felt it was the right way to go. I argued with her about it, but she was adamant on the whole 'less is more' theory."

I can picture Aunt Jo's fingers stabbing quotes in the air.

Her words trigger a memory of Mom and me enjoying a free event day in the Art Institute of Chicago one cold Saturday afternoon. We strolled through several exhibits—the miniatures, impressionists, and the European renaissance art—analyzing each magnificent piece. By the time we reached the contemporary and modern art wings, I groaned, not wanting to put a stain on a perfect day. I remember telling Mom the impressionist art beautifully captured light and movement, eliciting emotion while setting creative trends, unlike most modern and contemporary art. I claimed the later art to be too sharp, too dark, abstract, and uninspiring for the discerning artist like myself. Mom laughed, noting my argument, but fought for the rights of the nontraditional art admirers. She used those same words as she defended the artists' choice in embracing a "less is more" approach. I remember her saying that too many details can jumble up the essence of the overall effect or interpretation. I didn't agree. I loved the details, but she praised the overly simplistic and bold approach.

Aunt Jo's voice comes back into focus. "She thought it'd be better for you to submerge yourself into their world, that this was your best option for the life she always wanted for you—"

"But I don't want to be here!" I yell. "I want to come home."

Aunt Jo's tone is strained. "I know, sweet girl. But, Marni, this is your chance to have a father!" She pauses. "You have a decision to make, young lady. You can be miserable for the next six months, or you can give the Mercers a chance and see what your future holds with them. Make the right choice." Silence fills the air, signaling she's done with this conversation.

I sniffle loudly, but I know better than to keep pushing Aunt Jo. When she's done, she's done. And obviously, she is done.

"So, tell me all about the Mercers," she says.

"They're stinking rich," I say, my voice devoid of any emotion or excitement as I recap what I've already said.

"All right then." Aunt Jo's reply is sharper than I expect. She pushes out her frustrations with an exaggerated exhale and tries again. "Maybe you can tell me a little bit *more* about the Mercers?" I can almost see her eyebrows raise up as she cocks her head with her typical "get on with it" expression.

"Um ... their two little girls, Lila and Annabelle, literally live and breathe in a magical world of princesses. They seem to like me for now since I'm still a novelty to them. But let me tell you," I pause for effect, "they are balls of energy." An unexpected burst of laughter catches me off guard.

"I bet it'll be a fun change being surrounded by constant commotion and noise. I know that when you came along, you rocked my quiet world, and I'm so glad you did." Her glittering smile can be heard, reaching my ears and touching my heart. "What's their house like?"

I should've guessed Aunt Jo—an HGTV junkie—would be interested in their house. I tease her with a vague description: "It's like nothing I've ever been in before." I pause before adding, "I mean, in real life."

"What does *that* mean exactly?"

"They live in a massive mansion that's, like, sixteen stories tall and stands all by itself. They don't share a wall, a driveway, or anything with anyone else. Remember how we used to look up as we walked past the towering apartment buildings where we figured millionaires must live, and wondered about how much space they must have up there?" I pause to let her conjure that image in her mind before continuing. "The amount of space here is unfathomable. There is space everywhere. The girls and I each have our own rooms and bathrooms upstairs! Can you believe that? My own bathroom! My room sits on the opposite side of the house from the girls. It's like I have my own private wing. And their yard!" I exclaim. "They literally have a park for their backyard with huge trees, tons of flowers, even a swing set and a giant pool!"

"Sounds pretty amazing to me," Aunt Jo says.

"It is ... but it's just so different." A sadness creeps into my voice. Of course it's amazing—who wouldn't be impressed by all this stuff? I'd be stupid not to recognize the blessings staring me right in the face. But it's all so flashy. In one day, I went from having next-to-nothing to living with very polite strangers in their humongous mansion. "We're just so different, Aunt Jo. I mean, how am I supposed to live here with these people?"

"Just take it one day at a time, and you'll see, it'll all work out."

"But I don't even know how to pretend to be like them." My voice quivers.

"You just be you, Marni. That's all anyone can ask." I hear a smile in her voice as she adds, "They're gonna love you, sweet girl. It sounds like they've gone to great trouble in making this transition special for you, which makes my heart happy."

I look around and silently nod, appreciating having this beautiful new room all to myself, but I'd trade it in a heartbeat to be back home.

"I want you to know how much I already miss you, Marni. So very much! But this is where your mom wanted you to be, and it sounds like she was right …."

A series of staccato breaths escape my nose as I cry. "I feel so alone and out of place." I sniffle then add, "It's just not home. You are my home. My friends and Chicago are my home, not this place. Not these people. They're nothing like me." I plead for her support, hoping she may see how wrong it was to send me down here.

"Marni, trust in your mom's love and wisdom. She would never send you somewhere that she didn't believe deep in her bones would be the best place for you. We both need to trust her," Aunt Jo urges.

"I miss you so much, but I miss Mom even more. Everything reminds me of her—even the things that normally wouldn't have now remind me of her. This has all been too much to swallow at once … losing Mom, then you and everything else in my life being turned upside down. I keep wondering when I'll go numb to it all," I whisper through the knot in my throat. "I wish you were here with me, Aunt Jo. I need you." I cry softly into the phone.

"Shhh, shhh now. Honey, a numb heart is not what you want to wish for. You will always remember and love your mom because you loved each other so deeply. And yes, the pain will lessen with time. But never strive to numb your heart's voice because doing so would mean that you just don't care anymore. Don't be numb to your mom's memory or your life together. Try to give your father and Texas a fair chance—do it for your mom. And always remember, sweet girl, that I'm here for you and lovin' you to pieces no matter where you are!"

"I love you too, Aunt Jo." I yawn into the receiver as we exchange our goodbyes and promise to talk again in a few days.

As I set my phone down on the nightstand, I roll on top of the cushy bed and stare at the ceiling fan spinning in a hypnotic trance. In my old room, I dreamed of having a fan that buzzed loudly to drown out the sirens and chaos from our neighborhood. But this fan doesn't need to mask outside noise. Instead, it hums a mellow tune, which adds a soothing element of sound to the otherwise silent night. Lying still, I think about Mom and what Aunt Jo said. Mom would want me to try, so I will, even if it's only for her. I will do my best for Mom.

My eyes start to yield to the weight of exhaustion and unexpected twists of my new reality. I beg the Lord to take me back home, to Chicago. Even if it is just in my dreams … I want to be home.

Home. Four letters constructed into a simple word describing a place, family, feelings, and level of comfort. My home embodies unconditional love while creating a solid family identity, a place I belong without question. But to *belong* has proven to be another arbitrary phrase that can change with circumstance. I know where I used to belong, but that's not where I am. Circumstances have forever flipped my whole world on its head. Losing Mom meant losing my best friend, my provider, my protector, my home, my friends, and everything that shaped me into me.

CHAPTER 12
Marni

D reaming of what-ifs, my body slowly starts to wake up. I am semiconscious when two little tornadoes fly into my room, disturbing any semblance of peace. The girls pounce on my bed, giggling as they squeeze their rowdy bodies under the covers on either side of me. Confusion and uncertainty wash over me as I become sandwiched between Princess one and Princess two. I try to shake off the light fog that clings to my brain and the back of my eyelids as reality slowly sharpens into focus. Briefly, my mind blanks, blocking out my new surroundings, but of course, that lapse is short-lived. I had prayed the previous day was all a weird, bad dream. But this bouncy wake-up call is a slight punch in the gut. Contagious giggles spark into united belly laughter that fills the room. My head tips from side to side, finding two pairs of blue eyes sparkling up at me in anticipation. *Now what?* I wonder to myself.

All three of us pause when we hear the sound of shuffling coming down the hall. The girls tuck the pillowy covers over their head, pinning me in between their frozen bodies. Panic engulfs me, my fear of being trapped causes a flash of heat to ripple through my body. Not only am I trapped, but I know Mrs. Mercer is getting close to my room. I need a release button! My racing heart is instantly appeased when Mrs. Mercer peeks her blond head into my room.

"Lila and Annabelle, you leave Marni alone this instant! I told you not to wake her up," she whisper-yells at the girls, her expression a mix of *I'm sorry* and *I should have known*. "Get downstairs right now to eat your breakfast." She softens her tone as she dangles the carrot. "I made special cinnamon chocolate chip pancakes." She winks at me.

The girls squeal as they scissor-kick themselves out of the covers and off the bed, exposing my warm body to the cooler air. Mortified to be seen in my pajamas, I tumble out of bed and wrap the dangling sheet around my body. Mrs. Mercer lightly taps her hand onto the two sparkly rear ends that speed past her and down the stairs.

I must resemble a deer caught in the headlights. All the commotion and chaos of the morning's start is definitely foreign and overwhelming to me. I awkwardly stand in the middle of the room, unsure what to do next with her still in my doorway.

Mrs. Mercer turns her attention back to me and smiles. "Marni, I am so sorry the girls woke you. They have been so excited to see you this morning, but I promise, this won't happen again. We'll work harder to establish better boundaries. Please feel free to climb back into bed, or if you're ready, we'd love for you to join us for breakfast." And with those last words, she quietly shuts my door. My privacy is restored, but my sleepy solitude is shot. My empty stomach forces me to get this day started.

In awe of having my own bathroom, I take my sweet time getting ready. I wander around the large room, touching everything and turning on and off the faucets for both bathroom sinks and the giant clawfoot tub. I step inside the standalone shower, lifting my arms out to see just how big it is, amazed my fingertips never touch the smooth square tiles. I wash my face with the fluffiest washcloth I've ever felt and soap that smells like a combination of flowers and—I take another sniff—chocolate? I rub my tongue over the top of my teeth and smile at myself in the mirror, amazed at the shiny results of my brand-new electric toothbrush. The cabinet drawers are filled with a hair dryer, curling irons, flat irons, hair gels and creams, and an assortment of all kinds of other hair stuff and accessories. After I've opened every cabinet door and drawer and inspected all the linens in the closet, I know I cannot put off going downstairs any longer. I go to the walk-in closet to grab some clothes. My meager belongings look pathetic in a closet that rivals the size of my old bedroom. There are built-in white shelves, a full stand of dresser drawers, and cubical slots I have no idea what to do with.

I pull out my favorite shorts and pair them with an old Chicago T-shirt Aunt Jo gave me, then look at myself in the full-length mirror. Tugging at my too-short shorts, I pick at the hole in my worn shirt. I look at my secondhand sneakers before glancing through the handful of clothes barely taking up any space in this oversized closet. Nothing I own is much nicer. Shame and embarrassment wash over me, and I sink down to the plush, white carpet. Tears start rolling down my face before I can even process I'm crying. I lift my eyes up and ask, *How am I going to get through this, Mom?*

Sad to be embarrassed by the clothes Mom worked so hard to buy and terrified for my future, I give in to the tears for a few minutes. Then, with a heavy sigh, I pull myself up. I wash my face again before pointing myself in the direction of the noise and tempting smells.

Never in my life have I stayed in such a large place. Mom and I never traveled anywhere, but I can't imagine too many hotels feel bigger than the Mercer house. My nose tracks the smell of butter and cinnamon right into the large black-and-white kitchen. The girls sit at the kitchen island in their matching princess nightgowns. With mouths full of pancakes, they wave their sticky fingers, prompting me to join them. A smile reaches my eyes as I watch syrup drip out of the corners of Annabelle's mouth. It immediately hits me that if they are being this quiet and still, the pancakes must be great.

"Marni, can I interest you in a stack of pancakes?" Mrs. Mercer asks as she cleans up her workspace.

"Yes, ma'am. Thank you."

I take a seat next to Lila, thinking it might be a little cleaner and safer sitting next to the older one rather than the syrup-faced one. Annabelle, unbothered by my decision, keeps eating. Mrs. Mercer generously places a stack of three super-sized pancakes, bacon, and a banana in front of me, and reminds me there is plenty more. As I take my first forkful, the two chatterboxes next to me turn to watch me chew. It feels strange to have people staring at you when you eat, so I put my fork down and look behind me, wondering what they're seeing. Nothing appears unusual, so I pick up my fork and stab into the stack of pancakes for another bite. Again, they stare. This time, I rest my fork on the side of my plate, cross my arms, and meet the girls' gazes. Their faces beam up at me with huge expectant smiles.

"Okay, what's up, girls? Haven't you ever seen anyone eat pancakes with a fork before?" My words carry a snarky edge.

They both laugh, and Annabelle answers. "We just want to see if you like our mommy's pancakes. They're our favorite!" she squeals. She tries whispering across to Lila, but the effect sounds more breathy than hushed as she adds, "Mommy's a little nervous you won't like them." Her eyes dart to Mrs. Mercer and then back to me.

"Annabelle, stop that nonsense," Mrs. Mercer admonishes. "Marni, I wasn't sure what you would like for breakfast, so I made the girls their favorite. I would love to know what you like to eat so I can incorporate it into our meal rotation though," she politely explains.

I shove a large bite of the pancakes into my mouth. They are soft and fluffy and dotted with yummy chunks of chocolate. This breakfast tastes like dessert—it's better than delicious.

"Mrs. Mercer, these are amazing," I say as the fluffy pancakes effortlessly dissolve in my mouth. "I've never had pancakes like these, so I'd love to keep these in the meal rotation!" I manage to muffle between mouthfuls of sweet satisfaction.

The girls squeal and giggle, delighted we all love the pancakes. As they finish their breakfast, they twitch in their chairs as sugar starts to course through their system. Before running out of the room, they announce they are going upstairs to get dolled up. Confused, I stare blankly at the spot where they vanished. Are they going to come back dressed as a doll or get a doll dressed up?

Suddenly, I am both uncomfortable and nervous sitting in this huge kitchen alone with Mrs. Mercer. After hearing Lila's concerns last night, I wonder if my presence has unhinged Mrs. Mercer in ways I cannot fathom yet. I glance at her, wondering if I will ever feel at ease enough around her to be myself. Will she ever understand me? But maybe the better question is, does she even want to? My panicking brain swirls out of control with depressing thoughts and emotions, taunting me into thinking the worst is yet to come.

She must sense my turmoil because she stops fussing around the kitchen and puts down the dish towel. Her body language softens as she leans across the kitchen island and speaks to me in her slow, melodic Texas accent. "Marni, you've suffered a devastating loss, and I am so sorry you are going through so much right now. I know I'm not your mom, but I'd sure like to be your friend. I do know from personal experience how hard change can be, especially unwanted or unsolicited change." She waves her hand in a circular motion. "We know this is all strange to you, and we are all new to you, but we truly hope that, someday, you'll want to call us family." She straightens up and adds, "We will not pry or push or pressure you, but please know that if you ever need anything or just want to talk, your dad and I are here for you."

Staring into those hypnotic blue eyes, a glimmer of anguish reflects back at me. For an unguarded moment, her eyes reveal a deep pain hiding just below the surface. I wonder if my existence is the cause of the pain she's trying to conceal, but there's no way of knowing. "Thank you, Mrs. Mercer. Umm, but can I ask you a question?"

Her eyebrows perk up, and she calmly nods. "Sure, Marni. Anything."

"I'm not really sure what to do." I hesitate nervously before adding, "I mean, here, with your family, in Texas."

A half-laugh sneaks out of Mrs. Mercer's smile. "Well, what would you like to do? It's summer, so the options are limitless. We can swim, go to the movies, shop, sightsee, go to the zoo ... you name it! We were going to talk to you about our plan this evening at dinner, but why wait? Your dad and I have been talking, and we'd love to throw a barbecue to introduce you to all our friends and their kids. You know, school will be starting before you know it, so we want to introduce you to a few friendly faces, hopefully break the ice for when school starts back up. It'll be so much fun! Think on it, and we can discuss your thoughts at dinner. Okay?"

"Sure, Mrs. Mercer." I politely agree, but my insides twist, turn, and plunge at the thought of being surrounded by a bunch of snooty rich kids, laughing and talking nasty about me. I'm sure they'd make themselves look innocent from a parental distance, pretending to be friendly. But I've had my share of mean kids, so I know these privileged jerks will enjoy eating me alive. I feel my breath becoming shallow as I can almost hear them trashing my clothes and labeling me as Mr. Mercer's unwanted, one-night-stand kid. I need to tell Mrs. Mercer I'm not ready for that, but how? Will she understand?

Using the last remnants of my pancakes, I successfully sop up the remaining syrup on my plate. This seems to tickle Mrs. Mercer. "You and your dad eat pancakes exactly the same way." I cock my head as I absorb her observation, wondering how else we might be alike. She interrupts my thoughts by adding, "Once he's done, it looks like a dog has just licked his plate clean to the bone." The comparison makes her laugh.

Embarrassment slithers down my spine. I know I'm not sophisticated, refined, or educated in Southern graces, but I'm not on the same spectrum as a lowly dog. My mind flashes back to last night's confusion with the forks, wondering how many table rules I need to learn so I don't stick out like a sore thumb. "I'm sorry, Mrs. Mercer. I didn't mean to be rude. My mom did teach me better manners than to lick my plate. I'll try harder." I bury my chin into my neck to hide my flushing cheeks.

"Don't be silly, Marni. I'm thrilled you enjoyed your breakfast! Sop away anytime you want. You're in Texas now, and it's considered a compliment to the chef." She carries my empty plate and fork to the sink while I sit totally confused and anxious. After a few moments of silence, she twists her head in my direction and speaks over the sound of the water. "Marni, how would you like to meet your dad for lunch today with me and the girls?"

"Sounds good," I say, feigning excitement. All I really want to do is crawl back into bed and forget this day ever began. "Thank you for breakfast, Mrs. Mercer. If you don't mind, I think I'll go up to my room for a bit."

I walk upstairs and peek in on the girls, who are noisier than a herd of elephants. Disney think tanks could take notes from their combined imaginative play. The corners of my lips tip up as I watch a colorful world of princesses and ponies envelop their imaginations. They take turns directing each other in how best to bring their creative vision to life. Content in knowing they are preoccupied, I sneak into my room and quietly close the door, locking it to ensure total solitude. I admit that it hasn't taken me long to adjust to the amazing gift of privacy.

Sitting in my peaceful room, I try to anticipate what lunch with my father will be like. My mind travels back to the lunch I had hoped for every year on my birthday. I felt like the only girl in the world who didn't know her dad. I saw dads come eat lunch with their daughters in school, dads taking their little girls to restaurants, and dads just being around ... but not mine. Mine was dead—at least, that's what I assumed after years of disappointment. But the dream never died. Every year, I envisioned him finally being able to celebrate with me. He would surprise me at the park with a picnic lunch of cheeseburgers, fries, and two large slices of white cake with chocolate icing. We would laugh and play, I would tell him whatever secret I could think of, and he would tell me how much he loves me ... has always loved me. It would be the perfect start to a new beginning with him.

Since it's not my birthday, and the lunch isn't a surprise, I can't allow myself to think the lunch will be all that special. My expectations shift as I picture the two of us eating while he tells me stories I don't know or couldn't know about Mom. The heaviness in my chest starts to lift as I think of all the questions I now have about their relationship. But this will not be that lunch either. Not with Mrs. Mercer and the girls with us. I cringe at the thought of having a meal in public with these strangers. It was awkward enough in the privacy of their kitchen. What if they want to take me to some fancy-schmancy place where my ignorance and unpolished etiquette will surely embarrass us all?

Nervous about making a fool of them—and myself—I carefully fix my hair and change from my short shorts and holey T-shirt to my "nicest" outfit. I slip into the black dress and pumps I wore to Mom's funeral. My heart breaks as I wipe off a light layer of dirt clinging to my shoes, a reminder of her graveside. Hot tears sting my eyes. I feel humiliated that I have nothing to wear in between my funeral clothes and the tattered, secondhand clothes deemed barely appropriate for a school without a proper dress code. I swore to myself I would never wear this outfit again, but it's the very best one I have.

I'm so tired of being an embarrassment. And I'm so overwhelmed by all the unknowns and emotions. It's exhausting. A few minutes tick by before I give myself permission to redirect my brain. Then I shake my head and flap the tension out of my arms. Determined to forget about real life for a little while, I grab some supplies to escape in my art.

I walk downstairs, slouch in a plaid wingback chair in front of the wall of windows that faces the backyard, and open my sketchbook. Soon enough, the natural light washes over me, casting a sleepy spell on my heavy eyelids. I welcome the spell's full effect—a dreamy respite.

CHAPTER 13
Lauren

"I've already discussed it with Marni, and we're coming into town to have lunch with you today," I state with more enthusiasm than I feel. Kyle and Marni need to see I am on board with the new changes in our lives. But watching her practically lick her breakfast plate clean makes me question our lunch date. I know people are going to whisper and ask questions—I'd be shocked if they didn't. She looks like the poster child for an inner-city poverty campaign with her grungy clothes hanging off her skinny body. I can't help but wonder just how poor they really were. I shake that thought from my head and tell myself none of that matters.

"Babe, I don't know if I can. I have some important client meetings right after lunch." He lowers his voice and speaks directly into the phone. "Plus, we haven't told my parents yet. Can you imagine what Dad would say if someone else beat me to the punch?"

I puff out a ball of hot air as I silently scream to myself, *Who cares!* I should have been the hardest person he had to tell, but he acts like his dad's approval trumps mine. Who spent the past weeks poring through teen magazines, trying to decipher what fourteen-year-old girls like nowadays, then running around to purchase trendy bedroom décor, new linens, toiletries, and such, all to make Marni feel welcome? Me, not his dad. He needs to stop walking on eggshells where his dad is concerned and focus his energy on making Marni feel a little less terrified and lonely with every passing day.

"Look, Kyle, she's uncertain of us, of everything. She's your daughter, for crying out loud, who never met you until yesterday." My words gradually sharpen as I recall how her tear-filled eyes landed on mine for the first time. She was brave to get on that plane, brave to knock on our door, and the least he can do now is put on his big-boy pants and eat lunch with us. I grit my teeth. "Who cares a flying poop what your dad says. He's not the issue. Tell him something came up with the girls, and you have to meet me in town. Tell him your pants are on fire. Tell him anything you want, but you better get yourself to this lunch!"

"Fine, I'll be there, but just give me an hour to push back my meetings, okay?" He takes a deep inhale. "I'm sorry. You're right. I was thinking we should slowly let Marni adjust, but if we want her to be comfortable with us, she should join us by doing what we've always done. So where do I meet y'all?"

"At the club. We're going to go swimming afterward," I say.

Silence.

"Lauren. Can't we wait on the club?" he says, pushing me to rethink my strategy. "This is awkward, but does Marni have an outfit fit for lunch at the club? Does she own a bathing suit? Can she even swim?" He sighs. "We don't want to rush her introduction before she's ready. People will talk."

"Before *she's* ready or before *you're* ready, Kyle? Do you have something to hide? If they talk, they talk—"

"Don't you dare think I'm ashamed of Marni," he says, interrupting my snarky rant. "I just don't want the aftermath of gossip to destroy something that we're just starting to build. You of all people should know the devastating effects of malicious tongues."

After a heavy pause, I nod my head in resignation. He can't see my reaction, but he knows how to interpret my silence. At the back of my throat, an old knot reappears and starts growing, choking out any utterances of sound or words. I sit in a state of shock, reliving my tattered past as I mentally take inventory of our new family structure.

Kyle understood my endgame today was to call him out, but that isn't what my heart truly desires, is it? I can't wrap my finger around the exact pain that has triggered our heated discussion, but we both know the issues here are deeper than a lunch date. His hurtful words hit a chord that resonates deep in my soul. I don't want to be bitter like she was—I won't be like her. I look around my room and focus on a framed picture of us on our wedding day. My mood softens as I think back to the plans we mapped out for our future. None of this was in the cards, but it's time to play the hand I've been dealt. I will play it safe for Marni because he's right, no one deserves the wrath of hateful and judgmental tongues.

"Fine, instead of the club, let's get hamburgers at Whizzbang's. Nothing says welcome to Texas like a greasy burger and fries. And afterward, I'll take the girls shopping."

"Great. Looking forward to seeing all my girls in a bit." His words bounce lightly as he adds, "Lauren, I love you."

As I hang up the phone, shame instantly casts its shadow over me. Why am I taking this out on Kyle? It's not like he purposefully kept Marni a secret from me. He never knew she existed until a couple of weeks ago.

My past self-doubts resurface as I wonder whether I'm truly good enough or am just some decent substitute for a true love that never panned out. My mind drifts back to my dad. I remember hating him for finding love outside his marriage and was baffled he chose a woman the polar opposite of my mother. The stark differences between them always bothered me, just like it unnerves me now, threatening my confidence in Kyle's love. The deep-seated fear of being a girl whose heart is broken by the first man she ever loved still haunts me as I ask myself, *Am I good enough*?

There's only one person I can completely trust, one person who truly understands. I close my eyes and see her beautiful face staring at me with huge glassy tears filling her eyes. She was lost, scared, and needed a friend. It's funny to think about it now—I never saw her as my enemy, which probably had more to do with our friendship than my ability to rise above the ugly drama. The honest truth is, I never blamed her. How could I? None of it was her fault. I cast all the blame, hatred, heartache, and loss on her mother and my dad. She was innocent.

Reaching for a truth I can cling to, that memory hits my heart like a dart in a bullseye. I need to remember Marni is not the enemy. In fact, like Rosemary, she's a victim of a series of terrible circumstances and misfortune. Rosemary never had a father until her mother actively hunted mine down. I still think that woman had some nerve! Similarly, Marni never knew she had a father until after her mom passed.

Turns out Marni's mother understood her relationship was over, so she deliberately denied Kyle his first chance at fatherhood. My blood boils as I think of how selfish she must have been to have deprived any child the love of a parent. I can't imagine Kyle missing a single spectacular moment in our girls' lives—I wouldn't allow it. Being a present parent is far too important, so the fact that she kept Kyle in the dark until now makes me nauseous.

Until a couple of weeks ago, I hadn't imagined I would ever need to walk in my mother's footsteps, wear her shoes, feel the uneven road underfoot. But now I can honestly say I have thought about her reaction to Rosemary. It took years for her to accept Rosemary as my dad's other daughter. Mom always referred to Rosemary as "the illegitimate." She couldn't even add the noun "daughter" after it. What a strain her drama and hatred put on all of us and our family gatherings. For years, my mother punished my dad privately and publicly with her sword-like tongue and general hostility. Finally, time and my grandmother's gracious actions paved the way for some family healing. My grandmother, a woman who strongly believed in the power of God's love, proved through her example that genuine love is greater than any pain or lingering bitterness. Grandma took the time to get to know Rosemary and happily flaunted their relationship to the world. She made a point never to end a conversation with my mom without expressing her joy and love for Rosemary.

Walking into the laundry room, I start another full load of the girls' pink-and-purple clothes. They go through outfits like the cast of a Broadway production, constantly changing costumes. Wishing

Penny was here instead of being on a long summer vacation, I pull out a clean load of whites, dump them on the long counter across from the dryer, and begin sorting. I methodically match and roll pairs of socks, tossing them into their designated baskets. This mundane task proves to be therapeutic. My thoughts swing back and forth from the past to the present as muscle memory keeps my hands busy and productive.

Eventually it hits me: I need Rosemary's help. I can't keep my thoughts and feelings bottled up inside. So, I walk to my room, close the door for privacy, and dial her number, softly admitting to myself, "I need my sister." I send a silent prayer up, hoping for a renewed perspective and the determination to not react to Marni like my mother.

"Rosemary? It's me, Lauren. How are ya'?" My eyebrows lift in arches as my voice comes across too airy, too fake. I shake my head to refocus and ask, "How's California?"

"Oh, busy and beautiful! I do miss the family, but the beach life here is pretty hard to beat. What's going on with y'all?"

I pause, and my left palm grips the base of my neck as my fingers dig into the spastic trapezius muscle. I knead at the deep knots in a circular motion, hoping to relieve the ache that stabs at my neck and shoulders. I need a vacation from all this, but that would only be a temporary fix. I take a deep breath, deciding to tackle this dilemma head-on. "Actually, Rosemary, I'd like to talk something through with you if you have a minute?"

"For you, always. What's going on?" her voice softens with sincerity.

I tell her all about Marni. By the end of my monologue, I am emotionally tapped. I didn't realize how hard divulging Marni's story and my initial response to her was going to be, especially to Rosemary. Even though decades have passed, the bruise my father and her mother stamped on our hearts remains sensitive, like the lingering effects of a nasty bone bruise you can't see but desperately protect against the slightest insinuation of touch. We're sisters now. But when did that start? I'm not sure ... not sure of when she finally felt like one of the family.

"I guess I'm telling you all this because I need advice. What do I do with Marni?" That came out wrong. I try again, "Specifically, how do I avoid making the same mistakes my mom made with you? How do I let her know we want her around when I'm struggling to accept all this change?" My exhausted pleas evolve into emotional sobs of defeat.

"Look, Lauren. You've been dealt a pretty interesting hand—not once, but twice. It seems that God might have used me as a warm-up for Marni. It was hard moving to podunk, East Texas my junior year just to be closer to a guy my mom claimed to be my father." Her voice sounds distant. "Life is never the perfect fairy tale we dream it will be. We both know better than that, right?" She lets her question bounce lightly through the air like a bubble.

I close my eyes, trying to picture where my life got off course, but she interrupts my thoughts.

"You can't imagine what it was like growing up without a dad. It was lonely, devastating, and segregating. I saw dads engaged with their kids everywhere—everywhere except at my house. I always dreamed I'd have a dad who would play soccer with me, laugh at my jokes, tell me stories, help me with homework, take me on adventures, and just be there for me and my mother. That was my dream."

"I'm sorry, Rosemary. I know that was hard."

"The hardest part, Lauren, was your mother."

"I know ... and it wasn't just you. I walked on eggshells for years, trying to assuage her bitterness. But that's just it. I don't want to end up like her, don't want history to repeat itself through me." A slight whine creeps out of my voice.

"You won't. You're aware, and that's the first step."

"Tell me, when did you finally feel accepted, like one of the family?"

"Jeez ... it's too long ago to pinpoint a specific time, but I do remember how it happened." I sense her smile stretch across her narrow face as she says one word. "Grandma."

My eyes mist over as Grandma's cheerful image pops into focus.

"Thank goodness for Grandma." Rosemary laughs quietly, almost to herself. "You know, she saw me ... I mean, *really* saw me. I was just a scared teenager stuck in the middle of a nasty soap opera. All I ever wanted was to be loved and accepted, a part of a family, and she knew it." The warmth of her words radiates through the line as a smile touches my face.

"How did she do it?"

"She chose love over her own disappointment. Do you remember how she treated Dad after it all?" I shake my head no, but without waiting for my response, she continues. "She let him have it. She ripped him up and down, but once she said her peace, she closed that door and moved on."

"That's right." My eyebrows furrow. "I forgot about that. How do you even remember that?"

"Because I asked her what she thought about me being her son's daughter. I asked her if she was disappointed and resented me like your mother." I cringe at the word *resented*.

"That was gutsy."

"I needed to know where I stood, so she told me the truth. She told me how she held nothing back when she confronted him—her disappointment, her rage, her pain. But then she surprised me by admitting that she forgave him. Remember how she used to say, 'Don't go to bed with a bitter taste in your mouth?'"

A tear slips out of the corner of my eyes as I hear her perky voice through Rosemary.

"She chose love. You have a chance to pick a path. Your family's story will be changed forever with Marni's presence, but you have the power to shape the environment for all of you. Will you be like your mother—a resentful woman who caused years of unnecessary drama and pain for all of us? Will you travel the road Grandma chose and accept this innocent girl, choosing to love her? Or will you sulk in denial and straddle the fence, like Dad did at first?"

We sit in silence for a moment. Deep inside my body, a sinister emotion pumps through my veins and up into my head, flushing my cheeks. It feels wrong sympathizing with my mother right now, but I kind of do. Until now, I never thought I would be able to have such a strong distaste for someone else—an innocent someone else like Rosemary. My head floats and spins, and I register just how justified my mother's reaction must have felt. I can't admit this to Rosemary. I can barely be honest enough with myself to confess such terrible thoughts. My heart pounds so hard in my chest, it feels like it's threatening to jump ship.

I balance my forehead on the palm of my free hand as I attempt to take slow and steady breaths. I think Rosemary must understand the turmoil I'm feeling because she finally adds, "Lauren, all the storylines eventually come to the same conclusion. Some just take the harder and longer paths."

"I know."

"Marni needs a relationship with her father and you. Fourteen is still just a child. Can you imagine what it would have been like to lose your mother before entering high school?"

I hadn't thought about that. I hadn't thought about any of the milestones she wouldn't get to share with her mother.

"There's no question that this is going to be extremely difficult, but for everyone's sake, *you* have to try to forget the past. Forget Kyle's past. Forget Dad's past. Don't transfer your past pains onto your family's future potential." Rosemary methodically slows the tempo of her speech, emphasizing these last two words: *future* and *potential*.

I let her words tumble inside my head as I mentally compare the family I always envisioned next to the family I now have.

"You haven't lost anyone, Lauren. She has."

The truth of her words sting instantly.

Rosemary continues, "Sometimes moving forward can feel obscure in more ways than one can articulate. I've seen clients who are so scared of the future's unknowns that they physically can't function. But while I'm encouraging you to forget the past, I'd suggest Marni do the opposite. I'm sure she's terrified not only of the future but of letting go of her past. I think that's your answer."

"What's the answer?"

"In order to move forward, don't let her forget her past, her mother, and who she is. Embrace her into your family, scars and all. Talk to her, ask her questions, and be intentional in getting to know her."

She's right. I know she's right. "Thanks, Rosemary. I'm so blessed to have a sister who'll speak truth to me, especially one that's a psychologist." The irony of life tickles me just enough to produce a little chuckle.

"Ha, ha. Oh, and don't listen to anything those small-minded, snobby Southerners say. You know there will be whispers, but don't let their ignorance influence you or your precious family. Stand your ground and support this new family of yours. Be true to yourself."

"Well, we're thinking of having a barbecue in a few days to introduce Marni to all our friends. Fingers crossed, but I'm hopeful for a positive reaction."

"You're on the right track. Start by putting a positive spin on your new family, and everyone else will jump right on that Mercer merry-go-round."

"You're the best, Rosemary. Maybe the girls and I can squeeze a trip out to California before too long to see you. I miss you so much!"

"I'd love to see you, Lauren, and to meet Marni! Give my love to Kyle and all the girls in his life."

I feel her wink through the phone, which makes me smile. "Will do. Give our love and a big Texas hug to yours too."

I hang up the phone and balance my elbows on my knees as I hold my clasped hands to my face. My thumbs catch and release my bottom lip as I raise my head up and down, thinking. I feel like I'm at the end of one of those pick-your-own-adventure books. I loved being able to try out different endings, but life doesn't give us that option. I know once I make the choice, there's no turning back.

I think about the past and Rosemary's life and how my life was altered through the lies, drama, and change. Will our new family dynamics negatively impact my girls or my marriage? I don't want that, not for any of us. I think about the possibility of our future as a new family. Can we be a family? Do I want to be her mother? I cringe as I think of what I would want for my girls if I were gone. Deep in my gut, I understand both paths have the potential to adversely affect my family, one way or another. Closing my eyes, I take a deep breath and choose my own ending.

CHAPTER 14
Marni

After my brief nap in the den yesterday, I woke up calm—not completely at peace but definitely calmer than I'd felt in weeks—and resolute. I decided lunch would be an investment—a down payment in building a relationship with my dad and his family which would allow us to open the door Mom sealed for fourteen years. I hadn't considered what going to lunch with the Mercers might look like since that luxury wasn't in Mom's penny-pinched budget. Surprisingly enough, lunch turned out to be infinitely better than I anticipated.

They took me to a burger joint, which Mrs. Mercer had insisted was very casual and encouraged me to change out of my funeral clothes. Whizzbang's was a blue-collar burger joint with 1950s-inspired checkered floors, vinyl booths, and air thick with the smell of fried grease. There was nothing uppity about it. I breathed a sigh of relief yet still hoped we wouldn't run into anyone the Mercers know, anyone who could easily confirm I don't belong. Our lunch was not heart-stoppingly humiliating—nor was it life-altering; we did not become one big happy family over cheeseburgers. However, it did give me another little glimpse into their lives. Their casual ways astonished me as the sophisticated elegance I had assigned them dissolved before my eyes like a fading illusion. I couldn't believe how down-to-earth and normal they appeared.

I sat wedged between the girls on one side of the booth, trying desperately to figure out their family dynamics. I willed myself to keep an open mind, which turned out not to be that difficult. I listened as the four of them debated which burger I should order—the Double Whizz-pigg, it was!—then Mr. Mercer treated "all my girls" to thick strawberry milkshakes. The girls couldn't wrap their brains around the fact that I'd never tasted a milkshake before, let alone a pink one. I smiled at them, my mouth watering in anticipation as they talked it up insisting "it's the best thing ever!" And, yeah, it was delicious.

Relaxing into my seat, I watched how easily Mr. and Mrs. Mercer conversed and the gentle looks and touches they shared. I noticed how confident the girls were in speaking their minds and how often they, too, showed affection for each other. I was envious of their obvious love and how they made it look so easy and effortless. I felt a strong magnetic force tempting to pull me into their circle, but I warned myself not to fall under their spell, no matter how easy it could have been.

I noted everyone's individual food preferences and inwardly smiled at some of our quirky similarities. Like when Mr. Mercer and I both ordered our cheeseburgers well-done with onion rings instead of tots or fries; or when I squirted globs of ketchup on my burger, then dragged it through another pile of ketchup on my plate—and so did he, Lila, and Annabelle. Mrs. Mercer shocked me and made me laugh by ordering jalapeños and egg on her burger. Who does that?

Nothing earth-shattering was discussed, no revelations were shared, but by the end of the meal, I couldn't believe how much more relaxed I felt with them all.

Afterward, however, was a whole 'nother ball game.

When Mr. Mercer went back to his office, Mrs. Mercer and the girls took me shopping "in town," meaning Waco, for clothes suitable for school and the miserably hot Texas weather. We shopped for everything—including a bathing suit, even though I told her I couldn't swim.

"Well, we'll just have to change that," Mrs. Mercer claimed.

We spent hours in and out of little shops they called "boutiques," the girls' thick accents drawing out the first syllable twice as long as necessary. I know Mrs. Mercer meant well, but our first stop was the catalyst that pushed me over the edge.

I was 100 percent out of my element despite the dazzling effect the racks of brand-new clothes had on me. A giddy feeling came over me at the prospect of trying on such beautiful clothes. The girls anchored themselves on a tufted couch, demanding a fashion show. I tried on outfit after outfit, absolutely loving more than half of them. When Mrs. Mercer asked to see my favorites, I showed her the stack, secretly hoping to get one thing. She snatched up the entire load and handed them to the cashier. Coming out of the curtained room, I heard the woman put an absurd price tag on the pile of clothes, but Mrs. Mercer didn't bat an eye. Just whipped out her plastic and paid for it all, without ever flinching. Heat began building inside my ears, embarrassed by the obscene amount of money she just spent. Before I could say anything, before I could challenge her unnecessary spending, she ushered us out the door, saying, "Next store, here we come!"

That was the pattern. Look. Buy. Spend more money. Repeat. Repeat. Repeat. My head spun as Mrs. Mercer slapped her credit card down like she was playing a game, happily buying as many clothes as she could. I kept saying, "Please, I don't need all of this."

"Nonsense. You need some new things. Besides, your dad and I want to do this for you."

Her reckless spending made me extremely uncomfortable. Even though it felt like I had just won the lottery, buying an entirely new wardrobe, it was utterly embarrassing. Obviously, she needed to make me more presentable, more polished like them. I didn't fit into their world with the clothes Mom had worked herself to death to provide. None of it was good enough for their world.

The ride home was quiet. Mrs. Mercer listened to her favorite radio station, the girls passed out in their car seats, and I fumed all the way home. With a trunk filled with bags of new clothes for every occasion and new shoes to match, you'd have thought I would be elated. But anger was burning holes in my belly. It was difficult to understand my feelings because I was truly excited about my new clothes. I was mad, not ungrateful. Mad at Mom for everything she did to keep me, and us, from their world. She was the only person who kept us from rising above the slums. She knew she held the power to change our station, and she didn't do a damn thing until she died. I was struck dumb by her stupid pride! Mr. Mercer would have helped her. He would have made sure we weren't one step away from living in a shelter. She wouldn't have had to worry so much or fight so hard just to barely get by. Maybe *we* could have had a mother-daughter shopping trip in a real store with new clothes instead of scavenging for secondhand finds. I wrung my fingers in frustration.

When we arrived at the house, I helped get the girls inside before returning to the garage to grab all the shopping bags from the car. Mrs. Mercer came to help me but stopped short as she saw me practically vibrating with anger. My breathing was hard and irregular. I clasped my hands behind my head, trying to keep myself from having a full-blown panic attack.

"Marni, what is it? Did I do something to upset you?"

I turned to her, intending to blurt out whatever hit my lips first, but the kindness in her eyes was my undoing. The tears rolled down my face, and I shook my head, letting my hands slide down the sides of my neck. "Mrs. Mercer ... I ... I cannot thank you enough for today, but I'm not feeling so great right now. I think I'd like to skip dinner and just go to bed, if that's okay?"

"Of course, Marni." Concern was etched across her face, but she remained silent. She simply gathered my shopping bags and ushered me into the house.

I whispered goodnight and lugged all my shiny-new belongings upstairs. I was so darn tired.

Maybe tomorrow, the tears will stop, I thought before crawling under the covers.

Here's a hint: the tears didn't stop. And the days kept ticking by ....

***

Friday arrives without fanfare. It's the day of my barbecue reveal party, and I've spent most of the week finding comfy places to read, both inside and out. Annabelle and Lila have transformed their playroom into a mythical palace where colorful sheets and blankets drape over furniture and large toys to create a massive tent with several rooms inside. From the doorway, I watch the tent coverings flap as the girls move around inside their palace, their voices muffled but happy. They know to stay out of Mrs. Mercer's way until she needs our help.

The Mercers said they invited their closest friends and Mr. Mercer's parents, but I'm not quite sure how to gauge my expectations for this party. Mrs. Mercer insists it will help me make some friends before school starts. She called it an "icebreaker." She has assured me everyone is anxious to get to know me. I've never been what Mrs. Mercer deems the "guest of honor," so how will I know what to do at a party full of strangers? My nerves start to eat away at my courage as I suddenly feel very unprepared and out of place. I'm not sure I like the idea of being the fish in a glass bowl tonight.

I know Mr. and Mrs. Mercer thought they prepared me for this evening, but how do you psych yourself up for the meet-our-new-daughter barbecue? What am I supposed to do? Tricks? Sing? Tell jokes? Ugh! I'm so stressed out. Unsure of how to spend my day, I walk downstairs to offer Mrs. Mercer help.

She smiles politely, thanks me, and says, "It's fine, I've got it under control. You go and relax for a while." She bends down to grab a rag and a bucket of sudsy water before walking out the patio door. She scrubs down the outdoor table and chairs as I turn to head upstairs. I sneak into the playroom where I go completely unnoticed and grab a pad of sketch paper and a tub of pencils. I head to my room, plop onto my bed, and scoot to the head where I arrange my pillows just perfectly behind my head and back, propping myself up. I dig through the pencils until I find the sharpest point and begin drawing.

There has always been one picture I gravitate toward and attempt to draw—a picture depicting Mom, me, and my father ... finally together. Creating our family portrait used to soothe me. I'd sketch my father much bigger and stronger than Mom. He'd hold his arms open wide toward me, and we'd all wear smiles. It's funny, though, I never thought of him having wavy, blond hair. His hair and eyes always matched mine. And I *never* pictured him with another wife and two other daughters; it was always just the three of us. I marvel at how far reality is from my preconceived vision of my family. I had created the perfect family of three on paper, but now I see the truth. So, I sketch something completely different: my lonely feet at Mom's gravestone with a complete stranger watching in the distance.

As my pencil lightly grazes the surface of the paper, leaving charcoal lines and curves, my emotions begin to mellow. I concentrate on each pencil stroke, erasing the unwanted markings as I analyze my handiwork. After a couple of hours, my hand starts cramping. I put my pencil back in the container and study my drawing. Satisfied, I close the book and sink into the pile of pillows and rest my eyes.

A light tap on my door rouses me to consciousness. Mrs. Mercer pushes the door open, asking me if I'd like to help her in the kitchen and suggests I wear one of my new sundresses this evening. She reports that the girls are ready, primped, and in the playroom until the party. I want to see how the girls look to assess how I should get ready.

I peek into the playroom where they play quietly, trying their best to follow Mrs. Mercer's only instructions: "No tiaras in your hair—don't mess it up." The girls wear matching sunshine-yellow-and-bright-blue-checked dresses. Lila's braided hair frames her face as two french braids symmetrically weave down the sides of her head, landing on her shoulders. A rubber band adorned with a yellow, plastic daisy secures each braid in place. Annabelle's hair is swept up into a high ponytail where a huge blue-and-yellow bow sits neatly positioned on top of her head. However, Lila and Annabelle have wrapped pink boas around their necks, piling them on top of their heads as a feathery cushion to the tiaras they're wearing. I smile as I walk back to my room, wondering how long it took them to find a way to sidestep Mrs. Mercer's instructions with a technicality.

I open my closet and grab each sundress, hold them up under my chin, and study each look in front of the mirror until I finally decide on the baby-blue dress trimmed with white eyelet lace. I carefully twist my hair into two small sections at the front and pin them down with several bobby pins. After applying a touch of blush and lip gloss, I put on my silver cross necklace from Mom. Satisfied with my reflection, I decide to give Aunt Jo a quick call. I need to hear her voice. I need a pep talk.

"Hey, Aunt Jo."

"Well, sweet girl! What a wonderful surprise to hear your voice today. What's going on with you?"

"Actually, the Mercers are throwing a barbecue party for me tonight. They want to introduce me to their friends and my new grandparents. But I'm nervous, Aunt Jo."

"Wow, that's really nice of them. This is a good thing, Marni. They're excited to show you off, and who wouldn't be? You're an amazing girl. I'm so proud of you."

"Aunt Jooo," I say, drawing out her name. I need sincere help and advice, not flattery. "Seriously, what do I do? I'm going to feel so out of place!"

"I know it's going to be overwhelming, but take the night in bite-sized increments and follow Mrs. Mercer's lead. Everyone is going to be anxious to meet the guest of honor." I sense her signature sideways smile through the phone. "Just be yourself and don't clam up."

"But what if they all hate me? What if the Mercers see that I am too different from them and their friends? What will happen next? Can I come home then?"

"Slow waaaay down, Marni. Don't wreck this train before it leaves the station. It's not important what all those other people think anyways. It's important what you think of the Mercers and how they treat you. And it sounds to me like they're treating you like a princess, hosting this party for you." She pauses briefly for me to chew on that thought.

"Well, Mrs. Mercer and the girls did take me shopping for some new clothes."

"Well, that does sound like fairy-tale livin' down there. Anything in my size?" Tickled, Aunt Jo lets out a burst of laughter.

"Ha, ha," I reply sarcastically.

"Seriously, Marni. Go enjoy the party and meet everyone you can with the open attitude you'd want from them."

"Thanks, Aunt Jo. I am pretty excited to meet these grandparents. The girls absolutely love them and are thrilled to introduce their new big sister to them."

"I can't wait to hear all about your night. Call me tomorrow with a full report, sweet girl." Before we get off the phone, Aunt Jo reminds me, "Oh, and don't worry about remembering everyone's names tonight. They will all know yours, but they're supposed to. You just have fun!"

We tell each other how much we miss the other and say our I-love-yous. I sit on the edge of my bed for a few quiet minutes as I mentally prepare for the night ahead. When the doorbell starts ringing, I decide to give myself ten more minutes to build up my courage before heading down to join the party.

CHAPTER 15
Lauren

People are starting to arrive, but where is Kyle? He said he'd be home over an hour ago to help with all the last-minute preparations. All the cooking prep work and baking is done. The three girls actually helped me bake yesterday afternoon, which was a big timesaver. And the hours together in the kitchen provided a great bonding experience.

I couldn't help but notice how stiff Marni appeared when we were pulling out the ingredients to bake. She told us she rarely baked and never made anything that didn't come in a box. Lila and Annabelle were baffled, so they asked her how she made desserts.

"We didn't have dessert often, but when we could, Mom and I loved buying a box of yellow cake mix and a tub of chocolate icing," she answered. "We'd bake the cake and then coat it with a thick layer of icing."

"Well, today, we will all bake from scratch," I declared.

We made several large pans of homemade brownies. Lila and Annabelle were over-the-moon excited to share the highly coveted brownie batter with Marni. The three of them kept dipping spoons into the batter when I wasn't looking, or so they thought. Although, to tell the truth, it was such a sweet and fun moment, I practically encouraged the sneaky taste-testers!

After the brownies, we agreed that every great brownie deserves to be paired with homemade vanilla ice cream—a menu must-have.

So, we pulled out the electric ice cream maker. Marni was fascinated and kept giggling with the girls as the paddle swirled the creamy ingredients into sweet, thick ice cream. Another warm memory made.

This morning, I mixed gallons of tea and lemonade and set out all the plasticware, plates, and napkins on the furniture I had just cleaned. A short time ago, I finished assembling the cheese, fruit, and veggie trays waiting in the fridge; Grandma's famous baked bean and hash brown casseroles remain warm in the oven; all that's left to do is grill the meat! So where is Kyle?

I look at my watch—twenty minutes until the party. I can't wait for him. I need to freshen up. I reapply some powder and blush just as Kyle walks into our room and closes the door.

"Where have you been?" I bark, frustrated before I even have a chance to gauge his mood. When I take notice, I soften my tone. "Everything okay?"

Kyle slumps onto the edge of our bathtub, his entire demeanor emitting defeat. "They're not coming."

"Who's not coming?" I ask, mentally calculating all the RSVPs I'd already received. "Almost everyone is planning on coming. It's going to be a full house. Who are you talking about?" When we sent out the invitations, we put a little blurb at the bottom announcing Marni, who she is, and how happy we are to introduce her to our friends and family. Both Kyle and I didn't want to have the same conversation over and over again, especially in front of Marni. We hoped this would make the evening more comfortable and manageable. And so far, everyone seems excited and curious, definitely more than understanding, considering the situation. There has been no backlash or nasty talk. So, as my mind runs through our guest list, trying to imagine which of our friends changed their minds, he answers my question.

"My parents. Specifically, my dad," he states. "He's furious. He says they're not coming." I watch him pull his chin into his neck as he tries to steady his breathing. I imagine the harsh words his father used, notorious for never approving of anything that didn't fit neatly into his perfect mold. I always admired that quality, even though its ripple effect means Kyle lives to please his father, which is beyond frustrating. But now there's something different in his eyes—shame? Suddenly, I can see it all, and I know. My heart hurts for him—a son ashamed of his father's callousness and ignorance.

"What? How did this happen? Tell me what was said exactly."

Pacing the length of our bathroom, Kyle quickly relays everything his dad said to him. My jaw hangs open as he tells me exactly what happened. After all these years, his dad admitted to orchestrating his move from Chicago back home because someone leaked Kyle's "unsavory" relationship to him.

"I told Dad all about her once I got the transfer notice. I told him everything, and that I might be falling for her. He told me that it was not a relationship that a well-respected Southern lawyer would ever condone, marrying a random girl 'off the streets' with no parents, no background, no social standing, and no formal education—it was unacceptable. He even went so far as to accuse her of using me, which I never bought. I always knew my transfer back to Texas was hasty. Dad assured me the Chicago firm was sending me back because they didn't need me anymore, didn't want to pay my salary any longer. My livelihood and career were at stake. What was I supposed to do? I had to leave. I went willingly, understanding that it would most likely end my relationship with Marni's mom."

Kyle looks exhausted from rehashing the argument. "Dad is disgusted by the entire 'fiasco,'" he says, putting air quotes around the word his father used. "He insists that Marni is a disgrace." He pauses, trying to get his emotions under control. "And that there's no room for Marni in this family, just like there was no room for her mother." Kyle stops pacing and sits back down on the edge of our free-standing tub. His tired face and exhausted eyes add years onto his deflated body. He looks up at me like a lost puppy before he rests his heavy head on the palms of his hands.

I am dumbstruck. How can anyone be that stupid and arrogant toward another person, let alone a fourteen-year-old girl? This is not how the party is supposed to move forward. *Wrong vibe*, I tell myself. For Kyle's benefit and my own, I say, "We don't need your dad's approval to live our lives."

His eyes rebound up to meet mine.

"It's fine," I say, peering down at him. "I don't want them here if they're going to treat our family like that. This is their loss, not ours." I take a deep breath. "We have a fork in our road, and I don't need permission from anyone to decide which path I choose." I cock my head slightly to the side, raise my eyebrows, and wait a beat to ensure I have his full attention. I slowly squat down and balance on his bended knees. "I choose you, Kyle. You, Marni, and the girls."

His eyes well with tears as he leans forward to lightly brush my lips with a kiss.

I stand up, pulling him up with me. "Now, let's start this party with a positive attitude. We are proud to have Marni with us, and I need our whole world to see that firsthand."

The disappointment Kyle carried with him now ebbs away, an unwanted tide he forces off our family's protected shoreline. I think back to my conversation with Rosemary at the beginning of the week. I hope he realizes that his wife, his teammate and partner in life, will always stand beside him. His dad hurt him deeply. In time and with plenty of prayer, I hope his parents' attitude toward Marni and our new family unit will mellow, and they come around.

With relief in his eyes, he wraps his comforting arms around me and whispers in my ear, "You're right." We quietly hold each other close, fueled by the strength of our love. No words are spoken as we both hit an imaginary restart button, vowing we won't get on that emotional rollercoaster again.

Finally, Kyle breaks the silence and whispers, "I love you, Lauren. I can't imagine my life without you." He leans down to tenderly kiss my lips.

"Okay now. Don't mess up my face before the party," I tease. "Oh, by the way, I got Marni signed up for those swim lessons at the club starting next week."

"Great. Let me take her though."

"I think she'll appreciate spending the time with you. Now, get ready."

He grins as he walks toward his closet, unbuttoning his dress shirt. "Just let me change out of these stuffy clothes, and I'll get the grill started!"

CHAPTER 16
Marni

At the top of the stairs, I pause, taking in all the people walking in and out of the house. Everyone looks so confident and beautifully put together. Anxiety fills my chest as I ponder running back into my room to change my outfit. I know how ruthless girls my age can be in these situations, especially if they don't approve of your outfit. Before heading downstairs, I bend over, put my hands on my hips, and take deep breaths in and out while praying, *Lord, help me to fit in.*

Strangers arrive through the front door and join the party in the backyard through the patio door, all of them carrying some sort of appetizer or dessert to add to the increasingly lavish buffet. I slip outside unnoticed and drift around aimlessly as I try to figure out where to stand. Mr. Mercer mans the grill while several men crowd him and discuss their predictions for some college team's football season. I can't decide why they all gravitate to a hot, smoky grill, but it appears to be the guy zone. Mrs. Mercer mingles, seamlessly moving from one small group to another. She elegantly waves me over to meet several new ladies. One very animated woman, boisterous in her enthusiasm, squeezes me in a side hug that leaves me a little breathless. She whoops and hollers to a boy named Blake who tries unsuccessfully to ignore her. Reluctantly, Blake slides into the circle of women. His mom, disregarding both of our embarrassed faces, starts the awkward introduction process.

"Blake, this is Marni. She's new to Texas and will be in your grade this year. Isn't that exciting?"

"Sure, Mom. Can I go now?" Blake turns to leave as his mom yanks him back by the collar.

"Please introduce Marni to the others." Her emphasis on the word *please* is more of a command. "She doesn't want to listen to us old ladies chitchat. Okay?" Her suggestion feels more like a direct order. Thankfully, he knew to quickly follow her instructions, allowing us both to escape her watchful attention.

"C'mon. It's Marni, right?" Blake beckons with a wave of his hand and turns to flee the scene.

My shoulders slump forward as I reluctantly follow him. "Yes, it's Marni. You don't have to do this, you know," I say shyly, trying to let him off the hook. He just shoots me a glare. This party is going exactly like I predicted, and I'm so embarrassed. He doesn't want to know me; I'm sure none of them do. I look back at the house, wondering if anyone would notice if I hid inside.

"My mom's got eyes like a hawk and manners like Ms. Priss on steroids. I will be quizzed on this later," he says through gritted teeth, obviously annoyed by his task.

I follow Blake to the back of the huge yard where kids close to my age gather away from the adults. A group of preppy boys, interested only in the football they are tossing, wear brightly colored shirts embroidered with a small alligator and khaki shorts. I watch them flip their skater hair out of their eyes in between throws and wonder why they don't use their hands instead of jerking their heads constantly.

I zero-in on the girls my age, laughing and talking near the boys. A shiver runs up my spine as I place them in the same category as the popular girls from my old school, unapproachable and snobby. It's obvious they collaborated with each other before the party since everyone's expensive, magazine-worthy outfit is some shade of pink. I catch glimpses of perfectly painted pink fingernails as their hands animatedly wave through the air. Suddenly embarrassed not to be wearing a stitch of pink, I adjust my baby-blue dress as I try to grin and bear the irritation welling up inside me. They're sending me the message I'm an outsider, and they aren't looking for another friend. I stare at these popular girls who expertly ignore me. I silently whisper to myself, *Message received*.

I can tell everyone already has a solid place in this group. They have probably known each other for years, maybe since birth. I promise myself that I'll go back inside and hide until everyone's gone. But first, I force myself to stand up tall, ready to get this little charade of an introduction over with.

"Hey, y'all. Come meet Marni. This is her party. She's new to Texas," Blake blurts without much thought or emotion.

I stand frozen, while the short Marni infomercial he vomits to the group instantly validates the feeling that I'm out of place. Butterflies fill my stomach as everyone stops talking and turns to look at me, their eyes examining me from head to toe. My eyes widen as I watch Blake steal the football from another boy's hands and run the opposite direction, pulling the guys back to their game. Sweat beads trickle down the curve of my neck. He did exactly what was asked and no more. Typical guy. His lack of legendary Southern genteel manners stuns me. I guess I falsely assumed manners and expectations were bred into these people, knotted into their DNA. Obviously, that is not the case. Clasping my hands in front of my waist to hide my nervousness, I quietly squeak, "Hi. Nice to meet you." The statement comes out more like a question though.

Embarrassed, I drop my head and start to pivot back toward the patio where the adults mingle around the food. I stop at the sound of one of the girls actually speaking to me. She makes quick introductions of herself and the other four girls standing nearby. I immediately forget everyone's name, probably because I'm so shocked they're actually talking to me, including me. I feel my eyes growing bigger by the minute as their circle opens up to allow me inside.

One girl says, "Sorry about Blake. He can be such a tool." The other girls chimed in with their agreement.

Another girl says, "I love your dress! Who's it by?" But without wasting a single second, she fishes out my dress tag and squeals with delight. My head whips around, surprised to feel her nosy little fingers at the base of my neck.

Ashamed I'm not in their dress code, I apologize for not wearing pink. They laugh, seemingly embarrassed by my observation, and one girl claims, "It was a total accident."

A different girl, clearly frustrated, adds, "I hate matching other people. It's the worst! My mom still makes me and my little sister dress alike for church and pictures." She starts getting even more worked up but takes a deep breath before insisting, "This won't happen again, right?" She peers around the circle, reassured by her friends' nodding heads.

"So, you didn't all plan to wear pink?" I ask, confused.

"Heck no!" they answer, almost in unison. My shoulders start to relax, realizing maybe I misjudged them.

Changing the subject, I ask about the boys playing football. Immediately, their excitement gains momentum as they point out and name each boy from a safe distance away. They tell me about the good, the bad, and the even better ones I'll meet at school. A smile lifts at the corner of my mouth as their conversation feels familiar, like something my friends and I would discuss.

My mind drifts back to the friends I left behind and how natural our connections were to one another. I can't figure out if this feels artificial and forced, which makes me leery and uncomfortable. Unable to hold back, tears fill my eyes, and I debate whether or not they really want another friend. One girl, Nicole, silences her friends and says, "Hey, Marni, are you okay? Is something wrong?"

I wipe away the few tears that dribble down my cheeks and somberly tell them the truth. "I just miss my friends back in Chicago, and meeting you all reminds me of them. I'm sorry, I didn't mean to get upset."

"Don't worry, it's what we do. At least one of us always ends up crying for one reason or another. My mom says it's our hormones, but I think it's because we can finally be real with each other without our nosy parents constantly monitoring everything," Nicole comforts me with a friendly wink.

"Thanks," I say with genuine sincerity. "So, what do you normally do at a barbecue? This is a first for me."

With that open-ended question, I follow the girls' lead and move to sit under the shade of a huge oak tree, out of the way of the boys. The girls happily fill me in on the latest gossip about boys, their excitement about starting ninth grade, moms and dads, and what foods to avoid. "Never eat anything Blake's mom brings!" This is a no-fail rule in their book. But since Mrs. Mercer is the host, all the main food is expected to be exceptionally tasty.

They ask me about Chicago, why I moved to Texas, and if I'm excited to be here. Of course, I give them a brief synopsis of why I left Chicago and how I just discovered I have a dad living in Texas.

"Wow, that sounds like something straight out of a soap opera!" a girl named Becca says, then corrects herself. "Except for the fact that it's really sad about your mom." She's right, it does feel like I'm trapped in a family saga where sadness, loss, and mystery captivate lonely housewives while they fold endless mounds of laundry. I cringe just thinking of the comparison.

But I can't exactly tell them how I feel about being in Texas. The Mercers, this heat, their mansion and lifestyle, it's all still so new to me. I tell them how nice the Mercers have been by providing me with my very own room and new clothes, which prompts a classic teenage-girl reaction. Like any group of girls, they get excited and nosy at the mention of a new wardrobe.

"Can we see your room?"

"And your new clothes?"

"Pleeease?" They beg in giddy unison.

"Sure!" Glad to cast the attention on something else, I guide them inside and up to my room. We hang out there for the rest of the evening, minus going outside for dinner and the best homemade ice cream I've ever tasted! The girls seem to love my new clothes and were surprisingly eager to help me pick out specific outfits for my first week of school. I'm confused by how easily they usher me into their group. I wonder if my friends and I would have been this welcoming to an outsider.

I try to shake the thought as it occurs to me that maybe they're just being polite and doing exactly what their parents told them to do: to include me. I fix a plastered smile on my face as I watch the girls move around my room, comfortably talking at each other instead of to each other or to me. I start shrinking into my skin as fresh heat sweeps over my body, a toxic mix of panic and loneliness. I'm pulled out of my dark thoughts when I hear, "Did you draw this?" I look up and see Nicole studying the picture I had worked on before the party.

"Yes," I answer, embarrassed I left it out for someone else to see.

"It's amazing. Kinda dark, but ... wow, you're really good!" Nicole sounds sincere. Then she adds, "And I should know, I love to paint."

I smile, silently thanking God I have something in common—something in my comfort zone I can easily discuss—with one of these girls. My guard slowly breaks down again as we talk art, books, movies, and everyone's vision of what walking the halls of high school will be like. What a relief to hear that even these girls are nervous. The tone of the evening shifts as we barrel past being new acquaintances and start interacting and laughing as friends.

As people start to leave, the girls say goodbye one by one. My heart leaps with excitement when Nicole unexpectedly asks if we can trade phone numbers so we can hang out before school starts. I know she doesn't need another friend, but I do. And I'm more than a little pumped that I may have found one so soon. I quickly rip out a sheet of paper from the sketch pad and jot down my number. She grins and waves the paper in the air as she runs out the door. "I'll text you tomorrow."

After everyone leaves the barbecue, I help escort Annabelle and Lila up to their rooms. Chocolate brownie remnants and ice cream splatter a unique pattern across their dresses. They are sticky messes for sure! I help Mrs. Mercer get them undressed while she fills up their bath.

Downstairs, Mr. Mercer dutifully cleans up. He scrubs the grill, takes out all the trash, and puts away the extra chairs and tables set up for the day. As I head back to my room, the doorbell rings. I stop near the top of the landing to see who accidentally left something behind, but I don't recognize her face from the party. However, Mr. Mercer stiffens as he approaches the door. He obviously recognizes the woman peering through the glass. She is an older woman with auburn hair that barely touches her earlobes. He hesitates, takes a deep breath, and slowly opens the door.

"Hey, Mom." He doesn't invite her in, which seems strange.

Mom? Wait, wasn't she supposed to be at the party? I completely forgot about meeting the grandparents after I met Nicole and the other girls. Had she been here tonight and I didn't know it? The gut-wrenching feeling of messing up makes me feel woozy. But why is he acting so cold? And why does she seem so uncomfortable?

"Kyle, can I come in for just a bit? I'm terribly sorry I missed your party. But you know your father ..." She tilts her head as if he understands the gesture. "Can we please just talk?" Her voice cracks with emotion.

Mr. Mercer steps aside, motioning for her to come sit in the living room. I decide I need to know more about this woman, my grandmother, so I crouch down out of sight but easily within hearing distance. Normally, I'm not sneaky by nature, but something feels off about her late visit. I cross my fingers, hoping Mrs. Mercer and the girls won't catch me eavesdropping.

CHAPTER 17
Ann

"Can I get you a drink, Mom?" His voice is colder than I hoped it would be.

"No, thank you, son. I can't stay long."

"What are you doing here? Dad made it perfectly clear that y'all want nothing to do with us or Marni. So, why'd you come?" His question sounds more like a child's whiny reprimand.

"Can you please tell me the story of how Marni came to be here?" I ask. My mind swirls as I try to enlighten my son on just how much I hate the way his father always thinks he knows best. He's always tried to some extent to shape the world around him, but today, he's gone too far. "Sometimes your dad withholds information from me, only relaying what he wants me to hear. Over the years, I've found that I have to do some investigative digging if I want the full, unadulterated truth. In the spirit of discovery, I want to hear from your lips your version of this story." I pause slightly. "Please."

I watch him take a few deep breaths, possibly trying to balance an earlier conversation he had with his dad against what I'm asking. I sit perfectly still with my legs crossed at the ankles and hands clasped in my lap, staring. He holds my gaze for what feels like endless minutes until he concedes, knowing I will patiently wait for the answers I need.

Finally, his voice slices through the thick air of anticipation. "You already know the end of the story. It's Marni. That really should have been enough." His curt words sting.

"How did everything happen, Kyle? What happened?"

"Did he tell you? Did you know?" Pain glints in his eyes.

"Know what?" I play a little dumb because I can't afford to lose him or any of my girls.

"That the reason he engineered my transfer back to Texas was because of a girl he didn't approve of? He has always needed to control everything—my love life, my career, and my family. He's the domino that knocked down any chance I should have had to be Marni's father. Can you even imagine how gut-wrenching it is to know you've missed just about every single moment of your child's childhood? I never heard her utter her first words, watched as her eyes lit up with her first taste of birthday cake, or taught her to ride a bike. I never had a chance to be there for her." He inhales a quick breath and hisses, "It makes me sick! I lost fourteen years with her, Mom! Fourteen years. Because of him!" He tries to control his breathing before continuing. "I'm not saying her mother and I were the right fit for each other, but I one hundred percent would have been there for Marni ... and Gabby."

I watch him, unsure what to say, so I let him continue to air his thoughts.

"Gabby was special, Mom. Different from anyone I'd ever met. She was a spitfire, young and ready to conquer the world." His head drops ever so slightly as he softly shakes it back and forth. He whispers, "I truly cared for her, but she was so young. We both were."

My eyes widen as I meet his troubled gaze. "I didn't know that. I knew there was *someone* in Chicago, but I was under the impression it wasn't a full-on relationship. I remember your dad telling me you had a 'cheap fling,' so I stood beside him and supported his decision to have you transferred back home. I'm sorry I never asked you about her."

"Why didn't you? From the moment you learned about Lauren, you pestered me." He cocks his head to the side and furrows his thick, brown eyebrows.

"Your dad made it very clear that leaving Chicago was in your best interest. He said you wanted to return to your life in Texas, and that I should leave well enough alone." I pause, watching him twist his fingers into a mangled web of frustration. "How was I supposed to know? You never told me anything about her." I defend my ignorance with the hard facts. "Why did you hide her from us?"

Kyle drops his hand and walks into the adjoining kitchen. I hear cabinets open and close and then recognize the sound of ice chunks being dropped into crystal glasses. A couple of minutes later, he returns with two bourbon glasses filled halfway with an amber-brown liquid. He offers me one and takes a healthy swig from his. "It's Elijah Craig ... the good stuff. I thought we could use a drink."

I nod, sip the stout liquid, and enjoy the spicy burn that coats my throat. Then I raise my eyebrows, indicating I'm still waiting for his explanation.

"Dad didn't care that I had feelings for Gabby. Apparently, we weren't a 'proper Southern match.' Dad kept saying things like, 'How will you be able to bring her to business dinners and into society when she's so uneducated?' He tried to sound concerned for both of us when he said she'd be humiliated and I'd be embarrassed. He picked apart our differences and asked what kind of life I thought I'd really be able to build with someone so far beneath my station. He said she wouldn't be a proper wife, and I'd resent her for holding me back." He sighs and looks down at his feet. "He painted a convincing picture. Through his eyes, I saw a refined, Southern version of Gabby that *was* ready to be the wife I needed and deserved. He persuaded me to just let her go, reminding me that nothing was binding us to each other since we hadn't known each other long enough to build anything solid. Besides, wasn't she too young to be tied down or asked to give up her own dreams? I bought into it—everything he said—thinking maybe this was all for the best." He watches the bourbon swirl slowly as he traces tiny, imaginary circles in the air with his crystal glass. He looks up, his eyes rimmed with moisture. "I didn't fight him enough because part of me felt he was right."

"Oh, honey." My heart breaks for him.

He puts up a hand so he can continue. His words roll off his tongue like a sinner's confession. "Deep down, I knew he was happy having me back under his thumb. But I never imagined him capable of jeopardizing my happiness and manipulating my future to fit within his rigid parameters." A tear slips out of the corner of one of his eyes. He wipes the salty trail off his face. "The last conversation I had with her still haunts me. She was supposed to move back here with me after I settled in, but as soon as I left, I realized it would never work. I know I broke her heart, and she deserved an explanation, but I was young and selfish and immature ... with big dreams. And she was so young, too, just out of high school. I figured she had all the time in the world to find her forever love while pursuing her own dream. You know, she wanted to be a chef?" His voice trails off as his eyes cloud over with emotion.

I shake my head.

"Yep. Gabby had planned to study culinary arts in New York City. I didn't want to be the guy that stood in her way." A tear slides down his cheek and pools in his dimples.

I want to hush him, but I need to hear it just as much as he needs to say it. I wonder if he's been able to be this open with Lauren. My mind quickly detours to my daughter-in-law. How is she handling the news and this sudden change? I gather from what I have pieced together about her past that she puts tremendous stock in family stability and honor.

Kyle interrupts my thoughts. "Mom, I don't know if Gabby knew she was pregnant with Marni when we broke up, but believe me, if she did know, she never told me." I nod, catching a slight glimpse of the pain we all caused that poor woman. Somewhere deep in my bones, I feel certain she must have had an inkling that something was different in her body. Even if she knew Kyle's little girl was growing inside her, would she have told him, knowing he wasn't choosing her? A lump forms at the back of my throat, and emotion stings the edges of my eyes and nose.

"She did exactly what I told her to do: she vanished from my life without a trace until a couple of weeks ago."

"And how is Lauren handling all this ... change?"

"It's been tough, but she's okay," he says. "Telling her was one of the hardest things I've ever done."

"How so exactly?"

He tips the crystal glass of bourbon up to his lips, inhales its enticing scent, and slowly sips on the amber liquid. I recognize the habit; his father does the same when he's searching for the right words. I don't know if this is a distraction technique learned in law school or just a simple dose of liquid courage. Either way, I join him and take a delicate sip of Mr. Craig's bourbon.

"I messed up with Lauren, from the very beginning, which made everything so much harder than it should have been."

"What are you talking about?" My voice raises slightly.

"I lied to her. I never told her about my time in Chicago, let alone Gabby. So of course, she was blindsided to find out that not only do I have another daughter, but it's with a woman she'd never even heard of." Fresh tears start to roll in succession down his cheeks. I sigh deeply.

"Why didn't you ever tell her?"

"I've been asking myself that same question. I guess I felt so bad about the way everything ended, that I sealed up that part of my life. It was my secret to carry and my burden to bear. I didn't want to admit out loud that I had been such a coward, especially not to Lauren. All I've wanted to do since I met Lauren was love her and be worthy of her love. She's the love of my life."

I stare at my broken son, wishing we could all rewind time. I know Kyle. I know his heart and intentions are pure—not perfect, but whose are? I stand up and move to sit by him, lightly placing my hand on his back like I did when he was just a boy. He looks up. "She loves you, Kyle. She'll come around, and it'll all work out."

Kyle's smile tilts lopsided. "I hope so." He shakes his head and chuckles slightly. "I couldn't have asked for a more loving and supportive wife and partner."

I smile. Of course they're working it out. They've always been the perfect match for each other. But the real reason I'm here tonight is to learn more about Marni. I clear my throat, signaling a change in our conversation's direction. I ask cautiously, "Tell me more about Marni."

"You should have come to meet her in person."

"I don't disagree, but please indulge me." I glance down at my watch, knowing I should be heading back home sooner than later.

"I'm not sure how to describe her just yet. I know Marni misses her mom and life back in Chicago, but she's strong, like Gabby. I see a brave and beautiful girl who needs to be reassured that her place is in this family. She loves playing with the girls, who adore her. It amazes me how she seems to be taking everything in stride, which is more than I can say for you and Dad." I bite my upper lip as I listen to him, careful not to flinch at his words. "Dad was so concerned about me being with Gabby because she was poor." He laughs briefly. "Marni and the reason she's here with us ... none of it was an issue tonight. Everyone, except her grandparents, embraced her as one of their own."

"I see." My eyes drop to my lap where I nervously trace the elegant cuts in the crystal glass with my fidgety fingers.

"You and Dad are not going to ruin my family's chance at happiness. I'm tired of trying to mold my life around what Dad thinks is best. I don't care anymore. You can either be a part of our new family or not, but that decision is entirely yours." His firm voice threatens an ultimatum I know not to challenge.

"I hear you. You know your dad is a very difficult and demanding man. I'll be the first to admit that his standards are sometimes impossible to meet, which is probably why he's been so successful in business. He pushes hard but loves fiercely." I pause as I picture a giant teddy bear in my head because really that's really what he is. "He's an old-fashioned, stubborn man who struggles to accept change. It's just not in his wheelhouse.

"I love you, Kyle. It breaks my heart to know how much we've hurt you tonight and in the past." He gives me a gentle nod that encourages me to keep talking. "If it's okay with you, I would love to get to know Marni. If she's half of you and half of a woman that you adored, then she's bound to be beyond special. Unfortunately, your father will not partake in this relationship, but that's his loss. Let *me* handle him.

If you'd allow it, I'd be honored to take Marni out for a girls' day anytime this week. I have a lot of catching up to do as a grandmother ... fourteen years' worth."

I watch Kyle's body language, hoping to discern his thoughts. He seems surprised but in a good way. He opens his mouth to speak, but only vowel sounds escape as he searches for his words. He nods yes and takes a final drink of his bourbon. He sets the glass down on the table and smiles. Relief. That's what I see in his face.

"Very well." I stand quickly and make my way to the front door. "Please give my love to Lauren, Annabelle, Lila, and Marni." I mentally note to add Marni to the list of girls in my life. I will not be one of those grandmothers who plays favorites because I know what it feels like to not be chosen. The thought that I might have already started off my relationship with Marni in a way that makes her feel unwanted shames me. I pause at the front door. "I'll call tomorrow to make plans with Marni." I lean in to kiss Kyle on the cheek and quickly walk toward my car.

CHAPTER 18
Marni

For a few quiet minutes, I sit in the hallway, wrapping my arms around my bent knees, trying to digest everything I just overheard. I can't believe they could have been together all this time if only he'd had the guts to just try. All this time, we could have been a family, even if they weren't the right fit. They just needed more time, and then he would have known about me. I would have had him in my life from the very beginning, regardless of their relationship status. Instead, he's trying to make up for lost time; we both are. Why didn't he stand up to his father and be a man? And what kind of father brushes off his son's happiness? And why is his mother sneaking over so late just to ask if she can get to know me?

Just as these types of questions start to spin out of control in my head, Annabelle and Lila burst out of their door, completely naked and giggling. The wet blurs streak down the hallway and vanish downstairs, narrowly escaping Mrs. Mercer's attempt to towel them dry. Mrs. Mercer pauses as she rounds the corner into the hall, a towel in each hand. Her eyes lock on mine. I see an exhausted mother; she sees a girl crouching in the hall. I watch her catch her breath, sizing up the scene. Her quizzical look makes me nervous—how do I explain myself? But before she has a chance to ask what's going on, her attention quickly refocuses when she hears Mr. Mercer call out, "I'm gonna get my drippy little princesses!"

Her shoulders relax as she exhales. With a grin, she asks, "Marni, would you mind helping me catch those slippery monsters?"

I quickly come to my feet, thankful she doesn't ask me any questions about why I'm sitting in the hallway. She hands me one of the plush, pink towels, and we tiptoe downstairs. Mr. Mercer, enjoying a routine game of cat-and-mouse, smirks as the girls sneak up from behind trying to scare him. But the real game is to avoid being caught and clothed by their mother. When the girls catch a glimpse of their pink towels approaching, they scream, "Run!" But we're prepared. Mrs. Mercer snags Lila and rolls her wet body into a towel like a burrito while I capture Annabelle, draping her towel around her shoulders in queen-like fashion.

"Well, that was an eventful bath, right, girls?" Mrs. Mercer teases. "It seems we might have had too much sugar before bed. Brownies, lemonade, ice cream … hmm?"

The girls cut their eyes at each other and belly laugh until we all laugh so hard, we can barely catch our breath. Contagious laughter is the best medicine for the soul. I've missed that uncontainable joy, so this hysteria in the Mercers' family room comforts me. For a moment, I almost forget where I am and why I'm here. I'm just enjoying being a part of the fun.

"Girls, head on up to bed. Your grandmother stopped by while you were in the bath, and she wants to see you soon. So, let's get a solid night's sleep, okay?" Mr. Mercer tries to reason with them.

"Yes, sir," the girls answer in sweet unison as they prance up the stairs and into their individual rooms for the night.

Mrs. Mercer looks at Mr. Mercer and then glances at me. "When did your mom leave?"

"Oh, just minutes before the sugar storm hit."

I sense Mrs. Mercer may be piecing together the reason I was balled up in the hallway. It's obvious she wants to talk to him more about his mom's visit.

"Thank you for the barbecue tonight. I really had a nice time." I politely excuse myself and disappear into my room.

CHAPTER 19
Lauren

"What happened with your mom?" I ask Kyle. My voice is full of dread and concern as I slouch into the leather couch and prop my tired feet onto the coffee table.

"She came by and basically wanted to know the whole story behind Marni and her mother. Honestly, I thought she already knew everything, but it turns out that Dad only told her bits and pieces, vague and false information so she would support him. She ultimately said that it doesn't matter what Dad wants or is going to do, she wants to get to know Marni and develop a relationship with her." My eyes must have widened because he agrees with my reaction. "I'm just as surprised as you. I've never heard her so much as speak a negative word about Dad's wishes, let alone an outright defiance."

I watch a sly grin creep up his face. "Your dad has always been too controlling over everyone and everything in his life. I can only imagine how fed up she must be. I'm so proud of her for making this decision on her own! But I think you should know that whatever was said between the two of you, I'm fairly certain Marni overheard every word." I nod toward the upstairs hallway that offers an open view into the living room.

"What makes you say that?"

"Well, when I chased the girls around the corner, I found Marni scrunched into a ball in the hallway right where the overlook opens up. She wore a distant and confused look, like she was processing something. I wanted to ask her what was up, but instead of prying, I asked her to help me catch the girls. I thought maybe she was homesick or overwhelmed from the party. But now I'm pretty sure she had been eavesdropping."

"Hmm." His voice is more mellow than I expected. He glances up at the open walkway and shakes his head. "Well, nothing was said that should've upset her. If anything, hopefully she heard how vested you and I both are in getting to know and love her. Do you think I should ask her what she heard? I need to tell her that Mom wants to spend some one-on-one time with her. But I suppose I should I ask her first, right?"

I shrug my shoulders in response because who knows what the best protocol is when you are caring for your husband's child? I'm just trying to do the best I can at any given moment. I think for a minute, putting myself in Marni's shoes.

Hearing Rosemary's advice echo in my head, I say, "Remember what it was like being a teenager?" He cocks his head in question. "Wanting to be included in conversations? Talked to like an adult? Any of this ring a bell?"

"Sure, kind of," he admits, shrugging his shoulders slightly.

"I think we need to be very intentional with Marni, setting aside special time each evening to get to know her. Ask her questions, learn about her past, understand what makes her tick, ya know? Otherwise, we're all going to remain strangers." I watch him process my suggestion and wait.

Kyle nods, a slow grin filling his face. "That's a great plan."

"Great! You can start by talking to her about your mom. She's a teenager, Kyle. We can't gloss over these things with her like we thankfully can with our other girls. It's important that we establish open and honest lines of communication with her, just like we do with Lila and Annabelle."

Kyle pulls himself out of his comfy chair, and I finally muster the nerve to ask the question that's been eating away at me ever since I heard the name *Marni*. I look him in the eye, and my voice shakes. "Kyle?"

He stops. His face looks tired, but I can see I have his attention, so I continue. "If your parents had been on board with you being with Marni's mom, would you have married her?" I don't know if I really want to know the truth, but I can't take back what I've just said either. Nervous, I twist my wedding rings back and forth around my finger. "I just need to know if I am your second choice." Salty tears gently glide down my face forming tiny pools at the corners of my mouth. I am terrified of the truth ... or whether he would even tell me the truth.

Stunned, Kyle rubs his thumb and forefinger against his temple, a sure sign that he's worn out. He straightens his posture before joining me on the couch, where his warm arms wrap around my shoulders, pulling me safely into his chest. His heartbeat pounds an intense rhythm through his shirt into my ear. My heart starts to quicken as it tries desperately to match his fast-paced thump-thumping. I start to crumble under the weight of anticipation, feeling stupid for both needing and wanting validation.

Releasing me, he gently cradles my face in his hands, holding me inches away from his own face. "Lauren, I want you, to hear me. I am not your father. I did not choose someone over you and I didn't choose you because I couldn't have another. You are the love of my life!"

My eyelids close as my mind retorts a sarcastic response ... of course he'd say that. I can't decide if I'm embarrassed for me or disappointed in him. What can he say to me? *I've always loved another woman?* No. I've set us both up for a loss. He releases his tender hold on my face and gently grips one of my shoulders. My eyes open as I feel him take a large inhale of breath.

"Yes, I cared deeply for Marni's mother, but was it love? Maybe I thought it could have been at the time, but it wasn't." I roll my eyes, both of us knowing I deserve more. He nods, one corner of his mouth curving up into a lopsided smile. "Like I've told you, she was barely out of high school. Our lives were completely different. I was on my way up a career ladder while she had culinary dreams. We talked about our future, but I don't know that it ever felt real to me. I remember Gabby becoming giddy sometimes at the prospect of leaving Chicago, like I was saving her from a life she didn't know if she could escape on her own." He pauses, both us of picturing the life she did live. His voice quivers, hinting at the pain he must carry, probably guilt over how her life ended up. "In hindsight, I think I'd never been wanted or needed like that before, so I got caught up in the drama of being her prince charming. It didn't take much for Dad to convince me that we weren't the right fit because I think I already knew. I'm sure he had his own agenda, but mine was simple. I wanted to be free and follow my dreams and her to follow hers. I made the choice and I'm thankful every day I did because that choice, brought me to you." He stares into my eyes, holding my gaze to make sure I hear him. He adds, "Besides, if I really wanted to marry Gabby, I would have, with or without my parents' support."

I cock my head, silently questioning him.

"It's true. And I would have run away with you if it came to that, but thankfully, my parents love you. Don't doubt for a single moment my love and devotion. You are my partner, my world, my love, my whole life. I chose you, the promise of you, before I ever met you."

My thoughts mirror the emotion I see in his baby-blue eyes. His crystal tears sparkle in the dim light, and I search his face, trying to read the story imprinted on his heart. Somehow, I believe him. I can see he was never hers to have, which can only mean he never gave himself to her completely. I offer a soft smile as I think, *He was waiting for me.*

He leans into my body and gently showers me with tender, intimate kisses, starting at the tops of my eyelids, moving down to the corners of my mouth, landing romantically on my lips. My heart flutters with butterflies as his touch reassures me of his complete devotion. He has always had my whole heart, and now I see I have always had his.

CHAPTER 20
Marni

At breakfast, Mr. Mercer invites me to join him for a round of golf—a father-daughter outing with just the two of us. He explains we will start with golf, break for lunch, and finish the day with more golf. Apparently, golf takes a while to play.

"I don't know anything about golf," I reply woodenly. I've never played the game and certainly have never been on a golf course. I think back to the few times I've actually seen golf. Smiling, I remember how Mom would deliberately put golf on the TV, insisting it was a surefire way to get the best nap. The monotone voices that barely inflect with excitement lulled me to sleep on Sunday afternoons when Mom had to go to work. *Golf is boring*, I think as I smile somewhat uneasily at Mr. Mercer.

Mrs. Mercer must sense my anxiety, so she adds, "Remember, you two, the girls are attending birthday parties today. Marni, you are more than welcome to come and join us."

The girls' eyes widen with excitement as they squeal, "Can she?"

"Of course," Mrs. Mercer answers. "Just know that there will be a bunch of screaming kids hopped-up on cake and ice cream, fighting for your attention," she says to me with a sly grin. After seeing the girls' reaction to sugar at last night's barbeque, I am thankful for an alternate option and decide to give golf a shot.

Mr. Mercer says, "Don't worry, Marni, I'll teach you all about the game, and we'll have some fun out in the fresh air! Go upstairs and put on a collared short-sleeve shirt and some light-weight pants. We have a tee time in just over an hour."

Mr. Mercer drives us to "the club." He explains the club is private. But since the Mercers are "in" the club, Mr. Mercer excitedly tells me I can participate in any of the services or activities offered whenever I want. As he lists the club's amenities—restaurants, tennis, several pools, championship golf course, boat access to the lake, and an elegant ballroom—we slow down to turn into a beautifully manicured entrance. Ornate iron gates embellished with the club's logo welcome its members. Magnificent live oak trees line the main road that winds around the tennis courts, past the pools, and into the main parking lot. The natural-stone clubhouse sits at the end of the road like a stately monument. Splashes of vibrantly colored flowers pop out of soothing blue-green pots that trim the building's covered entrance and walkway. Gilded by the midmorning sun, the building's character glows with a timeless elegance that captivates me.

Mr. Mercer pulls up to a one-man stand and pops his trunk. The attendant immediately recognizes him and politely states, "Mr. Mercer, I'll have your clubs and beverage loaded onto cart number twelve for you."

Mr. Mercer nods in recognition and then quickly adds, "I'll need to borrow a set of women's clubs today. Will you please alert the pro shop for us, Shawn?"

Shawn nods and looks into the car, assuming to see Mrs. Mercer. His eyes widen as his head slightly tilts to the right. Obviously, Shawn has no clue who I am.

Straightening up, Mr. Mercer says, "Shawn, I want you to meet my daughter, Marni, here from Chicago. Please help her feel at home."

"Yes, sir. Of course. Nice to meet you, Ms. Marni." He sweeps his right hand into the air. "Welcome!"

I give a shy grin and lower my head, embarrassed by the attention. Thankfully, Mr. Mercer rolls up my passenger window and starts making his way to a parking spot. I shift slightly in my seat to watch Shawn carry Mr. Mercer's gear toward a line of matching golf carts.

Mr. Mercer ushers me into the golf shop. Again, he introduces me as his daughter to a guy called "the pro" who measures me and pulls out a bright-yellow golf bag with charcoal-colored ladies clubs. I watch as another young guy carries my loaner clubs to our cart, and Mr. Mercer orders me a large cola float, a Texas treat. The cart is already loaded with a couple bags of chips, two bottles of water, and all our gear. With all our stuff and provisions, it looks like we are going on a small trip, not playing a game.

It doesn't take me long to comprehend that the goal is to constantly hit my golf ball toward a hole I can't see in as few strokes as possible. After the first four holes, my frustration bubbles hot at the surface. Irritated, I wonder, *Why is it so hard to hit this dimply ball?* Mr. Mercer smiles as he helps me put away the seven iron I was just swinging. I try offering a smile back, but I'm just so annoyed at this game that it feels more like a grimace.

"Welcome to the most frustrating game ever," he says with a laugh. I look up at him, confused. "Look, Marni. I love golf for so many reasons, but it kicks my butt every time I'm out here. It's a challenge because it's just me against myself—I can't blame my performance on anyone else but me. I own up to my decisions and keep moving forward."

I tip my head up to meet his gaze, my eyes squint as new thoughts surge in my head. What's he trying to say? Does he see me as the exhausting result of a decision he made a long time ago? Am I here just because he's doing the "right thing" and owning up to a responsibility he never wanted?

Tears fill my eyes, blurring my vision. Seeing my emotion, he falsely assumes I'm upset at my golfing abilities. "Let's abandon all score-keeping and just have fun out here."

I nod, silently walking back to the cart. I tell myself to stop thinking about what he said, willing myself to have fun with the father I always wanted. It suddenly dawns on me that we're doing almost exactly what I had always envisioned I'd do with my father.

We are in a kind-of park together, playing a game. A smile brightens my face as I think, *I can do this.*

Halfway through golf, Mr. Mercer insists we break for lunch, and my stomach growls at the mention of food. We sit toward the back of the room in one of the club's restaurants and each order a fried chicken wrap with homemade salt and vinegar chips.

"I'm really enjoying this time with you, Mr. Mercer. I'm just sorry I stink at golf."

He chuckles. "No one is ever any good at golf. It's a game of chance. One day, you're on, and the next, well, you can't hit a ball straight to save your life. It's why this game is so frustratingly exciting. But you're doing great! If you ever decide that you want to take up the game, I'd love having you as my golf partner!" He winks. "I know that I have fourteen years of catching up to do. I want to know all I can about you—your life in Chicago, your interests, and what you want to do in the future. I'm just so thankful you are here."

By the time our food arrives, he has asked me some general get-to-know-you stuff, and I appreciate his efforts, but all this personal attention reminds me of Mom and how much I miss her. It's hard to put into words how much impact a little positive attention can make on a person's self-worth. For so long, Mom was my biggest cheerleader and supporter. She was my go-to for everything. I wonder if Mr. Mercer wants to fill that role because it feels like he may be trying.

My head drops as a weighted breath escapes through my slack lips. I know the only reason we know each other is because Mom is gone. The trade-off for me was too great, too final.

As if he can read my mind, he clears his throat and softly states, "But, Marni, I wish all this had happened under other circumstances. I would never wish for your mother to be gone. I hope you know that."

"I do. And I want you to know that I heard you talking to your mom last night about you and my mom."

With a deep sigh, he says, "I didn't know you were listening. I'm not quite sure what you heard. But I did care deeply for your mom. My mother didn't even know the extent of my relationship with her. It was my father ..." He pauses, taking a deep breath. "He's a difficult subject. My mother ... she's a gem," he says with a brilliant smile. "She would love the opportunity to know you as a grandmother if you'd allow her to spend some time with you." He reaches out his hand and touches the top of my arm for emphasis. "But this is your decision, so think on it for as long as you'd like."

We discuss the game of golf as we finish our meal, and I notice we are both much more laid-back with each other, laughing and talking. He answers my golf questions, using sugar packets and toothpicks on the table for strategy demonstration. After eating every last bite, we head back to the golf cart for the final nine holes. This time, I get to drive, and I quickly decide that driving the cart is definitely the best part of the game. After we're done, Mr. Mercer orders two milkshakes for the road. He admits with a mischievous laugh, "You never leave the club without a signature milkshake in your hand."

On the ride home, the grandmother invitation steadily runs through my head. I have never had a grandmother in my life—at least, not that I can remember. Mom's parents both died in a car accident before I was born. I have a few pictures of them with Mom and Aunt Jo, but that's all. I love those photos. The images of their glowing faces always fill my heart. I remember how Mom used to look up to heaven and back at me as she'd boast, "Oh, if your grandma could see you now!" The memory of her words, the excitement of what my grandma would have been like, casts a new light on this grandma offer.

Part of me is intrigued, but I need help. I don't know what grandmas do, or what she will expect from me. Most of my friends in Chicago didn't have grandparents close enough to see regularly, so I have no frame of reference. Will this be a fun thing or more like busywork? I need a friend's perspective, or at least someone that's a non-Mercer. I decide to call Nicole as soon as we get home and pick her brain on the subject. I really liked texting with her last night. Plus, this gives me a good excuse to call her. I cross my fingers, hoping she really wants to be my friend.

***

"Nicole, hi. It's me, Marni."

"Hey, Marni. What's up? Recovered from your first backyard barbecue?" She laughs through her words. She found it so strange that I had never been to one. Sure, we have skinny, tiny backyards in the city, but everyone we knew had very little money to host parties. We were always meeting friends at the park with a sandwich in hand or attending the occasional potluck gatherings at church. I don't recall ever being at a party where a guy stood sweating over a grill, cooking everyone's dinner. Then again, who did we know with a backyard like the Mercers' in Chicago?

"So, I need to ask you something. I guess you could say it's another new thing for me. Do you mind?"

"'Course not."

"Well, I've never really had a grandmother, at least, not one that I knew. My mom's parents died way before I was born."

"I'm sorry, Marni."

"It's fine. I never knew any different, but I used to imagine what it would be like to bake cupcakes with my grandma. Mom always said she had the magic touch in the kitchen." I shake my head like an Etch-A-Sketch, getting back to the issue at hand. "But here's the thing. Mr. Mercer's mom says she wants to be my grandmother. What do you think that means?"

"Are you serious?" Her voice jumps an octave in astonishment. "Okay, so you're a grandma virgin ... wow." She exaggerates her last word with a half-chuckle.

"Hey, don't make fun of me! It was always just me, Mom, and my Aunt Jo. It was perfect, okay?" My voice is starting to sound edgy, so I cover the phone and whisper to myself, "Keep it together."

"Hey, I'm not laughing at you—just tickled at the question. Here's the deal. Grandmothers are awesome!" she states with absolute authority. "They spoil us rotten! See, grandparents love to bypass parents, which means they'll let you do almost anything. Your grandma will take you shopping, out to eat at fun restaurants, to the movies—it doesn't matter to them as long as you're having fun together."

She pauses, waiting for me to respond. But how do I comment on something I've never even fully fantasized about? All this is so overwhelming. I never even did a lot of those things with my own mother. How could I contemplate doing them now with an utter stranger? Amid my confusion, an audible sigh slips through my lips.

"Hey, don't stress over this. I kinda know Mr. Mercer's parents, and you will love his mom. She's pretty spunky. All you need to know is that a grandparent will love and support you no matter what. It's in their job description. You don't have to do anything special or prove yourself. Just be open to spending time together. I'm pretty sure you're gonna love the whole grandma thing if you give it a chance."

"Thanks," I reply offhandedly, knowing I need more time to sort through my thoughts. I mean, Mom always made special time for me. I never felt deprived of her attention or love, so I'm not sure what to make of a stranger who is asking to be an older version of a mom I don't have anymore.

Without skipping a beat, Nicole changes the subject. "So, are you gearing up for school? There's a group of girls getting together to prepare for our back-to-school look. I was going to call you this evening to see if you wanted to join us. We're going to my friend Jenny's house to figure it out and watch a flick. Her mom makes the *best* junk food."

I can almost hear her salivating.

"Oh! I can already taste the chips and queso, iced brownies, and candied popcorn we'll eat while watching some awesome girl-power movie ..."

Nicole's words run together in a mashed-up blend of excitement and hysteria. My head starts to fog as I try to process all the things she's blurting out.

"... and experimenting with hairdos while trying out makeup tricks from magazines. Please ask the Mercers if you can come! My mom already said she can pick you up and bring you home. It's going to be so much fun!" I hear Nicole gasp for breath on the other end of the line.

"Are you sure they want me to come?" I ask quietly.

"What? Yes! Of course, silly!"

"Okay … um, sounds like fun. I'll let you know what the Mercers say," I answer before the conversation topic changes again.

As we say our goodbyes, Nicole reminds me to ask the Mercers about Jenny's party. I laugh at her persistence, and we finally hang up. I can't believe I was just invited to a party! Nicole seems like a potential true friend, which I desperately need. The terrifying thought of being alone in high school makes my insides flip upside down. I'm jealous of my friends in Chicago and the girls I don't even know here because all of them are already a part of a group. I hope they really want me to come, and this isn't some adult ploy to help me adjust. I lift my eyes to the sky and pray, "God, please let them accept me."

I curl up on my bed, staring holes into the white ceiling. "Grandmother Mercer. Hmm …."

CHAPTER 21
Marni

I must have dozed off because the next thing I know, my name is being whispered while someone gently nudges my shoulder. I force my heavy lids open to find Mrs. Mercer sitting next to me on the bed. "I'm sorry to wake you, honey, but dinner is ready. Didn't want you to sleep through it and get hungry after midnight."

"No, thank you for getting me up. I didn't mean to fall asleep. I'll be right down." My voice is groggy, trying to wake up as well.

Mrs. Mercer gracefully gets up to leave and hesitates in the doorway. She turns and looks me straight in the eye. Unsure of what she's about to say, my heart skips a beat. "Marni, I can't begin to imagine how overwhelming these past months have been for you. Saying goodbye to your mom and the only home you've known must have felt like a nightmare. I can't understand everything you've been through, but I know how it feels to lose your mom—it's gut-wrenching. I'm here if you ever want to talk." She pauses, lightly tapping her hand on the doorframe, before she adds, "Your mom was right sending you to us. She knew something we are all learning … she knew we needed each other." Her smile reaches all the way up to her eyes before she pivots out of the doorway.

Stunned, I lie there, fully awake with mixed feelings and questions filling the blank space around me. How could she say that? She barely even knows me. This is too much—too much change, too much pressure to fit in, too much family that isn't mine. Staring into space, I blurt out my thoughts to Mom, hoping she's listening to me. "Was this supposed to be easier for you or me, introducing us to each other after you've gone? I'm so angry at you, Mom, and I need you so much. I know the Mercers are trying to make this work, but it's just not the same ..." I sit up and look at the desk next to my bed. My eyes land on the newest version of the family picture I drew yesterday. "Do you think they will love me?" Tears flood my face, streaming down my chin and dissolving into my shirt. The emotions overwhelm me. This feels like too much for a fourteen-year-old to sort through and compartmentalize.

Collecting myself, I break the sad solitude and head to the bathroom to clean myself up for dinner. Taking inventory of my appearance, I notice my shirt is a soggy mess, and my face resembles a dry creek bed. I wipe a damp washcloth across my face, change into a fresh top, run my fingers through my hair, and head for the dining room. Sounds of laughter and love complement the delicious smells wafting my way. My stomach responds with a loud rumbling, and my spirits start to lift. I am hungry for the food and a family.

Mrs. Mercer's abilities in the kitchen are phenomenal. I catch the delicious smell of something familiar and follow my nose and grumbling stomach. To my surprise, dinner is not set up in a normal fashion around the dining room table. Instead, the girls are in the kitchen, elbow-deep in tomato sauce and shredded cheese.

"Just in time, Marni. We're making homemade pizzas," Mrs. Mercer says. "Just put it together however you like it, and they'll be ready to eat in about fifteen minutes!" She turns to monitor the girls' pizza creations. I step up to work at the island and grab a large, flat piece of soft, bubbly bread. The girls quickly inform me it's naan bread ... like that's supposed to mean something.

I layer tomato sauce all the way to the edge of my bread. Then I pile on the cheese, pepperoni, sliced onions, and green bell peppers. The final touch for a Chicago-style pizza is more sauce and more cheese ... at least, that's how I like it. The girls watch in fascination.

"Know why I added more sauce and cheese?" I ask the girls. Not waiting for their response, I inform them Chicago is famous for its pizza. "I'm not real sure how to make a true Chicago-style pizza, but it's kinda like an upside-down pizza with toppings at the bottom and the cheese and sauce on top. I love pizza!"

Mr. and Mrs. Mercer quickly glance at each other. Mr. Mercer winks at her, and she responds with a satisfied smile. Once we've assembled our own pizzas, Mrs. Mercer slides them into the oven. The enticing smell of pizza fills the house, reminding me of how our Chicago apartment used to absorb the Italian smells of the nearby hole-in-the-wall restaurants. The girls, trying to wait patiently, put on an on-the-fly show for us that proves to be a hysterical disaster. Lila follows a script in her head while Annabelle directs a completely different scene. Just when their tempers start to flare, the timer signals that our pizzas are ready.

"Wow, I missed my calling, ladies. I'm the best pizza maker of all time," Mr. Mercer exclaims with authority, instigating an immediate debate over whose pizza is the best.

"Marni, does your pizza taste like the ones in Chicago?" Lila asks with sincerity.

"Yes, Lila. Except it's not near greasy enough." That makes Mrs. Mercer laugh.

It feels strange falling into sync with the Mercers. The rhythm of their family slowly beats louder and stronger, enticing me to join them, be one of them. Even though it's tempting, I hesitate. I can't help but think that no matter how "normal" things may look, I am just an alien wearing a mask to blend in with its surroundings. I guess I've read one too many sci-fi books, but you get the picture. After I help Mrs. Mercer clear the dishes, I excuse myself upstairs to my room. I need privacy and some space to process the day. And I need to hear a familiar voice.

"Aunt Jo? Hey, it's me, Marni!"

"Heeeey, sweet girl! How's Texas treating you? Enjoying all that fresh space?"

"Yeah, I guess." I grunt and moan slightly before adding, "Not really. I'm just so ..."

"What is it honey? The Mercers bein' ugly to you?"

"No, it's not that. In fact, if anything, they're way too nice to me. I just wonder if it's an act that will dissolve once the get-to-know-you phase runs its course."

"That river will never run dry. It takes a lifetime to truly know someone, especially someone as amazing as yourself." I feel her warm smile transcend the space that separates us as she reassures me. We both sit quietly for a few seconds before she changes the trajectory of our conversation. She bluntly asks, "So what's got your skirt in a knot exactly?"

"My options. I want to know how we'll decide whether this trial period was a failure or a success. Will it just be up to me, or do the Mercers have to weigh in on whether I stay or go?"

"I guess that's up to you. Why? Is it that miserable? What's going on?"

Her questions irritate me. I can't answer the way I want to, and I can't lie. Plus, defining *miserable* is case- and person-specific, and I feel certain that feeling miserable and homesick isn't going to persuade her to bring me home any sooner. I opt for the truth. "No, they're treating me well. I'm just so confused ..." My mind starts to travel down a now-familiar path, but then I perk up enough to report good news. "I think I've made a new friend though. She's invited me to another girl's back-to-school sleepover."

"Well, that does sound promising! What other wonderful news is bothering you?" Her words are filled with sarcasm. But I know she's deeply concerned for me, so I let her snide remark slide.

Feeling frustrated, I gruffly answer her sarcasm with more good news. "It turns out that I have a grandmother who wants to get to know me. But it's complicated."

"How so?"

"Her husband, my would-be grandfather, is the one who encouraged Mr. Mercer to break up with Mom!" I wait for a gasping response, which she didn't offer. "It's weird, and it just makes me so sad to think about Mom and what might have been. You know?" I want to envision Aunt Jo nodding her head in agreement, but something inside me tells me she's not.

She says, "First off, having a grandmother is a treat, a blessing actually. If you think I'm pretty great, which we both know is indisputable, then I promise you, you'll love having a very present grandmother. Secondly, forget all the history behind your parents' fallout. It happened. Move on because everyone else did. You have been a part of the Mercer family since day one, you just never knew it. Why are you so scared of being a part of your father's family?"

With an audible sigh, I admit for the umpteenth time to Aunt Jo and myself, "I don't want to ever forget Mom or our life together. In Chicago, I can still see her in the places we visited, the friends we had, the smells of the city ... she's still there in all my memories. But here, she's just a memory that only I hold dear. I feel like my body has been transported to this happy, spacious place in Texas, but my heart didn't get the memo—I left it behind." Tears run freely down my cheeks and settle into the creases of my neck as I desperately cry out for help, for comfort, and for my idea of normalcy.

Long seconds of muffled silence fill the line. At first, I hear muted sounds of sniffling, then I hear her blow her nose. Pulling herself somewhat together, Aunt Jo says softly, "Honey, I can't let you come back yet, and you know it. But I have something for you." Her voice cracks through her words. "It's something I found, something your mom wanted you to have."

Gasping for air between my silent, hysterical cries, I manage to choke out, "What it is?" A hint of excitement creeps out as the thought of Mom leaving me something special to remember her fills my imagination.

"All I will tell you is there's a letter with it. I will put it in the mail for you ... soon. Look, Marni, I am going to fulfill your mom's wishes because I know she had your best interest at heart. Continue to give Texas a solid try, put yourself out there, and try to see what it is your mom wanted for you. Remember, I love you. Makes no difference to me where you are on this planet, I love you deep as the oceans."

"I love you, too, Aunt Jo. I'll call you in the next couple of days."
Exhausted from the emotional rollercoaster, I quickly get ready for
bed, tuck myself into the fluffy down comforter, and lie staring into
the darkness. My mind tries to envision what Mom could have possibly
left for me. Happily anticipating my last gift from her, I finally drift
into a sleepy stupor, dreaming about Mom.

CHAPTER 22
Marni

"I'll check the mail, Mrs. Mercer!" I holler, bolting out the front door. I had just seen the white boxy car pass by the front windows, which meant mail, and mail might mean Mom's gift—maybe.

Grabbing the mail, I quickly sift through it, looking for something addressed to me. Nothing, again. Deflated, I slip back inside and plop the unwanted pile of bills and magazines onto the kitchen counter.

"Thanks, Marni. I really appreciate you being on top of the mail these past few days. It seldom crosses my mind to go and grab it. There's never anything fun in it anymore. At least, not for me."

Mrs. Mercer keeps talking in a perky voice, but I stop listening. Ugh, why couldn't Aunt Jo have dropped my gift in the mail the very next day? This waiting game is going to drive me crazy!

I promised Aunt Jo I would try to be an active member of the Mercer family. I have thought and thought about this grandmother thing and finally decided to give it a try. Last night, I told the Mercers I'd like to spend some time with my grandmother. Mr. Mercer, trying to hold back his excitement, said he'd call his mom and make the arrangements. So here we are, one day later, and I'm about to be granddaughtered, or whatever you call it. Old Mrs. Mercer is planning to take me to a special lunch, and then we are just going to go do stuff.

I guess Old Mrs. Mercer isn't busy because she had the whole day ironed out in a matter of minutes over the phone with her son.

Nervous about this quick turnaround, I go upstairs to call Nicole. I need a friend's perspective and some advice.

"Nicole? What are you doin'?"

"Not much. Chores actually. So, thanks for the distraction! Hey! Are you able to go to the sleepover this weekend?"

"Yes, but that's not why I'm calling."

"Yesssss! It's going to be a blast!" Her excitement overpowers my words. She starts to ramble on about the sleepover when her brain finally catches up with her lips. "Wait, were you calling about something else?"

"Actually, I am." I take a deep breath. "I decided to give this grandmother thing a chance, and turns out, our first meeting is today. What do I do? What do I wear? What should I talk about or expect?" The questions fly out of my mouth at top speed before I pause. "I'm really nervous, Nicole. Is that crazy?"

"Marni, don't be scared of a sweet old lady who wants to get to know you. There are definitely worse things to do with your time. Trust me! As for your outfit, you want to wear something not too revealing or flashy. Old people like respectful. I'd go with a school outfit or sundress. Do you know what y'all are planning to do?"

"She's taking me to eat at some place called Sironia's ... is that any good?"

"Oh, yum! It's a total girl place with sandwiches, salads, soups. But the best part is the shopping. The restaurant part sits in the middle of a hodgepodge store of all kinds of things: clothes, jewelry, antiques, you name it. Every nook and cranny has stuff from a different vendor. It's pretty cool. What are your plans after lunch?"

"I don't know. You have any suggestions?"

"I always like to shop, but maybe you could go to the park, walk around downtown, or maybe even talk her into getting you a dog." After a huge intake of breath, she states, "Yep, that's what I would do. But that's because I've always wanted a dog, and my parents are pet-haters. Probably don't do the dog thing, at least, not on your first visit. Although, it doesn't hurt to go look at them, right?" Laughing at her dog-obsessed brain, we talk a bit longer until her mom insists she get off the phone to finish her chores.

Thankful for Nicole's fashion advice, I wear a dainty, soft-pink sundress that skims the top of my knees. I twirl a couple of times in front of the full-length mirror to watch the bottom hem flare like the petals of a blooming flower. I agree with Lila and Annabelle—any dress worth wearing must have a princess-worthy twirl factor. Pleased with my reflection, I make my way back into the kitchen where Mrs. Mercer works on the girls' chicken-nugget lunch.

"Wow, Marni! You look fabulous! Are you ready for today? Have any questions?" Mrs. Mercer asks, raising an eyebrow.

"I think I'm good, but I'm a little nervous." I sit at the island in front of a pencil and pad of paper where Mrs. Mercer started her grocery list. I pick up the pencil and start doodling and drawing grocery items along the edge of the paper. "What if this goes really bad?"

"I can't imagine how it could, but do you have your phone with you?"

"Yes, ma'am."

"Okay, if it's terrible, excuse yourself to the bathroom and call me. I promise to get you, no questions asked."

"You would do that? What if she gets mad at me or you?" I flip the sheet of paper over to continue drawing, an exercise that normally calms my nerves.

"That's not my problem. You, however, are my priority. I want you to have fun and be comfortable. To be honest, I think you're going to have a great time. The girls are jealous that you're getting a special afternoon with Grandma." Mrs. Mercer chuckles. "She really is a fabulous woman. But make your own judgments, okay? Just be yourself." Mrs. Mercer pauses long enough for me to stop doodling and look up. She smiles, looks across the island at the rough sketch I started, and nods approvingly.

"Okay, but, Mrs. Mercer? What do I call her ... Old Mrs. Mercer? I mean, I'm not ready to call her Grandmother."

I must have said something crazy funny because Mrs. Mercer busts out laughing so hard, she's literally crying and barely able to catch her breath. The girls sprint into the room, curious to find out what's so funny, and I make the mistake of repeating my question to the girls, which throws them into fits of laughter too. Whoever said laughter is contagious was right. At first, my laugh feels forced and uneasy since I'm not quite sure what's so funny. Within moments, though, my laugh effortlessly evolves into something I hadn't felt in a long time: joy. It has happened twice now with this family, and both times have taken me completely by surprise. While I still don't know if this arrangement will work out, I find myself hoping for more days and moments like this. A small voice in my head whispers Mom's words, "Laughter is the best medicine."

We're all laughing so loud, we don't even hear Old Mrs. Mercer come into the house. She walks into the kitchen, smiling, and innocently asks, "What's so funny in here?"

Sweet, innocent Annabelle blurts out before we can stop her, "Marci wants to call you Old Mrs. Mercer!" Immediately, my face flashes hot with color. I look from one Mrs. Mercer to the other for their reactions.

Mrs. Mercer, trying to contain herself, bites her lip. Old Mrs. Mercer just starts laughing. She looks at Annabelle and then winks at me. "As long as she promises to call my mother-in-law the Oldest Mrs. Mercer of All." Both Mercer women break into hysterics. Mrs. Mercer quickly informs me that the "Oldest Mrs. Mercer" is a thorn in everyone's side.

"Well, since the ice has been broken, Marni, will you join this old Mercer for a fun day? Oh, and please just call me Ann," she says in a warm and welcoming tone. I hear Mom's voice cautioning me to always put Mr. and Ms. in front of an adult's name as a sign of respect.

"Yes, ma'am. I'm ready." I follow Mrs. Ann to her sporty red convertible. Nicole said she was spunky, but who knew grandmas drove convertibles? I slide into the leather front seat, buckle myself in, and wait for her to drive off.

Before Mrs. Ann pulls the car out, she smiles at me and says, "I think we're both a little nervous, but I want you to know I'm so excited to get to know you! Thank you for giving me this chance."

Nicole was right, Sironia's is the definition of the perfect girly place. In fact, the only men in there are a couple of husbands less than thrilled to mix shopping with lunch. The inviting atmosphere is quaint and sophisticated. The smells of their "signature" carrot cake muffins and pink iced strawberry cake drift through the store, tempting shoppers to treat themselves. The beat of high-heeled shoes clicking against the concrete floor muffled by the faint hum of female conversations and laughter creates Sironia's melodious atmosphere. This truly is a girl haven … Mom would have loved this place.

As we are being shown to a table, some friends of Mrs. Ann frantically wave us over, their eyes critically sizing me up as we approach. Without skipping a beat, Mrs. Ann proudly introduces me as her granddaughter, Marni, from Chicago. The ladies' eyes widen, and their mouths slightly fall open, obviously baffled. Their stunned reactions seem to humor Mrs. Ann as I watch a smile gradually spread across her face. She politely excuses us from the awkwardness and ushers me to our table.

"Mrs. Ann, who are those women?"

"They're just a couple of pretentious old hags who live miserable, hoity-toity lives, looking down their noses at everyone. They pretend to be everyone's friend and ally, but, honey, it's all an act. They live in a shiny, glitzy bubble that I just love to pop every chance I get. Funny thing is, they're no better off than us or half the people they judge."

I glance over her shoulder and notice them leaning heavily on their forearms, whispering and unapologetically staring at us. They catch me watching them and quickly turn their shoulders inward, creating a blockade.

Mrs. Ann looks over her shoulder, turns back to me, and says, "Don't give them a second thought. I'm sorry for the abrupt introduction, but I want everyone to know how proud I am to have you in my life. Better to shock 'em with reality than let their tongues spew wild falsities all over town."

"Oh, okay. So that was damage control?" I ask, suddenly putting two and two together, realizing her true motivation for today's outing. It's not about getting to know me; this is about how to handle me.

As if my thoughts had just been broadcast to the entire room, I notice the tip of Mrs. Ann's nose turning red with emotion. I feel the tingling sting of sadness bloom at the edge of my nose, exposing my insecurities. I know without looking in a mirror that our noses match, which makes me wonder if I inherited this obnoxious trait from her.

"Marni, no, of course not! First of all, you are not damage, you're family. I am thrilled to have you here in Texas and on a girls' date with this old Mercer." She points her thumb at her chest. "However, this is a small community, and you're in the South now. People talk, whether they have something of true importance to say or not. So, I was only trying to stop those tacky-talkers from putting their feet in their mouths. I know you don't know me, but I want to know you so badly, and I want to know who your mom was." With this last statement, my eyes must have doubled in size. "Yes, I love *young* Mrs. Mercer, but I want to know all about the woman I never knew—the woman who raised you, your mom. Not only did she mean a lot to my son, she's my granddaughter's mother."

Surprised, I swallow the knot in my throat and lightly bob my head in acknowledgment. Since I got here, no one has asked me about Mom. Thank goodness Mrs. Ann understands Mom will always be a part of me, living in my heart and memories. I want to be able to share our precious memories because I know remembering her will keep her alive in me. I don't want to close the book on the last fourteen years of my life. "What would you like to know first, Mrs. Ann?"

"You pick. What do you want to talk about? I want to know everything." I see a soft twinkle in her eye.

I tell her all about my school, my old friends, and what I like to do. I draw a mental picture of our little apartment in a crowded, grease-stinky corner of downtown Chicago. She laughs at my comparisons of the sounds and smells at the Mercers' house versus my old neighborhood. I confess that I really miss the greasy pizza joint just up the street. Then I finally tell her about Mom's sickness and how I ended up here. When I look up, her eyes are glistening.

"I'm so sorry, Marni. I know how hard it is to lose someone you dearly love. I am thankful to have you in my life, but I wish for your sake that it was under different circumstances."

"Do you think you would have wanted to meet me if my mother was still here?"

"A million times yes. Why ever wouldn't I?"

"Well, I overheard you talking with Mr. Mercer the night of the barbecue. It seems to me that I might be the cause of some social disappointment to you and your entire family." Unable to meet her eyes, I focus on the ice floating in my glass of pink lemonade. What if her expression tells me I'm right? I don't think I can handle more disappointment when I already feel so alone.

She reaches across the table and touches my hand. "I'm sorry for so many things, Marni. I'm ashamed and incredibly sorry that I didn't come that night. I'm sorry that I never knew your mother or the special bond she shared with Kyle. I hate that she was so hurt by my husband's stupidity and my son's immaturity, and that she felt she couldn't share you with us until now. I'm sorry that I am married to a grade A, stubborn mule. I'm sorry your life has been turned upside down. But most of all, I'm sorry and heartbroken that you doubt your importance to this family!" She squeezes my hand and then returns hers to her lap. "You are family—a true blessing to us all."

We hold each other's stare like kids in a contest, only to be broken by the waitress depositing the check. Mrs. Ann pays the bill and asks for our drinks to be put in to-go cups. "Mrs. Ann? Have you ever felt ... like, um, completely alone and lost before?"

"Yes, Marni. I have." She stands up and swings her purse onto her shoulder. "Let's shop while we talk. Sound good?"

We spend the next hour or so shopping. I pick out a flowy, striped top with a slight boat neck Mrs. Ann insists I need for school ... it's beautiful! Then Mrs. Ann spots a necklace in a display case near the register and cautiously asks me if she can buy her granddaughter her first pearl necklace.

"That's not necessary, Mrs. Ann. This has been too much already!"

"Nonsense! This is what I want to do. Grandmothers love to buy fun things for their granddaughters. I'm just lucky it's something I know well: jewelry." She giggles with delight.

As soon as money exchanges hands, she clasps the dainty gold-and-pearl beaded necklace around my neck. I admire my reflection and how these two necklaces complement each other.

Mrs. Ann lets out a satisfied exhale. "My, my, my. Marni, those necklaces are gorgeous together."

I reach my hand up and gently roll my new jewelry between my fingers. Out of sheer habit, I move to give her a thank-you hug but awkwardly stop myself within inches of her body, suddenly reluctant. Instead, I say shyly, "Thank you … for everything."

Getting back into Mrs. Ann's car, I ask, "Where are we going now, Mrs. Ann?"

"Well, if you don't mind, I want to pop one more bubble."

"Huh? What do you mean?" I rub my arm, trying to soften the prickling hairs standing rigid and tall along my forearm.

"Look, Marni. I've only spent about two hours with you, and I'm already so proud of the young lady your mom raised you to be. But in order for you to have the full experience of grandparents, you need to meet your stubborn, ole mule-headed grandfather. Your dad may not be able to make him see the light, but if he wants dinner and clean underwear, he'll listen to me. It's always easier to put something or someone out of your mind if you've never been personally introduced to it. So, I'd like for you two to personally meet."

"But he hates me."

"Fiddle faddle! Hate you? How can he? He's never even met you!"

"Isn't he mad at you for being with me?"

"Marni, if he's upset, it won't last past supper, knowing how much that man depends on me. Besides, when you've been married to the old goat as long as I have, you learn how to *play* him. I know how to discreetly manipulate him so that when he does come around, he thinks he did it on his own terms. Just another trick of the trade," she says, a little too chipper.

I stare at her, somewhat awed by her confidence and somewhat terrified by her plan.

She shoots me a devious grin and asks, "Do you like to drive golf carts?"

I raise my eyebrows apprehensively, but she continues.

"He's at the club right now, playing golf with an old friend. It's the perfect place to introduce you."

CHAPTER 23
Marni

We walk up to the golf pro shop, and Mrs. Ann asks what hole her husband is on. She quickly herds me into the passenger seat of a golf cart, but once the pro shop is out of sight, we switch seats. I drive the cart right up to the golfers on the fifteenth tee. We quietly watch as both men tee off. As they're heading back to their cart, Mrs. Ann hops out to greet Old Mr. Mercer and his friend. Without hesitation, she introduces me as their granddaughter, and their friend politely shakes my hand. However, Mr. Mercer's hands grip his club, clenching his fingers until the color drains from his fingertips. I watch his stern-set jaw and hard eyes try to recover from Mrs. Ann's surprise visit. His eyes meet mine. The uneasiness I feel agitates every fiber in my body and causes my heart to plummet. I turn to look at Mrs. Ann, silently pleading with her to get me out of there. Instead, she smiles and subtly makes a fist, like she's encouraging a player on a team to keep going.

Mrs. Ann lightly touches the friend's arm and says in her sweet, grandmotherly voice, "I know this is the end of your golf round, but would you mind terribly if Marni rode the next two holes with her grandfather? We really can't stay long."

"Of course. Time with your grandchildren is precious and hard to come by sometimes." The friend hops in Mrs. Ann's golf cart. "Mind driving so I can look for my ball though?"

"It's a plan," Mrs. Ann says and walks up to kiss Mr. Mercer on the cheek. The kiss lingers long enough for me to hear her growl out "be kind" in his ear. His shoulders relax as he cocks his head to the side as if he's preparing a rebuttal but then seems to think better of it.

"Well, come on. Slow enough game without us just standing around, looking at each other," Mr. Mercer barks. I obediently jump into the passenger seat and brace myself, not knowing what to expect next. After a few awkward moments of silence, he finally looks over at me, resigning as he makes a *humph* sound. "So, you're Marni?"

"Yes, sir."

"Play golf?"

"Only once with Mr. Mercer."

"Like it?"

"Yes, sir."

And that was it. His interpretation of kindness felt more like an interview, firing off basic questions in succinct succession without any emotion. It is obvious he's trying his best to do what needs to be done—the bare minimum—as quickly as possible. As my mind tries to process his terse tone and behavior, confusion clouds my head. How can someone like Mrs. Ann be married to this man? I watch silently, like an obedient pet, as Mr. Mercer plays out hole fifteen, refusing to engage with me. This is humiliating! We are both relieved to start hole number sixteen since Mrs. Ann had already promised we would leave after the sixteenth.

I look over at Mrs. Ann and watch her stare at us. Her eyes send mixed messages. Darts fly out of her pupils, hoping to drill some sense into Mr. Mercer, but it feels like hearts radiate off her eyelashes like a cartoon drawing when she looks at me. She catches my attention and pumps her fist lightly in the air again. Since this is our last hole together, I hoist up my courage, take a deep breath, and decide I have nothing to lose in being direct with Mr. Mercer.

Mr. Mercer and his friend hit their golf balls and start making their way back to the carts. Only this time, I remember Mrs. Ann asking me, "Do you like to drive carts?" I firmly plant my rear in the driver's seat, waiting for Mr. Mercer to sit down. He looks at me, then back at his friend and Mrs. Ann. Resigned to his position, he flops into the passenger seat.

Mrs. Ann pulls up next to me and says, "Take your time driving, dear. We don't want to rush the game of golf." Then she speeds off.

"*Humph*. Well, let's go then," he grumbles. Seems we both knew what she was up to.

I head down the cart path and drive to where his ball lays in the grass. He carefully selects a club, lines up, and knocks the ball into a white sandy pit.

"Good job, Mr. Mercer."

He slams his club into his bag, grits his teeth, and mumbles, "That was not a good hit; it's a mistake. But how can I expect a girl like you to know the difference?" With fiery-blue eyes, he stares intensely at me and continues. "It's hard to recover from mistakes," he says sardonically as he slows his speech to emphasize his last word.

So that's how it is. Without thinking, I take the bait, "You mean just like me, right? You think I'm a mistake, and that it'll be hard for you and your family to recover from being tied to me. Right?" I give him a second to think and add, "That's okay, you're not my favorite either. So don't worry about trying to hide your true feelings from me because I see you clearly."

Whether it's from what I've just said or the fact that I was gutsy enough to even say anything, I watch a cherry-colored flush bloom across his face. He replies, "Maybe you're right. We both know that your dad and mom's fling was not a blessed union, which means quite literally that you are a bastard child, not family. I cannot accept you and don't see how Lauren can either."

The remark about Mrs. Mercer hurts, but I'm not going to give him the satisfaction of a reaction. "You have a pet, Mr. Mercer?"

"Yes." His expression softens a touch. "Cutest, fluffiest poodle mix you ever saw. Ann saved it from somewhere ... name's Bruno." He's practically boasting over Bruno.

"I've never had a dog. You love him?"

"Of course. He's spoiled rotten."

"So, Bruno was born from your blessed union with Mrs. Ann?" His eyes snap up to meet mine. "Or is he what *you'd* like to call a bastard, like me?" Mr. Mercer's face twitches as he stares at me. "It just seems to me that Bruno and I are one and the same. You're just choosing to love a mix-breed mutt while passing judgment on people like me who are the product of a loving, yet not-so-proper, union."

"There's a big difference between dogs and people. We have the gift of choice—we're not animals with mere instincts."

"Exactly. My parents made a choice to love each other even though it wasn't forever."

"They didn't choose this," he says, shoving his hand in my direction. My heart sinks at his directness. "Nobody would ever choose to start a family with someone they never intended to follow through with, especially not my son."

"What are you saying?"

"He was never going to marry your mom. She came from a different world, a lesser world. It's just not done like that down here. He had his fun, and now here you stand. You're not a Mercer. It's that simple."

"Actually, I am half of your blood, which makes me half Mercer, and I can't tell you how much that bothers me." I glare at him, hoping to hide the pain in my own heart.

"Touché." His attitude softens slightly. "Although, I wonder why your mom kept you a secret for so long. Could it be because she knew her bastard child could never really belong here?"

Tears sting the edges of my eyes. "My family may be different than yours, and we certainly did not have the money you all do, but that doesn't make us *inferior*, and it doesn't make *me* less strong, smart, or lovable. No one has ever labeled me a bastard, until you. That's not my identity, it's your dog's. Don't ever get us confused again," I say harsher than intended.

With his tongue temporarily tied, I drop my head, deflated by all this candor.

"I'm sorry. That was disrespectful," I whisper. "I just miss my mom so much … and now I have a dad, I'm living so far away from home with a bunch of strangers, and I'm not sure any of them truly want me here." A tear escapes and trickles down my cheek. "You, obviously, don't want me here. That ... I get."

Silence fills the cart as I drive us to the sand pit. He retrieves his sand wedge, hits the ball onto the green, and hops onto his seat, looking at me with what I presume is shock. I drive him up to the green near his ball. Looking a little paler than earlier, he pulls his putter out of his bag and glances in my direction. "It does seem like you inherited the Mercer ability to argue and get your point across," he says approvingly. "I'll give you that."

After they finish the hole, Mrs. Ann and I leave the men to finish their game alone. She doesn't ask how it went; I think she senses it was intense. I can't offer her any information because I'm too busy shaking on the inside. I have never been so bold, especially to an adult.

We get in the car and drive off to finish our date. The rest of the day is filled with more shopping, ice cream, and plenty of lighthearted conversation. At the end of the day, Mrs. Ann asks, "Would you like to come over to my house one day this week? You said your mom loved to cook, right? Well, I love to bake. Maybe we could make some tasty treats for you to take to your sleepover this weekend ... if you'd like?"

"Thank you, that sounds great!" Nicole was right—this grandmother thing seems pretty wonderful.

CHAPTER 24
Lauren

"She's back! She's back!" the girls call out a second before the front door slams. Looking out the kitchen window, I watch as Ann steps out of her convertible, laughing at the noisy mob running her way. A smile dances across my face as I silently thank God for blessing these girls with such an amazing grandmother.

I quickly walk to the door inviting Ann inside, which she politely declines. "It's been an exhilarating and exhausting day," she says, winking at Marni before sliding back into her car and driving off.

After ushering the girls back inside and upstairs, I turn my attention to Marni. "So, how was your day with Ann?"

"Good! Kinda awkward at times. But you were right—she's really nice. She even bought me a few things for school and this beautiful necklace." Marni pulls out the necklace, running her index finger and thumb over the smooth pearls.

"That's beautiful, Marni. And I know it made her so happy to spend the day with you. But what was awkward?"

"Mrs. Ann is a little crazy. She sort of hijacked me and forced me to play two holes of golf with her mean husband," Marni says, scrunching her face like she's just eaten something incredibly bitter.

"What? Your dad is going to flip! What happened?" My voice sounds breathless as my eyes widen. What was Ann thinking?

"Well, he really didn't talk except a few short questions about golf, and then he got mad about a mistake in the sand. So, I decided to be crazy like Mrs. Ann and called him out on accusing me of being a big mistake. We went back and forth a little." She hesitates, diverting her eyes to the fidgeting hands in her lap. "The only thing that hurt was when he told me he couldn't believe you were okay with having me around."

I nearly pass out from shock, but before I can respond, her eyes lock onto mine. Her words are honest and childlike as she quietly asks, "Do you want me to leave? I understand if it's true. I mean, I miss my real family too."

Marni stares into my eyes, looking for a reaction that would confirm she's busted my charade of acceptance. Anger starts to flare inside me. How could he do such a thing? It seems low, even for him. But I can see a tidal wave of pain building behind her eyes, which means he succeeded in breaking her confidence in us. Flustered, I touch my fingertips to my burning ears, knowing the intense heat radiating from them must have turned them bright red. I sink down on the living room couch and motion Marni to join me.

"Marni, he has no right to speak on behalf of me or my feelings. He assumes what he wants, fitting it perfectly inside his mold, and then he broadcasts it like it's the absolute truth." I shake my head in disgust and add, "But I do have a history that I've tried to bury. And to be honest, when I learned of you, old feelings of insecurity resurfaced. But that has nothing to do with you; it's between your father and me." I stretch out my hand, softly touching her arm. "But we're better than good. There's nothing to worry about, I promise you."

Marni tilts her head slightly. "What exactly does my being here remind you of that's so terrible? What history?"

I could strangle that grumpy old fool! Thanks to the Grandpa encounter, I have no choice but to answer the questions he malignantly planted in her head. But how? How do I delicately explain the turmoil I personally faced when Kyle first told me the news? No. Why would I put her through that? She needs to feel at home. I need to reassure her she's safe, welcome, and part of this family. I decide that if I have to,

I'll tell her only what's necessary about my past. Ironically, my past has been my burden to carry, but somehow, knowing her, watching her, and putting myself in her shoes, I find her presence is helping me bury my insecurities daily.

I blow out my breath. "Sooo, once upon a time, my dad cheated on my mom ... and I got a half sister out of the deal. However, I didn't find out about her until the beginning of my senior year of high school. Living in a very small East Texas town—even smaller than this one—you can imagine how fast news travels, especially reputation-damaging news. Well, the local gossip train got a hold of my dad's secret and Rosemary's identity, and the scandal left deep scars that devastated my entire family. The biggest baggage strapped to my back translates to some pretty major trust issues." I drop my eyes, suddenly thinking of how trivial this all sounds to a girl who has lost everything. "My dad's actions have long since been forgiven and mostly forgotten, but I still struggle with my own self-worth."

"Why would you doubt your self-worth?" Marni asks. "Your dad loved you, right?"

"He did." I bite at the inside of my cheek as I think of how to proceed. "When someone cheats on you or your family, it sucks you down a black hole of despair. He had a choice just like we all have choices. Some are good while others leave destruction in their wake like a tornado. But I interpreted his affair as evidence that he was chasing after something *more*—more exciting, more extraordinary— something different ... better ... than what he already had. It was obvious that we just weren't enough for him." I take in a deep breath. "I can still hear Mother's bitter tongue spewing in my ear, 'If it could happen to me, it will happen to you.'" I cringe at the thought of her words, so negative and foreboding. "So ever since, I guess you could say, I've been waiting for another 'Rosemary' to throw my world off-balance."

"You think my mom was your Rosemary?" Her voice lifts in confusion.

"Not exactly. This is different since your mom and Kyle were together before I was ever in the picture. However, your dad failed to ever mention his relationship with your mother. Seeing your beautiful face for the first time reawakened my insecure feelings of inadequacy. As a wife, I want to be everything my husband desires, to be more than enough. And proof of your existence made me doubt that."

The butterflies in my stomach continue to flitter as I watch Marni digest my words. "Marni, the older you get, the better you'll understand the power one's past can hold over you if you let it. I've allowed my past to cast a daunting shadow over my life, dampening the hopeful glimpses of light up ahead. I'm tired of being a prisoner to fear, and I have you to thank." I squeeze the top of her hand tenderly.

She sits there for a few long seconds in silence before asking, "Did you ever become friends or even sisterly with Rosemary? Or was it too hard for you, Mrs. Mercer?"

"Before I knew the truth, we were friends. Then I pushed her away, which was easy thanks to my mother's litany of venom aimed at Rosemary, her mom, and my dad. But then something happened. My grandmother—my dad's mom—saw past the scandalous situation and discovered an innocent teenage girl suffering at the hands of her parents' poor decisions. My grandmother and Rosemary became very close, which trickled love and acceptance down the family tree, except for my mother." An audible sigh slips out of my mouth. "For ten long years, my mother harbored bitterness and anger toward Rosemary. She was a true sourpuss to the core. I don't want that kind of life for us—life is just too short. Don't you agree?"

"Yes, ma'am," Marni said. "So, you're not mad about me being here or that I'm Mr. Mercer's daughter? You and Mr. Mercer are okay?"

"Not mad at anyone, except Grandpa," I say with calm assurance. "Don't listen to that old man. He can be such a pain in the neck! Thank goodness we have Ann in our lives though."

"Yeah, she's pretty cool. Mrs. Ann invited me to come over and bake with her before the slumber party. Will that be okay?"

"Heavens, yes! Sounds like fun!"

"Thank you, Mrs. Mercer, for ... all of this." She gestures with a graceful wave, but her eyes betray her sadness as they travel across the bookshelves and walls, studying my proud display of family pictures.

She drops her eyes from the collage of our framed family memories, and I see a lost expression cloud her eyes, revealing a profound pain her honest face can't hide. In that moment, I ache for her. I resist a sudden urge to reach out and hug her, but I feel her journey deep in my bones. This poor child has been utterly blindsided. First, by the shocking demise of her mother—the single most important person in her life who lied to her all these years. Then, by being uprooted from everything and everyone she's ever known. Add to that the fear her father's family might not want her around ... her life must feel unrecognizable.

Marni stands in a slight daze as she processes whatever is going through her mind. I quietly observe her stoic demeanor without speaking. I want her to feel comfortable being herself without constantly fielding questions. Sometimes, a quiet space is worth its weight in gold. Upstairs, the girls' laughter breaks the silent trance. Marni carefully regains her composure. She tilts her head slightly and, with a sweet expression, politely thanks me again before walking upstairs.

I'll admit that my plan of action was to fake it till I make it, but I didn't have to pretend for long. Hoping Marni might feel the words I should have said, I whisper behind her, "We *do* want you here." I smile at the empty doorway, surprised by how easily she is winning me over.

CHAPTER 25
Kyle

"Your father is a monster!" Lauren spits at me as I come through the back door.

Oookay. Someone obviously needs to get something off her chest. "What happened? Something go wrong with my mom?" I ask, confused.

"Not exactly, except she hijacked Marni, took her to the club, and forced her to play a few holes with your dad! Pretty manipulative if you ask me," she states.

I can feel her frustration radiating off her like a furnace. "Wait … Dad met her?"

"'Met,'" she uses her fingers as quotation marks, "implies they had a proper, polite time together. He was horrible. He made her feel so unwanted by all of us, especially me!" she practically screeches. "He is deliberating undermining any speck of progress you and I have made with her."

I set my briefcase down and take her hand, leading her to our bedroom. After closing the door, I ask her to calmly tell me everything, which she does in full detail. Hearing about Marni's afternoon debacle infuriates me. The inside of my palms become raw as my angry thumbs release my agitation, rubbing aggressive circles into the soft flesh. I trusted my mother with Marni.

I pull my phone out of my pocket and quickly dial Mom's number. What am I going to say to her? What am I going to say to Marni? Just when I thought I'd have to leave a message, she answers.

"Mom, what were you thinking? Introducing Marni to Dad without me or Lauren? Are you crazy?"

"Kyle, it was no big deal. Besides, what better place than the golf course for your dad?"

Stunned by her stupidity or ignorance or something, I just look at Lauren, dumbfounded. "You don't get it, Mom. Things are hard enough without you causing trouble. Do you have any idea the things that he put into her head?"

She doesn't answer, so I continue. "Turns out, Dad made sure she felt unwanted, unaccepted … by *all* of us."

"He doesn't mean it. You know he's more bark than bite. Besides, there's an art to coercing your father into doing what he's supposed to do."

"Your version of coercion put my daughter and her feelings in a destructive situation. You manipulated her. I don't know what to say to you, except how disappointed I am in both of you."

"Kyle, wait."

"No. I have to go check on my daughter." Before she could say goodbye, I ended the call.

I look at Lauren and sigh. "Guess I should go talk to Marni."

She closes her eyes and takes a deep breath. "Want me to join you?"

I shake my head and walk into my closet to change out of my suit.

I tiptoe up the stairs, trying not to alert the girls of my presence. I'm not ignoring them, I just don't want them to intrude on this conversation or overhear anything they aren't ready to hear.

When we decided to tell the girls about Marni, we anticipated lots of questions now and somewhere in the future. One day, they will ask more detailed questions, but right now, they accept what they know: Marni's their sister from Chicago. But if they catch wind that their grandpa, whom they adore, is unreceptive to Marni, it will confuse them and might negatively affect them.

I lightly tap on the door and wait a few beats before gently opening the door a crack. Without invading her privacy, I whisper through the door, "Marni, it's me. Can we talk?" I hear her rustling some papers before consenting. I walk through the door, closing it behind me, and join Marni on the floor by her bed. She is surrounded by several crumpled-up pieces of paper, a spiral notebook, and colored pens.

"What are you drawing?" I ask.

"Nothing really."

I lean over and pick up one of her crumpled pages. I stretch out the wrinkles until I can take in the image properly. My heart falters. She's drawn some sort of cartoon reel. It starts with a scene at her mother's grave. The storyboard sketches out her journey to us, but it's the final scenes that stir the pot bubbling inside me. She's drawn my dad, evil and dark, with a golf club chasing her away, right into the arms of her aunt. The caption reads, "Go back to your kind." I feel her eyes watching me, waiting to see how I react.

"This is interesting. Disturbing but very creative," I say slowly.

I watch a smile perk up her face. "It's just trash."

"No, it's more than that." I pause, giving her a moment of silence to think about what motivated her to draw those pictures. "I hear you had quite a day," I say, raising one eyebrow.

"Being with Mrs. Ann was fun."

"And my dad?"

She tenses up and drops her gaze, unable to look at me.

"He's pretty intense, huh?" I prod.

"You could say that."

"What would you say? Don't worry, nothing you could say or think will shock or offend me, I promise." I cross my heart with my index finger and then watch her. I can't help but notice her facial expressions twist and scrunch up just like Gabby's did when she was concentrating.

"He's like a poked bear, mean and ornery." Her eyes widen, obviously concerned. "I'm sorry, I didn't mean to insult you."

I laugh. "Are you kidding me? It'd be an insult if you lied to me, telling me he's the greatest thing since sliced bread. I know the truth. I grew up with that man, and now I work with him. He's a piece of work." He points at my drawings. "And I don't mean that in an artistic, complimentary way."

She smiles. I watch her shoulders loosen up and drop into a more relaxed position. We spend the next twenty minutes talking back and forth. Marni tells me about her afternoon, and we discuss everything that happened on the golf course. I share some stories illustrating my own struggles with my dad. I need her to see that even though today was not ideal, there's always tomorrow.

"Even though Dad and I've had our ups and downs, you'll never meet anyone who fiercely challenges you and loves you with an intensity you can't imagine," I tell her.

She looks at me like I'm blowing smoke, deliberately misleading her. I get it, she doesn't see what time has shown me.

She asks me, "Did you ever miss my mom?"

Not expecting the sudden change in subject, I answer her as honestly as I can. "It seemed so complicated back then. Your mom and I were on different paths, chasing different dreams. But I used to wonder where she ended up every time I ate in a fancy Italian restaurant. So, yes, there were moments in my past when she came to mind, but …" I hold my breath for a beat and confess, "Until you, I assumed she moved on without any issues."

"She didn't."

"I'm so sorry, Marni. I never meant to hurt her."

Marni nods, but I watch as a single tear escapes down her cheek. She quickly wipes it away.

We sit in silence for a while until we hear Lauren hollering us to dinner.

"Marni, I'll be taking you to your swim lessons next week. How about I use that drive to tell you stories about your mom and me?"

Her face brightens as she smiles. We stand up to walk downstairs, and she stops me. "Can I ask you something?"

"Of course. Anything."

"You said you'd teach me to play golf. Is that still on the table?"

"You bet."

"I want to learn because I'm going to be a better golfer than your dad," she says, winking at me.

I can't help it; her fighting spirit makes me laugh. She's just like him, but I don't dare tell her that now.

CHAPTER 26
Marni

The summer days are flying by, and we are very busy. Mrs. Mercer constantly takes me shopping all over Waco, insisting on buying me multiple swimsuits, school clothes, church dresses, golf outfits, sneakers, sandals, and even cowboy boots. You name it, and the Mercers think I need it. They even bought me a brand-new pale pink and gray backpack with a matching lunchbox. Never once does Mrs. Mercer bother checking the price tags. It's ridiculous! And my goodness, they must spend a fortune on my swim and golf lessons at the club.

"It's so much fun shopping with you," Mrs. Mercer says to me on the way home from one such shopping spree. "I love seeing you in all the latest trends, things I wish I could still wear." She laughs, but I just stare at my newly manicured hands, unresponsive. Her lavish spending bothers me; it's like she thinks I've been so deprived, and it's humiliating. There's never explicit criticism, but with every purchase, she seems to be reminding me just how little Mom was able to provide me.

"Marni, is something wrong?" She glances over at me in the passenger seat of her SUV.

"No," my voice trails off, weak and unsteady. I glance at my fingernails, admiring the baby-blue polish and wishing I sounded more convincing.

"You can talk to me."

I turn to face her. Her soft blue eyes bounce from the road to me, trying to read past my one-word answer. She's been so generous; I don't think I can tell her the whole truth of what I'm feeling. "It's nothing really," I say with a sigh. "I just miss my mom. I was just wondering what it would have been like to have some of your money to really shop with her, ya know? Just once."

Her cream-painted fingernails grip the wheel as she turns onto the first side street we encounter. She pulls the car over, puts it in park, and adjusts her body to face me. I can see she doesn't know how to respond, but it makes me like her even more that she's trying.

"I'm sorry, Mrs. Mercer. I didn't mean to upset you or sound ungrateful."

She shakes her head and says, "I didn't take it that way." She looks down at her fingers and twists her wedding ring. "If you don't mind telling me, I'd love to know what shopping looked like with your mom."

My eyes widen in surprise, then my brows furrow as I wonder why she's asking.

Seeing my hesitation, she adds, "I just want to know how you and your mom spent time together. I have no hidden agenda. I'm just curious about your life back in Chicago."

I take off my seat belt and twist my body to face her, surprised at how much I want to tell her about Mom. "Our shopping was always in thrift stores, and even then, Mom was hunting or negotiating for a better bargain. I never had new clothes before coming here, let alone anything that you would consider fashionable." I smile, though, remembering Mom. "We made a game out of it—out of everything, actually. We tried to see who could find the best thing for the cheapest price." My eyes drift to the back of the SUV and my face falls. "We couldn't have afforded even the new pack of socks you threw in at the last minute."

She nods her head, possibly understanding my dilemma. "So, all that," she points to the backseat, "upsets you. Are you mad at me? Because that was never my intention."

"I know." I drop my head, ashamed to admit I'm mad at my mom for not allowing my dad to help us. "I'm not mad at you. I'm just embarrassed."

She turns to look out her window, obviously gathering her thoughts. "Marni, we can afford to buy you anything you need or want. It's our pleasure. Please don't be embarrassed or ..." she pauses, unsure if she should proceed, then adds, "ashamed of what your mom could provide. I know she did the very best she could. Whatever her reasons were, the fact is, she was a single mother, and she did a fantastic job raising you."

I wipe away the tears slipping down my face. Her intuition scares me, like she's starting to understand me. She reaches over and gently presses her hand onto mine. I meet her gaze and search her eyes, expecting to see her pitying me. Instead, all I find is compassion and sincerity. My lips gently curl up into a grin, grateful she seems to genuinely care about me.

CHAPTER 27
Marni

"You are coming Saturday night, right? I mean, you're not going to chicken out on me or anything?" Nicole asks, goading me. Then she practically screams into the phone, "It's going to be so much fun!"

"I'm not sure I'm going to feel welcome or even fit in, but Mrs. Mercer and Mrs. Ann already know about it. They're more excited about it than I am. All I keep hearing is, it's a 'rite of passage' and 'just put yourself out there.'"

"So, stop being a baby about it and get excited! You know, if nothing else, it's a night with me! And we both know that means fun!" Nicole busts out laughing, unable to stifle the high opinion she holds of herself. Her laughter is so contagious, we both start cracking up.

"Okay, Miss Know-it-All, what should I pack?" I listen as she lists what to bring, who's supposed to be there, and what to expect. After a bit, Lila and Annabelle skip into my room, interrupting our conversation as they swarm me. Nicole hears the girls' squeaky voices and tells me she needs to go, too, but reminds me one last time to get excited about the party.

I put the phone down and turn to the girls, each one carrying an armful of hair supplies. "What's going on?" I ask.

They shoot each other a devious look and announce, "We're going to fix your hair." I look at them quizzically, almost afraid to ask what they have in mind.

Annabelle laughs, running her fingers through my thick, wavy hair. "Was your mom's hair like yours?" Her question catches me off guard, but I nod.

"See, I told you so," Lila says. "Girls always look like their moms."

I smile, noting how confident she is in her misguided reasoning.

I turn to them both and ask, "Do you want to see a picture of my mom?" They drop their hair accessories and quickly cuddle up next to me. Their anticipation in seeing Mom warms my heart. I pull out a couple of photos to show them, carefully describing where each picture was taken and explaining what we were doing.

My stories mesmerize the girls and allow me to bring a little bit of Mom and Chicago into their world. I gaze into their angelic faces, appreciative they care enough to ask about my life before them. I'm sure they'll never comprehend how much their innocent curiosity— and talking about Mom so openly without fearing I will upset or offend someone—means to me.

Annabelle carefully plucks a photo from my hand. "She's beautiful, like you," she observes.

"Do you miss her a lot?" Lila asks.

I nod, unable to speak past the lump in my throat.

"I'd miss Mommy, too, if she weren't here," Lila says quietly.

"At least you have us, though … right, Marni?" Annabelle asks, apparently trying to verify that I enjoy being around them.

Smiling, I answer, "Who wouldn't want to be around you two— especially if you promise to fix my hair." They giggle, grab all their things, and pull me down the hall to their "princess hair studio."

After a fancy afternoon of sparkly makeovers by Lila and tiara-styled hair by Annabelle, I spend a little alone time in my room. I open the top drawer of my nightstand and pull out the folder where I store special birthday cards Mom neatly inscribed with a personal message, her funeral service brochure, and some letters from Mom, Aunt Jo, and my friends. I reread Mom's memorial card and order of worship for about the hundredth time. I know it all by heart, but I focus on the last words—the last words Mom wrote before she passed:

Loving mother to her beloved daughter, Marni. Marni, I will love you past the end of my days, forever and ever. I will be with you through every journey you take. This was not my choice, but God has a greater and more perfect plan than I could ever make. Remember you are loved, my love. Thank you for all the love and memories I take with me.

Forever your mother and now your guardian angel,
Mom

Sitting in a pile of pillows as tears sting my eyes, I hear Mrs. Mercer holler up the stairwell. "Marni, you have mail on the foyer entry table!"

I fly out of my room and down the hall, taking the stairs two at a time. This is not a delicate, ladylike, or quiet descent. In fact, all one hundred ten pounds of me sound like a herd of elephants on a mission. Mrs. Mercer stands by the front door, amazed at my instantaneous reaction. Her eyebrows arch over wide eyes as her mouth hinges slightly open.

"Wow! Are you expecting to win the lottery or something today, Marni?" A slight smile breaks across her face.

"Um, no, ma'am. But my Aunt Jo said she'd be sending me something. Is it from Chicago?"

"I believe so." She hands me the letter, then graciously excuses herself, extending me the privacy I crave without having to rush back upstairs.

I shove my pointer finger into the side of the envelope, ripping it open to reveal a small fold-over note with the letter *J* on the cover. It's from Aunt Jo! But as I read the note, I realize it's not what I was hoping to find. Aunt Jo has written me a pick-me-up encouragement letter. She wants me to know I am loved and missed a ton. She enclosed a picture of her, me, and Mom before Mom got sick. I smile, remembering the day we took that picture. We were at a park, eating a picnic lunch. Aunt Jo had brought her famous chocolate brownies with homemade chocolate icing on top. Mom had made her version of BBQ sandwiches stuffed with homemade crispy sour pickles. We played frisbee, took a long walk along the lake where I pet everyone's dog in sight, and we laughed for hours. It was one of the best last days I can remember with both of them, before the doctors' appointments and sickness swallowed us alive.

I walk back to my room and bury myself under my bed covers. I stare at the picture, lightly tracing the outline of mom's face over and over. Her image softens and distorts when the inevitable tears come. Memory fog blurs the edges of reality as I remember my old life. It's agonizing to acknowledge that while our life together was not perfect, it was still my once upon a time.

I have to escape the crushing weight of my devastation and the closing-in walls of my room. Enough is enough. I run downstairs and find Mrs. Mercer sitting at the kitchen table, sorting through the mail and making lists. Judging from her expression, I must have startled her.

"Marni, what's the matter? Is everything okay?" Mrs. Mercer asks, genuinely concerned.

Is she kidding? Nothing is okay ... everything is wrong. This is not how my life is supposed to go. I'm supposed to be in my snug Chicago apartment with a healthy mother, preparing for high school with the friends I've known my whole life. I'm supposed to be living a different life, not living here. So, yes. Everything is wrong. All my "supposed tos" have been shattered to pieces.

I open my mouth to speak, but nothing happens. I look around the room, my eyes landing on her refrigerator covered in painted handprints and crayon drawings. She patiently waits for me to speak, but my tongue is tied in knots as I remember how Mom used to display my art creations on our old fridge.

Mrs. Mercer softly clears her throat. "Marni, was there something upsetting ... in the letter?"

At the mention of the letter, tears well up and spill down my cheeks. "I don't want to talk about my letter." The words tumble out of my mouth sharper than intended.

She looks surprised but nods. "What would you like to talk about?"

"You have to send me back to Chicago, right now," I demand.

Taken off guard, she rests her forearms on the table as if to stabilize herself. "What? Why? What happened?"

"I want to go home ... not be here."

Mrs. Mercer's face drains of color.

"I'm tired of this facade. I'm sorry, Mrs. Mercer. I know you've tried, but this is not my home, and we're not a real family. I've had enough changes that were out of my control, so let me take control of this one thing. Send me home," I plead.

She remains silent for a while, composing herself. When she speaks, her voice cracks with emotion. "Marni, this *is* your home. We *truly* want you here with us." She clears her throat. "I know it's scary, but can't you try a little longer with us? To start over with a family that wants to love you? Don't you think we're worth the risk?"

"Aunt Jo is my family. She loves me and wants me back," I lie, hoping to strong-arm my way back to Chicago. I watch her eyes widen in disbelief, like she's already talked to Aunt Jo and knows I'm bluffing. My voice drops to just above a whisper. "I want to go home. You can't tell me your life and family wouldn't be better off without me because I know I'd be happier with my aunt and my friends back home. Please understand. This is what I need."

Mrs. Mercer's shoulders round as she lets out the breath she's been holding. "Everything you've experienced recently has been beyond difficult, we know that. But we're here for you. We may not feel like family to you yet, but please give us a little more time."

"Just, please! Send me back! There's nothing here for me ... no memories, no friends, no history, nothing!" With a lump in my throat, I walk up to the table and slap my hand next to her pile of mail to secure her full attention. "You are not my mom, and this is not my home."

Shock and hurt color her face in marbling shades of pink and red. Her eyes lock onto mine, unblinking and overly calm. "I'll talk to your father, Marni," Mrs. Mercer says. She turns her attention back to the pile of mail and quietly adds, "I understand what you think your reality is, but you're wrong. You are family to us."

CHAPTER 28
Lauren

My head continuously replays Marni's sudden demand on a steady loop. It floors me that she has such strong feelings against me and our family. I thought she was starting to feel somewhat comfortable here. But she made it perfectly clear she sees us as an obstacle to her happiness. Of course, I empathize with her situation, knowing she's a lonely and scared fourteen-year-old girl who has lost the only parent she's ever known. But keeping a neutral composure at the kitchen table, trying not to panic or take the attack personally proved very difficult. My gut instinct was to throw my arms around her and hug out all the pain built up like plaque in her system, but maybe she doesn't do hugs? Her sharpened eyes exposed a raw determination to fight, which was a far cry from "comfort me," so I stayed firmly planted where I was. She took a stance against me, Kyle, the girls, Texas ... the whole kit and caboodle. But none of this was our idea—it was all her mom's.

From the first moment I heard about Marni, I knew I had two choices: push her away or redefine our family. Exiling her was my very first instinct because, let's be honest, what woman wants her husband's love child constantly thrown in her face? But we're committed and have been doing whatever it takes to firmly enfold Marni into the family.

We knew the transition wouldn't be all roses and sunshine. The teenage years are tumultuous enough as it is, never mind having to navigate the grief and all the unknowns Marni has piled on her. I remember that age and how tightly I held onto what I knew or loved when everything around me appeared to be morphing into something unrecognizable. Still, up until now, things seemed to be going better than expected. But apparently, that's not how Marni sees things.

Can't she see we love her just like we love the girls? That thought almost takes my breath away because I realize I *do* love her, really and truly. I do love her, like she's my own. It hits me right between the eyes, and she doesn't see it.

I sink down into my chair and tuck my head into my folded arms. *I'm failing her.* I let the disquiet overtake me for a few minutes before the little voice in my head whispers an idea. *New territory demands new perspective.* I grab the phone, walk into my room, and quietly close the door. I turn on the television, ensuring no one, not even Kyle, will be able to eavesdrop. I dial the phone as I silently ask God for reinforcements.

"Ann, thank goodness you're home. I really need your help. We've got to bring the family together."

Ann and I speak for over an hour about what we refer to as Project Keep Marni Home. As we discuss our hypotheses, strategies, and collective sympathies, I scan my bedroom, smiling at a smaller collection of family memories shamelessly flaunted across my walls and dresser. My heart swells every time I take a few moments to remember the people and moments that hang frozen in time along my wall. With sudden realization, a tightness reappears at the back of my throat, a new idea permeating my thoughts. I tell Ann what I'm thinking, and we devise a plan.

Later in the evening, Ann delights the girls and Kyle with one of her classic surprises. Without knocking, Ann waltzes into the dining room as we're wrapping up dinner, cradling a decadent, three-layered chocolate cake on her crystal cake stand. She places the cake in the middle of the table and slides gracefully into the last seat at the table. Grinning, she says, "Would anyone like to eat some cake with me?"

Annabelle and Lila immediately bounce in their seats with the palms of their hands lightly pounding the table for emphasis. "Me! Me! I want cake!"

Ann smiles and then looks at Marni, who has been sullen all evening after her outburst in the kitchen. "Marni, would you like some too? I made it special for all my beautiful granddaughters," she says, tilting her head as she anticipates Marni's reaction.

"It looks great, Mrs. Ann. Thank you," Marni answers softly.

"Well then, all right." Ann nods her head. A sneaky smile plays at the edges of her lips as I imagine she's thrilled with the positive reception her love gift has received. "Lauren, can I borrow a knife and cake server?"

While I fetch the utensils and fresh plates, Lila and Annabelle pop out of their chairs and run to the back fridge in the laundry room. A moment later, the girls hand me a tub of old-fashioned vanilla ice cream, a not-so-subtle prompt. Tickled that their reaction to Ann's chocolate tower was nothing short of "here, add more sugar," we all agree a couple of scoops of ice cream is necessary if we're to achieve a full sugar overdose.

Ann slices the cake while I generously top each wedge of chocolate delight with ice cream. We watch carefully as Marni laughs at the girls' sugary silliness and even participates in light conversation. Ann and I steal a few glances at one another, reassuring the other we're in this together. Marni belongs here with us; we are her home and family. I am determined to prove this to my newest daughter.

Once every crumb served has been devoured, Kyle helps me with the dishes, and the girls dart upstairs to put on their fourth princess outfit of the day. We all know a sugar-induced show is in the making, but it gives Ann a little time alone with Marni to discuss what she would like to make for her upcoming slumber party. I hear them discussing cupcakes, brownies, cookies, and they finally settle on Ann's famous decorated almond sugar cookies in the shape of purses and shoes.

Soon thereafter, the glitzy pink-and-purple tornadoes swirl and twirl down the stairs. The night quickly gets out of hand with two sugar-crazed kids, one mercurial teenager, and an overtired husband. It's exhausting trying to bring order to all the chaos ... it's just been an emotionally exhausting day. The girls perform an on-the-fly skit, mandating applause. With elevated egos, they link their arms together and, as gracefully as possible, escort themselves off center stage, blowing kisses to their admirers and sashaying upstairs toward their bedtime routines.

Through her subdued giggles, Marni yawns. "What a night. Mind if I go upstairs as well?"

"Of course, Marni," I reply.

"I'm about to leave, but I'll see you tomorrow," Ann says. "How about I pick you up around lunch-ish? We'll eat, then start baking and decorating. Sound good to you?"

"Yes, ma'am. I'll be ready," Marni says with a delicate smile.

"Goodnight, sweet girl."

Marni's eyebrows pitch up in surprise and confusion.

Ann notices her response and quickly adds, "I mean—good night, Marni."

Marni tips her head slightly to the right and squints at her with an unreadable expression. I see the wheels turning and grinding in her head as she contemplates whatever has momentarily thrown her off-balance before giving Ann a polite smile with a simultaneous head nod.

Progress? I silently wonder. I really don't know, but at least she knows Ann cares for her. We just have to keep convincing her we all do.

From the corner of my eye, I notice Kyle analyzing this interaction. It was clear to me he knew something was up earlier in the evening, like he was trying to find out the real reason for his mom's visit. Thank goodness he didn't ask any questions or make a big deal about her faux surprise. Instead, in his quiet wisdom, he savored his mom's cake while trying to decipher the synergetic effect of dessert combined with female conspiracy. He is silent yet attentive, as if he's witnessing animals in the wild. But now that all three girls are upstairs, Kyle's eyes flash back and forth between his mom and me, as we all enjoy the silence.

"Okay, spill. What's going on, Mom?" Kyle whispers, sensing a secret that sits on the verge of a scheme.

"Walk me to my car, Kyle. I need help taking some cake home to your grumpy old dad," Ann says. Cool as a cucumber, Ann casually dismisses Kyle's initial attempt at extracting information and walks into the kitchen to gather her stuff.

Kyle eyes me carefully, silently searching for answers. I simply arch my eyebrows to shrug off his inquiry. Kyle expels an exasperated sigh and follows his mother. I hear Ann give him some light orders on what to grab, then there are distant footsteps that end with the garage door opening and closing. Silence. I relax onto the couch, thankful to have Ann on my team and grateful for a quiet moment.

Before I get too relaxed, I head upstairs and put the girls in the bath. My wheels continue to turn—slightly less frantically now that we have a plan—as the bubbles dissolve, signaling it's time to get the girls into bed.

Tucking the girls into bed is a ritual that cannot be overlooked. It's not just about saying good night, there's an entire program one must follow. As always, I start with plopping each clean girl in her bed. Then they each name off the stuffed animals they have requested to cuddle with them. I grab their assorted friends and place them in a rainbow around their heads. Why they have to sleep around their heads is anybody's guess. Once they have everything just so, the girls snuggle farther under their covers, waiting for their individual time alone with me. We briefly share our favorite things from the day, say our prayers, and finally end in an array of kisses, always finishing with me kissing their sweet eyelids shut for the night. It's an in-depth process, but I love it, knowing that one day, they won't want me to put them to bed. That thought alone devastates me.

As I close Lila's door, I notice Marni's door is shut. I can't help but wonder what her routine used to be. Did she snuggle under the covers with her mom reading books? Did they plan out Marni's future before saying prayers out loud? Did she ask her mom to tell her stories about her father? Could she sleep at night if she didn't have the right number of kisses and hugs? I walk to her door and lightly tap on it, prompting Marni to allow me in. "I just wanted to check on you before you went to bed."

She looks at me like I might be crazy but nods anyway.

Of course she's fine, she's fourteen, not four. "Look, I know your mom must have done things so different from me. It's just that I'm a hugger, and I like giving hugs goodnight. So, I thought I'd ask if maybe I can give you one too?"

She visibly stiffens. Shaking her head, she rejects my attempt at mothering her. "No, that's not necessary."

Acknowledging I've crossed an imaginary line, I smile to let her know her response is perfectly okay. "All right, well the offer stands." I tell her goodnight and gently close the door behind me.

Tired but satisfied, I tiptoe downstairs to find Kyle sitting in his oversized chair, sipping on his favorite bourbon. "Sorry that took so long—"

"What is this plan my mom is talking about?" Kyle interrupts.

"Well, what'd she tell you?"

"She said you two have concocted a plan to keep Marni in Texas and make her happy. Is she not happy here?" Kyle asks, his voice wavering between confusion and uneasiness.

I take a deep breath before trying to fill in the blanks for him. "Marni asked me today if she could go back to Chicago to be with her Aunt Jo. She told me this isn't her home, and we're not really her family. Bottom line"—I lightly clear my throat—"she is *not* happy." I watch as this news sucks the wind out of his sails. "Look, it's not a perfect plan, but I am working on something that I think will help her start to identify us as home. I want her here, Kyle, I do! She's just lost so much, so quickly—her mom, her friends—her whole life is unrecognizable. I can't even imagine how overwhelmed and lonely she must feel. It's not hard to see she's struggling under the weight of her grief. She's confused, scared, and mad—and trying so hard to hide it while not letting us in. But we're on the cusp, I can feel it in my bones. We're making headway; we're just still a ways away from sealing the deal." Tears fill my eyes as emotion floods my voice. "This is breaking my heart." I feel the tears spill out and roll down my cheeks.

Kyle swirls his amber drink, takes a lengthy sip, and tries to absorb the brunt of the news I've just delivered. Typical male.

"Our home is made up of memories," I continue, "both physical and emotional. I'm afraid the only memories that Marni associates with Texas and our home remind her of the loss of her mother and the life she once had. Come here, Kyle." I motion for him to follow me into our room. "Look around. What do you see?" While I'm waiting for him to reply, he stares blankly at the room. "Not a rhetorical question, Kyle. Tell me, what do you see?"

"Bed, pillows, decorations, pictures of the girls, cards and projects the girls gave us, some special things we bought on trips ..." His voice begins trailing as he sees it more clearly. "Okay, I get it. You're right. We need to bring Marni into this house as a part of our memories. But that's something that takes time," he argues in defense.

I spend the next half hour sitting on the edge of our king-size bed, laying out the plan Ann and I developed. With a genuinely grateful grin, Kyle sets his bourbon down, pulls me into his strong arms, and cradles me against his chest. The familiar smell of bourbon blending with the notes of chocolate still lingering on his breath dissolve the tension I've carried with me all day. I give in to the moment, completely melting into his arms.

A few breaths later, he pulls back, cupping my face in his palms and says, "I love you so much, Lauren. You know I'd be lost without you, right?" His lips lightly graze mine. "Thank you for loving me and our family with all your heart." With those last words, he tenderly showers me with his kisses until we both fully release into each other's embrace, decompressing from a long, emotional day.

CHAPTER 29
Marni

"All right, Marni. You ready for some girl time and baking?" Mrs. Ann chirps enthusiastically.

"Yes, ma'am ... I think so," I say, my voice quivering slightly. My heart starts racing as a cloud of fear suddenly overwhelms me.

Mrs. Ann lifts an eyebrow, analyzing my body language.

I can feel her gearing up to speak when I shake my head and add, "I'm pretty nervous about tomorrow night. Maybe I shouldn't go? Besides, I only barely know Nicole, and these are all her friends who probably don't even want me to come." I feel embarrassed saying all this out loud.

A dagger of jealousy spears my heart as I imagine jumping at any opportunity to spend the night at a friend's house with a bunch of girls ... if only I were back in Chicago. I practically knew every girl in my grade and not to toot my own horn, but they all really liked me. A sleepover would have been a piece of cake in Chicago. However, tomorrow night's actual setup terrifies me, being dropped off at a stranger's home with a bunch of girls I've never met. To make matters even more stressful, I'm confident these girls don't want or need another friend, especially since their group is already defined so perfectly. I imagine an awkward night where I stick out like a sore thumb, hunched in the corner, watching the fun from a safe distance. I don't think I can go to the party. Anxiety fills my gut as I realize that, I'm sunk even before the night started!

Mrs. Ann waves off my melancholy mood. "Nonsense! It'll be a blast. This is going to be a weekend to remember," Mrs. Ann says with a wink. She quickly gives Mrs. Mercer a look that seems to boost their collective energy. I shrug my shoulders, feeling trapped. All I can think is, *Whatever*.

I follow Mrs. Ann out to her convertible, top down as usual, and buckle up before she whizzes away. As the sun warms my face, and the wind whips through my hair, I smile at the thought that Mrs. Ann is an oxymoron. I always imagined older Southern women as prim and proper bores, the type who tie scarves over their coiffed hair, constantly worrying about the state of their appearance. But Mrs. Ann's hair stands straight up like a mad scientist as we fly down the highway. She looks over and grins, a contagious smile that promises a fun day.

"Hope you're in the mood for a great burger! We're going to a small greasy joint that's just off the beaten path. Unless you'd prefer the country club?" Mrs. Ann asks, a little concerned. "I really love the not-so-obvious food joints, but that's just me. What are you up for, Marni?"

"Whatever you have planned is fine," I answer, remembering how Mom always said, "The less froufrou, the better the food."

We drive through town, crossing into an area I doubt the Mercers visit very often. Run-down strip centers line the street where exhausted businesses teeter on the verge of closing their doors forever. Iron bars encase windows and doors, creating an uninviting and sketchy atmosphere, amplified by intimidating groups of people hanging outside these places. This area of town appears neglected, like people have just given up trying, evidenced by the beat-up cars and old couches left to rot in abandoned parking lots.

I'm shocked Mrs. Ann knows this part of town exists. I watch as reckless drivers zigzag in and out of the traffic lanes around us. Surprisingly, she seems completely at ease. It's safe to say this is not a part of town I would ever expect to see her pass through, let alone dine in. After we cross a few more intersections, Mrs. Ann turns onto a side street, drives a few blocks, and pulls into a parking lot full of dirty, white work trucks.

"We're here! Let's eat!" Mrs. Ann exclaims as she pops out of the convertible with her fancy purse slung over her right shoulder. There's something funny about this picture, but I bite my lip, trying hard not to chuckle.

"Where are we exactly? I mean, where's the restaurant?"

"Oh, come on. It's in front of this parking lot. We better hurry though. It looks like they're busy." Mrs. Ann hurriedly waves me to join her as she picks up her pace. We round the corner to a very tiny, mostly white building. The windows match the neighborhood, decorated with iron bars. The restaurant entrance is no more than a creaky, old screen door that lost its springy, soft closure decades ago. The sign reads: Dubl-R.

We walk into a restaurant with about twelve tables plus a classic 1950s lunch counter that stretches the length of the open kitchen grill. At first glance, every customer appears to be a bearded man in work clothes. We are clearly not their regular customers, but that doesn't seem to slow Mrs. Ann's determination for a burger. She eyes two open seats, not together, at the counter and approaches a scruffy, dark-haired man, lightly tapping him on the shoulder just as he's taking a bite out of the biggest burger I've ever seen. With a full mouth of food, he turns his head, slightly surprised to see a woman standing next to him. Still chewing his burger, he tilts his head back a little, obviously wondering what she wants.

Without missing a beat, Mrs. Ann says, "Excuse me, sir. I'm here with my granddaughter"—she points over at me—"and I was wondering if you wouldn't mind shuffling down a seat so we can sit together?" Her tone is sweet and innocent as she points out that the only two seats left are on either side of him.

He glances at me, nods, and silently scoots his lunch over to the next spot. This entire exchange occurred without a single word from a man who looks quite large and scary.

"I so appreciate it! Thank you, sir." Mrs. Ann beams, waving me over to my swiveling red-leather barstool. "Marni, please hold this chair for me. I'll be right back."

I watch Mrs. Ann walk up to the cashier. She hands the woman a twenty-dollar bill, points in our direction, and then comes back.

"Do you have to prepay for food here, Mrs. Ann?" I whisper. Looking around, I wonder if people in this neighborhood just wouldn't pay their bills, so they had to initiate this policy.

"No, Marni." She half giggles. "I just thought I'd pay for our neighbor's food since he was so kind to accommodate our seating needs. Okay, now let's order!"

Marveling at Mrs. Ann's generosity toward a stranger, I stare at her for a moment as she studies the various burger options on the grease-splattered menu. After a few minutes, the cook comes over and takes our order of two cheeseburgers, one large fry, one large order of onion rings, and two sodas.

Mrs. Ann was right. The burgers are amazing! As we walk out of Dubl-R completely stuffed, Mrs. Ann flashes a devious smile and asks, "Ever had pecan pie?" A few minutes later, she parks in front of a large trailer with a sign that reads: Baked Bliss. We stand in line, order two slices of pecan pie, and devour it on the spot—a new and instant favorite. We waddle back to Mrs. Ann's convertible and drive twenty minutes across town to her beautiful soft-pink brick mansion situated on the golf course. What a stark difference from the neighborhood we just ate in! I wonder if Old Mr. Mercer ever takes Mrs. Ann for a burger at that grease pit?

Pulling into their driveway, I see Old Mr. Mercer's car in the garage. The heavy lunch tumbles like jagged rocks inside me as my nerves amp up at the thought of him ruining my time with Mrs. Ann.

"Mrs. Ann, is, uh, your husband home?" I ask, my voice sounding more timid than I intended.

"I'm not sure, dear. I think so, but he could be at the driving range. Sometimes he has a club employee come pick him up in a golf cart," Mrs. Ann says. "Don't you fret, he's really not so bad," she adds as if she's trying to convince us both.

She ushers me into a pristine house where I'm immediately greeted by a fluffy, white fur ball. "I'm guessing this is Bruno," I say. My voice lifts with excitement as I squat to the floor, petting him while he licks all over my arms and legs.

"Yes, this is Bruno. He's a mess, but we love him. And he sure seems to love you!" Mrs. Ann deposits her purse on top of the hall desk. I follow her into a kitchen skirted with white floor-to-ceiling cabinets cut in half by jet-black countertops and an ocean-inspired tile backsplash in varying shades of blue. An oversized, wood-stained island topped with a butcher block stands in the middle of her kitchen. The sophisticated space feels surprisingly warm and welcoming. It's obvious Mrs. Ann's kitchen is not one of those look-but-don't-touch rooms but rather a well-loved and comfortable space. She walks to the back of the kitchen. Facing a row of drawers, she shoots me a suspicious grin over her shoulder and spins around as she pulls two colorful aprons out of a drawer like a magician.

"Might as well look the part. Right, Marni?" She tosses one to me. I slip the smock over my head and look down, realizing I'm wearing a giant pink cupcake topped with rainbow-colored sprinkles and puff-paint confetti dots. She looks at me and winks as she adjusts a navy apron dotted with little white poodles flaunting pink bows. "Before we're covered in flour and sugar, how about a quick picture?" She asks, whipping out her phone. Without waiting for my response, she squishes up next to me and holds up her phone saying, "Smile!" as she snaps a few selfies.

I watch her gather all the necessary ingredients onto the butcher block counter. She pulls out a torn, stained piece of paper.

"This recipe has been passed down for two generations. I'm excited to teach you so you'll have it in your baking repertoire." With Mrs. Ann's patient guidance, she helps me make my first batch of from-scratch cookie dough. Mom and I used to bake but not like this. We never seemed to have the time to do homemade. Plus, mom liked to cook more than bake.

"Quality control check!" Mrs. Ann announces. When I don't move, she adds, "Go ahead, Marni. Grab a healthy pinch of the dough before we chill it. We need to make sure it's good, plus this is one of my favorite baking perks," she says with a sly grin.

I mimic her, grabbing a large chunk of dough and nibble on it, savoring the treat. Then she wraps the sugary dough in cellophane before popping it into the freezer. She explains that the dough needs to be cold and hard so our cut-out shapes will hold their desired form.

Mrs. Ann sets a timer for twenty minutes, which we decide is plenty of time to take Bruno for a quick walk. "He needs exercise and so do I. My burger feels a little heavy," Mrs. Ann jokes, rubbing her belly with a sideways grin. "Plus, we need to make room for more taste-testing. A baker always needs to be confident in her product."

After taking Bruno out, we put our aprons back on, and Mrs. Ann dusts flour over the butcher block. She plops the cookie dough in the middle, and we take turns rolling it out, then punching out purses and shoes. Eight minutes in the oven and, voilà, beautiful cookies! We repeat these steps until all the dough has either been baked or eaten. The whole time, there's not a moment of awkward silence. The kitchen reverberates with our laughter.

Ann tells me a story about my dad "helping" her bake brownies when he was about six years old. "My first mistake was leaving him alone in the kitchen with ready-to-pour batter," she says. "Because by the time I returned from answering the front door, he had brownie batter up to his elbows. His face, hands, and hair were covered in chocolate." She starts laughing. "You should have seen his eyes pop out when he knew he'd been caught."

I tell her the story of Mom teaching me to cook pasta. Recalling how I learned what utensils to use, how much water to put in the pot, and when to drop in the noodles, I begin to laugh. All I wanted was to surprise Mom with pasta after her long workday.

"Mom used to throw a noodle or two against the wall to test that it was done," I say. "However, to make sure the noodles were ready, I threw tons and tons of pasta noodles all over the kitchen cabinets and walls. Mom found pasta remnants around the kitchen for a solid week and told me that pasta was off-limits for a while."

Mrs. Ann and I continue chatting and exchanging stories while we wait for the cookies to cool completely. She tells me a hilarious story about her friends back in high school going "cow tipping." Amid my stomach-clenching guffaws, I tell her about our crazy neighbor's boys who got busted more than once for pelting passersby on the sidewalk with water balloons ... and not just in the summer!

Mrs. Ann teaches me how to make her homemade icing, sharing her special secret. "Always add both vanilla and almond extract to the mixture." We divide the sugary, white glaze into four separate bowls, allowing us to create our colors: turquoise, hot pink, bright yellow, and lavender. "Watch," she tells me, "as each cookie becomes a work of art."

I am in awe. The purse cookie in her hand becomes a miniature canvas. First, she dots and swirls colors in a pinwheel pattern. Then she accents the flat cookie by drawing in pleats and buckles before trimming the edges in pearl-like drops. Finally, she puts her finished cookie aside and looks at me as if she's just come out of an artsy trance. "Go ahead—grab one and start designing!" She picks up another blank cookie.

Mrs. Ann is right; this is by far the most fun and creative part of baking cookies. I'm halfway through my stack of cookies when I notice she has stopped decorating. I look up as she takes a picture.

"Just snapping a few candids while you're decorating your first cut-out cookies."

I offer a smile, slightly humored by her sentimentality and return my attention back to the cookies. We are almost finished when my stomach starts grumbling. I can't believe I'm already hungry again, but the clock on the oven alerts us it's close to dinnertime. We've been together all afternoon, baking, laughing, and sharing stories ... it's been so much fun! That is, until now, when Old Mr. Mercer interrupts us.

From the garage we hear, "Hmmm! Smells like sugar cookies, Ann. What's the occasion?"

It surprises me to hear his voice so light and happy, full of anticipation. Nervous to see him, the pounding of my heart drowns out the steady thud of his approaching footsteps.

"Can't wait to help with the quality control and—" As he rounds the corner, his sentence stops short in surprise and what I can only interpret as utter disapproval.

Mrs. Ann doesn't skip a beat though. She ignores his lack of manners and says, "Look who's helping me, honey. Marni and I are baking some special sugar cookies for her big slumber party tomorrow night! Don't they look amazing?" Mrs. Ann beams with pride while I wish I could find a deep hole to crawl inside.

"*Humph.*" He shrugs indifferently and scans the finished cookies. "Looks good, except for this one." And he quickly grabs the cookie Mrs. Ann had just decorated and walks out of the room.

"Well, we just lost one to Gramps. Want to lose two more? I'm dying to try these!" Mrs. Ann quickly attempts to lighten the mood.

I nod halfheartedly but stare down the hall where he disappeared. It's hard not to take his insolent behavior personally, especially since it's been such a great day. How can she stand him? I narrow my eyes and decide he's not worth it. I remind myself he can't ruin my day because he's unimportant to me. And I'm sure the feeling is mutual.

I push him out of my mind and grin at Mrs. Ann. "Absolutely, we should! You did say quality control is an important part of the process."

We both select an early decorating attempt since they're not as polished as the others. But they are delicious! Sinking my teeth into the soft, doughy cookie immediately triggers a memory of my ninth birthday when Mom and I walked to the bakery down the street from our apartment and carefully selected the two prettiest cookies in the display case.

A slight knot forms at the back of my throat as I swallow my bite. The satisfying sensation of the velvety cookie feels familiar, like home. This surprising emotion kidnaps me for a moment. Mom would be so impressed that I helped make these.

"I think I could eat all of these cookies before tomorrow's party," I confess, licking the crumbs off my fingers.

Mrs. Ann laughs, playfully shaking her pointer finger at me. "Oh! What a dilemma ... a belly ache or self-control?" Just then, her eyes pop open, widening in a sudden realization. "Of course you're hungry! Look at the time." She walks over to the fridge and pulls out a tray of cheese, sliced meat, crackers, and fruit.

"Thank you," I say. I stack a cracker with layers of cheese and meat and shove it into my mouth. "This is perfect," I add, the words muffled as I chew.

From down the hall, old Mr. Mercer hollers, "Ann, what's for dinner?"

"I'm not sure, but we're snacking on a charcuterie board right now. Why don't you come join us?" she asks sweetly.

"Nah, I'm good in here," he blusters.

Mrs. Ann looks at me and says, "He's probably too involved in some sporting event on TV to get out of the chair. But I know he's hungry." She pulls food off the tray and places it neatly on a large plate. "Come back here with me. I've got to feed this man."

Is she kidding? The look on my face must express my thoughts because she lightly rests her hand on my shoulder to reassure me.

"He's really not a bad man. There's nothing to be scared of. It'll be fine."

"He hates me! Can't I just wait in here?"

"No, because no one hates you."

I give her a sideways glance and want to remind her that just because you want something to be true, doesn't mean it is.

"He doesn't know you. There's a big difference."

"Well, he doesn't want to know me," I insist.

She shakes her head and says, "Remember what I told you. I have tricks up my sleeve when it comes to that man. I know how to play his games. Trust me," she demands, raising a single eyebrow.

I let out an audible sigh and try to release the tension building in my shoulders, signaling she won.

She picks up the plate, and I follow her into the back of the house toward the noise. As we enter the room, I see him sitting in a recliner with Bruno curled up in a ball on his lap. His eyes are glued to the screen while his hands softly stroke the dog. He feels her presence and says, "Thanks, babe," as he holds his hand out for the plate. It appears this is a regular service she provides, feeding him in his chair. However, this time, she withholds the plate until he pulls his eyes off the TV long enough to see us both.

"What are you doing back here?" he barks, looking past Mrs. Ann at me.

"James!" she spits out between tight lips. She shows him the plate and says, "We've brought you a snack."

He eyes me, then Mrs. Ann. "Just put it over there," he says, pointing to the coffee table.

She gently places it on the table, then turns to stand directly in front of the TV, blocking his view.

He drops his head to one side, shaking it in disbelief. "Ann, you're standing in the way."

"Well, we came in here to talk, not watch TV."

"But—"

She stops him before he can conjure up an argument.

"I've been telling Marni some funny stories from Kyle's younger years. What are some of your favorites?" His eyes narrow in frustration as she adds, "Any golf stories?" Just then, the phone rings in the kitchen. She stands and whispers reassuringly, "I'll be right back."

He stares me down before pointing the remote at the TV to turn up the volume.

"Why are you mad at me? I'm the one that deserves to be mad at you. I haven't done a thing to you."

"Is that what you think?" he asks, genuinely interested in an argument.

"You ruined my chances of having a real family." I pause, thumping my flattened hand onto my chest and adding, "My real family."

"Real family? You never had a real family to begin with." He practically laughs out his rebuttal.

"I think you kept my father from marrying my mom."

"It was his choice, but I nipped that in the bud before it could happen. So, yes, young lady, I'm better than good with my interference." He exhales and looks down at Bruno who is lightly snoring in his lap. He eyes me cautiously. "All this would have been fine if your mother hadn't gotten sick."

I can't believe he just said that to me. I look around the room, hoping to see Ann coming down the hall, but she's still gone. Tears bloom in my eyes, but I hold them back. I can hardly talk, but I finally say, "That's the only thing we seem to agree on. And it's exactly what I keep telling the Mercers. I want to go back home."

"But you're stuck here because you don't have a home anymore."

"Not with Mom, but I do with Aunt Jo," I say with more confidence than I feel.

Just then, Mrs. Ann sweeps back into the room. Immediately sensing the change in the room, she asks, "What did I miss?"

I look at her, wondering how such a nice lady can be with such an ornery man. I want to apologize to her or tell her *I told you so.* But I don't. I inhale a deep breath and tell him, "Believe it or not, people love me in Chicago." I fold my arms and add, "I don't want to be around you any more than you want to be around me."

He tips his head to the side, biting his lower lip. "It's not personal, Marni, I just think you'll be better off back in Chicago with your people."

"James, what are you saying? What's going on?" Mrs. Ann insists.

Without responding to her questions, he leans over to grab the plate, disturbing Bruno.

I scoff at him. *Not personal? My people?*

Bruno hops off his lap and makes a beeline for me. I bend over and scratch behind his ears, cradling his fluffy head between my palms. "You know what, Mr. Mercer? It's not a far jump from loving Bruno to accepting me. We're two bastards, alone in this world, in need of a family. But maybe there's only room for one in your life."

"Marni!" Mrs. Ann gasps, outwardly shocked. She only got the tail end of our exchange, but she gets the gist.

I slowly walk back into the kitchen, feeling the heavy weight of their eyes on my retreating back. I hear a heated exchange erupt but make no effort to eavesdrop. A few minutes later, Mrs. Ann joins me at the kitchen table, flustered. She notices my dour expression and immediately apologizes for his behavior.

"Pay no attention to him, Marni. He's an old fool—a stubborn old fool."

"Maybe, but we agree on one thing. I should go home."

"I'll take you home whenever you're ready."

I shake my head. "I mean, go home to Chicago."

I feel her energy deflate as she stands up and busies herself in the kitchen. I've made her uncomfortable, which was not my intent. We were having such a great day until he showed up.

"Marni, don't give up on us. Not now, not when we're just starting to get to know each other. Give us a chance." She flings her wrist toward the TV room and says, "Don't worry about him; he'll come around, you'll see. And when he does, you'll love him."

I flinch at the thought. His words sting like lash marks against my skin, but her loving insistence soothes the brunt of my pain like a balm.

Adjusting each cookie, she changes gears back to baking. "Look at all of our beautiful cookies!" she exclaims. "What do you think?"

"I can't believe I made these! They look too good to eat," I answer proudly.

She laughs and says, "I'll package them up nice and pretty before I bring them over tomorrow."

She drives me back to the Mercers' house and walks me to the door. "Marni, thank you for spending your entire afternoon with me! I had the best time with you, baking and talking and laughing. I hope you realize how special you are to me."

I study her sincerity for a second before responding. "Thank you, Mrs. Ann. I had fun with you too." Before I can leave, she pulls me into her chest. Wrapping her arms around me, I sink into her motherly embrace. I've almost forgotten how comforting it feels to be hugged. Tears sting my eyes as she lets go.

"Oh, I'm sorry, Marni."

"It's fine, really. It's just been a long time since I've been given a hug," I admit, feeling a little embarrassed. My head drops at the realization I might have just allowed her to see the true depths of my pain and loneliness. I take a deep breath, trying to regain my composure. I place my hand over the door handle and push it open. "Good night, Mrs. Ann. Thanks for today."

CHAPTER 30
Marni

"**Y**ou're going to a party! You're going to a party! You're going to a party!" I hear Annabelle and Lila's giddy chant down the hall, getting louder and louder like a runaway train picking up speed and intensity. I lie in my bed, still clinging to the last peaceful moments of sleep when it hits me—I *am* going to a party. I stir under the sheets, deciding whether I really want to get up. For a brief moment, I entertain the idea of staying in bed, pretending to be sick. Nicole might be disappointed, but she'll be surrounded by all her friends, so I'm sure I won't be missed.

I roll over onto my side, staring at the picture of Mom. I look at the edge of my bed and pretend she's sitting there, gently gliding the tips of her fingers along my arm. I hear her voice encouraging me to stick it out. I argue with her that I have—I've been in Texas for weeks now. She just shakes her head and whispers into my ear, *Trust me, you can do this. You are brave.*

The vision of Mom dissolves as the girls bolt through my closed door, flinging themselves onto my bed. Their legs spring like a frog's, jiggling me into full consciousness. I swipe at their quick ankles as they squeal, "You missed!"

Laughing, I ask, "What are you two so excited about this morning?"

Confused at my question, they drop right next to me and exclaim, "Your party!" I nod my head and twist and stretch underneath the covers. Waking up is not so terrible, but after last night's standoff with Old Mr. Mercer, who I now refer to as "Grumpa," and today's party anxiety squelching my confidence, it would be nice to pull the covers back over my head and just vanish.

Just as my eyes and brain start to adjust to the chaotic commotion, Mrs. Mercer whisper-barks at the girls from downstairs, "Pipe down! Leave Marni alone." The girls giggle as they hop off the bed and leave the room.

I am amazed two little people can produce such explosive levels of noise, popping my spatial bubble in the process, and yet, I don't even mind.

Smirking, I find it slightly funny how concerned Mrs. Mercer is about keeping a quiet house. *Quiet* isn't a word I'd use to describe our apartment in Chicago. Our Saturday mornings teemed with the constant racket of idling delivery trucks, rumbling dump trucks, people shouting, car doors slamming, and engines revving. I can't recall a truly quiet moment, which is why quiet is not an asset I safeguard. Actually, it's the opposite that's true. When the chaos subsides, small hairs on the back of my neck stand at attention as I wonder what's disturbed everyone else. But that's Chicago living. I'm still adjusting to the quiet and peaceful home Mrs. Mercer strives to create.

Mrs. Mercer peeks into my open room. I don't know if she is looking for the girls or checking in on me, but either way, she quietly turns to leave. I stop her by defending the girls. "Mrs. Mercer, I'm okay. I need to get up anyway." A gigantic yawn distorts my words.

"Well, you might want to sleep in a little more. You're going to be knee-deep in sugar, popcorn, and slumber party festivities. I'll be surprised if you girls get more than a few hours of sleep tonight," she says with a lighthearted wink.

I nod, securing the soft down under my chin and nestling back into the warm crater of my body's imprint. As I lie there, anticipating tonight, my brain replays the sleepovers Mom, Aunt Jo, and I used to have. Actually, it was Aunt Jo who did most of the sleeping over. It was their laughter I remember so vividly. Their contagious laughs, composed of the same rhythmic tones, made them sound like hysterical schoolgirls. To hear Mom and Aunt Jo carrying on with each other, barely able to breathe or even articulate actual words, was infectious. One would start telling a story from their childhood, the other one would add some complicated and entertaining details, and then they'd start talking on top of each other's words until the conversation was a mash-up of exaggerated hand gestures and hysterical laughter mixed with the occasional snort. And once we started down that road, I knew exhaustion would be the only remedy. Remembering Mom's laugh loosens the tension bottled up inside me. I close my eyes with a content smile and allow the peace of this memory to carry me into dreamland.

I wake up a couple of hours later and decide it's time to start my day. I make myself presentable, straighten my bed, and point myself in the direction of the soft chatter downstairs. As I walk into the kitchen, I freeze dead in my tracks. Sitting at the bar with Mrs. Mercer and the girls is Grumpa. To top it off, he has my cookies! And where is Mrs. Ann? I'm not sure how clearly my facial expression exposes my thoughts, but I'm pretty sure they can see I'm shocked.

"So glad to see you're up, Marni," Mrs. Mercer says, her positivity almost annoying. "Are you hungry?"

"I'll just have some toast, thank you." I'm irritated just being in the same room with him. "Where is Mrs. Ann? I want to thank *her* for helping me with the cookies," I ask, glaring in disgust at the old man. Part of me wants to remind him again that I was raised with manners and expected to be polite and courteous. But no amount of politeness will change his view of me, so I let my words sarcastically slide off my tongue. Mrs. Mercer acts like she doesn't even notice my mood or frustration as she hops off the barstool to refill his cup of coffee. My cheeks flush, thinking how upset Mom would have been at the slightest hint of disrespect. She would have colored my rear end until it resembled a red tomato. But she's not here dealing with him.

"Ann had some errands to run and asked me to bring these cookies over so you'd have them in time for your thing tonight," Grumpa states, casually sipping at his coffee, like polite conversations between us are normal.

"*Humph.* Well, please tell her thank you, if it's not *too* much trouble." My sneering words take Mrs. Mercer off guard.

"Marni, I think we need to get some food in you, okay?" Mrs. Mercer intervenes, her eyebrows shooting up in surprise. She obviously attributes my rudeness to the simple product of hunger and low blood sugar, although, let me go on record saying I have nothing against this old man. Except for the fact that he hates me and my mom, which I can back up with clear evidence. Every fiber inside me wants to scream, *I'm not hangry, it's him! He started this! I'm just the victim.*

I let out an audible sigh and reach for my plate. I sink my teeth into a slice of crunchy toast loaded with butter and honey. The sweet goo pools in the air pockets and drips down the outside of my hand onto the small white plate in front of me. I tear off a section of crust and dab it into the sweet, buttery puddle before tossing it into my mouth.

I guess this cookie delivery is about par to what Old Mr. Mercer expected because he responds with a whimsical smirk. "I appreciate the cookies that didn't make the party cut. My stomach thanks you both." He cocks his head like he's debating what to say next but instead puts his mug down and stands up. "Well, I'm off to the golf course." He pauses at the back door. "See y'all soon."

I nibble on my toast a little dumbfounded, wondering what in the world he means by *see y'all soon*? I ask Mrs. Mercer how long he'd been in the house. She stops wiping down the countertops enough to look me in the eye. "He's been here for over an hour, waiting for you to wake up. He said he wanted to thank you in person for his cookies. Seemed pretty sincere to me."

My lips won't produce a verbal reply, so I shrug my shoulders in a noncommittal response. As I finish my toast, I quietly evaluate his demeanor, his response to me, and his words. I can't put my finger on it, but it was more than just his words that seemed a little less harsh this morning. Mrs. Mercer's presence is the only rational explanation for his temperate behavior after our encounter last night where he happily accepted responsibility for keeping Mom and Mr. Mercer apart. The image of him sitting in his padded leather chair like a king, petting his perfect little dog, infuriates me. It's almost like he's proud of himself, like he's the sole person responsible for his perfect family. But it's not perfect anymore. Chills ripple down my spine as his words echo in my head: *Better off back in Chicago with your people.*

So why even pretend with me this morning? I know keeping up appearances is important to him, but he doesn't need to fake it with family. I admit, I'm confused.

"You know, Marni. People can come around to new things and new people. He might just surprise you. *You* might surprise you." Mrs. Mercer takes the empty plate in front of me and walks to the sink, rinsing it before depositing it in the dishwasher.

The day creeps along at a turtle's pace. The girls go to a friend's house for a playdate and return a few hours later. Mrs. Mercer runs to the store, then comes home to fold a bucket-load of laundry. I just sit around watching the clock. I try sketching but put it all away, too anxious about tonight. I pack, call Nicole, and decide to repack after she tells me what she's bringing. In a teal-and-navy quilt bag Mrs. Mercer bought for this occasion, I stuff:

Two outfits ... one to get dirty in and one to go home in

Two pairs of panties "in case we laugh so hard we pee," per Nicole's recommendation

Super cute pajama set

Toiletries

I set my pillow and sleeping bag next to the overnight bag, and I am all set. I just want this night to start so it can end. My pulse hammers rapidly as I nervously wait for Nicole to pick me up. I don't know if I can do this.

But at six o'clock, Nicole and her mom ring the doorbell. I bolt out of the back TV room and fling the door open.

"Ready to par-tay, Marni?" Nicole shrieks through a high-pitched giggle.

"Ready as I'll ever be. Let's go." I grab my bag, pillow, and sleeping bag.

Mrs. Mercer meets us at the car, running out of the house, carrying a white box tied up with pink and lime-green ribbon. "Marni, you're forgetting something."

"Oh, thank you!" I say, gently taking the box of cookies out of her hands. I set them in the back seat right before the girls practically tackle me. Decked out in full princess gear, they wrap their pink-and-purple bodies around my legs. "Have fun, Marni! We love you!"

I squat down to their level. "Thanks, girls. I love you too." I envelop them in a sisterly hug. "I'll see you tomorrow," I say, sliding into the back seat next to Nicole.

Before we pull away, Mrs. Mercer reminds me, "Call if you need anything."

I smile as we drive off, knowing that at least she will come and get me if it's a disaster.

Nicole rolls down her window, leans her head out, and yells to whomever, "Slumber party, here we come!" Her mother and I just laugh.

The drive to the party is fairly short—not even ten minutes. Thanks to Nicole's motormouth, the lack of silence means I can't be whisked back into the terrifying land of what-ifs that haunt me. Quick backstories, descriptions, and hobbies are spewed at me faster than I can possibly absorb. Nicole rambles about people and things I know nothing about, hoping to pre-shape my opinions to match hers as she secures my unassuming allegiance. Nicole's intensity proves to be a welcome distraction from the fears of my impending new-girl status.

"All right, girls, we're here," Nicole's mom announces, pulling up against the curb in front of a beautiful brown-brick and stucco two-story house tucked into the corner of a quiet cul-de-sac. The home is unassuming yet stately, masterfully outlined in tiered flower beds with varying plants and colors that add vibrancy to the neutral color pallet. This house welcomes us with the melodic tune of wind chimes swaying from a massive oak tree, a painted bird-bath-turned-herb-planter, and brightly painted rocks with kids' handprints scattered throughout the flower beds.

Nicole explodes out of the car, grabs her stuff, and squeals, "Come on, Marni!"

I carefully collect my gear and the cookies and take a deep breath before catching up with Nicole at the front door. Not sure what to expect, the sounds echoing through the house sound oddly familiar—blaring music fighting to be heard over high-pitched laughter. Nicole rings the doorbell. We can hear a stampede of animal-like feet behind the door. I step back, willing to sacrifice Nicole to whatever is about to pounce at us. My last thought before the door opens is, *Please let them like me. Please, please, let me have fun.*

CHAPTER 31
Marni

Mrs. Mercer shows up the next morning around ten, apologizing for picking me up so early by explaining we have errands to run.

As we're gathering my stuff, she asks the girls, "Did y'all take any pictures last night?"

Nicole answers, "Absolutely!" Then she turns to me and asks, "Did you get them all? I sent them to you last night."

I check my phone and see the unread message.

"Got them, thanks."

Within seconds of pulling away from the house, Mrs. Mercer blurts out, "Sooo, I'm dying to hear! How was the party? Did you have fun? What did y'all do? Tell me about the other girls." She fires question after question at me without pausing for my response. Somehow, each question elicits three more follow-up questions. I hate to admit it to myself, but she sounds just like Mom.

I wait patiently until she stops to make eye contact with me, her eyebrows raised, cueing me to talk. I can feel Mrs. Mercer's excitement, but there's something else too. Then it hits me. She was actually nervous for me. *Huh. That is so sweet.* I close my eyes briefly when a strange pang hits my chest. I'm not ready to decipher what it means—guilt, fear, relief, all the above?—so I shrug it off and start telling her about the party.

I admit to her how uneasy I felt walking into the house, skeptical of everything and everyone. But then Nicole said, *Y'all remember Marni? Been in Chicago, but she's home now ... in Texas!* "Nicole threw her arms in the air like I was back from an extended vacation and not the new girl in the group. All night, we laughed and never once did I feel like an outsider. I couldn't believe it!"

Mrs. Mercer softly clears her throat, prompting me to offer more details, but I don't have the energy this morning. It would probably take me all day to rehash last night's events, so instead, I offer her the highlight reel. "We did all kinds of stuff like watch movies, prank called some boys—"

She interrupts. "Which boys?"

I shrug my shoulders and tell her I honestly can't remember their names. "We also gave each other makeovers, and—"

She pops another quick question. "And hair? Did you do hair and makeup?"

I nod. "Yes, ma'am, we did both."

"How was your makeover?"

"It wasn't really my style." I grimace, and she laughs at my response. "But everyone loved the makeover I gave to a girl. Nicole even wiped off her clown face and insisted I do her makeup next," I say proudly.

"Oh, yes, that's a credit to your artistic eye! So, what else?"

"We ate junk food nonstop. We had pizza, chips and dip, popcorn, brownies, and, oh,"—I turn my whole body toward her, my voice lifting in excitement—"they totally loved my cookies!" I smile, remembering how a couple of the girls kept asking me, *You really made these? They look too pretty to eat!* I tell Mrs. Mercer, "They were impressed that we made the cookies ourselves."

I lie my head back against the car's headrest, wishing it were my pillow. A yawn floats out of my mouth as my eyes flutter against the morning's bright sun.

Mrs. Mercer says, "Are you okay? Just tired?"

"Yes, ma'am. Tired, but I'm really happy Nicole invited me to the party."

"So, *all* the girls were nice and welcoming?"

"They really were, which surprised me. It was like they had all invited me to be there, not just Nicole." A smile slowly stretches across Mrs. Mercer's face. "I promise you, I've never heard more or louder hyena-laughs in my life, especially when boys were mentioned. It was hard to absorb it all, but it was so much fun ... a night I won't forget."

"Did you have lots of sleepovers in Chicago?" Mrs. Mercer asks, cocking her head to the side.

"No, ma'am, not a lot. I would have one friend at a time spend the night—nothing like last night's party since most of my friends lived in small apartments. We hung out a lot, but most of the time, we'd all go back home to sleep. This was definitely a different experience for me." I say with a half-smile, leaning my head against the window to shut my eyes.

"Well, anytime you want to have those girls over, just say the word. We'll send Mr. Mercer and the girls over to Ann's house with Grampa. Ann would probably come over to hang out and be one of the girls with y'all," Mrs. Mercer says with a laugh, already forming plans for the future. "I bet she'd love to—"

I clear my throat. "Maybe you could be one of the girls, too, if you want," I offer quietly.

Mrs. Mercer quickly glances over at me. She smiles shyly. "I ... I'd love that."

Mrs. Mercer turns her focus back to finding a parking spot, and then she and I run into the department store to pick out some clothes: a new church dress for her, matching cotton dresses for the girls, and a flirty A-line skirt and silky top for me.

We continue to chatter about the party, and I tell her some more about all the girls as we grab a quick bite to eat. She shares some of her crazy sleepover stories, including one time when she and her friends snuck out to their principal's front yard where they unrolled a dozen rolls of toilet paper, securing white lines into his grass with plastic forks. I asked her what happened when they got caught, and she laughed, saying, "We never got caught! You're the only other person who knows," she says winking. "Oh! I can't wait to see your pictures from last night!"

I pause, a little reluctant, but since she's been so open with me, I decide to share my pictures with her. I set my phone between us and start swiping through the pictures, each image evidence of a successful night in vivid color. She barely catches her breath from laughing when she discovers just how bad my makeover truly looked. We throw away our food wrappers and then head out to the grocery store.

"You never go to *this* store on an empty stomach," Mrs. Mercer states as absolute fact. By the time our zillions of groceries are bagged and in the trunk, I am completely exhausted, both from the lack of sleep and a day on the town.

"Why don't you go up and try to recover a little from your all-nighter?" Mrs. Mercer suggests when we finally arrive home.

Music to my ears! I climb up the staircase, put my things away, take a five-minute rinse-off shower, throw on some comfy clothes, and dive straight into my fluffy bed.

***

A couple of hours later, laughter and a familiar sound stirs me out of sleep. Snuggled up in bed, I lie still for a minute, listening to what I quickly chalk up to my dreamy state of mind. As I start to give up consciousness again, I hear it—the sound I thought I had dreamed. I fling my covers off, bolting out of bed in a mad scramble, and dart out of my room. In my foggy stupor, I practically tumble down the stairs to find everyone watching my theatrical entrance with a smile. I freeze, taking in the strange scene.

Mr. and Mrs. Mercer sit comfortably in the high-back chairs facing the front entryway. Their seats offer the perfect view to my not-so-graceful dismount off the staircase. Mrs. Ann and Grumpa anchor themselves at either side of the couch with the girls between them, oblivious to everything else except their pretend world of princess Barbies. However, the standout character in the room turns out to be real! My mind isn't playing tricks on me. I know the familiar shape that captivates the room's attention. Stunned, I tilt my head to the side and slowly take a few delicate steps forward. A woman perches on the edge of the oversized chenille chair, sitting still as a bird with her broad back to me. Slowly, she shifts her body weight to the side and turns around to face me. Her smile lights up her face from corner to corner, and relief and comfort wash over me. I can't believe it! Finally, this can all end!

"Marni, sweet girl, I sure have missed your beautiful face! Come on over here and give me a big hug before I burst," Aunt Jo commands, flinging her soft arms into the air. I hurry toward her. She grabs my hands, and looks me up and down, impressed. "Look at you—you look like a million bucks!"

I look from her to Mrs. Mercer and fall into Aunt Jo's plump, familiar arms with tears streaming down my face.

"I've missed you, sweet girl! You bein' in Texas, this far from me ... well, enough's enough!"

Her words, her presence, and her embrace rejuvenate me. I relax into her, thankful we're on the same page. I lift my chin off her cushy body and glance over at Mr. and Mrs. Mercer. Their faces glow with happiness, which unsettles me even though I'm thrilled Aunt Jo has finally decided to take me home.

Aunt Jo repositions her head, lightly balancing it at an angle, her cheek resting on the crown of my head. She says, "Thank goodness for the Mercers' generosity. They were kind enough to fly me down here just to surprise you."

Her words sound a hidden alarm inside my heart. I look up at her and back to the Mercers, somewhat confused. Why do they keep insisting they want me to stay if they are so happy and willing to pay Aunt Jo to take me back? Without thinking, I blurt out, "Why would you do that?" I try not to sound hurt, but I am.

Aunt Jo answers on their behalf. "So I could see you."

I pull back, looking her in the eye.

"So? You're surprised?" Aunt Jo says half-joking, patting my thigh with her oversized hand as a twinkle of delight flickers in her eyes.

"More than you can know, Aunt Jo." Leaning in to whisper in her ear, I ask, "When are you taking me back to Chicago?" My mind races with anticipation as my heart struggles with a new loss I didn't expect. It's no secret I wanted to stay in Chicago, but now that I'm here with them, I'm not so sure where I want to be. Sensing an arrangement has once again been made without consulting me, the weight of their collective decision to send me away presses down on me. I never wanted to be unwanted by anyone—especially my father. With less enthusiasm than expected, I add, "It won't take me long to pack."

Aunt Jo looks over my head at Mrs. Mercer. I pivot to see Mr. and Mrs. Mercer watching our happy reunion as if the scene was scripted for an after-school special.

"I'm not here to take you home, Marni," Aunt Jo says, loud enough for everyone to hear. Stunned by her news and the volume it is delivered, I watch the Mercers for confirmation. Their smiles fall from their faces.

Relieved, yet puzzled, all I can mutter is, "Oh."

I watch Mrs. Mercer and Mrs. Ann exchange incredulous looks. I turn back to Aunt Jo just in time to catch her shrugging her shoulders in response to the other women. She tries diverting my attention by saying, "Marni, you didn't come close to doing this place justice." She lifts both her arms up into a jiggly *Y* and exclaims, "It's magnificent!"

I scan the room, trying to decipher what's going on when my eyes land on Grumpa. He sits, straight-backed and uncomfortable, hands clasped in his lap, and his head slowly slides back and forth as he stares across the room at Aunt Jo. He shifts his uneasy gaze to me, his pupils dilated with awkwardness. I lift one eyebrow and slightly nod my head as I look back to Aunt Jo, signaling he's about to get what he wants—me gone. But he bites his bottom lip, turning his attention back to the girls.

"I can't get over the enormity of this place," Aunt Jo says, sweeping her arms in a rainbow over her head. "Everything is just so, so ..." she searches for the right word and finally adds, "opulent! Look at this room. It's bigger than my entire apartment. Right, Marni?"

I nod and notice Mrs. Mercer squirming in her seat. She wears a pleasant expression, but I sense Aunt Jo's observations make her uncomfortable. Oblivious of her faux pas, my aunt turns to Mrs. Mercer and says, "You must be cleaning and dusting all the time."

Mrs. Mercer shakes her head, but Lila pipes up and says, "That's Penny's job."

Mrs. Mercer flushes with embarrassment at Lila's innocent response but feels the need to add, "Penny's our maid, but she's off for the summer ... her vacation."

Aunt Jo nods, pretending this is all new information for her.

I need to refocus Aunt Jo and figure out the plan. "So, I'm not going back with you?"

"No, sweet girl, I'm just here for a visit. And I can only stay for a few days. Besides, why would you want to come back to Chicago and live in my cramped, cluttered mess?" Aunt Jo asks. Looking outside, she gasps, "You have a pool?"

The girls giggle at her excitement.

Aunt Jo looks around, taking in as much of her surroundings as possible, and utters in pure astonishment, "This place is like a hotel!"

"No, silly. It's our house," Annabelle corrects her.

Aunt Jo laughs and asks, "Can you take me for a dip in that pool?"

The girls shoot up, jumping up and down in excitement.

"Can we, Mommy?" they ask in unison. Mrs. Mercer smiles and sends them upstairs to put on their swimsuits.

"Marni, I know we don't swim, but that pool sure looks refreshing. Let's cool off on the steps," she suggests, her voice lifts as she waits for my response.

"Actually, I can swim, Aunt Jo. Mr. Mercer drives me to swim and golf lessons almost every day."

I don't know why I kept that little tidbit from my aunt until just now. Maybe it's because I was afraid I'd have to admit that my favorite part about my lessons is the one-on-one time I get with my father as he drives me to and from the club. Our conversations have morphed from stranger small talk to friendly curiosity to comfortable banter. We trade stories with each other, learning about past experiences, like a real father and daughter would. Just the other day, he recalled a hilarious story from his high school days, concerning an incident he had on the golf course. Apparently, he tried, unsuccessfully, to sling his friends out of the golf cart. Instead, he ended up flipping the entire cart over directly in front of a full dining room where his parents dined with friends. He laughed, saying, "To this day, some of my dad's friends still razz me about my driving techniques on the course."

Aunt Jo flings her elbow into my side, her eyebrows shooting up in playful surprise. "Well, proof is in the pudding. Let's see how those lessons are working out for ya."

I start to laugh at her until I see Grumpa shoot Mr. Mercer a disapproving look. "Does that bother you, me bettering myself?" I challenge him. He looks agitated but doesn't bother responding. "Or are you afraid someone might actually like me at *your* club? What if I start to fit in?"

"Marni!" Aunt Jo snarls through clenched teeth.

"What? It's fine—he hates me. We all know it," I say, defending myself.

Appalled, Mrs. Ann finally breaks the Mercer silence. "Marni—"

I cut her off with a wave of my hand. Silently, I grant myself permission to untangle my emotions, releasing all my pent-up hurt and disappointment. I know nothing I say will ever change the past, but I owe it to Mom and myself to be honest.

I turn to the Mercers. "Just like we all know you never actually wanted me. I just landed on your doorstep because my mom had this crazy plan." Turning more squarely in the direction of Mr. Mercer, I say, "You never even *once* thought to check on the woman you supposedly loved. You abandoned us." I glare at Grumpa next. "And you *never* approved of my mother, even though you never even met her. You do know that your blood flows in my veins, right?" I ask, not pausing for a response. He jerks his head up, but I continue. "Maybe if my pedigree were Southern or in-your-face affluent, you'd have given me a chance. But I'm just a poor girl from the slums of Chicago who you don't want."

"Marni!" Aunt Jo barks, but I turn my face away from her, holding up my hand.

"*You* knew I wouldn't fit into this world, and you didn't warn me. You let me come here, thinking they might actually want me, that I could be one of them."

Aunt Jo sighs, not sure what to say.

I look at Grumpa again and add, "We both know I can't change what I was born into any more than you can change your old-man prejudices. You're right, there are consequences for doing things out of order. To you, I'm just a consequence born from a bad decision, not the blessing Mom always called me." I smirk a little. "At least I know where I stand. It's better to be a dog in this family, right?"

Mrs. Ann swivels in her seat, glaring at her husband, but then turns to me. "Marni, you're not making any sense," she says in her soothing voice like she's trying to talk me off a ledge.

Sadness washes over me, considering Mrs. Ann in all this. "I've never had a grandmother until you. I know you mean well, but what's going to happen when the novelty of me wears off? You'll go back to your canasta or bridge or whatever, and I'll just be that sad, orphaned girl who doesn't quite fit in." A lump blocks my words as Aunt Jo starts making guttural noises behind me, hinting at her disapproval. "Truthfully, Mrs. Ann, it's too painful to be around you. You remind me of Mom, a free spirit living each day to its fullest. I know you would have liked each other."

Looking at the Mercers, I admit, "I know I don't belong here." Wiping away the tears, I beg Aunt Jo, "Just take me back home. Mom was wrong, I belong with you."

"Marni, pull yourself together. That's enough out of you. The Mercers have bent over backward to welcome you into the family." Aunt Jo's tone is firm, indicating I really need to hear her. The deep frustration that rides the coattails of unfair treatment and betrayal exhausts me. I'm too tired for all this, but she's right about one thing: my presence forces them to bend over backward, hiding the obvious fact that I'm a huge inconvenience.

Mrs. Mercer sits across from me, shocked.

I recognize the pain that pools in her eyes. I never wanted to hurt her, so I say, "Thank you for bravely accepting me into your home. I can tell you're trying, but we both know I'm not what you signed up for, and I don't blame you for that either. I'm a mismatched wedge in your family pie. You deserve the family you always wanted."

She lets out the breath she's been holding and says, "Marni, you *really* don't know what any of us want. Stop pushing us away."

Twisting back to face Aunt Jo, who sits dumbstruck, I remind her of the deal. "You said I had to do a trial run—six months. I don't need that much time, we all know what the outcome will be." Not knowing if I could swallow saying goodbye to them now, never mind in six months, I add, "Let's not waste anyone's time and just get this over with." I punctuate my stance by crossing my arms, digging my knuckles into my biceps.

"Well, your attitude is about as sweet as rotten fish. I'm appalled at all this nonsense talk," Aunt Jo scolds, waving her pointer finger at me. "Read the room, Marni. Everyone in here cares about you and wants what's best for you."

"Not everyone," I retort, throwing a quick glance in Grumpa's direction.

My aunt's eyes narrow, warning me I'm on thin ice. She pushes out a guttural *humph* sound as she folds her body forward, resting her protruding belly on top of her wide thighs. She takes in a long breath, then exhales. "Give me a break, why don't you? This is my first vacation, and you're poo-pooing on my vibe." Her glare transitions from tired to irritated. "Now, I'm sayin' I want to secure myself in an innertube and float in that pool. So, move your tiny tush upstairs and put on a suit. We've all had enough of your lip, young lady." Aunt Jo growls like an overwhelmed mama bear.

I scan the room, taking inventory of everyone's expressions. Their eyes are wide, their faces are frozen, but they all silently nod in agreement with Aunt Jo—even Grumpa's playing along. My eyes lock onto his, neither one of us able to smile at the other. He knows I'm right, but something's got ahold of his tongue. I shake my head lightly from side to side, frustrated.

Just then, the girls yell over the upstairs banister. "Can we go swimming now?"

I look up, a genuine smile brightens my face, knowing these girls do actually love me, and I love them. We've been sisters from day one.

I stand up and answer in my sweetest princess voice, "Want to swim with me, girls?"

They glance at each other, squealing, "Race you to the pool!"

The girls thunder down the stairs as I slink away from the strange mixture of my two very different lives. Traces of hushed conversations drift upstairs, but my brain can't decipher the content. Questions swim around in my head, like too many goldfish crammed into a fishbowl. I need to find out why Aunt Jo came all this way, especially if she's not planning to whisk me away from this alien family. My heart and head play tug-of-war with my emotions. Of course, I want to go home to Chicago, but when I think of leaving them, my guts twist in knots. Confused by the battle raging in my head, it suddenly becomes clear. What if they've already made their choice, and Aunt Jo's presence is nothing more than a distraction meant to soften the blow of their rejection.

As frustrated heat builds in my chest, tears start to sting my eyes. I'm fully aware this arrangement was Mom's way of making things right and tying up her loose ends. I can't help wondering if she even considered how their rejection would affect me. I feel sick to my stomach, worrying they may not want me—may not love me. I walk into my room, pick up the framed photo of Mom on my nightstand, and ask, "Why did you do this to me?" I hug the rectangular frame into my chest. "You denied me all this—my father, a family, everything—until now. I'm not sure I'm ready to give them up—don't let them send me away," I beg, trying to stave off my fear of abandonment.

After throwing myself a pity party for a bit, I attempt to shake off my funk and change into my pink-and-turquoise striped swimsuit. I put on a brave face, bracing for whatever is happening outside. I tiptoe to the back door to size up the situation which appears to be a typical day in the backyard pool. I spy the girls splashing Mrs. Ann as everyone laughs, including Grumpa. I chuckle to myself, watching Aunt Jo floating in a giant sling chair, careful not to get her hair wet. Mr. Mercer fidgets with the grill as Mrs. Mercer plays the part of hostess like a pro.

Just as I am about to step outside, Mrs. Mercer catches my eye, smiles, and waves me over to join in the fun. With downcast eyes, I slip out of the house, embarrassed by my actions and uncomfortable with my current circumstances. But to my surprise, everyone acts as if this is the first time they have seen me all day. People are happy, eating, drinking, listening to music, and talking. Aunt Jo floats in the shallow end while Mrs. Ann plays water games with the girls in the deep end. Mrs. Mercer serves drinks and ensures the food will be "grill ready" for Mr. Mercer. Everyone seems so relaxed with each other, except for me and Grumpa. He sits alone under a dark-blue poolside umbrella, taking in the chaotic scene with a drink fixed in his right hand. He studies unobtrusively and with great focus as Mrs. Ann and Mr. Mercer interact with Aunt Jo. I'm sure he's noticed the peculiar tone out here too. Maybe he's trying to assess why everyone is so lighthearted and strangely unified. They're interacting with Aunt Jo like she's family, but they just met. It doesn't feel right, but strangely, it doesn't feel forced either. As I wonder how they can be so comfortable with each other, a new thought hits me. Maybe they're up to something? Before I can contemplate what that could be, the girls suck me into a game of their imagination.

Annabelle points at me and screams with theatrical fear. "Oh, look, Lila-mermaid! Marni is about to monster-splash us, the mostest beautiful mermaids in the world, with her long pink tail!"

Lila laughs and adds, "Quick, take cover!"

With such a dramatic introduction, there is only one thing left to do. With a devious grin, I run, jump, and tuck my knees into my chest, bombing them with my best cannonball splash. When I come up for air, Lila and Annabelle laugh hysterically as my rippling aftershock bounces them up and down. It takes me a brief second to realize I had practically landed on Aunt Jo which caused her to flip out of her float. She's soaked! I have never seen Aunt Jo swim until now. Panicking, she fights the water, trying desperately to reach the pool's edge before drowning, until she hears Mrs. Ann yelling, "Put your feet down, you can touch!" Suddenly, her frantic commotion stops. She straightens up, wipes the water off her face and uses a drippy hand to assess the condition of her hair. Once she recovers, everyone laughs as the girls take turns reenacting her flailing chaos.

"Glad to see your beautiful smile again," Aunt Jo says, gasping for breath on the pool's steps. As she regains her composure, she turns to Annabelle and Lila and asks, "So, what's next? Want to play colored eggs?" Annabelle and Lila, propelled by a new surge of energy, grab my arm and pull me over to join Aunt Jo and Mrs. Ann.

Savory smells of seasoned meat and grilled onions waft enticingly through the air as we play round after round of colored eggs. Bruno rambunctiously runs around the pool, barely missing Mrs. Mercer sitting on the edge, dipping and swirling her feet in the water. For a fleeting moment, everything feels ordinary—almost normal—like we're a real family hanging out together. But as soon as this thought materializes, it disintegrates with one look. Grumpa's unreadable gaze evaporates my smile, his bushy eyebrows drawing inward, accentuating two deep lines. His thumb and index finger pull intensely at his bottom lip like a TV villain concocting a plan. What is he thinking? Despite the Texas heat, a chill ripples down my spine as my mind replays the only truth we share … *I don't belong.*

At dinner, I sit between Aunt Jo and Grumpa. Don't really know how or why I got sandwiched there. As I am doctoring up my cheeseburger, Grumpa laughs and pokes fun at me. "Want any meat to go with that ketchup?" Looking around the table, he says, "Looks like all my granddaughters consider ketchup their main course." His observation produces laughter from all the adults. My eyes shoot up, confused by him lumping me into the granddaughter category. My eyes dart back and forth as I wait for him to backpedal, change his words to single out the girls. But he doesn't. Instead, everyone carries on eating and talking as if nothing huge was just said.

After dinner, the girls shuffle upstairs to play and wind down. I decide to stay in my seat as the adults enjoy their after-dinner coffee, secretly hoping I will learn something that would explain Aunt Jo's arrival. Instead, they just talk about nothing. Irritated, I decide enough is enough. Their charade masked as a surprise is over. I need answers, and I deserve the truth. I interrupt a moment of silence and ask, "What's really going on?" I eyeball each adult at the table.

"Marni, I'm not sure what you mean," Mrs. Mercer gently responds as she takes a dainty sip of her coffee.

"I'm pretty sure you all know exactly what I'm asking, so just answer me already." My rudeness starts to show its ugly face again despite the nice evening we've all shared.

"Whoa! Hold on, Marni. That is *not* the way you talk to adults. Your mom would be ashamed!" Aunt Jo barks with authority.

"Well, my mom should be ashamed of herself!" I say. "First, she throws away my father, then she asks *you* to throw *me* away." I pause, taking a breath to stabilize my emotions, but tears start to slide down my face. I wipe them away, upset at my situation and embarrassed to be crying in front of everyone.

Calmly, Aunt Jo crosses her hands loosely onto her lap. "Now calm down, Marni." Her familiar tone exudes gentle control. "You're right, sweet girl. I am here for a reason. I missed you!"

"Sure, that's it." I roll my eyes.

"*Humph.*" Aunt Jo looks at Mrs. Mercer and straightens herself in her chair. She leans into me like she's about to whisper and says, "Remember that thing that I was going to mail you?"

I nod, noting a lump the size of a toad clinging to the back of my throat.

"Well, when I called the Mercers a few days ago to check in on you, like I have been every now and then, they mentioned that you've been stalking the mailman and asked if I knew why. I explained that your mom had a last gift for you that I was planning to send your way. When I told them I hadn't had a chance to mail it yet, they offered to pay my way down here so I could hand-deliver it to you."

My eyes widen with excitement. "What! Where is it? Why have you waited until now to tell me?" Crumbling into my folded arms, I can't stop crying. I am overwrought, and the realization hits me hard that this will be the last tangible gift from Mom. The expectation I created for this gift and its potential meaning overwhelms me. Tears flow like streams down my face onto the table, releasing pent-up fears, confusion, and sadness. I sob for Mom, our past, and my undetermined future. No one makes a sound or moves.

When I finally lift my face, I look directly at Mrs. Mercer. "I'm so sorry, Mr. and Mrs. Mercer, for the scene I caused." Pausing to slow my irregular breathing, I continue in as sincere a manner as possible. "Thank you for helping Aunt Jo come here. It really means the world to see my family again." As the last words come out of my mouth, Mr. Mercer gently takes and squeezes his wife's hand as her smile clouds with sadness.

"Of course, Marni. This's what family does. We're here for each other," Mrs. Mercer says as tears form a glass wall against her blue eyes. She stands and pinches her forehead as if she has a headache. With quiet strength, she addresses the room. "I think we all need to give this child a break." She turns to face me. "You've been through a lot lately—more than most adults—and you've handled each unexpected curve better than I would have. I know you feel like Jo is the only family you have left, but you're wrong." Her eyes travel around the room as she says, "You have all of us."

I tilt my head, briefly digesting her words, then turn to Aunt Jo. "I'm ready. Please, can we go open Mom's gift now?"

Aunt Jo half chuckles as she says, "It's packed in my suitcase, sweet girl. If it's okay with the Mercers, I'll bring it to your room tonight. I think you're going to want some alone time once you've opened the box."

Looking across the table to the Mercers, they both nod in silence, agreeing to Aunt Jo's recommendations.

"Great! I'm finished, you're finished, let's go get ready for bed!" I bump the table with my legs as I erupt out of my chair. Aunt Jo's thick, trunk-like arm swiftly stops me in my tracks, surprising me and everyone else at the table.

"Hold on, missy! We are not about to leave all these dishes for Mrs. Mercer to clean up. No, ma'am. You are going to clear this table," Aunt Jo orders.

"It's no trouble, Jo. I do this by myself all the time. She doesn't need to hang around to clean up. It's fine, really," Mrs. Mercer quietly protests.

"What? Are you telling me that little Miss Marni doesn't have to lift a finger? Nope, that will not do! She needs to pull her weight in the Mercer family." And looking me hard in the eye as if she is about to put me in a trance, Aunt Jo quotes my mom. "Marni, if someone cooks for you, the least you can do is help clean up."

I can't help grinning at her, which puzzles everyone at the table.

Aunt Jo returns my smile, informing them, "That was Gabby's number-one rule in the kitchen, and she would scold me if I didn't remind Marni of it."

Grumpa's lips soften into an understated smile as he slowly bobs his head with an approving nod.

However, Mrs. Mercer insists she doesn't need or expect the help. Shifting my eyes from Mrs. Mercer to Aunt Jo, I give in and walk around the table gathering up empty plates. I hear Mrs. Mercer's tone shift as she orders everyone, "Just sit down and relax."

Stunned, I freeze in place, uncertain what to do, who to obey. Aunt Jo reaches out to touch Mrs. Mercer on the arm, trying to ease her nerves. She leans over and says, "Enjoy this mini vacation from dirty dishes, at least for right now. It'll give us time to talk."

Glancing over my shoulder as I walk away, I watch Mrs. Mercer sink back into her chair. Their conversation picks back up, laughing and sharing stories, like old friends catching up from where they left off.

After all the dishes are washed and loaded into the dishwasher, Grumpa comes up from behind me, pats me on the shoulder, and says, "Thank you, kiddo."

Turning around, I look him in the eye and make some incoherent grunting sound accompanied with a "whatever" shoulder shrug. He turns, says his goodbyes to everyone else, then politely takes Mrs. Ann by the elbow and escorts them both to their car. Before Mrs. Ann slips into her car, she eyes me in the doorway, blows me a kiss, and promises to see me tomorrow.

Finally, the evening has officially come to an end. Guests are gone, girls are upstairs in their own world, and the kitchen is clean. A surge of confidence bubbles out of my mouth as I announce to both the Mercers and Aunt Jo, "It's time!"

"Go on, Marni. Give me about fifteen minutes to get it together and bring it to your room," Aunt Jo says with a twinkle in her eyes.

I fly up the stairs, brush my teeth, jump into my PJs and flop onto my fluffy bed to wait. The waiting game is hard—it doesn't matter how old you are, it is just flat-out hard! I semi-patiently sit on my bed for what feels like hours, but finally, Aunt Jo carefully peeks her head into my room and whistles. "Ooooh, look at this room!" she exclaims, walking inside and spinning in a slow circle. "Can I live here? Maid, pool, private bedroom suites ... oh man!"

"Aunt Jo?"

"I'm just saying," she throws her flabby arms up and announces, "This is the life!"

"Aunt Josephine, seriously? The gift?"

Walking to the edge of my bed, her eyes glisten with unspent tears. "Oh, sweet Marni. I've missed you something fierce." Then she bends over me and wraps her entire body around me, engulfing me in her love.

I wiggle underneath all her weight. "Aunt Jo? I need air ... can't ... breathe."

She shuffles and plops down next to me on my bed. Waves of energy ripple through the mattress as her impact slightly bounces me up and down.

"Marni, I know you've been waiting for this gift ever since I told you about it, but I want you to understand something. This gift is your mom's way of guiding you and loving you. Your mom left instructions for after you've received it. You'll see what I mean."

"Okay, so where is it? I'm ready."

Aunt Jo pushes herself off my bed and walks out the door. She bends over to pick up an old shoebox covered in tattered, aged lace with different shades of pink, satin ribbon tied around it, keeping the contents inside safe. It looks like an arts-and-crafts project that was made long ago with love and then tossed in a closet and forgotten.

"Here you go," she says, placing the box in front of my crossed legs. She leans over me, gently kisses my forehead, and then silently turns to leave. She pauses at the door and wishes me good night.

As she turns to leave, I panic. "Wait! Aren't you going to watch me open this? Why are you leaving?"

"This is personal, between you and your mom. I want you to open it, take it in, and just be in the moment with memories of her. We'll talk more in the morning. Plus, I am pretty beat after all the traveling and swimming," she says, stretching her arms overhead to yawn.

"Good night, Aunt Jo. I love you," I reply, blowing her a kiss. Before she's out the door, I add, "Thank you."

She smiles as she closes the door behind her.

CHAPTER 32
Marni

Mom's last gift sits enticingly in front of my crisscrossed legs, but I'm paralyzed. Fear, anxiety, and unexplainable emotions have incapacitated me. This box—its importance—feels too big, too weighty for my teenage brain to comprehend. The tension in my body is knotting in my shoulders, as sweat pools at my nape. I'm afraid, and yet I want to remember every detail, relish every second.

I feel like such a drama queen, so I try to shake off my anxiety. What am I so afraid of? Is it the pain of knowing this is the last physical thing Mom will ever give me? Or am I truly scared of what I'll find inside? Her first posthumous "letter" was, er, bittersweet, to say the least.

I run my hands over the swatches of lace that cover every square inch of the box in different patterns. Once white, the lacy decor now shows its age with a slight yellowing around the edges once securely glued to the box. The top has an intricate cut-out of a heart within the lacy fabric. Inside the framed cut-out are the words "Our Memories" written in thick black ink in Mom's delicate handwriting. Three satin ribbons tied in perfect bows wrap around the box. The ribbons represent all Mom's favorite colors: a vibrant sunset pink, blush pink, and a pastel pink. She loved all colors, but pink was always her favorite. I smile.

I take a deep breath and gently untie the ribbons. I carefully lift the lid to find a letter with a bundle of journals and a framed picture neatly stored inside.

My dearest Marni,

Please read everything, take it all in, and share your thoughts with Aunt Jo, your dad, and whoever else you choose. Once you read everything, please also allow your dad's wife to read these memories as well. I want her to better understand all this too.

It comforts me to know that you are with family, and I know they will love you dearly. Always remember and know that I am with you in spirit ... always and forever.

All my love,
xoxoxoxo
Mom

Small streams cascade down my cheeks. I gently set the letter down before my tears dot Mom's letter. I pick up the old, brassy frame that holds a four-by-six picture of a young couple wrapped in each other's arms, smiling. It's Mom cuddled up beside a young Mr. Mercer.

Confused, I stare at their picture, evidence of a relationship she hid like a buried treasure. Why would she have kept this happiness from me for so long? I see their youthful joy and the promise of future possibilities in their embrace. They were full of life, ready to leap right off the picture to tackle whatever was thrown at them. Any kid would cherish this picture of their parents' affection.

"What happened, Mom?" I whisper to the picture before hugging the framed image to my heart. Wanting to understand this great love she never fully claimed as her own, I press their image into myself, hoping to evoke some feelings or emotions that mysteriously lie under the surface of their photo.

The effects of my picture-osmosis experiment leaves me wanting more from Mom. So, I gently prop the picture up on my bedside table and turn my attention back to the gift box. Inside the box are sixteen numbered journals full of Mom's cursive handwriting, pictures, phone numbers, letters from Mr. Mercer, and a small black-and-white picture of a weird blob-like image. *These are going to take some time to go through.*

I thumb through the first one and realize why she included their picture. She needed me to see them together. I stare at her youthful, healthy face, glowing with love as she looks up at him. I pull back the covers, fluff up my pillows, adjust my bedside lamp, and nestle into my bed, ready to read Mom's words.

> *I met a man today …*
>
> *We were both standing in a frantic crowd downtown, trying to flag a cab. As a vacant cab pulled over, we both lunged for the door. I hadn't noticed another person waving for the cab, let alone this man. We looked at each other and I smiled, hoping he would cave and give me the cab. Turns out, my stop was on the way to his stop, so we agreed to share the ride. We awkwardly folded ourselves into the cramped car, blurted our destinations to the driver, and then sat there in dead silence for what seemed an eternity. I guess we both couldn't handle the silent tension because we simultaneously turned toward each other and started talking.*
>
> *His name is Kyle Mercer, an attorney from Texas here on business. The next twenty minutes flew by while we filled up the back seat with friendly chatter and laughter. As the driver pulled over to let me out, Kyle said, "I'm in town for a while. Would you care to show me the sights? You know, an insider's tour of Chicago?" His words slowed with timid hesitation. Grinning, I agreed and bowed my head a little so as not to show him my blushing cheeks. We have an official meetup late tomorrow afternoon after my lunch shift. Seems crazy, right? But you know what? Something about him just feels right ….*

Fascinated, I turned the page.

I had a wonderful time with Kyle tonight. We walked the streets, rode the rail, and enjoyed the local sounds and tastes of my not-so-commercialized Chicago. Our agenda was not all that impressive, but the conversations were deep and meaningful. Am I crazy seeing this man? I mean, we are so different ... in every aspect. For starters, he's wealthy. Not only rich, but from an old-money Southern family as well. We live polar opposite lives.

Strangely, though, it feels like our differences are compelling a transparency between us that feels so natural. Our curiosity about each other's lives quickly led us to dive below the superficial surface and into uncharted waters, and tonight I felt my inner self come alive. Honestly, I really don't know what people thought seeing us laughing and carrying on together, but who cares? It's like he's unlocked something inside me that I never knew existed. We have plans for tomorrow ... lunch by Lake Michigan! I wonder if he is as intrigued with me as I am with him. Fingers crossed!

Mom's words fill my heart as I watch their story unfold like a fairy tale full of magical moments, endless kisses, and her unmistakable joy. My heart pounds as I read each entry. Mom's words vividly float off the pages and soak into the gaping hole in my heart like a thirsty sponge. I marvel at their romance, feeling her happiness deep inside my core. Photographs scattered throughout the journal's pages validate their whirlwind affair. Proof. This journal, titled "One," reads like a romance novel, except I know it wasn't fiction. Their captivating story makes me pause to ask the question: "What if?" But there can never be a what-if because their story has already been written; the ink has long since dried with no possibilities of a different ending.

At some point late in the night, my eyelids surrender to a deep sleep where my dreams animate Mom's journal entries. It was as if I had an out-of-body experience, but not as myself—as Mom. Her descriptions, heart-fluttering moments, and secret feelings were exposed to me as if I had the incredible ability to jump inside her body and experience her romance firsthand. It sounds creepy, but it wasn't.

In my dream, I saw their relationship more clearly as her vivid words send me back in time, witnessing their story unfold. I watched Mr. Mercer effortlessly flash his brilliant smile at Mom as they planned for their future, wrapped in each other's arms. I stood on the outskirts, stretching out my fingers to wake them up from their love-sick trance. They were oblivious to me, like I didn't even exist in their world. They were locked on to each other, blocking out all distractions. My heartbeat sped up, knowing my time was running out. I needed to tell them I'm their daughter and ask them questions only they can answer. They need to see we are a family. In the depths of my sleepy state, I am semi-aware of my vocal pleas breaking the barriers of my dream and filling the silent space around me. Crying, I beg, "Please, Mom, look at me! Please, Mom! I'm here."

The intoxicating dream slowly starts to slip away. With consciousness creeping into the edges of my mind, I fear I might forget everything the dream revealed to me. I desperately try to memorize their loving devotion and their obvious display of affection. I squeeze my eyes tighter, willing myself to stay in the dream and be near Mom. The vision of them together quietly resurfaces. However, my attempt at capturing her happiness to store it in my heart forever backfires. I watch her pull away from Mr. Mercer's arms with an understanding smile. She looks at me for the first time, peaceful and content, as she vanishes into thin air. I reach out for her, crying for her to come back, but she's gone. It's just me and Mr. Mercer, both left standing alone.

The morning sun's piercing light pries its way through my gauzy curtains, landing on my closed eyelids. I roll over, knocking the journal off the bed and suddenly remember Mom's gift. I lean over to carefully collect her journal and begin reading where I left off, but her tone now speaks of heartache.

Our plans are over. Our love, this child growing inside me, our future ... the slate has been wiped clean. I'm in shock! I just don't understand. He sounded so cold and legalistic, nothing like the man I knew and trusted. He said I can't join him in Texas because his family won't approve. Do they know I'm poor? Is that it? Do they not like the fact that I don't have a fancy pedigree? I don't know. The conversation ended almost as quickly as it started, without any explanation or real answers. Tears flowed like rivers from my eyes. I could barely speak, my throat tied itself in a knot. His harsh words wreaked havoc on my entire body. "Gabrielle, we can't do this anymore. It's time for me to get on with my life and get serious about my future—and you're not in it." I tried reminding him of us, and my love, but he tossed me aside like trash, claiming I was too young to understand, too naive, too wrong for him. The last thing he said was, "This isn't up for debate—you can't change my mind. Pretend like we never met. You disappear from my life and I'll disappear from yours. It's over, Gabby." And then he hung up ... a dead line and a broken heart.

I must have sat here crying and rehashing that agonizing phone call and our love story for hours. My hands cradled my stomach where proof of our love grows deep inside me ... and he has no idea. What do I do? This is not how this was supposed to happen. I wonder if knowing about the baby would make him fight for us? But do I really want to be with a man who only chooses me out of responsibility? If not, there's only one option left ...

My heart hurts for my mother as I swipe the angry tears off my face. I take a couple of deep breaths and wonder if I can handle any more of this story ... then I turn another page.

It's been a couple of weeks, and yes, I'm still incredibly sad. So, let's add insult to injury and tack on morning sickness and massive mood swings. I'm doing this alone ... pregnancy and planning to be a parent. Of course, Jo is by my side trying to keep my spirits up and cussing Kyle every chance she gets. But she'll never be the other half of this baby's parenting team. It's all on me. Never in a million years would I have imagined I'd be in these shoes.

Let's face it, this is never a girl's dream ... to be an unwed mother. I thought our love was real. We talked about starting a family together. I was ecstatic and so looking forward to telling him his first little one was on the way! Now he'll never know.

After the things he said to me, I'm not sure he would even want to know, but he's really not given me a choice. Why would I want my sweet baby to be around people who hate me even before they've attempted to get to know me? I would die before I let my child grow up around that kind of discrimination and ignorance.

As I finish reading a few more painful entries, the smell of pancakes and syrup drift into my room and awaken my famished stomach. I stumble out of bed, quickly freshen up, and head downstairs toward the cadence of Aunt Jo's booming laughter.

"Well, morning sunshine!" Aunt Jo greets me in an overly chipper mood.

"Morning," I grumble sleepily. Cheerful chatter with these people is something I don't feel up to, especially right after reading Mom's last few entries.

"Glad you finally decided to grace us with your perky disposition. I almost ate all those pancakes Mrs. Mercer's been saving for you," Aunt Jo says lightheartedly as she scrapes her fork across her empty plate, savoring the last taste of buttery syrup.

Mrs. Mercer smiles, shaking her head at Aunt Jo's nonsense. She stacks three very large chocolate chip pancakes neatly onto a plate, arranging hefty slabs of butter on each layer. The creamy butter slowly waterfalls down the stacked edges into a buttery moat I plan to sop up with my pancakes.

I shoot Aunt Jo an I'm-not-in-the-mood look, then silently cover my cakes with syrup before cramming a large bite into my mouth. I continue puzzling over Mom's journals. Why would Mom want me to know all her pain *after* sending me here to live with the people who inflicted it? She wasn't good enough for him so they ruined her life, and I'm supposed to somehow ignore that and embrace them?

As these thoughts roll through my mind, my blood starts boiling. I angrily shovel in the pancakes, mouthful after mouthful, trying to keep myself from talking while I try to pin down my whirling thoughts. When my chest starts to rise and fall faster than normal, I get up and throw my dirty dishes in the sink. I hear a few telltale cracks as I turn, ready to barrel upstairs to be with Mom. *I don't care. I hope I've broken them.*

"Hey!" Aunt Jo barks. "Did you just break the Mercers' plates? Apologize now, young lady!"

I stop but keep my back to them. "What do they care? They can just throw them away and buy new ones!" I say aggressively.

"Marni! You better get control of your tongue and attitude! Learn to treat those who care for you with respect." My aunt's voice slows down to let her words sink in.

"I would, *if* I had any of those people." I look from Aunt Jo to Mrs. Mercer. Aunt Jo's face flushes with embarrassment as Mrs. Mercer stands completely shocked. Granted, Mrs. Mercer hasn't read Mom's words, but Aunt Jo lived it with her. Can she really blame me? "Just. Leave. Me. Alone!" Hurling my words at them through gritted teeth, I storm out of the room.

At the top of the stairs, I hear Mrs. Mercer's voice as she tries to persuade Aunt Jo that everything will be all right. I am not sure what Aunt Jo is saying or doing, but by the way Mrs. Mercer sounds, I imagine Aunt Jo is wound up tight and ready to snap. It actually sounds like Mrs. Mercer is trying to comfort and console Aunt Jo, but that doesn't surprise me. She's perfect … isn't that why he chose her?

I listen to the muffled sounds through the walls, their words and sentences as indistinct as a kindergartener's words in a game of telephone. I half hope Mrs. Mercer will threaten to send me back with Aunt Jo, but it sounds like she's trying to buy more time with me. Whatever damage I intended to inflict seems to temporarily affect the wrong person.

Frustrated, I shut myself in my room and focus my attention back to Mom.

Perspective. It's been a hard few months since Kyle disappeared from my life, our lives. I found out yesterday that this bubble in my belly is a healthy, amazing girl! It was hard sitting in the doctor's waiting room, alone, while all the other expecting mothers cuddled up next to their men. But I did it ... I sat all alone. Jo offered to skip work so she could sit with me, but I knew I needed to do this on my own. I tried not to think of him, but I couldn't help but wonder what Kyle was doing. Was he happy? Would he have been here with me if he'd known about her? Blinking back the tears of all the might-have-beens, I made a choice ... to be strong. Acknowledging the fact that he's missing a backbone allowed me to put my future and my choices into perspective.

In my mind, Kyle is dead. The man I knew and loved died in a single phone call. I loved him, but I can't keep mourning a man who so easily abandoned me. It's just not worth any more tears. Besides, I have to conserve my energy for this sweet baby girl! I will always remember and love my "Chicago Kyle." Somewhere deep inside me, I hope he finds what he wants. It will be my goal to keep him in my prayers ... knowing that God's love is the only way to fully overcome the pain. For my sanity, this will be my last entry on the subject of Kyle. Lord, release me completely from this hurt, bless our baby girl, and make him happy.

I sit dumbfounded at Mom's ability to flip the switch, but she did exactly as she said ... she never mentioned Mr. Mercer, their romance, or her heartbreak again. Page after page detailed Mom's pregnancy like an autobiographical account of a significant event, which it was. She recorded how she felt, what she ate, and her excitement to meet me, leaving nothing she felt or experienced unaccounted for. My heart lightens as Mom's soft and familiar tone begins pulsing with the giddy anticipation of being my mom. She was on the upswing, riding the wave of hope into the unknown future.

I can't believe that tomorrow is the day. I'm being induced! I'd be lying if I said I wasn't nervous. I'm a tad bit scared. What woman isn't, though? It doesn't matter, she's worth it. I can't wait to hold my sweet baby girl! Jo is absolutely beside herself! She's been sleeping over the past few nights just in case this little one decides to come on her own. Thank goodness we all will meet her tomorrow because Jo is a nervous wreck. As I write these last words before I go to bed, Lord, I pray for this baby. Pray for her health, happiness, and a fullness in your love. I also pray that her father, name not to be mentioned again, is happy. I can't wait to cradle my sweet gift in my arms tomorrow!

Her entries transport me back in time, allowing me to walk beside her and fully experience the journey that is new motherhood.

Marni's first week at home has been a learning experience for us both. No one prepares you for being a new mom. The days and nights are long, but we're making it. When I hold Marni, my heart soars to heights unimaginable … a sweet peace settles deep in my soul. The sweet smell of her soft head as it rests on my chest fills my heart with joy. My heart continuously feels as if it's going to burst, I'm so full of love for this child. Thank you, Lord, for the gift you've blessed me with in Marni.

Over the next couple of hours, I pour through months of very short entries, tracking my growth progress and monumental milestones against her personal obstacles. Mom's writings are sporadic in style and content. Some entries were scribbled down quick and messy, whereas others were carefully recorded to a degree that pains me. She goes into great length about having to give up her dream of culinary school. Even though they offered her an extension until after I was born, Mom's constant money troubles held her back. My heart aches as I read her words. *My culinary dream is dead. My only dream now is Marni.*

She couldn't afford culinary school—she could barely afford me. She confides in her journal how hard it is to be a single parent. Her constant struggle was securing a decent-paying job and then keeping it without losing her paycheck to babysitting. She writes how she established an innovative bartering system to pay friends for babysitting—cooking, cleaning, childcare, whatever.

Despite all her obstacles, including sleep deprivation, she still managed to capture her unwavering love and devotion to me and us.

She wrote about quick outings to the grocery store, the mall, the park, and Aunt Jo's house. A giggle slips out from under my breath as I recall Mom always claiming neither of us slept for most of my first year. She insisted her goal was to "tire me out." Her voice echoes off the pages of her writings, captivating my senses and rational thinking.

A shiver ripples down my spine as I envision her sitting next to me, leaning in, her head slightly tilted to the side as she watches me absorb her words. Strange as it sounds, I know she's here. Looking up, I expect to see her dark-chocolate eyes staring back at mine, verifying my supernatural intuition. But of course, she's not there. At least, not physically. Long shadows fall heavy onto the brightness that surrounds me as I submit to the truth I know all too well. I will never be able to wrap my spindly arms around Mom's body. Not ever again.

I shut the journal and hang my head as fresh tears wet my cheeks. These journals are more than I can swallow. It just hurts too much to be inside her head and hear her thoughts when I can't talk to her about them. As a cocoon of sadness starts to envelop me, Aunt Jo's voice gets progressively louder and closer, which means she is heading my way. *Great. Just great.*

Aunt Jo uncharacteristically taps on my door with one knuckle as she gingerly swings it open. Audibly exhaling frustration, she inches her full presence into my room and plops down next to me on the bed. "Marni, honey, you've been up here for half a good day. Why don't you come down and join the family?"

"No," I squeak out sharply as my eyes dart away.

"What do you mean, *no*? You were unbelievably rude at breakfast. I think the least you can do is come join the living and be polite. Don't you?" She says in a matter-of-fact way. This isn't a question, but a command posed semi-delicately.

"No, they're fine without me. In fact, they prefer it that way."

"Why on earth do you think that? Did someone actually say those words to you? Have they hurt you in any way?" She pauses briefly, ready to hear my case, but I don't take the bait. "Seems to me these people really like you ... at least, the *normal* you."

I pull my knees into my chest and sit, stubborn as a mule, boring a hole through Aunt Jo's forehead. *Because you're fine without me*, I want to say, but she doesn't deserve any of my reasons. I do not have to justify my feelings to the woman who gave me up. I feel like Mom—loved then fully abandoned. My hurt and anger swirl like a tornado in my head. I am trying to stay calm, really I am, but my mouth just won't cooperate.

"I can't believe you, Aunt Jo! Trying to be all buddy-buddy now, talking about my feelings and this situation you let Mom sentence me to. You've called all the shots since Mom passed, but I'm through doing it your way. If I have to stay here with these hypocrites for the full six months, fine! But after that, I'm done! I'm not a Mercer and never will be. And by the way, I don't see myself going back to live with you either. You've broken my trust—forever." With tears squirting out of my eyes, I jump off my bed and shove at her hefty body until I have forced her into the open doorway.

She grabs hold of the doorframe and shifts her weight forward, blocking my attempts to push her out of my room.

"You done throwing yourself a pity party, missy?" she asks, looking both hurt and angry.

I furrow my eyebrows in thought while she inhales a large breath to sustain the rant I feel coming.

"Well, you are a foolish little girl if you think you're the only one missing the way life used to be. I fulfilled a promise I made to my best friend, my sister, but that doesn't mean that it doesn't hurt like crazy," she says.

Our anger has propelled us down the hallway into a more public arena, landing at the top of the foyer where Mr. and Mrs. Mercer are receiving his parents directly below us. They look up at the scene, but I don't care. I know I was foisted upon their family, that my presence is an unfortunate burden. I look down at the small crowd and target my ugly tongue on *him*.

"I'm sure he misses the way life was before Mom died even more than both of us," I spit out my words, pointing an accusing finger at Grumpa Mercer.

"Marni! Your mouth needs a good scrubbin' with bleach," Aunt Jo snaps, horrified.

"You'd like that, wouldn't you? Scrub the poor white trash right off my skin. Maybe the Mercers wouldn't be ashamed of me then?"

Aunt Jo gently grasps the edges of my shoulders and gets on my level. Something softens in her eyes as she says, "Honey, I feel deep in my bones that you're misreading this." She waves her arm in the air. Our eyes lock, her stare intent on deescalating my outbursts and easing the building tension downstairs.

I drop my head in defeat and say in a controlled voice. "I haven't misread a word. It's all in black and white in the box of journals Mom left me. I know how Mom was cast aside without a second thought or a fight." I turn back to face Aunt Jo and plead, "I know her hurt, her pain. I can't handle what he did to her! Can't you see? I've been living with the enemy. They loathed Mom and hurt her so badly, and now you're forcing me to live with them. I'm a constant reminder of the one thing, the one person, they wanted to forget—my mom." I spew the words over the banister toward the head of the Mercer family and bolt down the hall into my room, slamming the door with all my strength.

I sulk in my room, silently sobbing while thumbing through more journals filled with Mom's memories of our life together. Mom had stacked the sixteen journals in order, first for the year Mom found out she was pregnant with me, then one for each year of my life, and finally the last one that was only partially filled. I want to get to that last journal, but Mom's instructions were very clear: "Read the journals in order to receive your final gift."

After a couple more hours of reading, the scent of Mrs. Mercer's cooking floats upstairs, tempting my appetite. I grab at my growling belly, remembering I've only eaten a late breakfast today. But how can I possibly go down and face everyone? I can just hear the triumph in Aunt Jo's voice, "Well, well," she would say in a smug way. I weigh the pros and cons. Pro: I get to eat. That is a huge plus. Con: I leave

Mom alone in my room, not to mention, I'd have to see everyone and deal with Aunt Jo.

"Cons win," I say, squeezing my stomach and willing it to be quiet.

The scene I create in my head isn't so bad. I picture Mrs. Mercer expertly preparing and plating her delicious creation for the family, forks clinking against knives while glasses full of sweet tea land solidly on the wooden table. The aroma of the feast wafts upstairs, carrying with it soft laughter and murmurings of pleasant conversation. I am sure the girls are prancing around in their princess costumes, encouraging Aunt Jo to tap into her colorful imagination.

I prop myself up against the closed door and rest my heavy head in my hands. Now that I've gotten my runaway emotions under control, I'm simply overcome by sadness. I can't believe I've ruined everything, the little happiness I had here. Deep down, I know most of the Mercers are trying to accept me, but who could blame them if they all threw in the towel now? I look at Mom's picture and ask, "What have I done?"

Slowly, I hear a muffled disagreement creep up the staircase.

"It's fine. No, really. I want to," Mrs. Mercer states.

"Well, it is your house, but she doesn't deserve to be pampered," Aunt Jo argues.

"Knock, knock." Mrs. Mercer raps softly on my door. "Marni, I brought you some dinner."

I stand up, unlock the door, and open it to find Mrs. Mercer holding a tabletop tray with iced sweet tea, homemade lasagna, a green salad, wedge of watermelon, and a slice of warm, buttery bread. My body responds to the sight with a victorious growl, which puts a delicate smile on Mrs. Mercer's face.

She walks into the room, dodging the journal landmines scattered across the carpet. I watch her place the tray on top of the desk before looking around at all the opened books. "Are all these from your mom?"

"Yes." My one-word answer feels sufficient.

"What a special gift. I know you need time with her words and memories." She pauses, then continues once I make eye contact. "Marni, I don't know everything that happened in the past. And I don't want to presume I know all your thoughts and feelings. But, trust me when I tell you that just because I don't understand everything you're feeling doesn't mean I don't feel your pain. Believe me when I say that I hope, one day, you'll want to come talk to me and let me be there for you. You *are* part of this family, and we all understand how difficult this is for you. You're grieving, and we expect your emotions to be unpredictable, borderline irrational at times. There are no hard feelings for what's going through your mind and coming out of your mouth, okay? I get it—we all do—and we are here for you when you're ready." She walks toward the door, grabs the doorknob, and adds, "There's warm peach cobbler with vanilla ice cream downstairs if you'd like to join us for dessert. Come down and get some whenever you're ready." She smiles sweetly and then pivots out, closing the door behind her.

Just before she pulls the door shut, I swallow the knot in my throat to say, "Thank you, Mrs. Mercer." She gives me a gentle nod before leaving me in peace.

CHAPTER 33
Lauren

As soon as I leave Marni's room, I have to remind myself to breathe. I lean against the wall, and it's as if time has cruelly and violently thrown me back to my own formative teenage years where I felt I was drowning in shattered dreams. The ghost I've tried so hard to escape is alive in Marni's eyes. It's not the same ghost, but I recognize the pain and despair of what might have been. My story didn't write my mother into an early grave, leaving me with strangers in a foreign place, but I understand her pain.

It took years for me to even start believing I could trust anyone again. It's not fair, but the reality is that our perceived truths become heavily skewed based on our past experiences. So, for me to trust and fully love a man after my father's scandalous second family fiasco speaks volumes to how far I've come since my senior year in high school. Don't get me wrong, I dated plenty of eligible guys, but it was all a charade. My heart was never really searching for a perfect fit. It was too busy checking for leaks and holes, guarding me from the one thing that would eventually save me: love.

I pause at the top of the stairs, looking at the montage of framed pictures that cascade down the hallway. My eyes settle on one of my favorite pictures of Kyle and me—our engagement picture. I remember that day, that moment, like it was yesterday. We were sitting on top of an old rock wall, waiting for the photographer. Kyle was staring into my eyes, smiling as big as Dallas while I laughed at something he'd just said, my head slightly tilted back. One arm wrapped around my waist as his other hand secured my bent legs over his lap. We never heard the camera snap, but the image produced was so beautiful and organic. I smile at the memory, remembering how magical the promise of us felt.

I met Kyle in the fall of my senior year in college at a tailgate party before the football game. My girlfriends and I were on the hunt for some free food and drinks before the game. Bouncing and flirting our way from tailgate to tailgate, we finally decided we'd had enough entertainment and pointed ourselves toward the stadium. Kyle and his friends were near the party zone, practicing their spiral throws when a foam football got away from them and pelted my friend in the back.

"Excuse me?" I defended my friend as I picked up the spongy ball and chucked it at their heads. Kyle caught it and immediately ran up to apologize for his friend's terrible aim. He was handsome—not in a boyish, cute way, but more like the sophisticatedly rugged type. His brilliantly blue eyes contrasted magnificently against his long, dark lashes, sparkling intensely with a smile that accented his beautiful face. His blond wavy hair complemented his naturally tanned skin, which defined his muscular body. He was beautiful. I couldn't deny the instant attraction.

"Please forgive my friend's rudeness. Will y'all join us for sliders and beer?" Kyle asked with hopeful enthusiasm. And that was when it started—my heart's great thaw. It took a couple of months of dating, but the walls around my heart started to crumble. In all honesty, I knew he was different from the pack the moment we locked eyes. Kyle would later profess knowing I was his perfect match the moment he heard me confront the errant football-player wannabes.

Months went by, and we spent every possible moment together. He was a young lawyer in his father's firm, and I was finishing up school to be a teacher. I was quickly introduced to his family, whom I absolutely loved! They were the ideal package, complete with two parents still married after a lifetime of love and memories. I was enthralled by their legacy, which made it easier to let my guard down and picture a different family life than I had. I figured if a man was raised with parents devoted to loving each other, then the chances were solid their son would follow in their footsteps. And so, it happened ... I fell in love. We dated throughout my senior year, got engaged that spring, and married at the end of our first summer. To some, it might have seemed fast, but we couldn't wait to start our lives together. We had it all: love, romance, adventure, and each other ... until our idyllic lives were rattled with the news of another daughter.

I assumed I knew everything about Kyle, so I empathize with Marni and completely understand her anger toward all these surprises and huge life changes. I get she's hurting and feels lost. If only she could see we are in this boat together. It seems like we all got a little blindsided with her mom's passing. But it's too late to point fingers and dodge blame—this is just how it is. No matter how we got here, I took one look at a lost, scared girl on our doorstep and instantly knew we were her home. Now I just have to make her believe that.

They say hindsight is twenty-twenty, and I get it. Part of me wonders if everything I went through with my family was God's way of preparing me for Marni. Maybe it was, maybe it wasn't. Either way, I know now I must channel the turmoil of my past into helping Marni because I may be the only person in her life who can semi-relate.

CHAPTER 34
Marni

It takes every ounce of energy to put on fresh clothes and head downstairs for a late breakfast. The abnormally quiet house creaks against each footfall down the stairs. I startle at the noise, not wanting to disturb the silence. I begin tiptoeing toward the kitchen and realize it's too quiet. With Aunt Jo here and my unpredictable moods, I wonder if Mrs. Mercer decided to take the girls to the country club.

Carefully making my way through the house into the kitchen, I notice the dead silence. Where is everyone? Did they really all leave me here alone? As I turn into the kitchen, I see Aunt Jo sitting there, calmly sipping her fragrant coffee. Her back faces the garage, pointing her body and attention squarely at the main entrance into the kitchen. She waits for me, cool and calm. I know this look; Mom wore it well when she was disappointed in me.

"Well … good morning, sunshine. How are you feelin' today?" Aunt Jo asks, raising her eyes over the top of her coffee mug to meet mine.

"Fine. Where is everyone?"

"Mrs. Mercer took the girls out to run errands. I asked them to give us some time together, just the two of us. They were totally fine with that. I'm pretty certain they're all a little scared to be around you right now," she adds, trying to insert some humor. "They're used to the two little darlings, still in that sweet stage, not your unbalanced teenage hormones."

"Not in the mood, Aunt Jo," I say in my most grudging voice. "You know, you could have gone with them."

"Not today. But I did ask them to pray for us. Pray the Lord blesses me with energy and provides you with some good sense. Heaven knows we need all the prayers we can get right now." She pauses for effect before changing gears. "So, you hungry, sweet girl? Mrs. Mercer made lemon blueberry muffins for us. She sure is thoughtful, don't you think?"

I know this strategy. First, you state the obvious, something you know people already see. Then you make them agree to the understood statement and eventually use this against them later in an argument. Of course she made us muffins; of course she's thoughtful; of course everyone loves her ... ugh! I hate she is all these things because it means Mr. Mercer never gave Mom a second thought after he abandoned her. Instead of agreeing, I swipe a muffin, set it on a paper towel, and carry it to the table. I position myself directly across the round table from Aunt Jo, anticipating a heated conversation.

"Well, what's been going on in your room? Anything new to report?" Aunt Jo cheerfully inquires.

"Nothing I want to talk to you about," I snap, sinking my teeth into the fluffy muffin.

"Girl, do we really need to go another round? Surely, that last battle was just as exhausting for you as it was for Mr. and Mrs. Mercer and those poor old grandparents."

"You don't know anything," I say viciously, making her eyebrows shoot up in astonishment. "Yeah, that's right, you don't. But I do. I know the truth about it all, about me, about *them*, about Mom's disappointment and heartbreak. I know! Not you!" I can't stop the angry words as they roar out of my mouth and more tears are unleashed.

"You think I'm in the dark just because you have her journals? Looky here, sweet girl. I *lived* those journal entries. I know things she never wrote down. Your mom and I lived each other's highs and lows. Not a day went by that we didn't talk and confide in each other. And because of that, I can tell you beyond a shadow of doubt that this"—she waves her index finger like a tornado in the space between us—"is not how she envisioned life going for us, especially for you. She wanted to be with you forever, but since that wasn't going to happen, she made plans." She takes a deep breath to calm her frazzled emotions. "You have to try to look past what happened and see how your mom moved forward because that's what she wants you to do. I know you need more time, Marni, but you will have to acknowledge your pain, then push forward and live."

Silent tears pool in the creases of Aunt Jo's face. She picks up a loose napkin and dabs at the corners of her eyes. "You're right about one thing. I don't know what's in that last journal. I know it's something special and personal she wrote just for you. Please skip to that last one. I'm not here for very long, and I need to be sure of where we stand."

"Mom said I had to do them in order. I can't ... I don't want to ever finish reading Mom's words and thoughts," I admit, crying into the palms of my hands as I let the world around me go dark. That's when I feel her soft, cushiony arms wrap around my shoulders, cradling me while I bawl. After a few minutes, I catch my breath. With so much sorrow and remorse, I confess, "I'm so sorry, Aunt Jo."

She shushes me as her soft hands gently stroke my hair like Mom used to when I was a little girl. "It's okay ... it's okay ... it's okay," she softly whispers in my ear as if we both need convincing. "You know, your mom is always with you. Her words and love don't end with these journals; they're just something to help you get through this difficult time. Where are you in the journals?"

I temporarily pause my erratic breathing and snuffling to release a sigh of pure sadness. "I'm in my tenth year, so that would be the eleventh journal. I wish I was farther along, but her journey is taking a toll on me, like an emotional rollercoaster." Reading nonfiction is always more powerful than fiction because you know what you're reading really happened; those people genuinely had those thoughts and felt those feelings. So, multiply that understanding to the nth degree when considering how relevant her story is to my life.

"How am I supposed to process it all?"

"How do you mean?" Aunt Jo asks.

"Well, Mom retells her love story and breakup as this tragic fairy tale, which is almost more than my heart can handle. I mean, the drama around her breakup has left me with a sour taste, opening the door to more questions, concerns, and my personal paranoia of where I belong."

"I'm not sure I follow ..." her voice trails off, encouraging me to continue.

"It's been hard reading about every milestone and adventure in my life, knowing that Mom experienced parenthood alone. I know she was thrilled to be my mom, always proud of me, but I can't help feeling like her heart kept hurting a little each day, knowing that he was not a part of the family they created together." I look at Aunt Jo and confirm the question I see floating just beneath the surface. "She never says these things. It's just a feeling I get, a daughter's instinct."

"Marni, she was at peace with her life, and she loved having you at the center of her world," she says.

"Aunt Jo, I don't know if I can read any more words just now. I'm so tired of feeling sad and mad at the world."

"I know, sweet girl, but it will get better. With time, all wounds heal. You need to trust your mom. She was always a woman with a solid plan. Right?" Aunt Jo winks and smiles at the description of her sister.

"Yeah." A strange bubble of laughter pops out as I remember just how prepared Mom always was for anything. She always knew where we were going, what to expect, and never left home without an eclectic assortment of medicine and necessities tucked inside her enormous purse at all times. Surprises were only in the form of gifts. Other than that, she always seemed to know what was waiting around the next corner. Maybe Aunt Jo is right. Maybe Mom could see what I can't right now. "It's really okay if I read that last journal today and save the others for later? I mean, I do remember a lot of what's happened over the past four years anyway, and that's pretty much everything that's left. So, what do you think?"

Smiling, Aunt Jo flaps her free hand back and forth at me. "Go on upstairs, get cleaned up, and settle in to read that last journal. When you're finished, I'll be down here if you want to talk. Sound good?"

I grab another muffin, then bend down to kiss Aunt Jo on her cheek. As I walk out of the kitchen, I turn back and say, "Thank you. I've missed you so much."

"Missed you more, Marni," Aunt Jo answers, blowing me a string of exaggerated kisses.

A grin slides up my soggy face as I head upstairs. For the first time in weeks, my heart and attitude feel a little lighter. Clearing the air with the only other person who loved Mom almost as much as I did makes me feel like myself again—a girl with a family.

I walk into my room, quickly brush the fuzz off my teeth, wash my tear-stained face, and comb my fingers through my unruly hair. I am not put together, but I am in a lot better shape than before. I throw on some clean clothes, straighten my bed, and pull back my curtains for some natural light. Squatting beside my journal box, I carefully select the last book. This journal is different from the others—a red-leather journal with the letter *M* embossed in the center of the front cover. The binding cracks as I open it, evidence it has not been opened daily like the previous books whose pages easily lay open and flat. I hop onto my bed and arrange the large throw pillows behind my back and neck for added support. Then I tuck my plush throw blanket around my legs in cocoon fashion ... ready to read.

My dearest Marni,

How do you put a lifetime of love and adoration into a simple letter? I don't believe it's possible, but I'm going to try ...

It's been less than a year since we found out I was sick. We've lived and loved like tomorrow would never come, and I am so thankful for the gift of time with you. I know our separation will be hard on you—it tears me up inside to think of you in this world without me. You are and have always been my greatest gift, my greatest love.

By now, you've met your father, and I'm sure he already loves you with all his heart. Let him, and love him back. Love is a gift ... share yours! You'll be surprised how fast the heart heals when you choose to embrace love.

I will confess, Marni ... I am jealous of his wife. But not for the reasons you might think. I'm jealous that she's the one who will get to be with you, watch you go to college, get married, have your own kids. I wish I could tell her all about my precious, talented, loving, sensitive girl, but she will discover that and so much more on her own. She will see a girl who is brave and knows her heart and mind. A girl who I am so very proud of and know will do amazing things in her life.

Marni, try not to hold my mistakes against me or them. Life is just too short. This journal is my gift to you now. Use it to record all of your greatest moments and toughest trials. Use it to help you navigate your feelings, record your journey, and freeze your memories. Who knows ... you might have a daughter one day who wants to know your story too.

Remember, I will always be with you.
Mom

On the next page, turned sideways, Mom's hands are outlined in permanent marker with the words *I'll love you forever* written across her left palm and a full, red lipstick imprint inside the palm of her right hand. I gently trace her hands with my shaky fingertips, wishing they could lift themselves off the page so I can feel them hold me one more time. The letter, her hands, the kiss ... my heart and head swim in circles, trying to digest it all. I bundle myself into a ball, clutching Mom's hands tight into my chest and cry. Every pore in my body releases tears, tension, and sadness until my head begins to throb, and the room's edges start to resemble a watercolor painting. I lie back, resting my head against my pillow, as I try to calm myself enough to process everything I just read. Escaping the heartache and confusion,

I must have cried myself to sleep because I wake up to Aunt Jo lying next to me, gently combing her fingers through my hair.

"Hey, honey. You okay? You've been up here for hours. I was startin' to get worried," Aunt Jo whispers. "Is there anything you want to discuss?"

"I don't know. It hurts so much to try to do life without her," I say as fresh tears emerge. I reach over to the nightstand for a tissue and blow my nose forever. Finally, I look up. "She said they would love me if I let them, Aunt Jo, but I feel like an unwanted stray dog who's wandered into their yard, forcing them to care for it until the rightful owners can take it home. But I don't have a home anymore. And why should I even give them a chance when they didn't respect Mom enough to give her a chance?" Saying these words out loud bruises my already tender heart. "I mean, I don't hate them or anything. They treat me well, and I love those silly girls, but they don't know me yet. What happens when I'm no longer this new *thing* in their lives, and they realize what a burden I am? I'll just be a constant reminder of when Mr. Mercer went ... slumming." Aunt Jo and I both wince at my use of that word, but I continue on. "They're being nice right now, but they're all going to tire of me because I'm an outsider, not a part of them. They never planned on me."

"Well, that's the crazy thing about plans, Marni. They tend to change with or without our permission. Our plans are just our simple-minded concoctions of what we *think* we want and need, but God's plans are perfect beyond our knowledge, and they're concrete solid. They don't move ... it's set. You being here is not about their plans, your mom's plans, or anyone else's plans. God put you right here, in this family, for a reason. This family—the one *behaving* like a full-fledged family—*is* your family," Aunt Jo states with authority.

A grunt escapes as I roll my eyes and ponder the distinct difference between *behaving* and *being* someone's family.

Aunt Jo narrows her eyes, possibly detecting what I didn't say, and nods at me to explain myself.

"Grumpa is a problem," I tell her bluntly. I wait to see if she has anything to say to that. She just raises her eyebrows, encouraging me to continue. "The very first time we met, he compared me to a dog. Who does something like that? I can't unhear his words. Then he practically told me that he hates the idea of me and insists that I'll never belong." I chuck a small, ruffled throw pillow across the room. The gesture is bigger than the impact, but Aunt Jo understands my hurt and frustration. She softly rubs her hand in circles on my back, trying to soothe my nerves. "Aunt Jo, he is humiliated by me, claiming I have cast a social stigma on the entire family."

I don't know what she's thinking, but before my aunt can respond, I add, "I'm not stupid. I know they would all be a lot happier without me here. I'm like a puzzle piece you forcibly cram into the wrong space because you just don't want to deal with it anymore. Do you understand what I mean?"

"I do. This was never going to be easy, Marni. Your mom and I both knew it. But remember what your mom always said: 'Nothing good ever came easy.' Maybe you can't see it now, but time will be the judge."

With a deep sigh, I turn my attention out the window, mesmerized by the fluffy cloud formations drifting and morphing. Part of me knows Aunt Jo is right in trusting Mom. Until now, I always trusted Mom, but my confidence in her has dissolved into thin air. Her lying, her deceit, her betrayal—it can never be undone. She will never be able to answer my questions or explain herself. So, yeah, I question her now, why wouldn't I? I watch as a new blob of clouds begin to separate, revealing blue sky loosely shaped like a heart. I hold my breath, not wanting the wind to distort this beautiful image when the parallel hits me. Just like these clouds, life will never go back to the way it was. It's physically impossible. No matter what happens, my life is forever changed. I have to accept that.

I quietly lean into my aunt's embrace and swipe the jumbo tears balancing on the edge of my eyelids. Aunt Jo just holds me tight for a moment, then she picks up the journal and scans the room until she finds a pen laying on my nightstand. She opens the book to Mom's handprints and gently lifts my left hand, placing it on the adjacent page. She slowly and carefully traces around each knuckle and finger before switching to do my right hand.

"Marni, your mom will always be with you in your heart, thoughts, and experiences, just like I will always be with you, no matter what. And together, we will never forget her. One day, you will look back on these precious handprints and remember your pain and this time, but you will have survived and thrived through it all."

A tight lump in my throat blocks any verbal response, so I nod as tears flow freely. I hug her again, holding onto to her as tightly as I can. She readjusts my head, laying it against her broad shoulder like a baby while rhythmically stroking my back with her familiar touch. Patiently, she holds me until I pull away.

"Thank you, Aunt Jo. I love you so much."

"Aww, honey. Not more than I love you! But ... I am hungry. Do you think there's any decent grub in this palace?" Aunt Jo winks, and I laugh. Maybe the clouds are starting to lift ....

CHAPTER 35
Lauren

The sun is already up, perky and bright, bouncing its rays through the kitchen windows. I have been up for over an hour baking. I wrap up two egg, cheese, and bacon muffins and place them next to the large to-go cup of black coffee for Kyle. As he slips into the kitchen, I pass off his breakfast, and he lightly kisses me goodbye. I smile as he scoots out the door, knowing he'll be back in a few hours to take Marni to her golf lesson.

Ann lightly taps on the back door and sneaks into the kitchen. "Is anyone else up yet? Are the girls out of bed?"

"No, thank goodness! I want to talk through tonight's plan with you. Help me finish prepping these?"

"Of course," Ann says.

I cut the dough into pinwheels, and we begin to fill two round pans with extra-thick cinnamon rolls.

"So, are we all set?" I ask in a low voice.

"Yes, and I couldn't be more excited! It's supposed to be a beautiful night, and hopefully, a night we'll all remember," Ann says with a wink.

We cover the pans and set them aside just as we hear someone coming down the stairs. Jo rounds the corner, cheerfully greeting us with a smile and her peppy chatter. It amuses me how easily she enters a room and immediately claims the spotlight with such confidence and flare.

"We talkin' about tonight, ladies? Or something else on the menu … besides those sweet cinnamon rolls I smell?"

Ann and I both chuckle.

"Well, both actually. Have a seat. Can I get you some coffee, Jo?" Assuming a yes, I pour a cup and place the steaming mug in front of her. "We are all set for tonight, but do you think Marni will be up for it?" I ask, suddenly nervous the plan might fail or backfire on us.

"Oh yes. I think she might be turning a corner. We had ourselves a good talk and tear-fest yesterday. I think that poor girl has bottled up so much that reading her mom's love story might have been a little too much for her to fully process." Aunt Jo pauses, looking a little nervous for a second when she realizes whom she is talking to. "Sorry, yes. She'll be ready … I know it." She sheepishly brings the coffee mug to her lips and takes several long sips.

"Wait, why did her mom's love story upset Marni?" Ann asks as she glances in my direction.

"Gabby wanted Marni to understand that she was loved from the beginning. Loved by her mom and by her dad because Gabby believed there was so much love between them at one time." Aunt Jo stops and asks, "You sure you want me to talk about this?" She cocks her head, arching her eyebrows at me.

I slowly offer her a silent nod, encouraging her to continue. I need to hear what she has to say.

"Gabby's journals start off with a beautiful love blossoming. Then the stories describe my sister's heartbreak …"

For about twenty seconds, the room swallows up all the oxygen. I can't breathe. I glance at Ann who, like me, is sitting tall and stiff, like she's bracing herself for whatever comes next. My body feels both heavy and hollow as I try to push my feelings out of the equation.

Jo looks apologetically at us as she continues. "Unfortunately, it seems like reading Gabby's journals solidified Marni's sense of displacement. From the moment she arrived here, she kept telling me she didn't belong, didn't fit in. Gabby's journals reflect Marni's entire life, every memory and milestone. But, that first journal is not an easy read. Gabby was brutally honest with her pen, and Marni identifies with her pain."

"What pain is that?" Ann asks.

"Being unwanted and not enough."

I let out an audible exhale as I close my eyes and rest my palms against the table, hoping to steady my reeling thoughts. It's not as if I couldn't guess this was how Marni was feeling, but somehow, hearing it aloud makes it more painful.

"I'm not sure how to get Marni to see past the words my sister wrote in the heat of her broken heart."

I want to tell them both I understand feeling out of place and why I completely get where Marni is coming from, but this isn't about me. So instead, I simply say, "I get it."

Ann pats my hand tenderly and reaches across me for some napkins. She hands me one and clutches the other in her fist.

Clearing the knot in my throat, I add, "Marni is new to the family; she's new to us all." I take a deep breath and lean forward. "But it feels so right having her here. She fits, better than I ever could have anticipated. Don't you agree, Ann?"

Ann nods as she delicately dabs a tear from the corner of her eye.

Jo hesitates before posing her next question. "Do you, Ann? Do you think the whole family feels that way?"

Ann's head jerks up quickly, and her eyebrows furrow. "What did my husband do now?"

"Well," Jo says tentatively, "Marni told me some pretty awful things that he supposedly said to her. She said something about him comparing her to a dog?" Jo closes her eyes briefly and shakes her head. "She might have misunderstood him, but if he said anything like that, I might have a few words for him myself."

Ann looks like she might be sick. "I can't imagine that old goat outright compared poor Marni to a dog, but after learning about his interference with Kyle and Marni's mother, I'm not sure I know what he's capable of."

"Marni is convinced that he hates her and—"

"He doesn't hate Marni!" Ann exclaims. "He doesn't know her yet, that's true. But I've been with that man a long time, and I know that anyone willing to wage war and argue with him immediately gains his respect. I've seen him; he looks at Marni with admiration! Now, the old fuddy-dud probably did say hurtful things to that poor child, but I can guarantee he's feeling sorry about it now."

"Jo, I'm not going to make excuses for my father-in-law, but I do agree with Ann's assessment," I chime in. "I'm just not sure what to do about the two of them. Do you think she can move past whatever awful encounter they had initially?"

Jo lets out a sigh. "My sister wanted Marni to be surrounded by family who love her, living a life full of possibilities and happiness," she says, her voice starting to wobble. "I wanted that to be me, but I see now what Gabby already knew in her bones. Marni belongs here, with you."

Ann and I exchange a knowing look as Ann boasts triumphantly, "Oooo! I can't wait for tonight!"

I smile back at the two them, listening and daydreaming. My mind skips ahead, unveiling a future Marni's mom foresaw … a complete family. I picture us all together, celebrating birthdays, holidays, and all sorts of occasions as one big family, which includes boisterous Aunt Jo. I see me rolling my eyes at Kyle as our three girls team up against us, always protecting their sisterly bond. And when Marni comes home from college, I hear our family conversations starting with, *Remember when* … as we recall our favorite and funniest memories.

Another reality of Marni's situation strikes me. Marni and her mom had fourteen years of memories. She must feel like she's living in a deficit, always behind and unable to catch up. I, too, am feeling the paucity of a bond with my newest daughter, but that cannot be rushed. A smile touches my lips as I reassure myself we have the rest of our lives together to create loving memories.

Ann looks at me, then Jo, and smiles triumphantly. "It should comfort us all to know that Marni will not be able to escape a full-on Mercer family memory tonight."

The much-needed laughter breaks the tension, and as we drain the coffeepot, my two little princesses magically appear with the grace and silence of a small storm. We barely hold our laughter as they try to outdo each other by casting outrageous beauty spells from plastic wands onto the stuffed animals dangling from their tightened fists.

I get up from the table and slide both pans of cinnamon rolls into the oven. The girls bounce into two empty seats at the table between Ann and Jo, demanding their attention. They elaborately recount last night's dreams in imaginative detail, building on top of each other's vision like they shared the same dream sequence.

After we endure almost fifteen minutes of their storytelling, a sweet bouquet of cinnamon and sugar wafts through the air, eliciting toothy grins, and the girls squirm with sugary anticipation. Tickled, I pop out of my seat, retrieve both pans of gooey rolls, and promptly smother the tops with homemade cream cheese icing. In less than five minutes, a creamy, brown-speckled goo is smeared across the girls' faces.

CHAPTER 36
Marni

How can I face them? I ask my reflection in the mirror, a wave of insecurity washing over me. I'm sure my multiple Jekyll and Hyde performances have baffled and exhausted them—and embarrassed Mom—but that's really not me. That's not who I am.

Of course I know none of this is their fault. They didn't take Mom away from me and drag me down here. No, they're just as much a victim to circumstance and Mom's decisions as I am. And honestly, they've done so much for me and are trying so hard, it's overwhelming. Somewhere in the back of my mind, Mom's voice answers: *Own up to your actions, good or bad.*

As I wash my face and put on a new cotton dress, uncertainty consumes me. I feel myself straddling an imaginary fence with one foot firmly planted in the past while the other one reaches out, unable to secure a foothold in the present. The instability emotionally exhausts me. I fear picking a side of the fence will inevitably mean I have to let go of something so vital and fundamentally a part of me.

Before heading downstairs, I clasp my silver cross necklace around my neck. I gently run my fingers over the rounded-edged cross, aware of its sleek and sophisticated texture. Obviously, I never dreamed I'd live in a world without Mom. I can't help wondering if I'll ever stop asking, *Why Mom?* As I rotate the cross in my fingers, mesmerized by the light glinting off the silver, I remember something I heard years ago: "God promises rainbows after the worst of storms." Smiling, I tip my head down and kiss the cross pendant.

As embarrassed as I am about my behavior, it's time to face the Mercers. I understand what I need to do, but I'm scared. Banking on Aunt Jo's insistence that there really is nothing to fear, I head downstairs.

By the time I reach the kitchen, my heart pounds nervously, anticipating whether I'll be a disturbance or a welcome addition to their lively breakfast. Laughter echoes around the room, and my stomach grumbles a noisy demand just as my eyes land on plates of breakfast treats. I hesitate in the doorway, bracing for everyone's reaction.

The girls are too busy devouring breakfast and licking their fingers to notice me creeping into the room. But I see Mrs. Ann and Mrs. Mercer glance at each other. Was their look a wordless "Now what?" or a plea of "Please let her be okay."

Mrs. Mercer answers my silent quandary by meeting me more than halfway with her sincere generosity. I watch her place two large cinnamon rolls, an egg muffin, and mixed berries on a plate and set it in front of the open seat at the table, gesturing me to sit. My heart smiles at the realization that Mom would have liked Mrs. Mercer, seeing they shared the same love language: food.

I silently join the all-girls table without any reprimand or cautionary side looks from Aunt Jo. Could it really be this easy? Mrs. Mercer smiles at me, nodding slightly as she takes her seat.

"Good morning, Mrs. Mercer, Mrs. Ann," I whisper, my voice still groggy from last night's sleep.

"And what about me? Am I chopped liver?" Aunt Jo says, waving her hand at me. "You must not have seen my petite little ole self. Right, sweet girl?"

I roll my eyes, lips slightly parting in a deviant smile. "Of course, Aunt Jo. How could I ever miss you?" My sarcastic humor breaks the ice, permitting us all to laugh. Thank goodness!

Everyone devours their scrumptious breakfast, enjoying quality girl time while listening and laughing to the colorful stories the girls invent. Aunt Jo continually encourages them to embrace the spotlight by probing them to be more imaginative. More stories, more details, more expression. Obviously, she intends to keep the mood light.

After breakfast, Mrs. Mercer sends the girls upstairs to get ready for the day, and I volunteer to help them. As I'm heading up, a lightness sweeps over me as I watch Aunt Jo and Mrs. Ann plant themselves at the table and begin talking like old friends. I push back the dread of watching my aunt leave tomorrow. I think about what she said, how my mom wanted me to "just live." It's such a basic and simple statement, but when measured against her knowledge that her days were ticking off faster and faster, Mom's command feels monumental. She understood the value of time and the gift of another day. I take a deep breath and vow to seize this day.

CHAPTER 37
Ann

I pull into the garage and immediately notice James's golf clubs loaded onto the golf cart. I should have guessed—it's a beautiful day, a perfect "disciple day," which is a term my husband uses to describe the estimated twelve perfect days of weather we receive annually in central Texas. I am happy he'll be working from the golf course today since he insists his best thinking occurs on the greens. I know he's getting tired of the rat race, so today's change of pace will hopefully relax and rejuvenate him. Before that can happen, we need to chat. I wait in my car for a few long breaths, expecting James to run out the door, slightly flustered. When he doesn't appear, I know this means he's not hoping to make a last-minute tee time. We have time.

I gather up my strength as I head into the house. The smell of dark, rich coffee fills my senses as the bright, sun-filled kitchen greets me. I walk back to our bedroom and find him in the middle of his morning routine. He pops out a side grin and winks at me as he says, "Morning."

I echo his greeting, peel off my shoes, and head into the living room, waiting for him to emerge. I lean over the coffee table to pick up a small photo book stacked on top of travel picture books we've collected over the years. I flip through the pages that showcase Kyle, Lauren, and the girls' favorite memories from last year, and I smile at their precious faces. I can practically hear their laughter dancing off the pages as their joy radiates deep into my soul. As my heart swells with pride at their beautiful family, a terrible realization hits me. Of course I would prefer to deny any involvement or knowledge that Kyle's abrupt return home from Chicago all those years ago was anything but voluntary. On a deeper level, I knew something wasn't right. My mother's intuition suspected romantic trouble, but why ask? He was a man who surely understood what he was doing and why. But had I known the high stakes at hand, I think I would have encouraged him to follow his heart. My fingers stop flipping pages when they land on a picture of the girls laughing as they feed goats at the petting zoo. I flinch at the thought that if he'd chosen Gabby, then I wouldn't have these precious jewels in my life.

I stand up, set the picture book down before walking back to the kitchen to busy myself. An unrinsed coffee mug sits at the bottom of the white sink basin. Noticing the clean dishwasher hasn't been touched, I slide out the wire racks and begin putting everything back in its place.

I reach for my dish towel, run it under some hot water, and begin wiping down all the countertops. Crumbs litter the space where James ate a large bowl of cereal earlier this morning. As I rinse out the dirty dish towel and wring it out to dry, I hear James's footsteps coming down the hall.

"Hey, dear. I'm about to head to my office on the green. How was your breakfast with Lauren and the girls?" he asks with a grin. "Better than cereal?"

"Delicious as always, and very informative."

"Oh, really? How so?"

"Well, I got there early so Lauren and I could talk privately with Jo about Marni, without little ears present," I say, slightly over-enunciating those last words for emphasis.

"What could y'all possibly need to discuss further? You and Lauren are overreacting to Marni's mood swings. We can't walk on eggshells for six months."

"Not when *you're* the root of her problem."

"What?" James snaps, visibly irritated.

"Jo thinks Marni is ready to give this family a real chance minus one setback ... you."

He rolls his eyes and blows out a gust of hot air, like what I've said is either irrelevant or somehow taxing his patience.

Before he can interrupt, I continue. "Seems she's told Jo that she doesn't belong and isn't wanted in our family. You and I both know that's all you. I remember how you spoke to her here that afternoon."

He shakes his head, the silent response affording him time to formulate a respectable answer. "Well, it's true, and she knows it. She feels different because she is ... she's a whole world different from us. You can't bend over backward, trying to convince yourself, Marni, and the world that she's not. Because that's an impossible feat." His voice starts becoming edgy and defensive.

"You're such a hypocrite."

He flinches. I know he hates to be called a fraud, so my carefully chosen words hit him below the belt. His irritation shows as he slides his jaw back and forth, grinding his teeth.

"Do you remember where we started?" I prod. "Not here, not with all this ... we lived in a sloppy trailer park while you finished law school. Remember?"

He closes his eyes momentarily and shrugs. I know he would erase that part of his past if he could. No one knows about our trailer park days, and as far as he's concerned, no one ever will.

"That's irrelevant, Ann."

"I don't think so. You were always so antsy about fitting in—until you were at the top. Surely, you can understand Marni's insecurities, coming from nothing. It's not a far leap."

"I'm not saying poor people can't better their station in life."

"What are you saying, then?"

"It's simple. She's not one of us. She never has been and never will be a Mercer."

"Ugh! You infuriate me! How can you be so smart and so stupid at the same time?" I spit out. "She *is* a Mercer. She *is* Kyle's daughter. She *is* your granddaughter. When are you going to get with the program?"

"Ann, I know you adore that girl, but she and I have an understanding of sorts. Just leave it be."

"I can't because you're ruining that girl. You called her a bastard. I heard it with my own ears! You've gotten so hateful since Kyle told us about her."

"I—"

"I can't imagine saying the things you've said to anyone. Not anyone! Especially not my own flesh and blood."

James's face blooms with color. It's hard to know if he's angry or embarrassed, but at least I know something I said has gotten under his skin. "If you don't change your tune—"

"You're threatening me, Ann?"

"No, but Kyle might … with the girls."

He slumps against the kitchen counter, shocked.

"I didn't want it to come to this. I hoped you'd see how fantastic she is on your own, but you're too stubborn. Marni might be the best thing that'll ever happen to you, and you've ruined it, tossed her aside like trash." I shake my head, tear stinging my eyes. "Sticks and stones would have been kinder than the words you've thrown at her."

"What do you want me to do? I can't take back what's been said."

"Nope. Damage has been done. All I ask is that you talk to her like you would the girls. Be kind."

He glares at me, unwilling to admit he's wrong and I'm right. He lifts his wrist, shaking his watch loose, and peeks at the time. He's ready to end this conversation.

I take a deep breath, trying to figure out how to make this confrontation end the way I need it to. "I admit, there is some truth to what you said but only fragments of it," I concede. "Marni *did* grow up in a different world than our other grandchildren, but the reality is, James, she has as much of you in her as Lila and Annabelle."

Silence.

"You old, stubborn fool," I say, tossing my hands in the air. "Can't you see how alike you and Marni are?" Hot tears of anger bubble and spill out of the corners of my eyes. "She's a lovely young woman, and you've already missed fourteen years. Are you really willing to miss out on any more?"

"I didn't mean …" His voice trails off, uncertain of how to explain himself. He walks over to me and cups my chin in his hand, forcing me to look him in the eyes. "I do see, but it's hard, okay?" he admits. "I see all the little nuances and facial expressions that instantly remind me of Kyle. I hear myself coming out of her mouth sometimes. None of this, not Marni nor her mom, was what I had planned for Kyle. It's all gotten so complicated—the past and now—it's a tangled mess. I know what you think, but you're wrong. I don't hate her; I hate myself. Every time I see her, listen to her, and am near her, she brings out the worst in me because *I* know it's all my fault. I blame myself for all of it—her pain and Kyle's—fourteen years down the drain."

I watch his tough exterior crumble with remorse. His vulnerability softens his face, finally looking like the man I love. I reach up to hold his hands, but he drops them and turns his back to me. "I keep thinking about Lila and Annabelle. What if we'd missed it all? What if I was the reason Kyle missed out on fatherhood?" He turns back around; moisture rims his eyes. "We did and I am the reason … with Marni."

I grab ahold of his shoulders and plead, "So, do something about it."

He shakes his head, "You think an apology makes up for it? Marni's mother losing any chance of receiving support from Kyle or us? Marni growing up without her father, and Kyle not knowing he has a daughter?"

"It's a first step," I remind him, my tone firm and authoritative. He huffs and bites the inside of his cheek, a telltale sign he's mulling it over in his head. "Just give her an honest chance for both of your sakes. You two are more alike than you know."

"So, you think I'm the swing vote that will either persuade her to stay or go? That's a little ridiculous, don't you think?"

"You're her grandfather. You set the tone for this family; you have more power over this situation than you realize. She needs to understand she's welcome and belongs." I sigh, giving in to the emotional exhaustion that overwhelms my heart as he wraps his arms around me. I sink into his embrace, resting my head on his shoulder and wonder how I could love a man for well over half my life and still know what a cantankerous pain he can be.

I pull back enough to look into his eyes and ask one more question. "We both know what you've called her, but why did she tell Jo you'd love a dog more than her?" I tilt my head, raising an eyebrow as I wait with intense curiosity.

He drops his head and turns around, taking a few steps away from me. "That's not exactly what was said, but it's close enough."

"*What?*"

"It was the day that you submarined my golf game by forcing us to ride together for a few holes. I don't recall how it happened, but we started talking about how much I loved our dog, and she pointed out that I wasn't related to the dog by blood. She was pushing me, arguing my rationale! It was my golf time, for heaven's sake, not an interrogation. I didn't mean anything by it, I just wanted her to stop talking. We both know I love Bruno more than some people, but Marni was challenging me, and I didn't mean to do so much damage by meeting her head-on. I had no idea she'd take the conversation so seriously," he says in a defeated tone.

"I don't know what to say. Except, fix it. I don't know how, but you better find a way to fix things with your granddaughter. Dig deep and try for your sake and hers to make things right," I demand as fire blazes out of my eyes. I shake my head and start to walk out of the room. I turn to see him standing slack and unsure. "Go think this out on the golf course and don't you dare be late for this evening either."

CHAPTER 38
Marni

Earlier, Aunt Jo suggested we have a girls' day, just the two of us. "Show me the city!" she said. Mrs. Mercer swallowed a laugh, probably tickled, thinking how different Waco is compared to Chicago.

As I am getting ready for our outing, Lila and Annabelle run into my room and flop onto my still unmade bed.

"Marni? You wanna play dress-up with us?" Annabelle begs in her sweet, high-pitched voice.

"I can't today. How about tomorrow? I'm about to leave with Aunt Jo for the afternoon," I say.

"Oh. What are y'all gonna do?" Annabelle wonders.

"Shopping, I'm sure."

"Do you have time to fix our hair, Marni?" Lila asks, peering into the mirror at her wild, unruly hair.

"Hmm. How about you put on your outfits, and I'll meet you in the playroom in a few minutes to help you polish your princess looks," I offer.

Excited, the girls squeal as they flit out of my room like fairies. I finish applying some of the makeup Mrs. Mercer recently bought me and quickly tame my hair, trying to look extra special for my girls' date with Aunt Jo. Pleased with my efforts, I find the girls giddy and ready for my assistance in the playroom. Since I'm waiting on Aunt Jo to finish primping, I treat the girls to a glamorous makeover. They sit motionless while I swoop a peaches-n-cream blush over their cheeks, dab their lips with sparkly pink lip gloss, and paint their eyelids in rainbow arches of pastel pink, sapphire blue, and purple plum. I frame their dainty faces with two delicate braids and tie them together with oversized pink-and-purple bows. Ecstatic over their princess transformations, they decide I must introduce them to the royal court before I am permitted to leave with Aunt Jo.

I descend the stairs to find Aunt Jo and Mrs. Mercer sitting in the living room, casually chatting. With a loud, guttural sound, I clear my throat and announce, "Please welcome Her Majesty's royal princesses, Lila and Annabelle, as they grace our presence with their undeniable beauty." The girls not-so-gracefully rush down the stairs, eager to take center stage where they twirl like spindle-tops and admire the way their dresses flare. Within minutes, they become too dizzy to walk.

"Wow! Princesses in Texas! Who knew?" Aunt Jo teases.

"Princesses can be anywhere, Aunt Jo," Lila remarks with practiced princess swag.

"Yes, they can. Now, come over here and give me some princess hugs!" Aunt Jo instructs as she opens her arms.

Mrs. Mercer and I silently watch the blending of our families before she speaks. "Thank you, Marni, for fanning the princess fire with such beautiful hair and makeup. What an amazing big sis you girls have, right?" she says with a wink.

I meet Mrs. Mercer's eyes and smile, somewhat relieved the girls are oblivious to their mother's comment.

"Can I get a picture of the three of you?" she asks, pointing to me and the girls. Without hesitation, Lila and Annabelle strike their best poses while encouraging me to hurry up.

With my royalty duties temporarily suspended and pictures taken, Aunt Jo and I head out the door. Right now, today with Aunt Jo, is my time. It's my turn to enjoy the one-on-one time Aunt Jo planned for us before she leaves to go back home. Aunt Jo borrows Mrs. Mercer's car and drives us into town for a day of sightseeing, lunch, and window-shopping.

Before we walk into the first store, Aunt Jo says, "We aren't quitting until I've bought us both a special outfit to wear tonight for my send-off dinner."

Puzzled, I state the obvious. "You can't afford that."

"Well, with you and your mom not around, I've had a lot of time on my hands. I've been working a lot of extra shifts to keep my mind busy. My boss must've noticed 'cause I got offered a big promotion last month. My paycheck has gone up. I'm no Mercer," she winks playfully, "but I've got a little playing money now."

"Wow! Congrats, Aunt Jo! But you shouldn't spend money on me. Save it for yourself," I insist.

"Nah. It'll be way more fun treating us both, don't you think?"

I smile as I imagine Mom standing right beside us—just us girls, shopping.

We traipse in and out of stores, trying on the latest styles like we have unlimited time and money at our disposal until our stomachs remind us of the time. We decide to take a break at a local taco joint. My hot feet ache with exhaustion, so a chair and some food sound heavenly.

"Don't leave tomorrow, Aunt Jo."

"Oh, sweet girl." She hugs me tight and smooches my cheek. "Trust me, it's going to get easier. You're about to start school, make more friends, and before you know it, you'll be settled in here like a snug bug in a rug." She squeezes me tightly, then turns to sip her soda. "They're good people, Marni, who genuinely care about you. I hope you can see that."

"I know ... but it still doesn't make this any easier."

"Honey, these things take time, but it's all goin' to fall into place. God has a plan. We might not like some of His decisions, like Him calling your mom home, but He put you in the Mercers' home for a reason, and we gotta trust in that."

Inhaling, I nod slowly. "You sound like Mom. Always telling me that I'm not the one in the driver's seat. I know you're both right." I clear my throat and quietly add, "I worry that they may want me to forget who I am and become their version of Marni, a girl with a more appropriate past."

"What in heaven's name, child? Who's telling you to forget your past and us?" she screeches, waving her pointer finger in a triangular fashion to include Mom in the *us*. "First things first, you are loved more than you can handle. And we love *this* version of Marni, so don't go changing for anyone. And as for your past, you carry it with you. Cherish your memories, remember your past, and live in the present. It's your choice to make."

I'm so tired of all these feelings. I pick up my overly stuffed soft taco and take a huge bite, then shrug. Aunt Jo grins, satisfied. We are both ready to move on to other topics.

Throughout the rest of our lunch, we forecast what my new school might be like—the kids, the teachers, the activities, the outfits, my elective choices. It's nice to focus our attention on something different for a bit. My life has felt out of my control and truly exhausting for far too long now. I've been a victim of other people's actions, thoughts, or plans for what they thought I needed, without any input from me. But right now, in this very moment, my life feels almost normal, like I'm a typical teenager who holds about as much control over the options and choices in her life as the next girl.

We comb through several more stores until we finally discover the exact outfits Aunt Jo envisioned us wearing for her send-off party tonight. She decides on a butter-yellow blouse with ruffles on the sleeves and a loose-fitting pair of black pants. My dress, which she insists must complement her outfit, sits high on my collarbone with spaghetti straps that trace down my shoulder blades, stopping in the middle of my back, highlighting my bare shoulders. The trendy pale-blue dress is accented by a butter-yellow ribbon that creates the illusion of an empire waist. Small yellow-and-cream watercolor flowers dot the dress's skirt. It is a beautiful dress that makes me feel special. I stand next to Aunt Jo, concerned about the cost.

She shoves her hand into her purse and fishes out a wad of cash, grinning. "See? I told you not to worry. I've got us covered," she says and pays for the clothes. Pleased with our amazing finds, we load up the car and ready ourselves for one last errand, my errand.

"Okay, honey. Where to?" Aunt Jo asks as she backs the car out of the parking space and glides into the flow of traffic.

"I'd like to go to the art store ..." My reply sounds more like a question than a request.

"Sounds fun. Look up that address and guide us to it."

As we drive, Aunt Jo comments on the abundant natural beauty in what she terms my "new hometown." She marvels at how the massive oak trees allow their shade to relieve the sweltering roads and parking lots. She notices the splash of vibrant colors planted along the roads where countless butterflies dart from flower to flower. But the most amazing observation is the blessed absence of invasive buildings, stacked one right next to the other. Sure, there's a downtown here, but most of the buildings are compact in size and only take up a few blocks of space, unlike Chicago's downtown cityscape. She's always loved the old architectural buildings of Chicago. But here, in Texas, abundant space complements the classic architectural heritage. She says it's a breath of fresh air for her since walking through downtown Chicago can make you feel as insignificant as an ant.

"I envy you being in this place. It just feels so relaxed, like everyone's enjoying life at a slower pace. I love the thought of that, don't you? Makes me think of a simpler time ...." Aunt Jo's voice trails off as her mind no doubt recalls some long-ago memory.

After a ten-minute commute, we pull into the local art store. Since this is my first time inside the place, I have no idea what to expect. We step into a beautiful, massive space bursting with color that begs me to come and explore every nook and cranny. Aunt Jo and I weave in and out of aisles, mesmerized by all the pretty things that demand to be seen until we finally end up at the back of the store, staring into an overwhelmingly colorful inventory of art supplies.

"So? What are we in the market for, sweet girl?"

"I'd like to get some colored pencils ..." I hesitate before I continue. "I was thinking that's how I want to record my journal entries."

"Oh!" she exclaims, clasping her hands together in front of her chest. "What a wonderful idea!"

I smile. "You know drawing is like a kind of therapy for me. I feel like this art journal might be the perfect distraction that'll help me navigate life without Mom." I pause, looking at the white labels that line the row of the pricey colored pencils in front of me. "Art is my brain-break, my escape route. Am I making any sense?"

"Makes perfect sense to me. I know this will make your mom smile, knowing that you're making the journal yours, personalizing it with your creative touch. You know, she always treasured every picture and semblance of art you made for her. And she used to get such a kick out of your special Marni's Creations box you kept under your bed." A tear glistens in her eyes. "This idea is perfect, just perfect."

We browse for a couple of minutes until I lock on to a twenty-four-color set of pencils. I always wanted one of these "professional" pencil sets but had to settle for whatever could be found in the dollar store or Goodwill. I pick up a set and imagine my fingers wrapped around each color as I fill in the pages of my journal, crafting pictures and perfecting my doodling.

Aunt Jo's eyes watch me drift deep into art paradise. I know I'm being watched, but I'm not ready to leave the fantasy just yet. She bends over my shoulder and cheerfully asks, "Those the ones you want?"

Shocked and confused, I just look at her for a few seconds before I hang it back onto its silver hook. "They're too expensive," I state, matter-of-factly. "We should look in the school supply section, not in the artist area."

"No skimping today, not with all my promotion cash burning a hole in my purse. We're splurging, remember?" She grabs a sharpener, a special eraser hanging nearby, and a zippered carrying case. She pauses and looks me seriously in the eye and adds, "My only stipulation is that you show me some of your drawings in the very near future. I need to keep *my* Marni's Creations box current," she says, winking as she places the items in our basket.

I fling my arms around Aunt Jo's neck, incredibly grateful for her generosity. She chuckles as we both relish in the intoxicating happiness that envelops us like a bear hug.

We enjoyed a wonderful day together. But on the way back to the Mercers' house, I sink into the darkness that haunts the edges of my mind as I'm reminded my number-one fan and biggest supporter in the world is about to be thousands of miles away from me again. My head clouds with uncertainty. Why can't I push all the what-ifs out of my mind and choose to look ahead to the future Mom envisioned?

The car is too quiet. Aunt Jo looks at me, concerned. "What's wrong, Marni? Didn't you have fun today?"

"Of course!" I answer with a wobbly smile. "I'm just sad you're leaving. I need you here with me, Aunt Jo. Can't you stay and find a job here?"

"Marni, listen closely. There's nothin' I'd like better than to be with you always. I'd move in a heartbeat for you if that's what I thought was best." Her voice softens as she admits, "But I don't think that's what's best right now for you or the Mercers. You all need to make a go of being a family, and I don't want to be in the way." Trying to break the tension, she adds, "No one needs the added pressure of having to compete with little ole me."

"You're not in the way! Mrs. Mercer and Mrs. Ann love you, not to mention the girls."

Aunt Jo glances over and shushes me. Embarrassed, my cheeks burn red, like I've just had the back of my hand slapped. "Marni, if I was here with you in Texas, do you really think you'd give the Mercers a fair chance? They need time with you, just you, so they can discover what an amazing person you truly are. And *you*," she emphasizes, "need time to do the same with them."

"But, when will I see you again?" I burst out.

"Well, the Mercers have already asked me to come back Thanksgiving week." She cocks her head to the side.

Knowing her plans to return are already set in stone gives me hope. It isn't next month, but it isn't terribly far off either. "Okay," I say with more pluck in my voice than I feel. "Then tomorrow, let's say 'see you later' instead of 'goodbye.'"

By the time we pull into the driveway, it is late afternoon. Mrs. Mercer fusses over the girls' hair and outfits upstairs while Mr. Mercer is still at work. With the party only a couple of hours away, I hole up in my room, testing my new pencils on a loose piece of paper— drawing, coloring, and escaping. I spend an hour creating a quick sketch of Aunt Jo and I in our new outfits, walking in a park. I want her to have something special to take back with her to Chicago as a thank-you for her visit.

About half an hour before the party, I gently place each pencil back inside the box in rainbow order and start to get ready. I'm not sure how many people they're expecting, but it seems to be a big deal to Aunt Jo and Mrs. Mercer. After I get myself together, I head into the playroom where the girls invite me to play a new round of Candyland with them. We play Candyland once and a princess memory game twice. Playing the same games I once played with Mom stirs up feelings of being home and comfortable. Being with the girls is refreshing. There are no unasked questions, no underlying concerns, no hidden agendas— just fun. While we try to decide on a third game to start, Mr. Mercer calls us downstairs. The girls quickly run out while I spend a couple of minutes putting away the games. Aunt Jo comes in just as I am standing up to walk out.

"Ready for a good time?" she asks in a tone that foreshadows nothing but her optimism.

"With you?" I raise my eyebrows with a questioning smile before I add, "Of course!" I wink.

We stroll downstairs to find the entire Mercer family waiting for us by the front door. Everyone is dressed in shades of cream, yellow, blue, and gray. We look like we belong in a Southern magazine spread. It feels a little odd.

Mrs. Mercer shoos us out the door, and we load into two cars. Grumpa and Mrs. Ann drive the girls while Aunt Jo and I hop in with Mr. and Mrs. Mercer. We drive for about twenty minutes, farther into the country, until Mr. Mercer stops at an old park across from an even older-looking cemetery. The parking lot sits almost abandoned, except for a black SUV where a woman is unloading equipment.

"Is this where the party's supposed to be?" I ask hesitantly.

They all laugh a little as Mrs. Mercer delicately shakes her head back and forth, a subtle answer I almost miss. Grumpa, Mrs. Ann, and the girls wait patiently in the gravel parking lot as they watch Mr. Mercer park. As soon as Mrs. Mercer opens her door, though, the girls take off running toward the abandoned swings. Without missing a beat, Mrs. Mercer hollers, "Stop your feet and come back here this instant!"

Once the girls are back in step, I follow everyone down an old stone path that has been laid beneath a canopy of ancient oak trees. The stones drop down in an uneven stair-like fashion that leads us to a grassy landing in front of a curved bank along a river. It is a beautiful setting for a party, but where are the tables, the food, the decorations? Besides all of us, the only other person with us is the strange woman I saw earlier, unloading her SUV. She rifles through several bags of equipment near a grouping of large boulders, pulling out and assembling things I don't recognize. Mrs. Mercer and Mrs. Ann interrupt her progress to initiate a private conversation.

While they talk, I direct my attention to the river where a decent waterfall cascades just upstream. Downstream, trees line the river on one side while limestone cliffs dramatically drop into the water where cream-colored bluffs hang over the water's edge. The stark beauty is picturesque. I wish I could capture these vivid colors on my sketch pad—the baby-blue sky, lush green grass, and gray-and-white marbled limestone. I snap a few pictures with my phone and breathe it all in when Grumpa wanders up next to me.

"I used to go swimming in this river and would jump from that waterfall"—he points upstream—"over there when I was about your age." I hear the smile in his voice. I stare up at him, surprised he's talking to me but also curious to hear more about this place. He continues, unfazed by my silence. "Nice to see Tonkawa Falls hasn't changed much over the years. Still as beautiful as ever." Grumpa smiles slightly as he reminisces.

Interested in his story, I decide to press the unbalanced conversation forward. "You can swim here?"

"Oh, yeah, people do it all the time. But Ann prefers the cleanliness of the pool." He chuckles. "Would you ever try swimming in this river? Or canoeing in it even?"

I look up at him, puzzled at the idea. "I don't know. The Chicago River is not a place I'd ever swim, so ..." I pause for a few beats to think on the question.

"No is an okay answer. Most girls your age and older wouldn't do it either."

I can't tell if he's goading me or just expelling hot air. Either way, I know my answer. "Sure, I'd try it."

He grins. He lifts his hand out toward my shoulder, stopping it awkwardly midair before making a loose fist. "You know, your dad has always been full of adventure too. I can see so much of his spirit in you ..."

I watch as he lightly bounces one of his knuckles off his bottom lip, still staring into the dark river below our feet. "This hasn't been easy for anyone ... especially you. And I've not made things easier. It's hard to admit you were wrong about something you can't undo, but I am glad you're with us, Marni. I'd like for us to get to know each other, if that's okay with you?"

Stunned he's admitting he was wrong—even in a backward sort of way—I turn to face him, incredulous. Why is he changing his tune? Before I can ask, he shifts his weight and meets my gaze. We lock eyes. He doesn't blink, doesn't look away, doesn't taunt me with hostility or regret for my presence. Somewhere between us, the deadbolt on a distant door unlocks, cracking the seal to shine a beam of light onto this new possibility. With a tight knot developing in my throat, all I can offer him is a single slow nod up and down.

About that time, the mystery lady begins waving her hands to direct traffic. Still puzzled by what we're all doing, I walk over to Aunt Jo and ask, "You know what's going on?"

She half hollers, "Mrs. Mercer, can you tell this confused child what in heaven's name is going on?" Aunt Jo wears a sideways grin. Everyone stops, looking to Mrs. Mercer.

"Well, Marni, we are taking our first-ever it's-the-whole-family picture. It's a tradition for the Mercers to mark important moments and milestones with photos. You and Aunt Jo are now part of the Mercer family, which is a very important milestone in our lives," Mrs. Mercer says.

"Oh … okay," I respond hesitantly.

Of course, I noticed all the treasured family photos displayed around their house. Honestly, it amazed me how well they've been able to preserve such a thorough photographic timeline of their lives. The Mercers' wedding photos, the girls in matching holiday outfits, and fun family vacation memories captured for all to remember. None of this had escaped my attention, but I can't figure out why Mrs. Mercer wanted to schedule this family picture on the day of Aunt Jo's party. But it does explain why we are all so color coordinated.

Then it hits me. "Wait, are we going to a send-off party after this?" I ask, concerned Aunt Jo isn't getting the party that was promised.

"Oh, sweet girl!" Aunt Jo laughs. "This is my party! You know, hanging out with all the family I now have in Texas. We just told you it was a party for me so everyone would get ready without too many questions. But I do expect a really good steak after this," she says, shooting a playful wink at Grumpa, who laughs out loud at her honesty.

"Wouldn't have it any other way, Jo," he says.

About that time, the photographer informs us we are going to lose our "good light" if we don't move the shoot along. First, she shoots a ton of pictures of the entire group with the limestone bluffs in the background. Then, she whittles the group down, keeping me as the one constant in all the pictures. I take pictures with the entire Mercer family, then with Mr. and Mrs. Mercer and the girls, then with just the girls, then one with just Mr. Mercer and Mrs. Mercer, another one with Mrs. Ann and Grumpa, some with just Aunt Jo, and finally some of just me. After the hour-and-a-half photo session, I rub my tired cheeks, exhausted from all the smiling. By the time we are finished, the light has transformed from a warm golden glow into the cooler blue tones of evening. Along the river, swarms of tiny flickering lights from the fireflies magically blink on and off.

"So, James. How about that steak?" Aunt Jo teases as the photographer finishes packing up her equipment.

"Let's go. I have reservations waiting at the club," Grumpa announces as he starts guiding everyone back up the path to the cars. "We can be there in fifteen minutes if we hurry," he says, encouraging everyone to move it along.

I can't help but notice how comfortable everyone is with one another. I sit in the back seat, lost in my own thoughts while Aunt Jo and Mrs. Mercer fill the empty space with lively conversation. Seeing everyone act so friendly and accommodating and hearing all the lighthearted teasing makes me think they all truly like each other. I try to shake off the feeling that this is starting to feel like a real family—with professional pictures to prove it—as a terrifying notion sweeps over me. I look around at the people who could be my new family and wonder, *If I conform into a Mercer, how will I continue to keep the identity I've always treasured as Mom's daughter?* Trying to sort out the confusion bubbling up in my head, I spot Mr. Mercer watching me through the rearview mirror, his eyes crinkling slightly at the edges as he smiles. Holding my eyes, he gives me a reassuring nod as if to say, *It's going to be all right.*

Turning into the gated club, we drive under a canopy of white twinkly lights elegantly intertwined around the arms of the old oak trees that line the windy entrance. The ambiance of the soft light promises magic and happiness at the end of the trail. Aunt Jo *oohs* and *aahs*. We both know she has never experienced anything like this. A beautiful building with a covered drive-through, called a porte cochere, anchors the private drive. The colonial-inspired club showcases deep-red brick with a whitewash that softens the red tones. Huge flowerpots full of pink, yellow, and purple flowers dot the wide stair entrance while potted ferns flank both sides of the iron and glass double-doors. I've been to the club countless times but have never come through this entrance or been here at night. My heart pounds with excitement, noting how the atmosphere hints at a special and sophisticated evening.

We all walk in and are seated at once in a private alcove that showcases a beautiful view of the golf course. The girls and I quickly demolish several small bowls of hush puppies and flower-stamped butter. While the adults quietly talk about boring things, I entertain the girls by playing I Spy.

After a few games, the hairs on the back of my neck prickle as I sense someone is looking in my direction. I glance up, hoping to catch them in their socially awkward act before they have time to avert their stare. My eyes meet Grumpa's, and I search them, trying to uncover what lies behind his intense expression. The honesty of what I see stuns me. I blink away the connection. *What does he want from me?*

CHAPTER 39
Marni

Seven in the morning. My alarm irritatingly breaks the silence, repeating a pattern of sounds designed to dissolve any chance of continued peace. Tapping my alarm off, I suddenly remember why I need to get up and bolt upright. Aunt Jo is leaving today, so I can't waste any time we have left. My chest tightens as fear presses in on me like a heavy weight. I need time to slow down. I silently pray, asking God to stretch my time with Aunt Jo. *Don't take her away too fast.*

Pulling myself together quickly, I tiptoe down the hall and creep into Aunt Jo's room where she sleeps as peaceful and still as a hibernating bear. A mischievous idea tickles me, and a grin grows across my shadowy face. I run and flop onto the bed next to her, startling her as I demand, "Get up, Aunt Jo! Get up!" I flop around her like a fish out of water.

In a complete tizzy, her arms flail through the air like she's trying to grab hold of something. "What in high heaven are you doing waking me up like this? And this early? Don't you remember that I'm on vacation?" she barks.

"I just wanted to spend as much time with you as possible before you leave," I say, pushing my fake pouty face closer to hers.

She half smirks, snorts once, and rolls to the opposite side of the bed from where I perch before aggressively pulling several layers of covers over her head. I sit there, staring at the large mound of covers, bummed for a couple of seconds, until the entire bed starts shaking under me. I yank the covers off her head, exposing her jiggly body desperately trying to stifle her laughter. Within seconds, she pounces on me, faster than anticipated, and starts tickling me under my arms.

A few exasperated breaths later, Aunt Jo's body produces a series of loud and perturbed rumblings. She glances at her bedside clock. "Sweet girl, we can't do anything fun today until I eat a big breakfast."

My stomach seconds that with a loud growl.

Aunt Jo smiles, snaps her fingers, and says, "I have the perfect idea! I'll make breakfast for everyone in that fancy-shmancy kitchen. You know, as a thank-you to the Mercers for their hospitality."

I lift my eyebrows, wondering if I should remind her she's a notoriously bad cook. Mom never let her help in our kitchen, insisting she was always more trouble than help. *Jo, you could burn water*, Mom used to tease. Who knows? Maybe she can cook now. She's already in her bathroom, getting ready and determined to surprise everyone. I bite my tongue and head downstairs into the silent kitchen. When Aunt Jo joins me, we rummage through the pantry and refrigerator and pull out all sorts of ingredients that look breakfast-worthy. We decide to whip up french toast with a side of bacon. Aunt Jo lays the bacon in a pan before sliding them into the preheated oven. Then she mixes a few eggs, a splash of milk, and some cinnamon and sugar in a bowl, then beats the ingredients together with her fork. I pull out twelve slices of bread and melt some butter in a skillet. Aunt Jo dips the bread slices into the egg mixture and gently lays them into the sizzling pan, flipping them over after a few minutes. In no time, we're done and pleased with the minimal mess we've made.

Hints of cinnamon and caramelized sugar perfume the kitchen as we load the table with bowls of powdered sugar, pre-sliced slabs of cold butter, and a mini pitcher filled with warm maple syrup. I stand back, impressed with our creation, and silently chide myself for doubting Aunt Jo. But alas, as I turn away from the table, heavy ribbons of smoke pour out of the oven. Before I can alert Aunt Jo, the smoke alarm starts to scream throughout the house. Panicking, I run and open the patio door, fanning it back and forth to encourage the smoky beast outside. Aunt Jo rushes to the oven, slings the burnt bacon into the sink yelling, "Ow!" as she waves oversized oven mitts frantically in the air.

Mr. and Mrs. Mercer fly around the corner, probably thinking their entire house must be on fire. Shocked by all the smoke, they are instantly at my side, checking to make sure I'm okay. Satisfied that I'm unharmed, Mr. Mercer immediately swings the front and back doors wide open and raises the garage door, creating a wind current to carry the smoke away.

After a few hectic minutes, the smoke drifts outside, and the noisy alarm stops, which helps to ease the tension in the house. Mrs. Mercer, however, looks around the kitchen, assessing what happened to start the chaos. Her eyes settle on a full sink of dirty dishes. "What's all this?" she asks.

I can't tell if she's pleased or upset we've been cooking in her kitchen. We almost destroyed her kitchen, not to mention the horrific alarm that woke them up.

"Aunt Jo made you breakfast," I answer, looking beyond her to the mess we haven't touched yet. I suddenly see our good intentions mean more work for Mrs. Mercer, which completely defeats our purpose. I shift my gaze to the table we just finished setting and nervously add, "We wanted to thank you for bringing her down here and everything." I know Aunt Jo is more than capable of answering for herself, but I can't stop the words from tumbling out of my mouth.

Aunt Jo looks at Mrs. Mercer. "Cooking was always my sister's thing, but I figured I'd try." She wears her 'I'm sorry' smile. "Sure did want to wake you up with pleasant smells, not scary sounds. But I can promise you one thing … that bacon is done." She laughs, unable to control herself, which ignites contagious laughter from all of us. She is right, that bacon is burnt black!

"Well, thank you, ladies! I can't wait to eat my breakfast," Mr. Mercer says, plopping himself at the table, visibly relieved the house isn't actually on fire.

"Yes, what a special surprise. I never have breakfast fixed for me. This is a treat! Thank you," Mrs. Mercer says.

The four of us sit down to enjoy the french toast and some very burnt bacon. We talk and laugh about the fiasco, another memory made with Aunt Jo. Everyone is pleasantly surprised by her french toast. Especially me. Mr. and Mrs. Mercer crack up when they discover we had overheated the oven by one hundred degrees.

Since it is a beautiful morning, Aunt Jo and I decide to walk off our sugary breakfast. As we walk down the street, we talk about Nicole and the other girls I met at the sleepover. I tell her Nicole and I are going to try out for the golf team. I laugh with Aunt Jo as I reveal Nicole is only playing golf to get to know the boys. When she asks me why I'm interested in golf, I shrug my shoulders. I'm not sure why I'm doing it, but I explain I need an athletic credit in my schedule.

"I'm most excited about art class. Nicole likes art, too, so hopefully we'll have it together. I promise I'll make you something right away," I say, sealing my promise with a wink.

As we walk along, I listen to Aunt Jo talk about her job, and my mind wanders back to Mom and her journals. I am starting to see how therapeutic it was for her to record her emotions and thoughts on paper. She never held any unclaimed anger toward anyone. She was always just full of love, and now I understand why. Journaling was her therapy. It gave her heart and mind an avenue to release so she could move on and live her life. I don't share her love of writing, but I think, in my own way, I can find the peace Mom wants for me.

Looking ahead, I picture my journal full of colorful sketches and shaded-in doodling. Someday in the future, I will flip through those pages and see how art brought me back to myself. Like Mom's words did for her, I know my drawings will allow me to escape whatever is pinning me down at the moment. Even sketching Aunt Jo and I in our new outfits yesterday relaxed me. It was the first time in a long time I actually felt like myself—the person I was before Mom passed.

After a few blocks, Aunt Jo's voice sounds winded, giving me an excuse to head back. I woke up this morning excited to give Aunt Jo her gift, the drawing, and now I can't wait to see her reaction. We only have a couple more hours left.

As if she feels the shift in my sails, she leans down and wraps an arm around my back and pulls me in close. "I'm sure gonna miss you. But I'm happy how things are turning out." She pauses, shakes her head back and forth, and chuckles. "Your mom is definitely patting herself on the back right now. She always loved to be right." Looking up at the sky, Aunt Jo smirks. "And Thanksgiving is gonna be here before you know it. What with school and all, you'll be too busy with friends and stuff to miss me."

I look up at her with the words to insist she's wrong on the tip of my tongue. She stops me with a curt "uh-uh," pointing her index finger at me as her eyebrows peak into high arches. I shake my head and smile. Turning the corner, we see Mrs. Ann's convertible parked in the driveway. I'm surprised she's popped in for another visit when she intentionally said her goodbye to Aunt Jo last night. We walk up the driveway, pausing at the back door. We look at each other, both wondering why there's such a terrible noise coming from inside the house, like something's crying. Or maybe yelping? We crack the back door open to hear yelling and chaos. Aunt Jo and I shoot each other questioning looks.

"Honey, don't look at me. I have no idea what's going on in this house!"

Outside, Bruno barks incessantly at the windows to the living room. The girls squeal energetically, their pitch at least an octave above everything else. At the heart of the confusion, intense baritone sounds compete to be heard. Mr. Mercer scolds Grumpa, his weighted voice commanding respect as Grumpa combats him with miniature arguments. Mrs. Ann sits dead quiet in a chair while Mrs. Mercer sits on the opposite side of the room, obviously upset. Just when it couldn't get any louder, a terrible yelping cry slices through the air like a soprano trying to hit her signature high note. All goes momentarily quiet, then resumes without skipping a beat.

We slink into the back of the living room, unnoticed at first. As soon as Mrs. Mercer sees me, she claps her hand at the men, a signal teachers use to get children's attention, then she shifts her gaze to me. Mrs. Mercer instructs the girls to sit down and be still, and they both climb into Mrs. Ann's lap. Aunt Jo and I try to take in the scene, but from the looks of her, she's just as baffled as I am. Mr. Mercer raises both hands, calling his argument off, or maybe admitting defeat. Either way, he takes a seat on the couch, leaving Grumpa standing alone, staring at me and Aunt Jo. Mrs. Mercer breaks the uneasy silence and persuades Aunt Jo to take a seat. I watch her sit down on the couch and spot a large box in the corner of the room.

Okay, so what is going on? Two thoughts enter my mind. Either this is some kind of intervention where both Grumpa and I need to be coerced into caring about each other, or this is our moment of truth where we both publicly profess our hostility toward each other with no-holds-barred tactics. I'm not sure which I prefer—both options make my knees wobble underneath me. My stomach starts to twist and turn as I brace for whatever comes next.

"What's going on?" My words cut the tension like a warm knife in butter.

"I—I want to talk to you," Grumpa stammers briefly before recovering. "Would that be okay?"

"I guess so. What about though?" I sense I hold the power in this situation, though I'm not quite sure what that means, except that he's giving me a choice.

"Can we go outside for a moment? Just the two of us." His right eyebrow, graying with age, rises as he awaits my response.

I, and he leads me out the back door, gently pushing off his overly excited dog. Mr. Mercer quickly follows us outside, picks up Bruno, and heads back into the house.

Grumpa doesn't talk at first. Actually, neither one of us do. I can't help thinking I am stuck in enemy territory, captured by a foreigner who can't see me as anything other than an outsider. That's how I feel when he's around me—alienated. I stand on the patio, waiting. Grumpa walks around the pool and toward the swings, casually flicking his wrist, encouraging me to follow, which I do.

"I always loved pushing your dad on the swings when he was younger. Did you like to swing as a child?" His tone is softer than I anticipated. It sounds like an innocent icebreaker question, but I can't help thinking he's up to something. I don't really care either way because I jump at any chance I get to talk about me and Mom.

"Yes! When she had time off, Mom used to take me to this park near the lake to play on the swings. She'd sometimes buy me an ice cream." I smile at the memory, temporarily forgetting who's listening to me.

"Sounds like she was a good mom," he says.

I look up to study his face and am surprised by the smile that touches his eyes. "She was. The very best!"

"Look, Marni," he says. "I'd like a fresh start with you, a do-over, if you will. I've been a terrible grandfather, and that's really not who I am or want to be. Truth is ... being around you has been harder on me than you could know. I was wrong all those years ago to interfere with Kyle and your mom. And seeing you and knowing how much we've all missed out makes me hate myself even more. I've dealt with my regrets very poorly, but that's still no excuse for my behavior."

I turn to one of the swings, sit in the plastic seat, and let my toes drag through the worn-out grass under me, thinking. "Are you asking me this because you want me around or because Mrs. Ann, Mr. and Mrs. Mercer, and Aunt Jo put you up to it?" Before he can answer, I remind him, "You made it pretty clear to me that I don't fit into your family ideals. From day one, Mom and I have always been the wrong 'pedigree' to be a Mercer," I say, hoping the bite in my tone stings.

Grumpa drops his head a little and sinks into the swing next to me. He pushes his swing back, digging thick lines into the soft dirt with the backs of his shoes. "For starters, you need to know that no one has or will ever force me into saying or doing something I don't want. I'm too bullheaded to let anyone steer me off the path of my choosing." He twists his swing toward me, crossing the chains at the top. "You know, I see a lot of myself in you—headstrong and determined."

Squinting, I watch the bright, puffy clouds move through the sky, constantly changing in the wind. "Mom was determined too."

He nods in acknowledgment as his swing jerks back into position, facing forward. "Yes, I heard she was, but the Mercer blood runs through you too. I know I've been slow on the uptake, but I see it ...

the family resemblance, personality quirks, and the Mercer gumption." He cocks his head to the side like he's pondering what to say next. "Your arrival, the entire situation, threw me at first. I'm ashamed to admit this to you and myself, ashamed of what happened in the past." He clears his throat, looking uncomfortable. "It's time to clear the air."

Taking a deep breath, he swivels his head, his eyes sharply fixed on my face. Knowing I am not ready to meet his gaze, I focus my attention on an emerging weed pushing through the dirt several feet in front of me. Unfazed by my indifference, he says, "I learned Kyle was seeing your mother from a fellow colleague in Chicago. Kyle never mentioned your mother to us, which was a red flag. So, I stepped in, essentially persuading him she wasn't worthy of him and forcing him to leave her, putting him back on track to achieve the life we envisioned for him. I put him in an unfair position, insisting that the Chicago office release him from his job and send him back to my Texas firm. I convinced myself he had a choice: either her or everything else—his family, job, security, and social status—but it wasn't a fair choice. I feel confident the only thing that caught his attention was the mention of pulling his family out from under him, ironically enough."

I pull my eyes off the sprouting weed and stare at him, open-mouthed and horrified. His eyes glass over with emotion as he registers my disgust.

"It was not the best feeling in the world, watching him crumble under my pressure. But from the bottom of my heart, I thought I was doing the right thing. And, honestly, I never thought he and your mother were as serious as they apparently were," he says, lifting his hand in my direction. "So, imagine my surprise when fifteen years later, you appear out of thin air. I never questioned whether you were Kyle's daughter, but that didn't take the sting out of my initial shock. Was I upset? Definitely. And for more reasons than you probably think. After the shock settled into my bones, I began to fume with anger at myself and your mom. The bottom line is," he pauses for dramatic effect, "we've missed out on so much with you because of what I did."

His admission surprises me. I turn my head to look him square in the eyes, trying to gauge his sincerity. As if detecting my reluctance to believe him, he says, "Make no mistake, Marni. You are my first granddaughter." He blinks back the tears pooling at the bottom of his eyelids. "I guess all I'm asking from you is a chance to be your grandfather." His words hang in the air between us.

I lift my feet up, granting the swing permission to sway back and forth while I consider his proposition. He didn't have to tell me what he did back then and why, but it fills in some of the holes. Mom always said, *Confronting the truth is the first step to acceptance and moving forward.*

I stare into his eyes as I say, "I don't know how to start over." The honesty of my answer hits me in the gut. The chains creak above my head, following the gentle rhythm of my swing as my heart asks, *How do I start over?*

"You know, I never wanted this. I lost everything when Mom died, including the story I created in my head about my father," I tell him, my voice barely escaping the closing knot in my throat. "I remember landing in Texas, full of nerves and excited anticipation tumbling around like a bag of rocks inside me. It was Aunt Jo who constantly assured me that your family, my family, was anxious to know and love me."

I raise an eyebrow, purse my lips, and shake my head. I'm not trying to start an argument, but I need him to understand. "Imagine my surprise when my new family falls very short from the distinct picture I'd envisioned." He stares blankly at me, so I add, "But I guess Aunt Jo was right about some of it. Most of you did accept me."

"We all want you in our lives," he insists.

Thoughts swirl inside my head, but my mouth is glued shut. At a crossroads, we swing in silence. As the summer breeze skims across my cheeks, Mom whispers her command in my heart, *Live, Marni.* I slow down, planting my feet in the channeled-out path, and ask, "You've been my number-one nemesis, so why the sudden change of heart?"

He reaches over, pulls the chains of my swing closer to him, and asks, "Why not now? It's never too late to try, Marni." His head dips down as his clear eyes peer at me before releasing his grip on my swing.

Feuds are hard to dissolve without leaving a wake of hurt feelings. But I know Mom wanted me to become part of their family, not just live with them. Exhausted from maintaining my guard around him, I say, "I'm sorry too."

A puzzled expression flashes across his face. "For what?"

"Calling you Grumpa," I reply, embarrassed.

His laugh takes me by surprise. "Well, it was a fairly accurate assessment. I actually find it quite clever and gutsy," he admits. "There's one more thing I need you to understand, Marni. How I reacted to you, even though I know it must have felt like a personal attack, was never really about you. The bottom line is that you are proof that I messed up. Big time. And that's a hard pill for this old man to swallow," he says, poking his finger in his chest.

A grin tips up at both corner of my lips as I dread telling Aunt Jo she was right about him. I guess he is right, we may be cut from the same stubborn cloth. The air brightens around us like a rainbow after a storm.

Clumps of hard dirt litter the worn-out patch of grass under Grumpa. I imagine the girls running full speed into the plastic seat, plopping tummy-first onto the curved swing while their feet fly into the air, trying to out-fly each other. With the toe of my right shoe, I trace a random pattern into the dirt below my seat. The monotonous motion clears my head as I unintentionally make room for this new possibility.

"You know, I've never had a grandfather."

He stops the motion of his swing and eyes me in a sideways glance. A smile lights his face. "Well, you'll never have a better grandfather than me," he claims as a tear escapes the corner of his eye. He stands up and hesitantly asks, "Can I give you a hug, Marni?" I nod as he helps me out of my swing. He wraps his arms around my back and lets out a relieved exhale. A sigh of relief washes over me too. All is quiet for about thirty seconds until Mrs. Ann breaks the silence. We laugh at the sight of her running toward us, clapping and squealing like an uncaged bird.

"I want in!" she demands, barging in.

"There's one last thing, Marni," Grumpa says, his voice hinting at mischief. "I don't know what all you heard in there before we came outside, but I seem to have caused a little raucous earlier ... it involves you."

I furrow my brows and look to Mrs. Ann for confirmation. She smiles and nods, affirming what he is saying.

"What'd you do?" I ask.

He smirks. "I got you a special gift," he pauses for effect, "without asking." He shrugs off the hysteria from earlier that must have been his fault. "But my theory is, ask for forgiveness, not permission."

Confused, I lean in, encouraging him to continue.

"Of course, I know what Kyle and Lauren would have preferred, but in this instance, I decided that I'm a new grandpa, so I can give you whatever I want."

My curiosity is piqued. Mom and I couldn't waste money on frivolous things, so the idea of getting a special gift when it's not my birthday or Christmas excites me. My mind wonders with giddy anticipation. What could he have gotten that's stirred up so much trouble?

"You didn't need to get me anything, especially if it's going to get me in trouble," I say, but he just smiles.

"This is something I wanted to do for you. I hope this little gift will be something that we can enjoy together." He looks at me expectantly as he asks, "Are you ready for it?" His excited voice jumps an octave like a kid on Christmas morning. My grin stretches from ear to ear, matching his. He turns to Mrs. Ann. "Cover her eyes so she can't peek." Mrs. Ann turns me around and places a folded scarf over my eyes, knotting the ends at the back of my head.

Once they are sure I can't see, he slips inside the house. While he's away, Mrs. Ann tells me how much she's enjoyed having Aunt Jo here. She is overcome with the giggles as I recount this morning's breakfast debacle. It is not long before I hear Grumpa clearing his throat. Mrs. Ann takes a deep breath and lightly spins me around by my shoulders, pointing me in the direction of the house. She loosens the scarf at the back of my head, and it floats to the ground. Shocked and tongue-tied, I see Grumpa cradling a curly-haired brown puppy in his arms.

"I picked her out especially for you. She's a sweet girl looking for a home. What do you think?" he asks, holding her out for me to take.

"Is she really for me?"

"Only if you want her."

I immediately reach out to claim her, tucking her soft paws into my arms. I lift her up, admiring her teddy bear face with amber-flecked, chocolate eyes. Our eyes meet. Hers seek some sort of reassurance ... love, family, happiness? I know the look; I understand. Her big brown eyes promise me unconditional love and companionship. I pull her into my face, giggling as she tries to lick the tip of my nose. I tuck her perfect snout into the crook of my neck as I whisper into her fur, "Hi, sweet girl." She wriggles her body out of my bear hug and licks my chin.

"I love her so much! Thank you!" I blurt out, mesmerized at how silky her curls feel between my fingers. After a few minutes, I sit down, ready to watch her explore her new backyard. Uninterested in everything around her, she immediately crawls into my lap to gently gnaw on my hand.

"She loves you already!" Mrs. Ann exclaims.

Grumpa squats down next to me, giving me the specifics about her. "She's a non-shedding poodle who's going to get plenty bigger. She's very smart, which should make potty training fairly easy." He stops to look at the faces watching us from inside the house. "Your dad and Lauren are a little miffed at me, but I've already promised to help you with her training if you'd like."

"Yes, please." Then I panic briefly. "I've never had a pet before— just one goldfish that died after only two days." The thought of messing up scares me.

He shushes me, explaining every girl should have a dog to call her own. "One that will run and play with you, cuddle up next to you when you're sad, comfort you when you're sick, and be happy to see you every time you walk through the door." He pauses momentarily before he adds, "Kind of like a grandfather." He leans over to stroke the top of my puppy's fluffy topknot. "I want to be there for you, Marni, in every possible way."

I bend over to kiss my little girl puppy and smile. "Maybe we can take walks together, you, me, Bruno, and her?"

"It will be our pleasure," he says, looking up and reaching for Mrs. Ann's hand.

Finally, the house doors fly open as the girls run and squeal toward us. They plop down onto the thick grass, enamored by my puppy's playful personality, overactive licking, and velvety hair.

Aunt Jo allows the girls a few minutes to play with the puppy before she insists it's her turn to hold my baby. She picks her up, squeezes her into her chest, and declares, "My, what a beautiful puppy! If your mom could see this, oh, why, she'd be so happy for you!" She hands my squirming puppy back to me. "So does she have a name yet?"

The girls pipe in with their princess suggestions, one Disney character after another. I study my sweet puppy's chocolate-brown hair and matching eyes and decide she deserves something more than a Disney name. I want it to be special. "Not yet."

Mr. and Mrs. Mercer walk up, hand in hand. I know they never wanted this puppy, but I ask them if I can keep her.

"Marni, she's yours. Of course you can! Your grandfather, however, is responsible for helping you train her," Mr. Mercer says, shooting his dad a look—a truce.

"Can I hold your little fluff ball?" Mrs. Mercer asks, stretching out her hands as my puppy willingly lunges into her arms. In puppy heaven, she says, "Oooh, don't you just love puppy breath?" As if on cue, the puppy's tongue curiously laps at the air around Mrs. Mercer's face until it finally licks the length of her nose. We laugh at her expression as she wipes puppy slobber off her face.

I take her back and place her on the grass next to me, thinking she might want to walk around a bit and explore. Instead, she tumbles clumsily into the hole I created with my crossed legs and immediately falls asleep, exhausted from all the hands-on attention. Mrs. Ann snaps a photo of the pup sleeping on me while everyone chatters with each other, and a special memory Mom used to share with me springs to mind.

I remember our walks in the park, watching kids play fetch with their dogs and laughing as rambunctious pets dragged their owners behind them in a sprint. Mom's smile would broaden every time she recalled her childhood memories playing with her beloved dog, Gigi. Her highlight reel comes to life in my mind's eye as I clearly see her memories come alive. They were inseparable friends. For Halloween, Mom hand-sewed costumes for Gigi. On rainy days, they played dress-up. When she was sick, Gigi cuddled up next to her in bed. And on long summer afternoons, they explored together. "We were two peas in a pod," Mom used to say. With every retelling, Mom always ended her stories with an apology, sad she couldn't give me that same experience of having my very own dog.

Dancing shapes of light bounce around us as the sun's rays filter through the canopy of the massive oak tree we're sitting under. In this moment, I feel Mom next to me. She is happy ... happy for me and the journey ahead.

Mom always said the best gift we can give to each other is the time we spend together. My time with Mom has come and gone. All I have left of her is a heart full of memories and her treasured journals. I look around this yard and understand this is my new life, my new family, my new home. It's time to take a leap of faith and live—like Mom wanted.

I look up into the heavens, warmth filling me from within, and smile. I whisper to my new best friend, "Gigi, I love you so much. Welcome home."

EPILOGUE

Completely shattered and empty, I stare at the familiar glossy box. I know what happened, but part of me still holds out hope that all this is just another bad dream. It's been sixteen years since I stood at Mom's graveside, lost and devastated, yet my wounds still feel fresh. And now—he's gone too. Water blurs my vision as I remember the memories we made together over the last sixteen years.

Grandma reaches over and grabs my hand, gently squeezing my fingers as she works to control her breathing. I feel her pain. The weight of his death pounces on my heart like a mountain lion, unexpected and ferocious. I can't believe he's gone; he was just here. Silent tears slide down my face as I faintly comprehend the preacher's words meant to comfort and console us. I should feel relief he's in a better place, but right now, I want to interrupt the preacher and tell him to stop wasting his breath on typical funeral words and talk more about the man who set the bar of life higher than I ever imagined. Through glassy vision, I stare at the picture propped next to the coffin. I can't help but ask God, *Why did you take him? Don't you know that we didn't have enough time together either?*

Sensing my distress, Grandma wraps an arm around my shoulders, pulling us into each other as she whispers, "I hope you know that he loved you more than life itself." My lip quivers as I meet her watery gaze, answering her with a solemn nod. I look down the row of people, at my family. The girls, no longer rambunctious princesses but young adults, fall to pieces next to Mama L as she consoles them. Pulling pre-folded tissues out of her purse, she hands them to the girls, then dabs at her own eyes. But it's the sight of Dad that breaks my heart. Our eyes meet, and I watch as fresh tears well up in his eyes. He gives me an encouraging smile as a line of tears trail down his cheek.

I wonder how any of us are going to move forward when we still need him. I tilt my head up and squeeze my eyes shut, feeling sticky tears slip down my cheeks.

Once the preacher finishes checking all the funeral agenda boxes, he volunteers the podium to anyone wishing to share a special memory. Soft noise builds in the tent as the crowd of people shifts and mumbles to each other until they notice Grandma standing next to the coffin, not behind the podium, staring at them as she prepares to address the now-hushed crowd. I'm in awe of her strength and poise, and I admire her determination to honor him despite her trembling hands.

She clears her throat, intentionally looks at each one of us—her family—and starts, "Thank you for being here today. It means more to me than I will ever be able to express to see how much he was loved. I don't want to take up too much of your time because, honestly, there's not enough time in the world for me to properly recount his life and how important he will always be to me and his family." She lifts her hand, wipes away fresh tears, and half laughs as she continues, "And let's face it, he would absolutely hate all this fuss anyway. Heavens, given the chance, he would have preferred to be on the golf course or at a family barbeque."

Laughter lightens the mood of the tent as I hear the people behind me whisper, "That's so true."

"So, I have just one thing left to say, and they're his words. I'd like to read you his final love letter to you." She reaches into her sleeve to retrieve a hidden, dainty handkerchief she uses to blot the corners of her eyes. She takes a few steps to the podium, pulls out a folded letter, and slips on her stylish reading glasses. The air in the tent goes still, as if everyone is holding their breath in anticipation. She takes a deep breath.

Dear family and friends,

Thank you for making my life and journey on this earth so incredible. I am blessed to have had the time to know and love each one of you in different and significant ways. God gave me the gift of a wonderful, healthy life with an amazing family. Take comfort in knowing that I loved every minute God granted me and every person He placed in my life. My heart is full, and it's because you let me love you. Thank you for walking beside me on my journey. I know we will see each other again someday. Until then, I carry you all in my heart."

Her voice quivers as she whispers his last words. I sit there, unable to move, unsure if I am even breathing. Sniffling and rhythmic sobs ripple through the reverent tent. Either unable to move or unwilling, Grandma remains frozen, looking from the podium to the picture beside his coffin. It takes me a couple of minutes to recognize she isn't ready to say goodbye.

I remember not wanting to leave Mom's graveside. I know Grandma must think if she sits down, it means he really is gone, and life as she knew it is over. Understanding her dilemma, I carefully join her at the front, wrapping my arms lovingly around her neck.

She sniffs loudly into my ear and whispers, "He was so proud of you." Her weight collapses against my body as her frail arms envelop me. I guide her to the edge of the tent, fully aware of her need to keep standing. The preacher reclaims his podium, ends the service in prayer, and then invites everyone back at my parents' house.

Later, after the last person leaves, we all go off to our own corners, emotionally exhausted. I climb upstairs, close myself in my old room, and change into my comfortable loungewear and fuzzy socks before rejoining everyone downstairs. The girls reminisce about old times and funny stories, but I can't make myself participate. I sit isolated, alone, and dazed, studying the family pictures that fill the bookshelves and walls. There are years of framed memories displayed on the shelves, but my favorites are the early ones, from my first summer here. I love that Mama L intentionally took all those pictures just to make me feel at home. I've told her to take them down, but she refuses. I think those pictures mean something different to her, but whatever that is, she keeps them framed for everyone to enjoy. Finally, Grandma approaches me and asks, "Marni, where's Gigi?"

"In the yard," I answer, nodding my head toward the backyard as fresh tears cloud my vision. I think back, remembering how Grumpa insisted we take Gigi on daily walks so he could teach me about dogs. At first, it was a chore, just being around him. Before long, we started to let each other in. Tears slide down my cheeks as I remember how much I enjoyed those walks, our time together, our honest talks, and his dry humor.

"Let's bring her in," she says, walking toward the back door. I'm about to protest, but it's too late. I hear Gigi's collar jingling as she walks over to me. I smile as Gigi leans up against my legs, insisting I pet her.

She scoots a folding chair next to me and runs her fingers through Gigi's soft curls.

"Thank you for letting her in," I say, rubbing my cold hands along her warm body.

"You know, Marni. You were the sun and moon to that man," she says, smiling. I feel my chin quiver as I fight to maintain my composure.

A knowing look passes between us, and I nod. "I loved him so much, but I don't think I can do this again. I can't handle losing another person I love this much," I admit as my voice cracks.

Then her cold fingers cradle my chin as she gently lifts my face up to meet her gaze. "You can, and you must. Life moves forward, and we need you. Don't shut down on me." She pauses as a familiar light sparkles in her eyes. "Isn't it funny how things change and work out?"

I cock my head and ask, "How do you mean?"

"Remember the first summer you were here? The first time you met him on the golf course?"

I nod and chuckle, suddenly missing the standing tee time he used to set aside for us every Sunday afternoon. I sigh at the thought of never golfing with him again.

"I wonder what would have happened if you could go back and tell yourself that the one person you disliked the most in the world would become your best friend?"

I can't speak. My lips tremble as I try to smile.

She gets slightly tickled, saying, "You wouldn't have believed yourself."

She's right. We didn't always see eye to eye, but he learned to listen to me. Looking back, I see how formative he was in my life. He pushed me to be the person I am today—competitive, strong, independent, and, believe it or not, full of compassion. He was always there, and now he's gone.

I look at her and confide, "He gave me the greatest gift of all—his love and acceptance."

Tears pool in her eyes as she nods.

"He saved me, Grandma."

Grandma's tired face brightens as she tells me what I already knew. "He adored being your Grumpa."

Knowing his love will never leave me, I feel peace washing over me. As the sun reaches through the nearby windows and warms my cheek, I picture my two favorite people finally meeting each other face-to-face for the first time. I imagine Mom hooking her arm through Grumpa's as they both watch over me, smiling.

ACKNOWLEDGMENTS

I remember the first time a voice in my head said, I'm going to write a book. It was one of those surreal moments where you find yourself teetering between reality and fantasy. Almost immediately, I chalked it up to a fleeting, hairbrained idea that wouldn't amount to much. Surely, the thought would go away ... but I couldn't shake it. The sentence grew roots until I finally voiced it out loud to myself and, eventually, to my family and friends. I had no idea how to accomplish this monstrous dream except to start writing.

But publishing a book takes a village ... so, let me start by thanking all the people in my life who've walked this journey with me and kept me on-point. You always asked me about my writing and the never-ending editing process. You were early beta readers who offered unbiased and honest feedback. You have been my loudest cheerleaders and the best PR team a girl could have. Thank you for all your invaluable support.

Thank you, Warren Publishing, for taking a chance on me. It has been such a dream working with you and your team. You've educated me about the industry and successfully guided me through each phase of the publishing process. It's a tough industry with lots of moving parts, so thank you for helping me get this book off my computer and into readers' hands.

Thank you to my phenomenal editors!

Karli Jackson, you answered a random email from an aspiring author and agreed to edit my manuscript. What a gift! I love the fact I found you in one of my favorite author's acknowledgments! Thank you for helping me polish my manuscript, which turned heads at Warren Publishing and several other publishing houses.

Erika Nein, I had so much fun editing with you! Thank you for helping me bring depth and definition into my writing. You pushed me to be a better writer, and I will forever be thankful. Together, we cleared the hurdles, and I had a blast doing it with you!

Katherine Bartis, thank you for your eagle-eye editing expertise! You made me look like I actually remember every grammar rule ever taught, which I clearly did not!

To all my editors, y'all are amazing! Working with you was truly a privilege ... let's do it again!

To my New York Pitch Conference friends—you know who you are—I love each of you! Thank you for your open and honest opinions, comments, and writerly support. What a magical week it was spending time with fellow fiction writers. You hold a very dear place in my heart.

To Christie Talbert, Laura Schmeltekopf, and Kay Fromm, thank you for always asking about the book's progress and breaking up the hours I spent at my computer—grabbing lunch, going out to dinner, taking caffeine breaks, or going on walks! Your love, support, and excitement mean more to me than I can ever express! Y'all are the best!

Thank you to my wonderful family!

Mom and Dad, I love you and am beyond thrilled at how excited you've been for this book release! I love how you tell everyone you meet about this book. Thank you for all your support, enthusiasm, and love.

Melissa, thank you for always being more than my sister. You're my best friend, supporter, encourager, and the daily phone call I can't live without. I love how we will never run out of words with each other!

Codi and Cara, I love you both so much! I am so thankful God gifted you to me. You are my inspiration. I hope you always remember you're never too old to chase a new dream. I'm so proud of you and am honored to be your mom.

Aaron, you are an incredibly loving and supportive husband, my very best friend, my partner in everything, and the love of my life. I thank God for you and your love every day. Thank you for encouraging me every step of the way! Your love always gives me the confidence I need to keep pushing forward. With you by my side, I know I can do anything.

Finally, to my readers, thank you for buying books, reading books, and posting about books. I am so appreciative to have the opportunity to share my book with you. From the bottom of my heart, I hope you enjoy my debut!

Printed in the USA
CPSIA information can be obtained
at www.ICGtesting.com
LVHW040822151023
761015LV00051B/536